The master of
medical suspen

FRANK G. SLAUGHTER
—creates his most
fascinating characters!

GUY REED: The renowned archaeologist who loves antiquity—and Lael Valdez.

LAEL VALDEZ: Guy's alluring young fiancée. Must her only chance to live come at the cost of Guy's death?

GRANT REED: The heroic doctor who must choose between loyalty and love as he pits his modern technology against an ancient scourge unleashed by his brother's hand.

SANTOS: The ruthless Peruvian witch doctor whose jealous rivalry may thwart Grant's vital research.

SHIRLEY ROSS: The glamorous network reporter who discovers how devastating a plague story can be.

Are there paperbound books you want but cannot find in your retail stores?

PLAGUE SHIP

by

Frank G. Slaughter

A KANGAROO BOOK
PUBLISHED BY POCKET BOOKS NEW YORK

PLAGUE SHIP

Doubleday edition published 1976

POCKET BOOK edition published July, 1977

3rd printing.........................July, 1977

This POCKET BOOK edition includes every word contained in
the original, higher-priced edition. It is printed from brand-
new plates made from completely reset, clear, easy-to-read type.
POCKET BOOK editions are published by
POCKET BOOKS,
a Simon & Schuster Division of
GULF & WESTERN CORPORATION
1230 Avenue of the Americas,
New York, N.Y. 10020.
Trademarks registered in the United States
and other countries.

ISBN: 0-671-80938-5.
Library of Congress Catalog Card Number: 75-36611.
This POCKET BOOK edition is published by arrangement with
Doubleday & Company, Inc. Copyright, ©, 1976, by Frank G.
Slaughter. All rights reserved. This book, or portions thereof, may
not be reproduced by any means without permission of the original
publisher: Doubleday & Company, Inc., 245 Park Avenue,
New York, N.Y. 10017.
Printed in the U.S.A.

MUTATION: A sudden variation in some inheritable characteristic of an animal or plant, as distinguished from a variation resulting from generations of gradual change.

Webster's New World Dictionary

CONTENTS

BOOK ONE

The
CASA YANQUI

I

THE LOCAL PLANE of the Compañía del Aviación Faucett had been field-hopping up the northern coast of Peru from Lima during the morning, nearly always in sight of the Pacific Ocean stretching endlessly to the west. To the east the heights of the Andean Cordillera sharply defined the coastal plain, now quite close to it and again many miles away.

Except where a river tumbled from the heights to its destination in the broad Pacific, the strip between sea and mountain was mostly desert. Flanking the river courses, however, extensive irrigation systems built centuries ago, long before the coming of the famous Inca civilization, enabled the inhabitants to produce vegetable gardens, vineyards, and the large fields of cotton, corn, and other agricultural products grown in this region since ancient times.

The plane banked sharply above a small mountain and revealed a large bay, the largest Dr. Grant Reed had seen during the flight northward from Lima. The southernmost point of the almost enclosed body of water was marked by a low mountain, and to the north, where a town was located along its northeast course, a mountain of almost the same height marked the other end of the protected bay. Offshore a large island, bracketed by several smaller ones, gave further protection to what Grant recognized as the most ideal anchorage he had seen since leaving Lima and its own nearby port of Callao.

From the pilots' cabin a Texas drawl—most Faucett pilots were American—announced: "We are approach-

3

ing Chimbote. Please fasten your seat belts. The large anchorage you see below us is Ferrol Bay."

The dark-haired stewardess repeated the announcement in flawless Spanish, which Grant Reed spoke and understood almost as well as English. She followed with another announcement in a language that was unfamiliar to him, however, although his work as senior epidemiologist with the Center for Disease Control in Atlanta, Georgia, took him all over the world.

"What was that last language?" he asked the stewardess when she came down the aisle, checking seat belts.

"Quechua, Dr. Reed—the tongue of the Incas spoken by many in the uplands of the Andes. Have you looked out? This coast is obscured by clouds most of the year, so we hardly ever get so clear a view of it as today."

"It's very beautiful."

Grant picked up the pamphlet on Peru he'd bought last night in the Miami International Airport, shortly before taking off for Lima, where he'd transferred to the local flight. The industrial center of Chimbote and its port—one of the best, according to the pamphlet, on the north coast of Peru near the equator—was charted in detail. As the plane made a wide curve over the Pacific in preparation for landing, he could see the port itself very clearly exactly as charted.

"The large white vessel docked at the long pier is the famous hospital ship *Mercy*." The stewardess paused beside Grant's seat on the way back up the aisle. "It has been berthed at Chimbote for several months."

"My brother's a patient aboard it—seriously ill."

"I'm so sorry, Dr. Reed. Perhaps you'll find him better."

"I hope so, I certainly hope so."

Grant Reed had last seen the *Mercy* at Tanjungperak, the port for Surabaya in Indonesia, nearly two years ago. Both he and the ship had been there on the same business then, combating an epidemic of a strange fever that threatened to spread throughout the Far East.

For the *Mercy* and its complement, the task had been part of its far-ranging mission to help train native medical personnel and fight disease where needed. Grant's own assignment had been that of chief investigating epidemiologist for the World Health Organization, to whom he was often on loan from the Atlanta Center of the United States Public Health Service. His specific task had been to identify the disease threatening to rage beyond control and plan specific measures to hold it in check while a cure or a preventive vaccine was being found in the laboratory.

The call that had brought him three thousand miles to northern Peru this October morning had caught him as he was debarking from an Eastern Airlines flight that had brought him from New York to Atlanta yesterday, less than twenty-four hours after leaving Lagos, Nigeria. His departure from Africa had ended a six months' battle to control the insidious virus of Sudan fever in the uplands of the Jos Plateau—during which time he'd almost lost his own life, until saved by a transfusion of immune blood from a mission hospital nurse who had survived the virulent fever herself and was, fortunately, of the same blood type as he.

He'd not been surprised to hear the voice of the paging operator as he came into the airport at Atlanta yesterday; it happened to him often in airports at the distant corners of the world. In the busy corridor leading to the baggage claim area, he'd gone to the nearest white telephone as directed, lifting it from the hook.

"This is Dr. Grant Reed. You were paging me."

"Hold the phone for the overseas operator, Dr. Reed. You have a call from aboard ship."

"I have Dr. Grant Reed for you," he heard another operator say moments later—this time with a Spanish accent. Almost immediately, too, still another voice had come on the line.

"This is Lael Valdez in Chimbote, Peru, Dr. Reed . . ." The speaker paused momentarily as if she expected him to recognize her name.

Somewhere back in the recesses of his mind he suspected that he should, too, but like a stubborn piece of a jigsaw puzzle it failed to fall into place. That she was of at least part Spanish origin, he didn't doubt—there was enough of the lilting Latin quality to her voice, even without the name of Valdez, to tell him that. But something else in her tone—perhaps the peculiar sound of the *a*—sounded almost like New England.

"We've never met, but I thought perhaps Guy had mentioned me in one of his letters." Again the tantalizing hint of two accents. "I've been his secretary and photographer for the past year."

"Oh yes. I remember Guy writing me perhaps six months ago about you, Miss Valdez."

The note from his older brother had been waiting for him when he had reached Lagos on a Sudan Interior Mission plane from one of the Nigerian upland stations. Guy had mentioned a new feminine name, but Grant had paid little attention, judging that she was only another in his brother's long string of conquests.

"Are you still there, Doctor?" the voice of Lael Valdez inquired somewhat coolly.

"Yes. I was surprised to hear that you and Guy had arrived in Peru, Miss Valdez. His last letter was from Buenos Aires."

"We've been in the Callejón de Huaylas area in the Peruvian Andes for several months, but I'm speaking from the hospital ship *Mercy* at the port of Chimbote on the north coast of Peru near Trujillo. Guy became severely ill several days ago and I brought him here. We've been trying to reach you on the ship's radiotelephone since the day before yesterday."

"I was en route from Jos in the interior of Sudan. What's wrong with Guy, Miss Valdez?"

"Dr. Smithson—"

"Is that Jack Smithson?"

"Yes. I believe you and he were in Indonesia together. He's standing beside me and can tell you more about Guy's condition than I can."

"Hello, Grant." Even over roughly four thousand

miles of land and ocean, Grant Reed recognized the voice of an old friend. "I'm afraid your brother's in bad shape."

"When did all this happen, Jack?"

"Miss Valdez and Guy were excavating in the Andean Altiplano east of here when he developed a severe fever. She brought him down to Chimbote as soon as he would let her. Naturally we admitted him as a patient."

"Thank God the *Mercy* was there!"

"At first I thought he might have picked up something like that Paraguayan hemorrhagic fever you identified and won your Nobel Prize for, but the complement fixation is negative for both that and the Bolivian variety. Actually, his symptoms resemble the pneumonic form of bubonic plague more than anything else," said Smithson, "but neither the Peruvian, Bolivian, nor Paraguayan health authorities know of any plague reservoirs in South America. All our cultures and complement fixationists have failed so far to identify Guy's fever or the organism causing it. He's losing ground, too, so I suggested to Miss Valdez that she get in touch with you."

"I'll be there as soon as I can get a plane."

"Miss Valdez has been looking up the plane routes. Just a minute."

Lael Valdez's voice came back on the line. "How soon can you leave, Dr. Reed?"

"In a few hours. Is Guy conscious?"

"Only intermittently. When he is, he asks for you."

"Tell him I'm on the way—and please brief me on how to reach Chimbote."

"You'd best fly directly to Lima on Braniff. They have a service out of Miami daily. In Lima you can pick up a Faucett local plane that stops at Chimbote when there are passengers for this point. I will meet you at the airport."

"That sounds perfect."

"The Braniff flights leave Miami at different times on different days, but I was hoping to reach you today,

so I have the airline holding a first-class seat in Miami
on a flight leaving there at two-ten tomorrow morning.
It arrives in Lima at six-twenty and your flight to
Chimbote on Faucett leaves at nine, so even if there's
a delay out of Miami, you ought to be able to catch
the local plane easily. I'll meet you at the Chimbote
Airport at ten-thirty. Good-by."

The girl was efficient, no doubt about that, Grant
thought as he hung up the telephone. She was obviously deeply concerned about his brother, too—which
wasn't unusual either. Guy's relationships with women
always had a special quality, either in brief romantic
liaisons, of which there had been many, or with the
two he had married. No matter how the relationships
eventually ended, however, none of them ever blamed
Guy.

Which said a lot, Grant supposed, for Guy; but certainly not for him, six months divorced *in absentia*
after five years of marriage, whose only period of peace
had been when he was away from home.

II

Grant had gone directly to his apartment in Atlanta
yesterday, after reporting in at the Center for Disease
Control and holding the usual press conference. He'd
realized Shirley was there the moment he opened the
door.

The well-remembered fragrance of her perfume, the
rush of water in the shower, the pile of feminine garments on the foot of the bed in the small apartment
he'd moved into, after they separated almost a year
ago—any one of them would have identified her. But
she identified herself just then by coming through the
door to the bathroom, rather precariously clutching the
nubby bath towel wrapped around her with one hand,
while drying her short red hair with a smaller towel in
the other.

"Hello, darling," she said brightly. "You took so long getting here, I decided to take a shower."

"A gaggle of reporters and cameramen was waiting at the center."

"I know. Setting up your press conference was my last official act as public relations director for the center."

"You're leaving? Why?"

"You're not the only one who likes to be famous, or travel about the world. I've been a local stringer for CBS since you went away and now I'm embarking on a career as a free-lance photo-journalist."

"You've a flair for it," he admitted.

"Thanks. No hard feelings?"

"No. Should I have any?"

"That depends. My first feature, already sold to CBS, will be on your work. After all, you're the most famous member of the center staff now."

"Famous, squamous! You know damn well I couldn't have done it without the Center for Disease Control, the Pan-American and the World Health Organizations behind me. Did you know I damn near died from Sudan fever?"

"We're using that, too; the CBS correspondent in Nigeria has already interviewed Marie Toussaint, who gave you the blood. Incidentally, Marshall Payne at the center has added another five million to his budget request for the next fiscal year, using you as an example of what's being done there."

"I may need that much extra to work out a vaccine for Sudan fever virus, if I ever do."

"You will. The only thing I ever knew you to fail at was marriage—and with the proper start, we might even still make a go of that." Moving closer to him, she added in the familiar mocking tone, "I dare you to admit that you wouldn't find the idea of having me in your bed again too repulsive."

She was still as beautiful and as desirable as she'd been in his fevered dreams, tossing on a hospital cot surrounded with mosquito netting, while the tropic heat of Central Africa made sleep next to impossible. What was more, however angry her presence and her plans to utilize his accomplishments to further her own career made him, he couldn't control the sudden surge of desire that flooded through his body at her mocking invitation.

"How did you get in here anyway?" he demanded.

"The building superintendent opened the door; after all, my driver's license still reads 'Mrs. Grant Reed.' In case you've forgotten, too, you won't be legally shed of me for another six months."

"I hadn't forgotten," he said, somewhat ungraciously, hoping to keep her from realizing the effect seeing her again after six months had produced in his hormones and autonomics.

"Don't you think I look better, darling?" Tossing away the small towel she'd used to dry her hair, Shirley shook her head vigorously and, just as he remembered, every wave fell into place. "I've put on a little weight —mostly under the towel."

"You know damn well you look fine."

"Maybe not that good. But to someone who's been in a jungle for six months away from contact with white women—"

"I'm in a hurry. What do you really want, Shirley?"

"*You,* darling. What else? Since you've been away, I've realized how lonely a divorced woman can be."

"Come off it. You always drew men like sugar draws flies."

"I suppose you meant that as a compliment." She shrugged and almost lost the towel that was her only garment. "Of course it's shameless of me to admit it, but I do want you back sometimes—even with all your faults."

She came so close that only the towel was between them. And her eyes mocked him as, rising on tiptoes, she put her arms around his neck, pulling his head down—not at all unwillingly—until her eager, avid mouth was against his. In the process, of course, the towel dropped to the floor, and since there was no longer any use pretending he didn't want her, he'd let his demanding body take command, savagely and without any restraint.

Her eyes had been mocking just before she kissed him, but there'd been no mockery in them as she strained against him. Or in the frenzied grip of her hands upon his shoulders and back as her body arched in response. When it was over, she lay on the bed under the sheet, looking up at him with a smile that was almost tender—and almost close enough to being honest to make him believe she really was sincere.

But he knew her too well after five years of alternate quarreling and passionately making up. Of watching men smile at her knowingly in the hospital, where they'd both worked while he was finishing his graduate work in microbiology. Of coming home unexpectedly from work to find her out, only to hear her call "Good night" hours later outside the apartment door—and a masculine voice answer.

She was dressed when he came out of the shower, in a blue pants suit that made the most of an already striking figure.

"Six months of abstinence certainly built up your libido, Grant. You made love just now like a lover —instead of a husband."

She applied lipstick and studied the result briefly in the dressing table mirror. "I don't see any bruises, at least none that show. By the way, was a message from a Miss Valdez in Peru waiting for you at the center?"

"She was paging me in the airport when I got off the plane. Guy's ill with a fever in a city on the coast of Peru, so I'm leaving for Miami and Lima tonight." He stopped short in the midst of knotting his tie. "But you already knew about Guy, didn't you?"

"The call came to my apartment yesterday—from the hospital ship *Mercy* in some South American port."

"Why the apartment where you're living now?"

"I'm still listed in the phone book as Mrs. Grant Reed, remember? Your phone here is temporarily disconnected, too, so Information must have given the overseas operator my number. The woman who called said Guy was sick; she sounded young—"

"Her name's Lael Valdez and she's been Guy's secretary for about a year. They met in Spain—"

"Guy always did select beautiful secretaries."

"According to Dr. Jack Smithson on the *Mercy*, he has a serious fever. I'm flying down to Lima tonight and on to Chimbote tomorrow."

"Give Guy my love. I've always been fond of him. We have a lot in common—the roving instinct, an intolerance for smug middle-class morality, a love of adventure—"

"You should have plenty of that in your new assignment with CBS."

"I'm counting on it," she said. "And since I'll be specializing in medical epidemiological questions, our paths are sure to cross."

"Possibly," he admitted.

"I spent five years of my life married to you, Grant, and they weren't exactly Paradise—typing reports, writing interviews with dull people for the center newsletter, so you could take a low-pay government job when you could have been out making a fortune in private practice. I never held it against you, though. We'd never have made a success of marriage anyway—our temperaments and ambitions are too different—but that's no reason why we can't be friends—perhaps even lovers on occasion."

"Do you think that would be wise?"

"Maybe not wise but a lot of fun. You always were good in bed—when you took time off from your damned microscopes and cultures to really work at it." She held out her hand and he took it. "Shall we say '*Auf wiedersehen*' then? I'm counting on you to let me know when any good stories break in the public health field."

He stopped short with her hand in his. "Was that the reason for the big seduction scene you just staged?"

"Not entirely," she said airily. "But it never hurts a reporter to have reliable sources."

"*Auf wiedersehen* then," he said, shaking hands— but neither of them could possibly have foreseen the bizarre set of situations that would bring them together again.

III

While Grant Reed had been flying from Atlanta to Miami the night before, Carlos Ganza had been busy at the trade for which he had developed a special skill —that of a thief. In the United States he would have been called a second-story man, but in the village of Yungay almost in the shadow of one of South America's highest peaks, the Nevada de Huascarán, the houses were largely one-storied structures, many of adobe bricks. Easy to get into, for a thief of Carlo's light-fingered ability, they were for the most part, however, poor pickings.

For the past decade, Carlos's favorite field of operation had been Lima, where the spreading bougain-villaea vines espaliered against the walls of so many houses gave easy access to balconies. These, in turn, opened upon bedrooms, and emptying a lady's jewel case into his pocket without even disturbing her sleep was almost ridiculously easy for Carlos Ganza—or it had been, until he'd made the mistake of stealing jewels belonging to the wife of a fence, to whom he had tried to sell them the next day.

Seizing the loot, the fence had also set the police on Carlos's trail, forcing him to find refuge in a district where the *guardar el orden* were unlikely to look for him, the outskirts of the village in the Callejón de Huaylas where he had been born.

Pickings in Yungay had been light for a thief, however, so Carlos had been forced to find work at one of the new hydroelectric plants being built in the Cañón del Pato—Duck Canyon. There the River Santa, after traveling over a hundred miles between the Cordillera Negra and the Cordillera Blanca, plunged almost to sea level in a distance of not much more than eight miles. In its fall it produced the electricity counted upon by the Peruvian Government to make Chimbote and nearby Trujillo into busy industrial centers and seaports.

On the bus riding back from work in Duck Canyon, Carlos had heard some of the men speak of a rich *yanqui,* who was crazy enough to be drilling for oil in the foothills of the snow-clad peak of Huascarán itself, a few miles from the village of Yungay. The American, it was said, lived in a rented villa just outside town and drove back and forth to the drilling site in the foothills of the Cordillera Blanca every day.

More important, the yanqui and his assistant—according to the bus riders a lovely young woman considerably younger than he—had been seen carrying expensive cameras and other equipment to and from the drill site. Moreover, the American was reported to have become ill a few days earlier and had been carried down to Chimbote, where the hospital ship had been anchored in the port for several months.

It was reasonable to suppose, Carlos had decided, that one might find something of value in the temporarily deserted Casa Yanqui, so that afternoon he had not left the bus at his usual stop at the edge of town. Instead he had ridden into Yungay itself, carrying his kit of burglar's tools in his lunch box, and had spent the evening in a *cantina* on the square. He drank little but asked casual questions here and there about the *gringo* who was crazy enough to drill for oil at an elevation of more than eight thousand feet. Word from the drinkers was that the American had stopped drilling just before he became sick, but all agreed that his departure for Chimbote with his assistant and the Indian drilling foreman, Augustine Almaviva, had been abrupt. It was quite probable therefore, that everything of value had not been removed from the villa.

About midnight, Carlos Ganza, walking unsteadily and pretending to be drunk, had lurched through the

town and taken a street leading up to the deserted Casa
Yanqui. Once beyond the main part of Yungay, however, he'd stopped pretending to be drunk. When he
reached the small villa, he moved carefully around it,
determining first that it did indeed appear to be deserted.
And second that, as he had hoped, in her haste to take
Señor Guy Reed down to the coast, the young señora
had neglected to lock one of the windows. From that
point, entry into the house was simple, and Carlos had
examined the bedroom carefully by the light of a small
pocket torch.

He'd found only some costume jewelry that was
hardly worth trying to sell, however, plus a gold fountain pen which he dropped into his lunch box, a disappointing haul indeed. But moving to the second bedroom, which had apparently been turned into a laboratory, he had better luck when his torch showed him an
unusual object to be seen in this part of the world, a
binocular microscope. It was located on a table near
a closet from which a faint light came, but when Carlos
opened the closet door, he saw a peculiar sort of
case inside.

The case had a glass front, somewhat like the new
ovens he'd occasionally seen in the homes of the
wealthy he'd robbed in Lima. The light came from a
small bulb inside the cabinet, which seemed to contain
nothing except a metal rack filled with glass tubes
plugged with cotton and some small dishes with glass
covers in which something that looked like mold was
growing. Disappointed, Carlos shut the door of the
closet but took the microscope to the kitchen counter
just beside the back door, where he could reach it
quickly if he had to leave in a hurry.

Returning to the laboratory once again, Carlos continued to search and was rewarded to discover, lying
against the wall at one side, a strange object indeed.
About ten feet long, the device appeared to be made
of aluminum, for it shone brightly in the light of the
torch. Moreover, it was extendable like an old-fashioned
telescope, and with each section sliding from the one

outside it, the entire device appeared capable of expanding to a considerable length. Actually, when he tested the device by extending the tube, it reached across the room, and even then, he had not come anywhere near extending the shining cylinder to its full length. Realizing that whatever the object was, it was much too big for him to carry around on foot, as well as far too unusual to be sold easily, Carlos laid it down on the floor to continue his search.

When he saw the camera attached to the smaller end of the aluminum tube, Carlos knew at once what he had found. Almost tiny, the camera bore the trademark of a German manufacturer, and having stolen a number of these small but very valuable cameras in Lima, Carlos knew it would bring a good price. Working carefully so as not to damage the delicate instrument, he separated the camera from the end of the strange aluminum tube to which it was attached. It appeared to be in perfect condition, although some dark material had stuck to the case, but he was able to remove most of it with his handkerchief. Wrapping the tiny camera in the handkerchief, he placed it carefully in the lunch box and continued his survey of the room.

The clothes in the two bedroom closets, especially the señora's dresses, were obviously expensive, and under other circumstances, he might have taken them with him. But he had no wish to be caught by the police of Yungay carrying an armful of stolen clothing, so he left them hanging there. Lastly he opened the bottom drawer of the chest in the bedroom and shone the light of the torch into it to make sure the señora hadn't hidden something of value among the lingerie stored there, as women often did. It was then that he saw the picture, and the horror of it fixed even Carlos Ganza, who had seen his share of horrible things, in a state of frozen immobility.

In the light of the torch a large color print was revealed, vivid, sharp, and as real as if the subject were staring him in the face, even though it was obviously only a photograph of a painting. The big staring

eyes were those of a shaman, or witch doctor, for the
headgear had been fashioned out of skin taken from
the head of a stag. The horns had almost the appearance of coming from the witch doctor's head, too, so
the mask was obviously of a time far older than Carlos
Ganza ever remembered seeing, although he had more
than once evaded the guards to prowl the museums of
Lima at night after they were closed, seeking anything
of value that might be sold or ransomed back to
museum authorities.

The *brujo* himself had obviously been painted in the
act of pronouncing the most awful curse he knew, and
the camera had faithfully recorded everything. The
horrible eyes, glaring with the reflected light of the flash
bulb used to photograph the picture, shone almost as if
the witch doctor were actually alive. In fact, even
though he knew it was only a picture, Carlos almost expected the lips to move in the words of the curse and,
suddenly shivering, shut the drawer quickly, closing
away the horrible photograph.

Stopping only to pick up the microscope and his
lunch box with the camera in it, he headed for his
room in the village.

IV

The nightly sea breeze had still been blowing when
Lael Valdez stepped out of Guy Reed's stateroom and
leaned against the rail of the *Mercy* to breathe deeply
of the morning freshness in the air. Even though the
port of Chimbote lay close to the equator and this was
only October—the beginning of spring in this southern
clime—the night had been cool. Looking down from
the deck of the old liner—long since having seen its
best days as a passenger vessel and wartime hospital
ship and destined now at the end of its life for the
scrap heap—Lael watched the people of the town begin
to move about as the port city came alive for another
day.

The strong breeze from the Pacific outside the protected harbor bent the fronds of the sentinel trunks in
the long allée of royal palms, making them look oddly
like a parade of feather dusters across the morning
sky. The sun, often hidden by fog and mist during
much of the day here on the northern coast of Peru,
was breaking through with the promise of something
rare—a clear day.

From the dock below came the cry of a woman
selling roses, and taking a coin from her pocket, Lael
tossed it to her. The coin was caught in the odd upside-
down-shaped hat the vendor wore, like most of the
mestizos, or mixed breeds, of the lowland population.
In return a bunch of roses, exquisite and dewy fresh,
was tossed expertly up for Lael to catch. She held
them for a while to enjoy the fragrance before taking
them into Guy's stateroom and putting them in a vase.

Across the street that paralleled the long dock pro-
jecting into gleaming Ferrol Bay, a bed of red and
yellow cannas reminded Lael of Monte Carlo, half a
world away and, it seemed, more than half a universe
in custom and civilization. She and Guy had driven
through Monte Carlo about six months ago. It had
been the beginning of spring there, too, and they'd
been on the way to Genoa and the ship that had taken
them, with Guy's oil prospecting equipment and her
cameras as almost their only baggage, to Buenos Aires.

She'd been happy that spring day on the Mediter-
ranean for she'd been setting out on a journey of adventure with the man she loved. From Buenos Aires,
in the Land Rover that now stood patiently across the
street from the gangplank connecting the ship with the
pier, they had started upon the almost unbelievable
journey, literally across the top of the Western world
below the equator. It had been an adventure in search
of an ancient treasure in this region where archaeologists, bemused at first by the magnificent remains of
the Inca dynasty, were just now starting to look beyond
it into the shadowed haunts of man's beginnings in the
New World.

She and Guy had already discovered the first evidence that in the uplands of the Cordillera Blanca and its environs—the very heart of the Andes that formed a watershed at many places in sight of the Pacific—civilized man had existed far longer than anyone else had thought possible. Far beyond, in fact, even the Chimu, the Mochica, and the Tiahuanaco civilizations of Peru, and long before the coming of either the Inca or the Spanish conquerors. The discovery had promised to be the crowning feat of Guy's already brilliant career—until he had been stricken down by the strange fever that even the medical genius of Dr. Jack Smithson and his dedicated staff aboard the *Mercy* had so far been unable either to name or contain.

The door of Guy Reed's cabin opened and Smithson came out. Stocky, almost ugly, in rumpled whites with the inevitable stethoscope hanging from his neck, the bearded older doctor had quickly come to represent the only rock to which Lael, in a situation for which she had no training or experience, could cling.

"Any change?" she asked.

"None since last night." Smithson paused at the rail beside her. "Except that his temperature has stopped climbing."

"Isn't that a good sign?"

"Not always. It's sometimes part of a shock picture that hits Paraguayan and Argentine hemorrhagic fever cases around the fifth to the eighth day after onset, but as I told Grant on the telephone, neither disease is the villain here. What time are you meeting him?"

"About ten-thirty. It's a local Faucett plane and may not be on time." She turned to face him. "What do you expect him to do that you and your staff haven't already done, Dr. Smithson?"

"Perhaps nothing," Smithson admitted, "but Grant Reed is the leading world authority on obscure fevers. He received his M.D. and his Ph.D. in the same year and won the Nobel Prize four years later for his work on the Paraguayan hemorrhagic virus. Maybe he can think of something we've missed."

"I don't think so." Her tone was somber. "Anything I ever really loved either died—or went away."

Startled by the quiet conviction in her tone, and not knowing what to say, Smithson glanced quickly at the girl. She was looking at the palms and, he was sure, not seeing them at all. Yet, in spite of her natural sorrow at the prospect of losing someone she loved very deeply, he could not help marveling at her extraordinary beauty—the product, she'd told him, of a Bolivian father and a Boston-Irish mother. Or at her courage in the face of what must be the most crucial challenge in her life.

His own daughter back home in Indiana, he thought, would be only a few years younger than the twenty-six he remembered seeing listed on Lael Valdez's passport, when she was registered as a hospital assistant on the *Mercy* so she could be assigned to a stateroom.

"At least you've done everything for Guy anyone could have done under the circumstances," he assured her.

"Fortunately Augustine Almaviva, our drill crew foreman, has a sister who runs a restaurant here in Chimbote. He wanted to visit her, so I was able to hire him to make the trip down from Yungay with us. Augustine held Guy on a mattress we placed across the back seat of the Land Rover." She nodded toward the dock where the battered vehicle, showing scars from the rough tracks of the Andes on practically every square foot of its surface, was parked. "The road was pretty rough until we got to the Pan-American Highway."

"I still admire your courage."

"A year ago I probably wouldn't have been able to cope, but Guy taught me you do what you have to do, without complaining."

"By the way, you can bring Grant directly to the ship. I've already registered him in as a consultant and assigned him the stateroom beyond Guy." His large hand covered her smaller one on the ship's rail and gave it an affectionate squeeze. "Have you had breakfast?"

"Not yet. I didn't feel like eating."

"Better eat something and lie down until you have to leave for the airport. We've got capable nurses, you know; it really isn't necessary for you to sit by Guy's bed every night."

"He often asks for me when he wakes. I don't want him to think I've deserted him."

"Delirium is common with these fevers. I doubt that he'll ever remember whether you're there or not."

"I'll remember," she said simply. "And please don't try to reassure me when there's no change for the better, Doctor."

"This fall in blood pressure isn't a reassuring development," he concluded. "Neither are certain signs of neurological involvement."

"Like the tremors of his tongue that make it almost impossible for him to talk intelligently any more? Or take food by mouth without danger of strangling?" Again he was startled by her ability to go directly to the heart of the situation—and to face even the most unpleasant possibilities.

"With hypotension—low blood pressure—and the shock syndrome we're seeing develop now, chances of recovery are decreased," Smithson conceded. "Particularly if we're dealing with a new disease."

"I'm sure we are." Her voice had a strong note of conviction.

"Then God help us all."

V

At Boston, Massachusetts, in a Harvard University physics classroom more than four thousand miles away from the Peruvian port city of Chimbote, where Grant's plane was beginning its descent to the airport, Dr. Philemon E. Mallinson of the Institute of Radiation

Physics was addressing an early morning class. On the table before him, beside an ashtray holding his pipe with its still glowing coals, lay a small piece of what appeared to be bone, with a blackish substance stuck to it.

"Bishop James Usher—sometimes spelled with two *s*'s—was an Irish divine who lived and wrote in the first half of the seventeenth century," Dr. Mallinson opened the class by saying. "Between 1650 and 1654, Bishop Usher produced what was long considered to be his most important work, the *Annales Veteris et Novi Testamenti*, propounding a system of biblical chronology that placed the creation of the world at somewhat less than six thousand years ago—in the year 4004 B.C., in fact, on October twenty-third, at nine A.M."

A titter of amusement went through the class, which consisted of both undergraduates and a few graduate students needing a general science course to fill out their schedules. Picking up the bone fragment and examining it briefly, Professor Mallinson passed it to a student in the front row, to be handed from person to person until all had been given an opportunity to study it. Taking up his pipe, while the students were studying the fragment, Professor Mallinson drew upon it several times before continuing, wreathing his massive head with a cloud of smoke, like some latter-day Moses on a mountaintop in the wilderness.

"Fortunately, the origin of man has been placed accurately some millions of years earlier by means of the technique of radiocarbon assay. Popularly known as the 'atomic clock,' this method has become one of the most important tools of the archaeologist and anthropologist in calculating the chronological sequence of man's residence on earth, as well as the age of almost anything that once possessed life. Are any of you familiar with the procedure from your high school physics studies?"

Perhaps half the class raised their hands, but at the end of the row, a thin-faced young man with an unruly mop of red hair said, "I'd appreciate it if you would go over the method again, sir."

"All right, Mr. Prentiss, I'll go slowly so please make notes. Carbon, as you all know, is the basic ingredient of all living matter, so naturally it is found in all animal or vegetable life. Living things eat other living things, so there is a constant intake of carbon into the body, along with an equally constant outflow as waste. As it happens, carbon is not always the simple element it appears to be in the form of a lump of coal, or even a diamond—its purest state. Am I going too fast for you, Mr. Prentiss?"

"No, sir," said the red-haired student. "Not at all, sir."

"Actually, ordinary carbon consists of three isotopes, chemically indistinguishable from each other," Professor Mallinson continued. "They do, however, show quite different characteristics upon more sophisticated study, particularly a variation in atomic weight ranging between twelve, thirteen, and fourteen. Most of everyday carbon is C-12, but it also contains about one part to several million of C-13 and C-14, the latter all manufactured in the upper atmosphere, when the carbon dioxide expelled in breathing is exposed to showers of ionized particles called cosmic rays that rain down upon the earth from the vast reaches of outer space.

"When a cosmic particle happens to collide with an atom of carbon in the atmosphere, some of its energy is absorbed and the atom of C-12 is converted into C-13 or C-14. When this 'heavy carbon' is then absorbed by a plant and later eaten by man, or by an animal that is subsequently eaten by man, C-14 becomes a part of the body.

Mallinson paused, then added, "But with this difference from the rest of the tissue carbon: C-14 is radioactive."

There was a sudden stir of interest in the class, a few of whom had been dozing.

"I thought the news that all of you are radioactive would wake some of you up." The teacher's voice took a sardonic note. "While alive you are constantly taking fresh C-14 into your bodies to counteract the gradual loss of what was already there and keep you in what might be called radioactive balance. When you die, however, you cease to take C-14 into your body, and inevitably, the amount in the tissues gradually decreases while the years pass. Fortunately for scientists, the degeneration rate of carbon 14 is fixed, and the half life—the period during which an atom of C-14 will lose half its radiation—has been determined to be—within an accuracy of point-five-four per cent—five thousand five hundred and sixty-eight years."

"Just what does all that mean, sir?" Prentiss asked.

"Simply that, when exposed to a Geiger counter in order to measure radioactivity, an atom of carbon from a tree or a person who died that many years ago would produce only half as many clicks as would the tissues and the C-14 of a tree or a man who died this morning."

From the end of the table where the last student to examine it had placed the small specimen, Dr. Mallinson once again picked it up.

"This fragment of bone, with what we take to be a small piece of woven fabric attached perhaps by dried blood was sent to me for analysis from Peru by Mr. Guy Reed—a well-known and highly successful petroleum geologist with a bent for archaeology. Not only has Mr. Reed accumulated a fortune by discovering oil where few thought it existed, he has also uncovered some rather startling archaeological finds in the process. I know nothing about this particular specimen—except what Mr. Reed himself wrote, when he sent it to us by Air Express for radiocarbon dating—which is that it was found somewhere in the highlands of Peru in a valley known as the Callejón de Huaylas. Unless some of you wish to examine it further, I shall now turn the specimen over to the atomic clock technician, and we should know the age, with considerable accuracy, before the period is over."

VI

In the somewhat dingy-looking building serving as a departure and arrival lounge for all flights to and from Chimbote, Grant Reed saw no one immediately who resembled his mental picture of the sort of girl Guy usually selected, either as a wife or traveling companion—until he noticed a young woman wearing a calf-length skirt, short leather boots, and a man's shirt open at the collar hurrying down the corridor toward him. She possessed one of the loveliest faces he'd remembered seeing anywhere, and even before she called out to him, the unmistakable lithe grace of her body and the way she carried herself, as if quite unconscious of her looks or of what anyone thought of them, told him this must be Lael Valdez.

"I'm sorry to be late, Dr. Reed." It was the same voice he remembered on the phone.

"You're not late, Miss Valdez," he said, shaking the hand she gave him. "The plane was a few minutes early."

"That's a miracle in this part of the world." She fell into step beside him, matching his stride easily. "Sand is always blowing across the Pan-American Highway, and when the road crews can't keep up with the piles, one is held up, as I was this morning. Do you have any other luggage?"

"None except what you see. I learned to travel light a long time ago."

"Our Land Rover's outside. The *Mercy* is docked only a few miles away at the north end of the bay."

"I saw her as we were coming in for a landing. Is my brother—?"

"Dr. Smithson is quite concerned because Guy's temperature and blood pressure fell rather sharply during the night," she told him. "He has some difficulty in swallowing, too, but I'm sure you know what that means far better than I."

He nodded, his expression grave. "It's a crisis these

hemorrhagic fevers often show about the eighth day. If the patient survives this backset, though, he usually begins to improve rather rapidly afterward."

"Pray God that will be true in Guy's case."

Her hand went instinctively, and quite unconsciously he was sure, to the cross hanging by a small chain from her neck. It was of gold, exquisitely fashioned, and obviously expensive, just the sort of gift Guy would select for this girl with her striking loveliness and obvious breeding.

They emerged from the terminal and Lael Valdez led the way to a battered Land Rover parked nearby.

"It was new when we left Buenos Aires six months ago," she said, "but the roads crossing the Andes aren't the Pan-Am Highway and the one from the Callejón de Huaylas down to Chimbote isn't much better. Toss your bag into the back seat; the door on your side is a bit hard to open since I slid into a bank coming down from the drill site about a month ago."

She was under the wheel and had the engine going by the time he opened the door on the other side and slipped in beside her.

"Would it be prying if I asked just what my brother has been doing in this part of the world?" he asked.

"Guy thought there was oil beneath the area we're studying. We've done some preliminary testing with the seismograph and drilled a couple of shallow test wells."

"Some travel literature I read on the plane mentioned the Callejón de Huaylas. Unless my memory fails me, the elevation there is around eight thousand feet."

"We were even higher." She broke off suddenly to shout a Spanish epithet at a goat that contested their passage; they had entered the narrow streets of Chimbote itself now, and all of Lael Valdez's attention was required to negotiate them with the Land Rover.

"Would it be too painful to give me a brief history of Guy's illness?" Grant asked when they were once again on a wider road leading to the dock at the northern end of the bay.

"It started about seven or eight days ago with a chill, some fever, and generalized aching. When it became obvious that he was getting worse, I brought him down to the *Mercy* in the Land Rover with the help of our drill foreman. By then Guy was half delirious, but he kept insisting that he didn't really need any help."

"My brother was always pretty stubborn—"

"I've often heard him say the same thing about you."

"Maybe I got mine from him. He practically raised me from the time our parents were killed in an airplane accident, when I was about twelve."

"I know. He's very proud of the record you've made in the field of public health."

Why, he wondered, was there a note of what appeared to be anger in her voice and a sudden stiffness in her tone? Then he thought of an answer.

"You blame me for not being available when Guy became ill, don't you?" he asked. "Just as you blame yourself for not bringing him to the *Mercy* sooner than you did."

She gave him a startled look and almost let the Land Rover drift off the highway, then pulled it back with a jerk.

"You're very perceptive—for a man."

"I'm a doctor, so I often see things other people miss and create a pattern of truth from them. As to the trouble you had finding me, though, if I hadn't been on the way from the Sudan Interior Missions to Lagos and the United States, you might not have reached me for weeks."

"And Guy would have been dead."

"Why are you so convinced that he's going to die, Miss Valdez?"

Seeing the sudden tears in her eyes, he recognized the depth of her concern for his brother—and envied Guy.

"I swore to Guy I wouldn't tell anyone—not even you," she said. "Actually, if he'd known what I was doing, he'd never have let me send for you."

"Why?"

"Because coming here may well cost you your life
—just as being here will cost me mine, before many
more days pass."

"I still don't understand—"

"Guy and I are under a curse, Dr. Reed—but then
I don't suppose a scientist could understand that
either."

It was a strange statement, but before he could
pursue its meaning, she made a sharp left turn onto the
long dock against which the *Mercy* was moored, divert-
ing his attention to the familiar profile of the old hospital ship and the familiar stocky figure of Jack Smithson waiting at the head of the gangplank.

VII

At a small table in the shade of a eucalyptus tree growing in front of one of several restaurants facing the
Plaza Central of Chimbote, Augustine Almaviva was
drinking a "pisco sour." A white grape brandy with the
juice of a fresh lime added, the drink was almost as
popular as the considerably cheaper *chicha,* a fer-
mented corn beer drunk by the less affluent part of the
population.

Although Augustine Almaviva was taking his ease,
he was far from feeling either relaxed or happy. After
only three days on the dry coastal plain, he was already
homesick for Yungay and the mountains looming over
the Callejón de Huaylas. The illness of Señor Guy
Reed seemed to mean he was probably out of a job,
too, but the señora had paid him well and he'd been
determined to enjoy his holiday—until day before yesterday. Since then, however, his head had felt as if a
thousand devils were boring holes in it, and his bones
ached worse than they had last summer when he'd had
a touch of a malaria that had swept through the lovely
upland valley like an avenging angel months earlier but
was now being controlled by the health authorities.

The increased headache this morning, Augustine decided, could be a hangover from the fiesta last evening at the *restaurante* of his sister, Conchita, and her husband, Juan Torres. The fiesta hadn't been his idea but he hadn't minded paying the cost, so Conchita could show off to their friends her smart brother, who had surely found a gold mine when Señor Reed insisted upon drilling dry holes where everybody knew there was no chance of finding oil.

He *had* drunk more corn beer than he should last night, too, Augustine freely admitted, but he had been feeling bad before the fiesta had even started. The headache had only grown worse until, drunk at last, he had slept on the floor of the *restaurante* after the fiesta finally ended. He had fled the house early, too, hoping to escape Conchita's insistence that, in spite of supplying money for the affair, he should also help clean up the mess.

This morning, Augustine Almaviva felt no urge to enjoy anything, not even his pisco sour. An ambitious man, who had occupied the position of foreman of Señor Reed's drilling crew that had been searching for oil in the upland plateau above his village of Yungay, Augustine had thought of looking for work in the oil fields to the north, around Trujillo, but now he was coming to believe Yungay was a paradise compared to this grubby port city.

Augustine had not yet eaten, waiting for the pain in his head and legs to be eased by the pisco sours. If he wished, however, he could still go down to the shore, where far better *restaurantes* were located than the one run by Conchita and her husband, Juan Torres. There he could dine on *chupe de mariscos* and *ceviche,* a fish delicacy best eaten in small pieces soaked in lemon or lime juice. Or since he didn't feel like catching them himself, he could purchase some of the large prawns called *camarones,* which would be cooked for him on the spot by the seller.

Or, again, since his stomach still felt queasy, he

could simply watch the sea rush in, cold from the
Humboldt Current that flowed north from the Antarctic, to break against the rocky shore. At another
time, he might even have enjoyed watching the huge
crabs, looking like colorful, and sometimes seemingly
evil, knights-in-armor of purple, green, and scarlet,
battling each other for no reason at all. The cold current brought a bountiful harvest of plankton into shallow water, generating plenty of food just for the taking
in the form of the bait fish and anchovies that schooled
in such thick layers in the shallow water that it seemed
one could walk upon them.

Today, however, Augustine Almaviva felt no more
like watching the things that had so entranced him on
his first days in Chimbote than he felt like observing
the cormorants perched on the rocks of the guano
islands. It was doubtful whether he could even have
seen all those things if he had gone down to the shore,
for the throbbing pain in his head, legs, and back was
growing worse by the minute. In fact, even the familiar
scenes around the square had begun to waver, now
appearing, now disappearing.

Signaling for another drink to the waiter watching
from inside the restaurant, Augustine sipped it briefly
but put down the glass while still three-fourths full.
Around the square old men were sitting, nursing the
single drinks they could afford each morning, while
talking endlessly about the same things they had dis-
cussed so profoundly yesterday and the day before—
and which they would discuss again tomorrow.

Their images wavered oddly before Augustine's eyes
and he shook his head to try to clear it, hoping to see
someone he recognized there who would listen to the
account of his own miseries. The whole scene only
coalesced into a phantasmagoria of light and color
however, and, suddenly conscious of a thirst far more
demanding than could be quenched by even a half
dozen pisco sours, Augustine lurched to his feet. Dropping a few coins on the table beside the almost un-

tasted drink, he staggered across the square toward the fountain playing in the center.

There, a policeman was talking to a girl with only one eye—uncovered by the shawl she wore over her hair—which was a strange thing, if Augustine had felt like considering it. His only urge, however, was to shove his head beneath a stream pouring from one of the llama-headed faucets of the fountain and allow the cool water to pour on his face and down his collar. Scooping up handfuls of water from the fountain itself, too, he drank in great gulps, seeking to assuage the fire searing his vitals.

"You there!" the policeman called. "That is forbidden!"

Augustine didn't hear, however, or know what he was doing. Suddenly pitching forward into the fountain itself, he lay face downward and unconscious with his nose, even his ears, under water. He would undoubtedly have drowned had not the policeman pulled him out and lifted him by the middle to drain water from his lungs.

Having had the good sense to keep Augustine Almaviva from drowning, the policeman was fortunately also intelligent enough to recognize that he was sick, not drunk. A shrill blast of his whistle brought help, and soon the man from Yungay was in an ambulance, careening through the narrow streets of the city with the siren going full blast, bound for the dockside and the white hospital ship moored there.

Placed on a pipe berth in the large admitting ward amidships, Augustine was examined briefly by Dr. Antonio y Marelia, a Bolivian physician attached to the hospital staff for further training. Busy with the hordes of outpatients who swarmed to the clinic on the *Mercy* every day, Dr. Marelia made only a tentative diagnosis of malignant malaria—to combat an epidemic of which the *Mercy* had come to Chimbote several months before at the request of the Pan-American Health Organization—ordered blood smears, and went back to the outpatient clinic.

Meanwhile Lael Valdez, who could have recognized Augustine Almaviva, and perhaps even diagnosed his condition, was on the way to the old white ship with Grant Reed in the Land Rover.

VIII

It had been a bad day for Manoel Allanza—but then most of them had been bad lately. Legless at birth except for small, badly deformed feet attached to short stumps, Manoel had made his living since he'd been able to talk by begging, propelling himself about on a small wooden platform with four casters that served him as legs, and mouthing curses at those who passed him by without tossing him a coin.

Through the years the crippled man had developed tremendous strength in his shoulders and arms from pushing his small vehicle and also from swinging himself up a slanting palm tree to the pocket in the crumbling wall of a deserted house that served him as home in the *barrio,* or slum, of Chimbote. Each evening on the way home he would stop to purchase food for his supper and a bottle of cheap *vino blanco.* He didn't need much food, for by day he fed, sometimes luxuriously, upon garbage discarded by the restaurants around the Plaza Central.

Carrying his small package between the tiny feet, Manoel would swing himself up into his elevated abode, proud that, unlike most of the adobe shacks in this district where it practically never rained, his own home had a roof. There he would count the money left from what had been given him during the day, hiding it behind a brick so cunningly fitted into the back wall of the hovel that he was confident no thief could have told it from the others. Then having eaten, he would sip his wine slowly, looking down from his elevated perch upon the seething, hungry, unhappy mass of humanity making up the barrio of Chimbote while telling the beads of his rosary, convinced that he, Manoel Allanza, though a cripple, was not like one of them.

Lately, though, the pickings had not been particularly good for Manoel. The steel and fish-meal factories driven by electricity produced from the swift current of the River Santa, as it descended from the Andes to the sea, were working only half-time. Word of the severe malaria epidemic that had brought the *Mercy* to Chimbote and of the pesky night-flying mosquitoes—said to have carried the often fatal plague from the other side of the world—had spread rapidly up and down the Pan-American Highway that passed through Chimbote. Even travelers had taken to hurrying through, when they could not avoid the area altogether, and ships bypassed the excellent port.

Both priests and brujos denied the claim of Dr. José Figueroa, the district health officer, and the doctors aboard the white ship in the harbor that mosquitoes carried the fever which could turn even a strong man into one of the living dead. The priests claimed the pestilence was a punishment for the sins of the people who, before the malaria epidemic that had now subsided, were earning more than a mere pittance for the first time in their lives. Doing so, they had been willing to spend much of it on chicha and the *tapadas,* women who, with heads covered by shawls leaving only one eye visible, prowled the city day and night in search of men with money enough to purchase their favors. The witch doctors, on the other hand, named the bone-shaking fever a curse upon the people for turning away from the ancient gods and from the support of the brujos themselves.

As for the great white ship in the harbor with its yanqui doctors and nurses, opinion was divided. A few in the barrio believed what they read or heard about the miracles performed on board the ship. Manoel himself had seen a baby, hideously deformed with its face practically split in half at birth, miraculously made whole by the surgeons working in the operating rooms of the *Mercy.* But others believed the witch doctors who claimed the norteamericanos were only there to experiment on the poor and the sick in order to learn ways to cure more of their own people in the land to the north, where every man was already rich.

This particular morning, one of the casters on Manoel's rolling platform had finally rusted through and come apart, leaving him only three. He never left home with money, lest the police search him and take it, so he'd been forced to limp, so to speak, on only three wheels, hoping to find someone compassionate enough to give him money to buy a new caster—or drunk enough to be robbed easily. He had circled the Plaza Central several times by ten-thirty, looking for a likely prospect, before he spied the dark-skinned man sitting before the Café Marisco, sipping his pisco sour.

The grape brandy, Manoel knew, was not likely to make anyone drunk enough to start tossing coins around before he had consumed at least a half dozen. But the solitary drinker swayed occasionally in his chair, indicating that he might have had something stronger before coming to the restaurant, so Manoel stayed on the alert.

Fortunately for his purpose, too, no one else was out on the square at the moment—except a policeman talking to a tapada—and inching a little closer to the small section of the square devoted to the outdoor tables of the restaurant where the man was sitting, Manoel studied him speculatively. The drinker was a full-blooded Indian, judging by his dark face and prominent nose. Probably from the uplands of the Sierra, he had perhaps come down to sea level to celebrate some piece of good fortune. The visitor didn't appear to be enjoying his pisco sour, however, and probably was, Manoel surmised, lonelier than he would have been if he had stayed at home.

On his third tour of the square, Manoel noted that the uplander had ordered another drink, which only made the crippled man more thirsty. He didn't dare to push his little platform over to the Central Fountain to drink from one of the llama-headed spouts, however, lest his action encourage the policeman to drive him away in a sudden show of authority to impress the tapada.

The stranger had barely tasted the fresh drink when Manoel saw him lurch to his feet and, dropping a few coins upon the table, stagger across the square toward the fountain. Moving quickly in spite of his missing caster, Manoel swooped past the table where the uplander had been sitting, poured the contents of the nearly full glass down his own gullet with one hand while, with the other, he scooped up the coins the man had left there.

Before the waiter watching the excitement around the square from inside the restaurant realized what had happened, the legless beggar was scooting down a side street safely away from the square. Thus Manoel missed seeing the stranger pulled by the policeman from the fountain into which he had fallen. He also missed seeing the ambulance that ground to a stop shortly afterward and the transferral of the unconscious man to a stretcher—although he did hear the clangor of its bell, as it sped away toward the waterfront and the great white ship docked there.

But what did it matter? The refreshing coolness of the drink was even then quenching the thirst in Manoel's stomach. And when he gleefully counted the coins, he saw that he had enough to buy the badly needed fourth caster for his means of locomotion—plus perhaps even a hamburger, that great gift of the gringos, at one of the new brightly lit eating places along the Pan-American Highway.

IX

The *Mercy,* Grant saw, as the Land Rover moved down the long pier, had weathered considerably since he'd last visited her while she'd been moored at Tanjungperak. The white paint was peeling off the high sides of the ship, with its three decks above the hull itself and three rows of portholes marking other decks below—six in all. Three hundred and fifty feet long, she had never been a large vessel and even before wartime necessity had turned her into an army-operated hospital ship, had engaged only in middle-cost cruises.

Paint was peeling, too, from the three lifeboats swinging from their davits on the dock side of the flat upper deck, whose red crosses of wartime, he'd seen from the plane coming in, had long since faded to a dingy brown. The double rows of life rafts swung along the sides were stained and worn, too, from exposure to weather and the sea.

Actually, as Grant well knew, the *Mercy* had always been, in spite of its age, an excellent hospital afloat. Usually it was manned by a very skilled complement of doctors, nurses, and attendants, many of them volunteers from the States who came and went for short periods of duty to supplement the small regular medical staff. The second deck, as he remembered it, was devoted to quarters for staff and crew, with staterooms both inside and out while below it was the heart of the hospital itself.

In the two operating rooms, many wounded, some taken directly off the beaches during battle, when she'd served as an army hospital ship in wartime, had been saved by doctors and nurses working sometimes for thirty-six hours at a stretch without rest. The smaller treatment rooms and adjacent X-ray department and laboratory were used for reducing fractures, putting on casts, and minor surgery, as well as doubling as examining rooms for medical patients. The decks below constituted the wards, some equipped with beds bolted to the floor, others with pipe berths that could be double-decked, if the occurrence of an epidemic made rapid admission of patients necessary.

Since the end of the Korean War, Grant knew, the *Mercy* had operated mainly as a training school for native doctors and technicians. Anchoring sometimes for months in a port, it had served as a center for treating patients who came to the ship, while teaching groups of medical personnel, doctors, nurses, and technicians, whose previous training left much to be desired. Lately, he'd heard, the activities of the Mercy Foundation, sponsor of the ship, had been sharply curtailed by lack of funds, a common experience with humanitarian nonprofit organizations. From the looks of the old ship, too, it was easy to see that not much money, if any, was being spent on maintenance.

Lael Valdez brought the Land Rover to a stop in a parking slot across the dock from the gangplank leading up to the main lower deck of the ship and swung herself down to the concrete surface. She didn't wait for Grant to get his bag, by which he judged that she did not intend to be questioned about the strange statement she had made as they were turning onto the dock. And respecting her right to be silent, he picked up his ValPak and raincoat and followed her across to the gangplank, where Jack Smithson greeted him with a smile and a warm handshake.

"Sorry your visit to the *Mercy* couldn't be under more pleasant circumstances, Grant," he said as they moved along the deck toward Guy's stateroom. "Your brother became ill just about eight days ago, with the usual picture of a general malaise caused by anything from flu to the onset of one of the severe hemorrhagic fevers. The symptoms grew steadily more severe over the next two days, according to Lael, and she finally persuaded Guy to have medical attention."

Smithson opened the chart he carried. "On admission, his temperature was a hundred and three degrees, pulse one hundred, respiration twenty-four. He was semiconscious and has remained so with intervals of delirium, in which he sometimes has to be restrained. The whole blood count on admission was thirteen thousand with an increase in neutrophil leukocytes."

"That's odd—for a viral fever."

"It was our first clue to the possibility of a bacterial infection instead of a viral one," Smithson agreed.

"Complement fixation tests with all of the viral antigens we have in stock, including Junin and Machupo, have also been negative."

"Any other positive symptoms or signs?"

"His pulse rate has been creeping up and the heart size has slowly increased. Do you know whether Guy ever had any heart disease?"

"He never mentioned it."

"Lael thinks he may have had some trouble before she met him, judging from some of the things he said. My guess from the electrocardiogram and the chest X-ray is that at some time in the past he had at least a mild case of rheumatic heart disease. It must have been compensated pretty well, though, for him to be able to live and work in the Andes."

"Did Guy ever show any signs of shortness of breath, or blueness of his lips and ear lobes at the higher elevations?" Grant asked Lael Valdez, who was walking ahead of them.

"Sometimes, but then a lot of people do. I was occasionally short of breath myself."

"Bleeding and clotting times are normal, so is the blood chemistry, and his blood type is A negative," Smithson continued. "None of our cultures have shown significant organisms either. Lung X-rays revealed a questionable haziness at both bases, but we've had to use an old portable X-ray machine. The pictures we get with it aren't always as clear as we would like."

Grant turned to Lael Valdez again. "Had you heard of much fever where you were?" he asked.

"The men working with us didn't say anything about it. I bought our food in the public market, so I'm sure I would have heard if there'd been much sickness."

"I spoke to Dr. Figueroa, the district health officer, but nothing unusual has been reported in the Callejón de Huaylas," Smithson added. "Shall we go inside now?"

"I'll wait out here," said Lael Valdez. "There's a deck chair outside my cabin."

"Good, you need the rest," Dr. Smithson told her.

"This girl has been sitting up all night with Guy ever since he was admitted, Grant."

X

Grant's examination revealed nothing new. During it, Guy's eyes opened once and he roused up, but seemed unaware of his surroundings, until his gaze focused on Grant's face. Then he tried to raise himself up in bed, only to fall back exhausted before anyone could make a move to restrain him.

"Gra-a-an-n—." The word was hardly audible.

"I came as soon as Miss Valdez called me, Guy. Do you understand?"

A faint pressure against his hand told him the answer was yes. But when the sick man tried to speak again, "S-a-ve . . . La-el" were the only words Grant could distinguish before he lapsed back into delirium.

"What brought the *Mercy* to Chimbote in the first place?" Grant asked as they were leaving the sickroom.

"An epidemic of malignant malaria," said Smithson.

Grant's eyebrows lifted. "It's a long way to the African Gold Coast—for a mosquito."

"More direct than you'd think at first glance. Chimbote is near the mouth of the Santa River, and Peru is building a massive hydroelectric system above here. Some of the equipment was flown in from Manáos, after being brought there by freighter from an abandoned project in Africa. Apparently some *Anopheles gambiae* from the Gold Coast stowed away aboard and made their way, across the Andes, to the Callejón de Huaylas—"

"Lael Valdez spoke of that place this morning."

"She and Guy were living in Yungay, a town in the valley. Dr. Figueroa found some *gambiae* mosquitoes there about six months ago loaded with malignant malaria parasites. Soon afterward quite a lot of the natives began to have chills and even went into comas when their brain vessels got plugged with the parasite-harboring blood cells. At the time we were at Guayaquil in Ecuador, but a hurry call came from Dr. Figueroa, and since Chimbote is the closest safe harbor to the uplands where the epidemic was raging, we came here. We lost a lot of patients at first, but once Figueroa and his crews got the *gambiae* invasion under control and people began to realize what had happened, we started seeing most cases early enough to destroy the parasites in the blood stream with chloroquine phosphate before they killed the patient."

"It's a good thing you and your staff had spent so much time in the Far East where malignant malaria is endemic."

"But none of that experience is any help to your brother. After three days of observation I still don't have the faintest idea what we're deaing with. It could be even a new disease."

"If that's true and Guy's condition is any indication of its virulence, we're in for real trouble."

Lael Valdez was pacing the deck outside when the two doctors emerged, and turned to face them.

"What do you think?" she asked.

"As of now the diagnosis can only be pyrexia of undetermined origin," Grant told her.

"PUO. I used to hear medical students in Boston use that term when I was working in a clinical laboratory there. But to them it was sort of a joke."

"This one is certainly no joke," said Grant. "Still, tropical fevers often burn themselves out. Fortunately, the patient's resistance mechanisms start functioning the moment a micro-organism invades the body and, given time, they can often overcome the infection."

"Can't you do *anything?*" she asked, with a note of bitterness, almost of accusation, in her voice.

"We can attack the causative agent with drugs, antibiotics, and what we call supportive medical treatment," he explained patiently. "But in the end, it's the patient's own immunological mechanism that enables him to overcome the invader. We can only pray that

Guy's strength will be enough to let him build up the necessary immunity in his blood to throw off the infection."

"Did he recognize you?"

"I think so, but all he said was 'Save Lael.' He's obviously more concerned about you than he is about himself."

"Dr. Smithson!" A plump young man in a white coat, with a stethoscope hanging from his neck, was hurrying along the deck toward them. "Could I see you for a minute, please?"

"Certainly, Tonio," said Smithson. "Dr. Antonio y Marelia, Dr. Grant Reed."

"I am honored, Dr. Reed." The young doctor gave him a ceremonial bow before shaking hands.

"What is it?" Smithson asked somewhat impatiently. "Dr. Reed and I were conferring—"

"A thousand pardons, but a new admission was brought in about an hour ago—in a coma."

"In coma, did you say?" Smithson was suddenly alert.

"Comatose and febrile—but not from malignant malaria as I suspected when I saw him brought up the gangplank," said Marelia. "I was busy with outpatients at the time, so I ordered admission and blood work. The patient is an Indian and was found lying face down in a fountain in the Plaza Central, according to the men who brought him in."

"He could be drunk—or even injured," said Smithson.

"I think not," said Marelia. "His symptoms and his blood picture are exactly the same as those of Señor Guy Reed."

XI

In the lecture room of the Harvard University Institute of Radiation Physics in Boston, Dr. Philemon Mallinson was just finishing his class when a technician in a white pants suit entered and handed him a single sheet of paper.

"I now have the report of the radiocarbon assay on the material I showed you at the beginning of the hour that was sent to me from Peru by Mr. Guy Reed," Mallinson announced. "According to our most sophisticated instruments, this material is five thousand years old, plus or minus two hundred years."

A murmur of amazement came from the audience.

"I have no knowledge of just where this specimen was obtained, except for the general area," Mallinson continued. "I believe, however, that it represents one of the earliest finds in the Peruvian Andes. Mr. Reed will be notified by radiogram immediately, as requested, and asked to send further details. Class is dismissed."

XII

For an instant after Dr. Marelia spoke, there was a startled silence, then Jack Smithson said sarcastically: "Don't be so dramatic, Tonio; almost all fevers behave the same in the beginning. What history does this patient give?"

"The police say he was drinking pisco in a restaurant on the square, when he suddenly lunged for the fountain and began to pour water on his head and try to drink."

"Sounds like he's drunk?"

"He babbles, but his temperature is a hundred and four. The police say he would have drowned if they had not pulled him out."

"What does *he* say?"

"None of us can understand him. He speaks Quechua—the Inca tongue."

"I both speak and understand Quechua," said Lael Valdez. "Perhaps I can talk to him."

"That makes sense," said Smithson. "Lead the way, Tonio."

The lower deck, which had been converted into hospital wards, was divided by watertight bulkheads

into several sections in which a number of patients lay
in pipe berths. They moved on to a smaller ward, however, equipped with hospital beds bolted to the steel
floor. A nurse was standing beside the sick man's bed,
and one of the natives employed as orderly was at the
other, ready to hold him in bed when he thrashed about
in delirium.

Grant was walking behind Lael Valdez when they
came into the ward. She caught her breath and appeared to stumble momentarily at the sight of the sick
man. When he put out his hand to catch her elbow
and steady her, however, she shook it off almost impatiently—but not before he saw the stark fear in her
eyes as all color drained from her face.

"Are you all right?" he asked.

She nodded, but the look of fear was still there.

"Sure?"

"Of course I'm sure," she said sharply. "Why would
you ask?"

"For a moment there it was almost as if you'd seen
a ghost."

"Well, I haven't," she snapped and he didn't pursue
the matter of her reaction further, although he was
almost certain that she'd recognized the sick Indian,
yet for reasons of her own didn't want to acknowledge
the fact.

Jack Smithson had been examining the chart and
spoke just then. "The patient's identification papers
show that he is Augustine Almaviva, a resident of
Yungay."

"Yungay?" Grant turned to the girl. "Weren't you
and Guy drilling somewhere in that area?"

"Yes." She had herself under full control now. "But
the valley is roughly a hundred miles long and thickly
populated."

"Please ask him when he became ill, Lael," said
Smithson.

When she spoke to the almost comatose patient in
the same tongue Grant had heard the stewardess use
earlier that morning, the sick man opened his eyes.

Seeing Lael, he tried to sit up, only to fall back on the bed. He also tried to speak, but only a babble of sounds came, with one word repeated several times.

"Doesn't that word mean curse, Señorita Valdez?" Dr. Marelia asked.

"There's another expression that sounds almost exactly like it," she said quickly. "He's trying to say he fell into the fountain."

"The tremor of his tongue obviously interferes with speech." Smithson's voice was sober now. "You may be right about the similarity of the two cases, Tonio."

"I'll wait on deck while you make your examinations." Lael Valdez was in full control of herself now. "It's rather warm in here."

"We don't seem to be getting anything out of him anyway," Smithson conceded. "If he does start speaking more intelligibly, we'll call you."

Lael Valdez was waiting when the three doctors came out on deck. The breeze from the broad bay made the early summer heat less cloying than had been the atmosphere inside the ship itself, but she was still somewhat pale.

"It may simply be a coincidence that Guy has been drilling in the Yungay area and that this man comes from there—or it may not," Grant said to her. "Are you sure there's been no mention of an outbreak of fever in Yungay?"

"None that I've heard of. Why do you ask?"

"I've got sort of an instinct about this kind of thing. Most epidemiologists develop it after a few years. It tells me there must be some connection between my brother's case and this one."

"An epidemic of two cases doesn't prove anything," Jack Smithson protested.

"I'd still like to check on Almaviva a little more closely. The best place to start is probably the square where he fell into the fountain."

"Take the Land Rover," said Lael, who was listening. "I usually sleep in the afternoons so I can stay with Guy at night."

"The plaza's in the middle of town," said Dr. Marelia. "Turn right when you leave the pier, Dr. Grant.
You'll go straight there."

XIII

Only three cafés were located around the Plaza Central.
Grant started with the one directly across from the
fountain to which the police had said Almaviva had
fled, apparently seized with a massive thirst because
of the fever burning within his body. The second waiter
he spoke to remembered the sick man, whose fall into
the public fountain had created quite a stir.

"For three days, señor, this man came each morning
and drank pisco sours at a small table out there." The
waiter pointed to the outdoor café that was part of the
restaurant. "He seemed lonely but he spoke only
Quechua and a few words of English. Only a few people—like myself—could understand him."

"Did he mention where he came from?"

"Once he spoke of being from Yungay. That morning, when I brought his first drink, he said the climate
here by the sea did not agree with him. He also said he
felt very bad and planned to go home the next day."

"Did he give any hint of where he was staying in
Chimbote?"

"He never spoke of it, señor."

"And no one ever drank with him?"

"No, señor. That is why I did not believe him a
thief, even after it happened."

Grant was suddenly alert. "What happened?"

"I had brought him a fresh drink, but he barely
sipped it before he put down the glass and rushed
across to the fountain in the center of the square. I
saw him drinking and pouring water over his head like
he had suddenly gone crazy, then the policeman on
duty in the square was blowing his whistle and pulling
the man out of the water. After that the ambulance
came and in the excitement I did not notice the drink

had been finished and the coins I saw the uplander drop on the table as he was leaving had vanished."

"Who could have finished the drink and taken the coins?"

"Who else but a *ladron*—a thief?" The waiter answered his own question. "A legless beggar named Manoel Allanza hangs around here all the time. While I was watching the disturbance at the fountain, the ladron must have drunk the pisco—the glass was almost full—stolen the money, and ran away."

"A legless beggar ran away?"

"This Manoel sits on a small platform with wheels and propels himself about with arms as long as a gorilla, señor. He can move faster than a man can run."

"One more thing." Grant took a twenty-centavos coin from his pocket. "Do you know where Manoel Allanza can be found?"

"In the barrio, of course, señor; everyone there knows him." The waiter pocketed the coin. "He's always boasting of his two-story house as if it were a *casa grande*."

Grant had no trouble finding the barrio of Chimbote; every South American city had its slums. Lima was the worst of all with, it had been reported, over two hundred thousand people living like animals.

Everybody in the barrio of Chimbote also knew Manoel Allanza, who lived in one of the few two-storied houses. When Grant saw it, he understood why the very mention of the beggar's name had brought smiles and even hoots of derision from the people he questioned.

He negotiated the trunk of the leaning palm tree with some difficulty, to find himself facing Manoel Allanza. Crouching inside his elevated hovel, the beggar was half drunk, surly and suspicious, though apparently healthy. He denied even having been at the square that morning, however, much less drinking the rest of the pisco sour left by a man from Yungay. And realizing that he was getting nowhere, Grant finally took one of his cards from his wallet, crossed out his own name and address, and wrote instead the name of the *Mercy* on it and the number of the pier where it was docked. Handing it to the beggar, he warned Manoel that he might become ill in a few days and advised him to bring the card to the *Mercy* at the first sign of sickness.

XIV

It was already past dinnertime when Grant returned to the hospital ship, so he ate in a corner of the main dining room set aside for snacks and coffee for the night crew. As he was finishing, Dr. Jack Smithson came in for coffee with Angus McTavish, the grizzled Scotch chief engineer.

"Discover anything in Chimbote?" Smithson asked.

"Only that if this fever proves to be very contagious, your Indian patient Almaviva had a good opportunity to spread it. We may be seeing the very beginning of a serious epidemic."

"You still have a series of only two cases," the chief engineer commented, "hardly enough to prove there's an epidemic."

"It may well have gone beyond that already." Grant gave them a summary of his interviews with the beggar Manoel in the barrio.

"Surely just drinking from a glass the Indian had been using couldn't infect a man," the engineer protested.

"It only takes one microbe, Chief," said Smithson.

"Like it only takes one rusty bolt to let a cylinder head blow and cripple an entire engine, I suppose."

"How's the work on that crippled engine going, by the way?" Grant asked.

"We're trying to weld a crack in the head, but we really need a new one. And that has to be air-lifted from the States."

"Why wouldn't a replacement be available from ship builders nearby, Chief?"

"That diesel electric is already a museum piece, Doctor—if the *Mercy* could ever make it to a museum. They stopped making equipment parts for them right after World War II."

McTavish finished his coffee and returned to his work in the depths of the ship.

"Guy seems to be holding his own," said Jack Smithson. "From all indications the fever has almost run its course, but I'm not that sanguine about his heart so I started oxygen. Working at high altitudes would have been tough on a healthy man, and with even the mild degree of rheumatic heart disease Guy seems to have had, he could have put a considerable strain on it."

"I imagine he did." Grant voiced a thought that had been on his mind increasingly, since his interview with the beggar that afternoon. "What about Miss Valdez? Has she shown any signs of fever?"

Smithson shook his head. "I just hope she doesn't realize how much danger she's actually in."

"I'd wager she knows a great deal more about how Guy came to develop this fever than she's told any of us, Jack. She's obviously holding something back, so I'm going up into the Callejón de Huaylas tomorrow to look for myself. What about the new patient, Almaviva?"

"He's approaching a crisis, may even already be beyond it. Are you still convinced Guy and this Indian have the same disease?"

"I'd bet on it. The signs and symptoms are identical and both of them have recently been in the same area."

"The Callejón de Huaylas is incredibly beautiful but heavily populated. An epidemic—of anything—would be worse there than down here on the coast, except perhaps in and around Lima."

"Don't forget the barrio of Chimbote. If Manoel Allanza is already infected, whatever we're dealing with could spread through that slum like fire through a shantytown."

"Pray God you're wrong on two counts," said the other doctor soberly. "First, that we're dealing with a new plague. And second, that there've been other contacts besides the two we have here."

"You've forgotten a third—Lael Valdez."

XV

The nurse sitting beside Guy's bed rose when Grant came in, but Lael Valdez only looked up dully and nodded. He checked Guy's chart and saw that the fever pattern was indeed starting to trend sightly downward as Jack Smithson had said. The heart sounds, too, although a little distant, were clear except for a murmur over the area of the mitral valve that often went with chronic rheumatic heart disease.

"Could I speak to you outside, please, Miss Valdez?" Grant asked when he had finished the examination.

For a moment he thought she hadn't heard him, then she rose and preceded him through the door he held open for her. The deck outside was deserted, but from the staff lounge forward came the sound of laughter and a hi-fi playing rock 'n' roll tunes.

"Guy's fever is subsiding," Grant told her. "But Dr. Smithson's somewhat worried about the strain it has put on his heart."

"He's going to die," she said tonelessly.

"You said the same thing this morning. Why are you so sure?"

She shrugged and didn't answer but seemed absorbed in watching the gurgle of water between the side of the ship and the pier.

"I'm going up to the area around Yungay tomorrow." He saw the grip of her hands upon the rail tighten until the knuckles were suddenly white. "I hope you'll go with me."

"And leave Guy when he's dying?" She turned to face him then, her body tense with anger. "You must be heartless."

"Jack Smithson is one of the most capable doctors

I know. He'll give Guy the best possible care available, and the facilities upon the *Mercy,* old as she is, are far better than they would be in any Peruvian hospital. My obligation now is to my duty as an epidemiologist."

"So you're putting your precious reputation as a disease fighter above your duty to your brother?" Her voice was taut and angry. "I'm sorry now that I called you."

He ignored the outburst, recognizing the strain she was under.

"Jack Smithson tells me the Callejón de Huaylas is thickly populated, with many small communities—all served, I imagine, by the same river as the water supply."

"It isn't the water—"

"If you know the answer why don't you tell me?"

She turned upon him savagely—and startlingly beautiful in her anger. "You're the expert who was called in to save Guy, but you're just as helpless as the rest of us."

"Admitted, but all my training and experience tells me a disease such as this must have a source. Occasionally it's a contaminated water supply, sometimes a virus transmitted to humans by animals like rats, squirrels, and chipmunks, usually through fleas as a vector. Or it may be airborne from person to person, which is the hardest type to control. If you look closely enough—"

"And don't die from it yourself—"

"Exactly. So far I've been lucky, although I would have died of Sudan fever in Africa if the blood of a nurse who had recently recovered from an attack of the disease hadn't provided the anti-toxins I needed to keep my body alive while it manufactured its own antibodies. When you reached me in the Atlanta Airport, I'd just been called back to the Center for Disease Control to attack the virus in the laboratory because my immunity from Sudan fever gave me a shield that allowed me to go on and study other diseases in the area."

"You won't have that shield here."

"Neither does anyone else, if my suspicion that this is a new disease proves to be true. I'm going to Yungay tomorrow to see whether more cases have come to light there. It would help to have someone along who knows the territory and speaks the dialect, so I'm asking you to go with me, but I'm going whether you go or not."

"Suppose I refuse to let you use the Land Rover?"

"Then I'll take it myself. I still have the keys."

All of the resentment seemed to go out of her at once and she slumped against the rail. "Do you realize that you're asking me to go back to the same danger that struck Guy down?" she demanded bitterly. "To perhaps risk my life?"

"You risked it when you stayed with Guy and cared for him, but you're obviously still afraid of something up there in that valley. I'm not going to force you to go, although I doubt that there's any danger up there you haven't already been exposed to. Are there any road maps in the Land Rover?"

"In the glove compartment. The tank's full of gas, too, and there are stations all along the road."

"I'll want to spend the night where you and Guy were living—"

"Why?" Her voice was suddenly tense and strained again.

"A clue to what I'm seeking may be inside the house."

"It's outside Yungay. The natives refer to it as the Casa Yanqui and anyone can direct you to it. The front door key is on the ring with the ignition keys to the Land Rover."

"I'd better get some sleep, then," he told her. "The sun rises about six o'clock and I want to be on the road as soon as it's light."

XVI

When Grant came into the hospital dining room about a quarter to six the next morning, he found Lael Valdez already eating breakfast. She was wearing khaki slacks and a khaki shirt open at the collar, leather hiking boots, and a scarf over her dark hair. A case containing a pair of sunglasses protruded from the breast pocket of her shirt.

"Good morning," he said. "I trust the way you're dressed means you're going with me to Yungay."

"Yes. I figured Guy would want me to."

"Did you get any sleep?"

"I asked the nurse for a sleeping pill right after you left Guy's room—and didn't wake up until a half hour ago."

"How far is it to Yungay?"

"About a hundred and twenty-five miles, from an elevation of maybe six hundred feet here at Chimbote to about eight thousand in the Callejón de Huaylas. It's several thousand feet higher at the drill site, if you intend to go there, too."

"I'm sure I will, unless I find what I'm looking for in the Casa Yanqui."

"Just what *are* you looking for?"

"A source of the fever."

"I can tell you now, it's a curse."

"You're too intelligent to really believe *that*. Besides, I've never seen even one so-called curse that was actually proved to cause disease. If Guy did manage to offend some local malevolent spirit, how could a simple Indian like Augustine Almaviva be involved, too?"

"Augustine was the drilling foreman on our project." She pushed her chair back and stood up before he could comment. "I'll be ready in fifteen minutes."

Once they were out of Chimbote and past the belt of irrigated land marking the course of the Santa River in its descent from the Andes to the ocean level, the road led across the desert that ranged along the entire coast of Peru and some of Ecuador to the north. Shortly after they started up the mountain, they ran into remnants of the cloud cover that hung over the area much of the time. The road was narrow, twisting, and climbed steadily, while the mist from the clouds often made it difficult to see around curves and left the pavement quite slick in many spots.

When the Land Rover rounded an outthrust escarpment on the side of the mountain a few thousand feet up, Lael Valdez braked it to a stop at an outlook where the road had been widened. From the elevation, the whole of Ferrol Bay stretched before them like a painting.

The town itself lay at the northern end of the half circle of protected water, with the rugged height of Mount Chimbote marking its northernmost point and the slightly higher Mount Division the southernmost. Offshore lay a chain of islands; the largest, Lael said, was called Blanca, the flashing beacon on its highest point helping to mark one of the several entrances into Ferrol Bay that made Chimbote one of the finest harbors between Callao, the seaport of Lima, and Guayaquil in Ecuador to the north.

At the northern end of the bay, a narrow passage between Chimbote Point and Blanca Rock led directly to the long pier and docks of Port Chimbote. Farther south, between the southern tip of Blanca Rock and North Ferrol Island, lay the much wider Main Passage into the protected anchorage.

Unlocking the glove compartment of the Land Rover, Lael took out a powerful pair of binoculars and handed them to Grant.

"Focus on the rocks just south of the Main Passage. You can usually see the seal colony there," she told him. "The cormorants and other sea birds that inhabit the islands have long since covered most of them with guano; that's why they look so white!"

In the powerful glasses Grant was able to find the seals—small dark spots—upon the rocks.

"I was going to do a photo-essay on the seal colonies out there before we moved on," Lael added. "But now—"

"Guy was holding his own when I checked on him just before I left the *Mercy*."

"What about his heart?"

"The digitalis Jack's giving him has slowed and strengthened the myocardium—the heart muscle. If it stops the heart from dilating until the toxins from the fever can be neutralized by the antitoxins his own body is manufacturing, he'll come through."

"I've prayed that he would." Her hand went instinctively again to the golden crucifix visible on its chain in the open collar of her shirt. "But I'm afraid I'm not as religious as when I was being taught by the Sisters in Boston."

She turned the car expertly away from the overlook and took the winding road upward once again.

"Where did you meet Guy?" he asked.

"At the University of Madrid. He was giving a series of seminars on some of the archaeological findings he uncovered while drilling for oil around the world and I was photographing the great paintings in the Prado to make up a traveling slide exhibit for a foundation in the States. One day I dropped in on Guy's lecture."

"He'd have made a wonderful teacher if he had chosen the academic field."

"How old were you when your parents were killed?" She changed the subject abruptly and he sensed that she was warning him away from inquiring too deeply into the relationship between her and his brother.

"Twelve. Guy was twenty-five, already through college and working on degrees in petroleum geology and archaeology. He took me to Boston to live with him and entered me in the Boston Latin School."

"I went to a convent school in Cambridge for a while, until my parents decided to send me to one of those girls' preparatory schools." She smiled briefly. "You know, the ones that get you ready to make your debut. When I graduated—"

"With honors, I'm sure."

She shrugged. "My grades got me into Radcliffe College. Then there was a divorce and after a year my mother married again. I worshipped my father, but he married again, too, and I haven't seen him for several years."

Which could be why you took up with an older man years later was Grant's thought, but he did not put it into words.

"My resentment against my mother for marrying again was enough to turn me into somewhat of a rebel," she added.

"I felt somewhat the same way about my parents for a while after they died," he admitted. "They were on a pleasure trip—"

"But *you* had Guy—"

"And nobody could have wanted a stronger rock to cling to. Fortunately our parents were fairly well off and were heavily insured, too. My part was put in trust with Guy as the trustee and he managed it well. There was enough to put me through medical school and the School of Public Health at Harvard, but all that schooling used up quite a lot of money, especially after I married."

"I talked to your wife in Atlanta."

"Shirley divorced me while I was in Africa."

"With your consent?"

"Yes. The decree will be final in another six months, but we'd been separated quite awhile before that. Being married to an epidemiologist isn't much of a life for an ambitious woman like Shirley. Now I keep a bachelor apartment in Atlanta near the Center for Disease Control, but you might as well say the world is my home."

"I didn't mean to be nosy." Her voice was more human and he was beginning to see why Guy would have been attracted to her, even if she hadn't been extraordinarily beautiful—which she was, with the mixture of an Irish and a Latin heritage that so often produced great beauties.

"Is your mother still living?" he asked.

"Yes—in La Paz, Bolivia; my stepfather is one of the richest men in the country. We stopped there on the way to Yungay and she was very happy that I had Guy to look after me."

"Then you're no longer bitter at her?"

She shook her head. "I've lived with Guy for a year

and you know what that can do for you when you're uncertain and without a purpose. But now—" Her voice broke on what was almost a sob, the nearest he'd yet seen her to breaking down.

He didn't intrude on her grief, and after a moment she added, "In Madrid I was considering drugs—there was a lot of that in the student area where I lived— but since I fell in love with Guy, all that has changed."

She smiled and was suddenly far away, gripped by memory. "The second lecture of Guy's I went to, he caught up with me as I was leaving the class and we went to dinner together. I'd never met anyone before who treated me like the complete person I was trying so desperately to be—but not succeeding very well."

"I felt much the same way when Guy took me to live with him in Boston. He has a charisma that draws people to him."

Women particularly, he could have added, but he knew that wouldn't have been entirely fair to his brother. Always a towering rock of personal strength and sure of himself in everything, Guy's attraction for other people went far beyond any casual—and with women, sexual—appeal.

"Guy was looking for a secretary and I type sixty words a minute and also take shorthand. Besides, even though he made wonderful discoveries, he's no photographer." She laughed softly. "The pictures he took of the important archeological finds he discovered before we met were atrocious."

"Was he planning to come to Peru even then?"

"No. I was responsible for that."

She said no more, and recognizing that it was a subject she didn't want to talk about, he, too, was silent.

XVII

The road had been climbing steadily since they left the coastal highway. Lael drove expertly, and the sturdy vehicle took the hairpin curves of the ascent without hesitation. About two and a half hours after leaving Chimbote the road broke through the towering Cordillera Negra near its northern terminus, where the Santa River turned sharply to enter Duck Canyon—the Cañón del Pato. Now that they had penetrated the lofty mountain range forming the western wall of the Callejón de Huaylas, the full beauty of the valley between the towering mountain ranges was easy to see.

The setting reminded Grant of the Swiss Alps, with mighty snow-clad peaks hemming in the valleys on two sides and the heights of Mount Huascarán almost directly eastward, snow-clad at more than 23,000 feet. They drove between lines of agave and ecualyptus trees through small native villages, each with its central market place lined with the shops of bakers, carvers, workers in leather and metals and many other crafts.

Along the road they frequently passed groups of Indian women in the colorful garb of dark skirts and blouses, from beneath which peeked several layers of the bright-colored fabrics that were obviously popular with the feminine population of the Andean uplands. As they walked, many of the women twirled hand spindles upon which they spun cotton thread for the looms of the weavers, the most famous and prosperous trades of the Andean uplands.

"This has to be one of the most beautiful valleys in the world." Grant was watching the glacier on the mountainside change color as the sun moved higher and the road varied in elevation, while following the Santa River. A relatively placid stream here, it was fed by melting snows from the glacier above it and provided water for irrigating the lush fields of flax, cotton, grain, and vegetables growing beside it.

"Huarás, toward the south, is the capital of the district and the largest city," Lael told him. "The elevation there is close to ten thousand feet."

"I can feel some effects even here."

"I did, too, when we first came to Yungay. It's about

eight thousand feet there, but you soon become used to it. The natives work as hard up here as they do along the coast; in fact, I think they're actually more thrifty in this area."

"The women seem to be. I never saw an African woman spinning cotton as she walked."

"The road to the drill site turns off toward the hills between here and Yungay," Lael said a little later. "If you want to go there first, we'd better take it and save time."

"By all means. I also want to talk to some people in Yungay who might give me more information about Augustine Almaviva."

"Many of them work, so you won't find them at home until they come in for the evening meal."

"Then we'll have to stay up here tonight."

"I don't like leaving Guy that long."

"Neither do I, but there's always the chance that other cases of the fever have occurred here and a local doctor might have already made the correct diagnosis. Serum from people immune to the disease may be available, and if it is, we could have it flown to the *Mercy* tomorrow, possibly in time to help Guy and Almaviva."

"We'll stay at the Casa Yanqui." She made no more objection. "You can sleep on a couch in the living room."

When a rough track turned off to the left, she swung the Land Rover into it and they began to ascend the slope of the Cordillera. The going wasn't easy and the elevation increased steadily, so it took them almost an hour to reach a small plateau high above the fertile valley, at a point just beneath the ice and snow line. Located at the foot of an escarpment that hung over it almost as a threat, the plateau was not a place where Grant would have chosen to work. Lael saw him looking up at the crag overhead and smiled.

"Guy said that cliff gave him the willies every time he set off a charge of dynamite for the seismograph."

"Then why take the risk?"

"Because all signs seemed to indicate that what we were looking for was here." She swung herself out of the Land Rover, ending the conversation for the moment.

The remains of a small drilling derrick stood in the middle of the small plateau, with the drill and the other equipment lying beside it already beginning to rust in the somewhat humid air at this elevation.

"How much higher is this than Yungay?" Just the exertion of climbing out of the car was making Grant pant for breath in the thinning air.

"About twenty-five hundred feet; we're close to twelve thousand here."

"How could you operate the drill?"

"Augustine and the other Indians did the work. They're accustomed to the thin air."

"I'm certainly not."

"We carry a small tank of oxygen in the Land Rover. I'll get it for you if you like."

"Don't bother—yet." He walked over to the derrick. "Has anything been disturbed—or taken away?"

"It's just as we left it the day Guy had his first chill. The Indians wouldn't come here unless they were paid; they consider this a sacred place."

"Why?"

"They say those who lived here thousands of years ago used this area as a shrine." She pointed to the dark mouths of several caves visible somewhat higher up on the mountainside. "Many of the caves are supposed to be burial places, but Guy examined several. If they were ever used as tombs, somebody rifled them years ago.

A sudden crash from high above them startled Grant, and he looked up in time to see that a chunk of ice with embedded rocks and gravel had broken off the edge of the snowcap perhaps a quarter of a mile away. It was sliding down the slope, piling up smaller stones and a ridge of dirt and gravel before it as it gained momentum.

"Does that happen often?" he asked.

"Frequently in spring and summer, when the icecap starts to melt."

"Then if there really were cave tombs in these hill-sides at one time, they could have been sealed off by avalanches centuries ago."

"Guy is sure many of them were. The city of Huarás in the valley was almost destroyed by an avalanche and flood only a few years ago."

At the foot of the derrick, the steel casing of the well jutted aboveground for perhaps a foot. When Grant moved to examine it closely, he saw that the open end had been sealed off with fresh cement.

"Why seal the shaft?" he asked Lael.

"Guy decided not to drill any deeper."

"How deep had he gone?"

"Not quite two hundred feet." She kicked at a stone restlessly. "Haven't you seen enough? There's really nothing here that would help you identify the fever."

"I'm still curious about two things. First, why would a petroleum geologist of Guy's experience even hope to find oil nearly twelve thousand feet up in the Andes? And second, having started, why did he give up at two hundred feet and cap the shaft?"

"Because it was obviously a dry hole." She was moving across the plateau toward the Land Rover as she spoke. "Why else?"

Once they boarded the battered vehicle again, she started the engine and thrust it into gear, moving down the rough track at a speed that threatened to shake the sturdy conveyance—and Grant—to pieces.

Why else indeed? Grant wondered when they reached the highway again and he was able to think of something other than staying inside the vehicle. For, knowing his brother, he was certain now that this must have been more than just another wildcat drilling operation. And when he learned just what it was, he suspected he would at last be on the track of the elusive fever.

XVIII

It was midafternoon when Grant and Lael entered Yungay, a picturesque town where the snowy crests of the two cordilleras forming the valley towered over the wide streets shaded by palm and eucalyptus.

"If you're hungry," Lael said as they approached the central square, "the wife of one of our workmen, Alfaro Mochas, runs a small cantina just off the square. She can serve us some bread and cheese with cold beer or wine."

"Sounds wonderful."

She drove around the square. Mostly it was empty but a few Indians were drowsing in the midafternoon sunlight. Halfway around, she pulled the Land Rover to a stop before a sign on a post bearing the word "Cantina." The door was almost hidden by a very large bougainvillaea vine, so they didn't notice the black wreath attached to the knob until they were almost at the door.

Lael saw it first and Grant heard her catch her breath.

"What's wrong?" he asked.

"There's been a death in the family. We'll have to go somewhere else."

She was turning away quickly when Grant stopped her with a question: "Didn't you say this woman's husband was in Guy's drill crew?"

"Yes. He rode up with us every morning in the back of the Land Rover. Augustine drove the pickup truck and carried the others, but Alfaro's home was right on the way, so Guy and I always picked him up."

"How large was the crew?"

"Four men from the village, six including Guy and myself."

"Then out of six who worked on the drilling project, two are gravely ill and a third is probably dead—"

"You don't know it's Alfaro," she said quickly.

"Let's ask."

"All right." All animation had gone out of her voice —and her body. Moreover he was fairly certain why, for whatever it was—curse or plague—that had stricken Guy and Augustine Almaviva could well be closing in on the other members of the drill crew—and upon Lael herself.

The story, when they talked to Señora Mochas, was brief. Alfaro, she said, had become sick the day after Señor Guy Reed, seized by a fever that seemed bent on destroying his body with an unquenchable flame. The local brujo, or witch doctor—there were far more of them than regular physicians in Peru, Grant already knew—sought to appease the demon that, he claimed, had been offended by Alfaro's part in pushing the hole into the mountainside. Sacrificing a chicken, he'd sprinkled its blood on the sick man while pronouncing a curse upon those who had paid others to carry out the forbidden act. He had also predicted that the other workers would suffer, just as the yanqui who had paid them to carry out the desecration was suffering.

Near the end, a medical doctor had been called and had injected drugs. He also charged a high fee, according to Señor Mochas, but the result was the same; the devil of fever eating at Alfaro's vitals had finally consumed his body. Fortunately, a priest had been called in time to administer the Last Rites and thus ensure that Alfaro's soul, at least, would not be damned. Señora Mochas herself, with the aid of other women in the village, had prepared his body for the wake, now in its second day, and the grave.

When the story was finished, Lael took out a wallet and, removing a bill, put it into Señora Mochas's hand.

"This cannot bring back Alfaro," she told the grieving widow in Spanish. "But it will help ease the burden of his loss."

"Gracias, Señora Reed. You and Señor Guy were kind to Alfaro and me. I hope your husband is better."

Lael didn't answer but turned to Grant.

"Do you have any more questions?"

"Ask about the other men working with you. Perhaps she knows whether any of them are ill."

Señora Mochas had been too busy caring for Alfaro during the week before he died to know much about what was going on in the village, but she did know where the men lived.

"I suppose you want to see them, too," Lael said as she copied down their addresses.

"Of course. Even you can see by now that there's a pattern—"

"Why do you say 'even you'?"

"Because I've realized from the very start that you've been hiding something about Guy's illness and—"

"What do *you* think is happening then?"

"Apparently a lethal agent of some kind was turned loose up on the plateau where you were drilling, so all six of you are in danger. You just heard Señora Mochas say a number of women from the village helped prepare the body for burial, too, which means they've all been exposed to whatever killed her husband. If the killer is a new kind of disease, as I'm beginning to suspect, it will almost certainly attack others —particularly you. Its spread is what I'm trying to prevent."

"Even if a plague *is* loose, as you say, only a small number of people are involved. And in this isolated valley—"

"The Callejón de Huaylas is far from isolated." He took the map from the glove compartment and, spreading it across his knees, traced the course of the Santa River northward with his finger. "At its northern end this valley has access to the coast at Chimbote by way of the Cañón del Pato. Both a railroad and a highway go down to the port, and near the center of the valley another road goes over the Cordillera Negra and down to Casma on the Pan-American Highway. To the south the central road through the valley joins the Pan-American Highway at Paramonga or Pativilca, with Lima not much more than a hundred miles away."

"A hundred and twenty-five or thereabouts."

"An easy jump for a highly contagious agent by any number of carriers; don't forget how easily the plague was carried down to Chimbote, when you brought Guy to the *Mercy*. Fortunately you went directly to the ship, so the possibilities of spread are limited somewhat. Unfortunately we have no idea where Augustine Almaviva was during the days after he first became ill, or how many people he may have infected already."

"He said he was going to visit his sister in Chimbote, and perhaps see whether anyone was drilling for oil again in the Trujillo field."

"Let's hope he didn't get there—and we can find the sister. Meanwhile, two other contacts are certain. One is the waiter who served Almaviva at a restaurant on the plaza several times. The other is a beggar who drank from a glass your foreman had been drinking from and stole money he'd put on the table."

"You make it sound dreadful—like the Andromeda Strain."

"Take my word for it, the real agent that killed Alfaro Mochas and is trying to kill Guy and Almaviva could be fully as dangerous as the fictional organism of the Andromeda Strain."

"How can you fight something when you don't even know what it is?"

"I've got to find out, which means we've got about enough time to check on those other two workmen and search the Casa Yanqui before dark. Did you leave any food in the house?"

"Enough to fix us a snack supper, and maybe make some toast and coffee for breakfast."

"Good. Let's go."

XIX

They drew blanks at the homes of the other two workers. One was said by a neighbor to have gone to Chavin in the foothills of the Cordillera Blanca east of Huarás to visit relatives. The other was well but remembered that he had not been working the last few days of the drilling operation, and when he'd learned of Guy's illness, he'd even been afraid to go to the Casa Yanqui to collect his pay.

It was almost dark when Lael Valdez pulled the Land Rover to a stop in the yard of the Casa Yanqui. The house was small, with the inevitable adobe walls set in a flower garden that was a riot of color, and also heavily overgrown.

"The garden is my project," she explained as they were walking up the gravel path to the house. "Since Guy became ill I've not had time to care for it."

"You've obviously got a green thumb."

She started to put her key in the lock but the door opened from the pressure alone. "That's funny. I remember locking this door carefully just before we left."

Grant reached out to take her arm and pull her away from the door. Kicking it open, he moved back quickly, but when no shot or sudden rush of footsteps indicated that a thief was inside, he entered carefully, holding the door so it couldn't be slammed against him if anyone was behind it.

A quick search proved that the casa was empty.

"Did they take anything?" he asked when Lael came back from examining the one bedroom used as such.

"Nothing I can—" She stopped suddenly at the door of the bedroom-laboratory and he saw that she was staring at something that looked like a piece of aluminum piping with a small but powerful light bulb set into the end of it lying against the opposite wall.

"What's that?" he asked.

"A Lerici—" She broke off and dropped to the floor to examine the end of the pipe. "My camera's gone! It was a miniature Minolta!"

She stood up and moved across to what apparently had been a worktable beneath a window, where the morning light would be upon it. "Guy's binocular microscope is gone, too! It was a Leitz—and frightfully expensive!"

"Are those two items the only things you can tell were taken?"

"So far. All our clothes were in the chest of drawers or the closets in the bedroom."

"This was obviously a professional burglar, seeking only small articles of considerable value," said Grant. "Did you keep any jewels in the house?"

She shook her head. "I don't like ostentation, so I don't own anything of much value. But my camera—"

"You have others, don't you?"

"A Konica and a small Rolleiflex, but I took them with me to the *Mercy*. The Minolta was a special camera, small so it could be attached to the Lerici—"

"You mentioned that word—Lerici—just now; don't you think it's time to tell me the whole story, Lael?" It was the first time he'd used her given name but neither of them realized it.

She looked at him for a long moment, then nodded. "I guess you're entitled to know everything—especially with one man dead and probably more to follow. It's a long story, though. Can you wait until I put some supper together?"

"Of course. Meanwhile I'll look around more closely."

Grant searched the house again before going outside. Part of the tool shed, he saw, had been converted into a small photographic dark room. The rest was crammed with drilling gear, including a small store of dynamite and Guy's seismograph—a portable instrument that had apparently been too bulky for the thief to carry.

What he did learn beyond any doubt was that Guy and Lael Valdez had been living together, if not legally as husband and wife. In a drawer of his brother's worktable, he also discovered what appeared to be a holographic will Guy had presumably written when he first began feeling badly, judging by the date:

Being of sound mind and in full possession of my senses, I make this my last will and testament. In

the event of my death from whatever cause, I
hereby bequeath all of my earthly possessions
unreservedly to Lael Valdez. I also designate my
brother, Grant Reed, as executor of my estate
without fee. And I direct that he shall liquidate
my estate—details of which are familiar to Lael
Valdez and can be found in a list of my safe-
deposit boxes to which she has the keys—paying
to her the entire amount after all of my just debts
have been paid.

> Signed this 1st day of October 1975
> Guy W. Reed

BOOK TWO

The
MICROBE

I

"Before I met Guy in Madrid, I'd been in a sort of a limbo for months," said Lael as they were eating pancakes and crisp bacon. "While I was at Radcliffe I'd done some photography at a dig site in Bolivia during one summer vacation and had become interested in Pre-Inca archaeology. I was going to take a night course at Harvard when I came back to Boston, but then I met Gerald Hartmann."

"A fellow student?"

"Boston University, we shared an apartment in Cambridge. I'd had some chemistry courses and one in bacteriology at Radcliffe, so I was able to work in a laboratory and help put Gerald through med school."

"That took courage."

"More than it took for him to ditch me the day he got his diploma," she said bitterly. "I was feeling pretty sorry for myself when I got the assignment to photograph the paintings in the Prado. Even in Madrid, though, I was still just drifting, until I met Guy. He showed me how resentment against Gerald and my mother were destroying the person I was really capable of becoming."

"No wonder you love him."

"I worship him," she said simply. "When he asked me to come with him to Peru, I was in heaven."

"Then you'd been living together before that?"

"Since a few days after we first met," she said on a note of defiance like a little girl who's been caught in a petty misdemeanor. "Does that shock you?"

"I'm not that naïve!"

"We'd have been married but Guy's last divorce hasn't ended officially yet. She's a Catholic and it takes the Vatican a long time to issue an annulment, but I've been happy with him and I think he's been happy with me."

"Here's proof of that." He handed her the sheet containing the will. "I found it in his desk."

She read the single page twice, and when she looked up, her eyes were filled with tears.

"Until this will was written you were Guy's sole heir," she reminded him. "You could have torn it up and I would never have known about it. I guess I'm going to have to revise my opinion of you."

"I hope so."

"When Guy became ill, he really needed me for the first time since the beginning of our relationship, and I'm afraid I took a selfish pride in being able to look after him. I even resented having to call you because I knew you'd take charge and I wouldn't be needed any more."

"I must admit that I felt much the same way."

"Then I owe you an apology."

"For loving my brother that much? I'm beginning to envy him, but one thing about this whole situation still troubles me. Guy's drilling ventures were almost always successful, so I guess the Callejón de Huaylas was almost his only dry hole."

"It wasn't either. You see, this time he wasn't even looking for oil."

He looked at the odd piece of aluminum pipe lying on the floor of the makeshift laboratory, then back at her. "He was really on the track of another archaeological find, wasn't he?"

"The most important in his entire career, Guy was sure. I was the one who got him interested in it and now he's dying because of me." The stark agony in her eyes made him want to take her in his arms and comfort her, as he would have comforted a child, but he also had to know the whole truth—and that, he was sure, she had not yet revealed.

"What did you really learn at Madrid that brought you and Guy halfway around the world, Lael?"

"Just a minute," she said as she left the table, "I'll show you."

She went into the bedroom, where he heard her opening and shutting drawers. When she came back, she was carrying a sheaf of large color prints. Pushing the dishes aside, she spread them out on the table before him.

"This," she said. "The greatest archaeological find since Schliemann excavated the gold of Troy."

II

The photographs had obviously been taken inside a cave, for each one represented a section of the wall. Each panel had been painted by some prehistoric artist as part of a mural, too, apparently using pigments mined from the mountainsides walling the valley.

A dozen men and women were depicted, but they were as different from the Indian population of the area as night from day. Tall for the most part, some were flaxen-haired, but all showed the sharply defined profiles of a Semitic heritage. They wore robes of woven cloth in which could be seen the characteristic patterns of the Phoenicians, and even the purple color of the dye that had made their empire famous the world over had somehow been duplicated in pigment by the prehistoric artist.

In the background, littering the floor of the cave, were a number of dark humps with the appearance of human bodies, some covered with what could still be distinguished as robes of fur. Several entire skulls showed through, looking oddly white against the darker background of the robes. On one of the bodies, a partially decomposed woven fabric was distinguishable, stained by spots of dark red. Looking at the bodies on the floor of the cave, Grant could almost believe they had been felled in their tracks, yet none of the skulls showed any signs of having been crushed or wounded, indicating that whatever had struck these people down had not been a weapon.

"This is unbelievable," he said in a tone of awe. "Who were they?"

"Guy thinks the bodies in the photographs are of natives who fled to this cave, where a prehistoric artist was painting the pictures of invaders from across the Pacific," Lael explained. "It may have been regarded as a sacred burial place. Or the people might have come there hoping to escape some plague."

"Perhaps the very one we're fighting now." Grant suddenly sat up straight. "Everyone we know of so far who helped open the tomb has fallen victim to a strange new fever. But it could really be a very old plague that attacked the people on the floor—and the artist, so his secret died with him."

"You could never prove that," she said quickly— then added on a note of desperation: "Could you?"

"We'll worry about that later." Aware of her concern—and the reason—he changed the subject. "What was Guy's professional opinion, judging from these photos?"

"He thinks the cave was presided over by a priest or shaman, which means it must have been regarded as a kind of temple."

He frowned. "Why?"

"This." She handed Grant a print she had been holding back.

His first glance sent a chill of dread through him, for glaring at him from the surface of the same print that had terrified Carlos Ganza the night before was the shaman—easily identifiable by the stag's head mask covering his head and most of his face. The glare of the flash bulb, reflected from the staring eyes at the moment the camera shutter was released, even made them seem alive and afire with hatred.

"How could Guy be certain the wall paintings weren't made perhaps centuries before the people lying on the floor died?" Grant asked. "They could have fled there because it was already a sacred place."

"Guy thinks not." She fished one of the color prints from the pile and put it on-top. "If you'll look closely at this, you'll see that it's incomplete, as if the artist were stricken while he was painting it. His body—or skeleton—is lying before the unfinished painting, too. Look real closely, and you'll see several small ceramic pots that must have contained the pigments he was using because the colors are still visible."

He studied the print more closely and nodded in agreement. "Did you ever see the cave paintings of southern France and parts of Spain?"

"Yes. That's how I recognized the purpose of the shaman's being painted there, signifying the curse intended for anyone opening the tomb. Guy thinks the cave was sealed off a long time ago, probably covered by an earth slide like the one that almost destroyed Huarás recently."

"No wonder he was excited about this find. In many of the cave paintings I've seen, a shaman has been depicted—and some of those were made twenty-five thousand years ago. But Guy couldn't have believed the curse theory of the natives."

"He was too busy thinking about the meaning of the pictures—until the fever struck him. Then it was too late; he became delirious almost immediately."

"Surely he had time to formulate some sort of theory about how Semitic people came to this part of the world—and when."

"I worked that out—in the archives at Madrid," she said proudly. "In 1966 Gene Savoy accompanied an expedition to the ruins of Pajaten near Chachapoyas, several hundred miles northeast of Huarás and the Callejón de Huaylas. He found natives there who were blond, blue-eyed, and considerably taller than Indians of the neighboring areas, with a generally aristocratic appearance like these, too. Most of them had long faces and high cheekbones, and in the same area, the expedition also found pottery containing figurines with mustaches and Semitic, or Phoenician, features. They could have been the ancestors of the people painted by the artist."

"I know some historians theorize that Phoenician ships visited the west coast of South America thousands of years ago. This could be the proof that their theories are true."

"Guy thinks they represent a much earlier visit," said Lael. "And what I discovered in the archives at Madrid tends to prove it."

"What makes you believe that?"

"A race of seafarers, who may have been the ancestors of the biblical Phoenicians, were centered at Dilmun—the present island of Bahrain. They traded with cities along the coast of India, taking advantage of the monsoon winds that blow in one direction for half of the year and then are reversed for the other half. It's known, too, that they visited the city of Ur, which flourished around thirty-five hundred B.C. before the Great Flood. So it's quite possible that Dilmunites, perhaps ancestors of the biblical Phoenicians, were making long voyages eastward—possibly as far as the coast of South America—thousands of years ago."

"What gave you the idea to look here?"

"Sheer luck," she admitted. "In the archives I found a previously untranslated account written in 1533 by a priest with Pizarro's army. It mentioned a belief—or myth—recounted to him by a native living in the Callejón de Huaylas area that burial caves there had been found to contain the bodies of people who lived long before that day. From the statements by natives, the priest was able to pinpoint the location in the area above Yungay."

Knowing Guy, Grant could understand how the girl's discovery would be a lure his brother could not resist —any more than Grant himself could resist reports of a new disease starting to spread anywhere in the world.

"I never saw Guy so excited as he was the day we located the burial cave upon the plateau where the drill site is." Lael's cheeks were pink, her eyes bright with memory. "It was what we'd come halfway around the world to find."

Watching her, Grant could understand why his brother had loved this girl who represented everything Guy admired in women: breeding, intelligence, and enthusiasm for the things that were so important in his own life she had in abundance, plus youth and a rare beauty.

"Once we knew the rough location from the priest's description," she continued, "it wasn't difficult, using the seismograph—"

"I found the instrument in the tool shed. It must have been too heavy for our burglar friend to carry away, but what about that aluminum contraption on the floor in the laboratory?"

"It's a periscope Guy made in the shops of the hydroelectric plant at Huallanca. He used plans of a similar one Professor Lerici explored Etruscan tombs with in Italy fifteen years or so ago. It fits into a drill casing."

"You were able to see into the tomb once you'd drilled into it?"

"Better than that. With a light source from this bulb"—she touched the small lamp he'd seen at the end of the extendable tube—"and with a small camera attached to the periscope controlled by wires inside, I was able to photograph the interior of the tomb and make those prints."

"Did Guy have any idea just when the people died?"

"No. But we should be able to pinpoint the date when the radiocarbon assay report comes back on a specimen he sent to Boston."

"Specimen? I thought you only took photos."

"When we removed the periscope, a small piece of what looked like bone with some fabric was attached to it," she explained. "Guy figured some clothing and a bit of bone from one of the bodies on the floor of the cave must have stuck to the end of the periscope. He was excited by the possibility of dating the material by radiocarbon assay and packed part of it off immediately by air mail to Professor Philemon Mallinson at the Harvard Institute of Radiation Physics. The report should be here any day."

Grant felt a sudden rush of excitement. "Did you send away all of the material?"

"All except the small amount I used to make the cultures." When he looked blank, she asked, "Don't you remember asking Guy to make bacterial cultures whenever he was doing exploratory drilling?"

"That was over a year ago, after some bacteriologists working with drill cores in the Antarctic found viable bacteria taken from sections of earth hundreds of feet below the surface of the ice—and probably a hundred thousand years old."

"I'd worked in the medical lab in Boston and had some knowledge of bacterial culture techniques, so I cultured the material that stuck to the periscope and the camera."

"How did you happen to have the equipment—and the culture material?"

"Guy intended to drill here so he bought it in Lima on the way to Yungay. We inoculated both culture tubes and Petri dishes."

"Using what medium?"

"The one you told Guy you wanted him to use— infusion agar plus a small amount of rabbit blood. I sterilized the tubes and Petri dishes in a large pressure cooker Guy bought in Lima."

"That was ingenious."

"But useless—all we got was a contaminant. It had been over a year since I'd done any work in bacteriology and I guess I wasn't careful enough about the technique."

"Where are the cultures now?" he asked quickly.

"In the incubator. It's still inside the closet in the workroom—or should be, if the thief didn't bother it."

Grant was out of his seat and across the room before she finished speaking. When he opened the door of the closet, he saw that the small incubator was still connected to the house electrical supply, for the bulb in the top that controlled the temperature inside the small glass-walled cabinet was still burning. He could see several racks of culture tubes on the bottom shelf and above these, on the second shelf, a half dozen Petri dishes. Removing one of the dishes, he held it under the light and what he saw set his pulse hammering.

The brownish culture medium spread over the bottom of the shallow glass dish was covered by golden patches of growth, many of them humped up in the center and hollowed out in the form of small cones.

"They look like tiny volcanoes," Lael said almost in a whisper. "What does it mean?"

"Each colony represents the offspring of a single microbe. They must have come from inside the burial cave; no contaminant I'm familiar with grows like that."

"How can you be sure?"

"These cultures are over a week old, aren't they?"

"More like ten days."

"In that time ordinary cultures should be covered by mold from spores in the air, but do you see even a speck of mold on any of these colonies or around them?"

"No. What does it mean?"

"This has to be an extremely virulent microbe, one capable of producing and releasing an exotoxin so powerful that it's able to kill everything with which it comes in contact."

III

Ingeniero Jara was proud of his new camera and particularly of the bargain he had struck for it, along with an ample supply of color film. He had not asked his friend from Lima where he had gotten the camera; knowing Carlos Ganza, he was quite sure of the answer. And what better time for taking pictures in color than during a fiesta in Huarás, a time for drinking, gossip, dancing in the street, and chewing coca leaf.

To the *sierranos* of the Andean uplands, coca suppressed pain, brought joy and sexual strength, while giving the chewer the energy to dance for hours, something mere chicha could not do. Under the influence of both, the plaza was alive with girls in *polleros*—brightly colored cotton blouses that showed off budding young breasts—gay ribbons hanging down their backs, richly woven hats, and many-tiered skirts of as many hues. Dancing here to the music of a native flutist, walking there under the admiring eyes of the younger men and the watchful gaze of the only slightly more sedately dressed older women, the young made the best of this day of fiesta, always a happy occasion for the upland *sierranos*.

As the afternoon wore on, the streets around the central square—freshly cleaned that morning by men with brooms made from the golden-blossomed retama bush that grew everywhere, giving a lovely fragrance to the very air of the city—quickly filled with people. Amidst the waving palms and eucalyptus trees moved dancers, strolling players, hawkers of sweetmeats, sellers of the many-colored fabrics worn by the Indian women whose spinning staffs went everywhere with them.

Wherever Ingeniero went, friends stopped him to have their pictures taken or to handle and admire the marvelous little camera. When evening finally came, his film supply was exhausted but his spirits had been elevated many times over by repeated cups of chicha and wads of coca his friends insisted upon giving him. Staggering homeward, Ingeniero shouted to neighbors that this had been the greatest fiesta day of his entire life—as indeed it had, although Ingeniero did not yet know the reason.

IV

It was almost noon when Grant and Lael reached the dock where the *Mercy* was moored and parked the Land Rover. They had found enough cotton batting in Yungay to pack the culture tubes and the Petri dishes safely for the rough trip down to the seacoast.

"Find something?" Dr. Jack Smithson had come on deck to meet them.

"The cause of an already spreading epidemic, unless I miss my guess," said Grant. "I've got cultures Lael and Guy made, so I'll need to use the facilities of your laboratory."

"Of course. Guy's temperature is down to a hundred and two. I only wish I could say as much for his heart."

"That's going to be our real problem from now on," Grant agreed. "The fever looked to me yesterday morning like it was breaking."

While Grant carried the package of culture tubes and dishes to the laboratory, Lael went into Guy's room with Smithson. When Grant came in a few minutes later, Lael was standing beside the bed, holding his brother's hand.

"He recognized me!" Her eyes were shining.

"The neurological complications seem to be subsiding, too," Smithson added. "That's usually a sign of recovery with hemorrhagic fevers."

Grant wasn't nearly so sanguine about the rest of the clinical picture, however. In spite of the oxygen being administered through a nasal catheter, the sick man's respirations were definitely more rapid and shallower than they'd been yesterday. The pulse rate had increased, too, evidence that Guy's damaged heart was having trouble supplying the oxygen needs of his body tissues.

As Grant finished listening to Guy's heart, the sick man opened his eyes.

"Grant," he whispered. "I knew you'd come."

"As soon as Lael called me. We've just got back from the Casa Yanqui."

"Then you know—"

"About the cultures? Yes. We brought them down. Lael told me everything, so don't try to talk."

"When I first saw—it growing—I knew you'd—

find the answer." The effort of speaking brought the bluish tint of cyanosis from oxygen lack to the sick man's lips.

"Don't try to talk, darling," Lael urged. "Grant's in charge now and everything will be all right."

"Lael—save her from—" The sick man's words faded but Grant knew what was troubling Guy, the near certainty that she would develop the dread fever.

Jack Smithson followed Grant from the sickroom. "We've pushed the oxygen delivery rate as high as it can go," he said, "but your brother's still developing some fluid in his lungs from gradual heart failure."

"The blood's backing up in the right side of the heart for sure," Grant agreed. "What they used to call plethora in the old days."

"My grandfather was a country doctor back in the mountains. I saw him bleed many a patient to relieve plethora."

Grant had been looking down at the dark water swirling around the pilings that supported the pier, half listening to the other doctor while his mind considered, and discarded one by one, the possible courses of action that might help Guy and save Lael. Jack Smithson's words suddenly gave him a possible answer.

"Would you recommend bleeding Guy now?" he asked.

"Perhaps not quite yet. Removing blood means taking out antibodies and he needs those to fight the fever, but we may have to use it as a last resort."

"I agree," said Grant. "I'd keep a pacemaker-defibrillator in the room, too, just in case."

"Good idea," said Smithson. "If he does go into failure, that could make the difference."

"I assume that you've made routine cultures—blood, sputum, stool?"

"Of course. All were negative."

"Did you use chocolate agar as the growth medium?"

"No." The bearded doctor frowned. "Do you think it might bring out something we've missed?"

"I learned long ago that chocolate agar will support more different organisms for routine broad-scale culture surveys than any other bacterial culture medium."

"I remember the name but not much else," Smithson admitted.

"It's made by mixing regular infusion agar with rabbit blood at ninety degrees centigrade," Grant explained. "That's close to boiling, so the heat turns the blood pigments brown and gives it the characteristic chocolate color."

"You spoke of bringing cultures down from Yungay. Were they made on this chocolate agar?"

Grant nodded. "I told Guy how to make it when I asked him to culture drill cores wherever he put down test wells."

"Why would you do that?"

"A couple of years ago some bacteriologists cultured cores brought up while drilling test wells in the Antarctic. They found two strains of viable organisms that may have been a hundred thousand years old."

"Were they pathogenic?"

"No, but we may have a killer microbe on our hands now. Guy and Lael accidentally opened into a burial cave up above Yungay and made cultures from a periscope she was using to take pictures inside the cave. The first cultures were made almost ten days ago, yet they show no molds or other contaminants."

"My God! It must produce one of the most powerful toxins known."

"An exotoxin released to circulate in the body while the bacteria themselves continue to grow."

"How can you be sure it's a bacterium and not a virus?"

"Did you ever see a virus grow that easily? Or release that powerful a toxin?"

"No," Smithson said thoughtfully. "If the bug wouldn't grow on the culture media we used, but did grow on this chocolate agar, it must belong to the

Hemophilus group, like organisms of whooping cough or influenza."

"Except that this one is far more toxic than either of those, which means it must be a brand-new organism." Grant moved away from the rail. "I'd better get busy and inject some rats to test the virulence. We'll have to prepare a large batch of chocolate agar, too, so we can make some new cultures from both Guy and Almaviva. I hope you can find rabbit blood—"

"For once we're prepared. We raise our own rabbits —for pregnancy tests."

V

As Smithson left to order preparation of the new culture medium, Lael Valdez came out of her cabin. She had changed to a blouse and skirt, making her look more feminine—and also more vulnerable.

"Guy's losing ground, isn't he?" she asked.

"He appears to be recovering from the fever, which means his immunological mechanisms are functioning well enough to produce antibodies against the infection." She had lived with his brother a year, so Grant could see no point in trying to delude her with false hopes. "But the toxins from the organism that's causing the fever have damaged an already weakened heart. Now his myocardium is slowly losing its ability to cope with the demands of keeping his body alive."

"He's not afraid." She reached suddenly for his hand. "Don't let him die, Grant. Not when he's shown me what it really means to be fully alive, while living with him."

"I'll do what I can," he promised. "We can only hope now that his heart will be able to hold up until his body can destroy the toxins from the new infection."

"Do you think it will?"

"I don't know," he admitted frankly. "But that's all the more reason why we must see that his wishes are carried out. Obviously it's our duty to open the burial chamber and reveal what's inside, once I've learned to control the microbe that was accidentally released."

She shivered suddenly and reached out for his hand, gripping it with a desperation that made her nails dig into his skin.

"I almost forgot." She took a folded yellow envelope from the pocket of her skirt and handed it to him. "This radiogram came while we were at the Casa Yanqui; Jake Porter, the radio operator, gave it to me a few minutes ago. It had been sent to Guy at Yungay, but the whole town knew he'd been brought to the *Mercy,* so the telegraph office sent it on to the ship."

The message was brief but startling:

RADIOCARBON ASSAY ON SPECIMENS OF BONE AND ATTACHED FABRIC SENT BY YOU REVEALS AN AGE OF 5,000 YEARS, PLUS OR MINUS 200. PLEASE WRITE OR CABLE DETAILS OF PLACE AND CIRCUMSTANCES OF FIND. THE HARVARD DEPARTMENT OF ARCHAEOLOGY IS VITALLY INTERESTED IN FURTHER DETAILS.

> PHILEMON E. MALLINSON, PH.D.
> PROFESSOR AND DIRECTOR,
> INSTITUTE OF RADIATION PHYSICS

"Five thousand years!" Grant exclaimed. "You and Guy have almost certainly rediscovered the oldest living micro-organism in history."

"I still wish we'd never opened that tomb."

"Somebody else probably would have, once you'd found the priest's account in Madrid," he assured her. "Fortunately you and Guy may have made the cultures in time for me to find a way to head off the plague. Meanwhile you've also produced the proof that men of Semitic ancestry, possibly from Dilmun or even a race of seamen earlier than they, reached the western shore of South America a thousand years before Abraham started on his journey along the Fertile Crescent from Ur, of the Chaldees, to Canaan."

"And Guy has to lose his life for *that?*"

VI

In the well-equipped laboratory of the *Mercy*, Grant Reed watched Leona Danvers, chief technician for the hospital ship, flick a cotton plug from the open end of one of the culture tubes he and Lael had brought from the Casa Yanqui and pass the glass mouth through the tear-shaped flame of the Bunsen burner. Both were wearing the working jump suits of tough paper buttoned down the middle in front that served as·uniforms for the nurses and orderlies when at work and could be discarded, or burned if contaminated, solving the laundry problem.

The tall blond technician held a platinum wire loop on the end of a long holder in the flame until it glowed red, killing any micro-organisms that might be on it. Reaching into the tube, she next picked up with the loop a small amount of the brownish-looking bacterial growth on the slanted, chocolate-colored surface of the blood agar medium. Then, holding a glass slide with a metal clamp, she smeared part of the culture from the loop upon it, flamed the open end of the tube, and plugged it once again.

Passing the slide itself through the flame, both to dry it and to kill the potent organisms there, she dropped a solution of crystal violet on the smear. Letting it stay long enough for the color to be absorbed, she then washed off the excess before flooding the area with Lugol's solution containing iodine. When the slide was then dipped in 95 per cent ethyl alcohol, the original violet stain largely disappeared.

"It's gram negative as I suspected," said Grant. "We can study the organisms better if you counterstain with carbolfuchsin."

"Yes, Doctor. That takes about ten minutes."

"I'll check on the agar, the temperature should be about right by now to add the rabbit blood."

The thermometer in the mixture of agar—a gelatin-like substance obtained from seaweed—with a potent beef broth in which micro-organisms liked to grow, showed ninety degrees on the centigrade scale, ten degrees away from the boiling point of water. Removing the container from the flame, Grant added the blood slowly, stirring the mixture with a glass rod all the while.

Next he filled a number of culture tubes about a third full before placing them in a wire rack in a slanting position to produce a large surface, when the medium cooled and hardened after sterilization. That done, he allowed enough of the brown mixture to flow into a dozen Petri dishes to put a film perhaps an eighth of an inch thick on the bottom of each before placing both tubes and dishes in a pressure autoclave to be sterilized.

"Slide's ready, Dr. Reed," Leona Danvers reported.

Grant took the now reddish-stained glass slide and, placing it under the highest power lens of a microscope, dropped a single drop of oil upon it.

"While I'm examining the slide," he told the technician, "would you make up that culture suspension I'll need to inject into rats for the virulence test?"

"I'll get to work on it at once, Doctor."

"By the way, do you have a heavy-duty centrifuge aboard?" he added. One that could be used for separating the blood components from plasmapheresis?"

"We had one but we weren't using it, so I asked Chief McTavish to store it away."

"Ask him to dig it out and make sure it's working, please."

"Certainly, Dr. Reed."

The technician moved away as Grant lowered the turreted objective of the scope until the highest power lens touched the oil. Looking through the binocular eyepieces, he moved the controls to focus on the material she had prepared and, almost immediately, a tangle of thin rod-shaped bacteria, stained sharply red by the carbolfuchsin, came into view. A few of the organisms had bulbous ends, as if they were about to curl up on themselves in the form of spores, in which state, he knew, they could live for long periods.

Jack Smithson came into the laboratory as Grant was studying the organism that had been resurrected after five thousand years.

"What is it?" he asked.

"A gram-negative rod. I'd say your guess that it would belong to the *Hemophilus* group was right on target."

"Hemophilus influenza?"

"Not likely. I'm getting ready to test this bug for virulence by injecting a suspension from the cultures we brought down from Yungay into some rats. I'll also reculture it as soon as the medium can be sterilized and let cool so that agar will set."

"Are you saying this is a new organism entirely?"

"For modern times, at least." Grant looked up from the microscope as a new idea struck him. "The influenza bacillus and the organism of whooping cough both affect the lungs. Which could mean *Bacillus yungay,* to give it a working name, may have its main area of growth in the lungs and do its major damage by flooding the victim's body with exotoxin."

"The pneumonic form of bubonic plague acts that way, but sputum cultures on both Guy and Almaviva were negative," said Smithson.

"On chocolate agar?"

"No. I'll have some more specimens sent down, so Miss Danvers can culture them as soon as your batch of medium is ready. By the way, how do you plan to identify the organism, now that you've got it in what appears to be pure form?"

"We should get fresh growth in our own cultures by tomorrow or the next day. I'll send a batch by air to the center laboratory in Atlanta and also to the arbor-virus laboratory at Yale."

"That's being smart. Their facilities are far better than ours."

"Take a look." Grant vacated the stool before the

microscope. "Nobody but us has ever seen this micro-organism before through a lens!"

The older doctor studied the slide briefly before he looked up, his expression grave. "If that slender rod growing there is as virulent as you think it is," he said, "I'd hate to be the mailmen who handle those packages going to Atlanta and New Haven."

VII

It was dinnertime before Grant finished injecting ten white rats—the standard method of determining virulence in a hurry—with suspensions of *B. yungay* prepared by Leona Danvers in ten dilutions. One cubic centimeter of the mixture was used for each of the animals, so diluted as to put one-tenth the number of organisms into each rat than had been injected into the one before it. The ten, frisking about in their cages, were fed by Esteban Gómez, the officers' cabin boy who doubled as animal keeper.

"Dr. Grant," said Esteban, "is it true that your brother loosed a curse from a tomb in the Callejón de Huaylas and everybody on the ship will die because of it?"

"Of course not, Esteban. Wherever did you hear that."

"The brujos in Chimbote have been telling it everywhere. The people in the barrio are very angry that the señorita and your brother should do this."

"Are the brujos stirring up the people against them?"

"They are saying if Señor Reed had been allowed to stay in the hills and die, it would all be over—except perhaps for Señorita Valdez, who is under the curse, too. But now the curse is on the ship, because the doctors are treating your brother, and all of us must die to appease the evil spirits."

"The brujos are angry because the hospital ship and the doctors cure people they have been letting die,

Esteban." Grant had a sudden inspiration. "Come look through this microscope and you'll see the only curse that has come from the Callejón de Huaylas."

The cabin boy stared through the binocular scope for a long moment; when he looked up, his dark eyes were glazed with fear. "They are so little! Can such things kill a man?"

"They are killing Augustine Almaviva, and they have almost killed my brother, Esteban. When you go into the barrio, tell the people you have seen what the brujos call a curse and it is a small thing, so small it can be seen only under the microscope. Tell them the doctors on the ship will control it as they controlled the *tercianas*—the chills and fever that were killing so many people before the ship came to Chimbote. Do that and I will pay you well."

"Sí señor!" Esteban was an ambitious young man. *"Muy bueno!"*

Lael was not at dinner, and learning that she had asked not to have a tray sent to her stateroom but had been given a sedative by Jack Smithson, Grant went there before stopping by to see Guy. He received no answer to his knock but the door was unlocked, so he pushed it open and went inside.

The curtain had been drawn over the porthole and the stateroom was in semidarkness, but he could see Lael lying on the fixed berth which, since the *Mercy* was an old ship, served as a bed. She had put on a white silk nightgown, leaving her arms and shoulders bare, and her dark hair was spread out on the pillow like a lovely fan. She seemed to be sleeping peacefully so he didn't disturb her.

The past two days, he knew, had been difficult for her, both physically and emotionally. They had forced her to face the truth that, however innocently, she and Guy were the source of the reappearance on earth of a deadly plague that still might kill thousands, including its discoverers, before it was brought under control. To Lael, sensitive and concerned as he had come to know her to be in the less than forty-eight hours since she had met him at Chimbote Airport, that knowledge could be a burden of guilt she would carry to her grave.

Tiptoeing from the stateroom and closing the door, he went in to see Guy. His brother was propped up in bed and quite conscious, though breathing rapidly.

"I've been wanting . . . to . . . talk to . . . you, Grant." The words came slowly because Guy had to pause every few syllables to get his breath.

"Don't talk, just listen," Grant advised. "Then, if you have any questions, I'll try to answer them, although there's a lot to this situation I don't know yet myself."

"I was . . . going . . . destroy . . . the culture . . . by boiling," Guy said when Grant finished a detailed description of their trip to Yungay and what they found at the Casa Yanqui, including theft of the camera and microscope.

"It wouldn't have helped, once you were infected. Besides, whoever took the camera and the microscope left a trail of bacteria wherever he went." Grant didn't mention Augustine Almaviva, knowing it would only distress Guy to learn that there were even more victims of the bacterial curse besides himself.

"I found the will," he added. "And showed it to Lael."

"She'll . . . be . . . well . . . taken care . . . of."

"Is Lael . . . sick?" Grant knew what was troubling his brother, the near certainty that Lael would develop the fever.

"She drove all the way and was tired after the trip," he said. "I looked in on her just now and she's sound asleep."

"You've . . . got to . . . protect her." The bluish tint to the sick man's lips and ear lobes had deepened from the effort of speaking. "I'm . . . de . . . pending . . . on you . . . Grant."

"I'll do everything I can. Now rest and save your strength. You seem to have licked the fever."

"It's . . . my . . . heart . . . now . . . isn't it?"

"Yes, but we'll probably bleed you tomorrow. It's an old-fashioned remedy, but it often helps an overloaded heart."

VIII

From the staff lounge forward came the sound of laughter, but Grant couldn't help wondering how much of the gaiety would remain if the hospital complement fully understood the danger that faced them all, with what he suspected to be the most virulent organism he'd ever encountered being breathed into the air by two patients aboard the ship. Ordinary isolation measures would prove to be futile, he suspected, just as they were futile against the pneumonic form of bubonic plague. Depressed by the thought of what was likely to happen, he climbed the metal stairway to the top deck, seeking fresh air and a chance to think.

The broad metal flooring of the deck was unbroken, except for the housing of the bridge at the forward end, and was brightly lit by floodlights. The deck, he'd been told, had served as a heliport for unloading the wounded during the Korean War. Now, except for some canvas lounge chairs and beach pads the nurses used while sunbathing, during the few hours in the middle of the day when the sun broke through the normal fog cover here on the northern coast of Peru, it appeared to be deserted. Moving to the edge, Grant looked out across the top of the palm trees growing on the shore to the town beyond.

From the Hotel Chimu on the bay front came the strains of guitar and accordion, while from the barrio that clung to the lowlands south of the city the steady popping of firecrackers could be heard. Both were signs that one of the almost continuous fiestas he'd noticed, when he and Lael Valdez had driven through Chimbote earlier, was still in progress.

In the seclusion of his second-story hovel in the barrio, Grant thought, Manoel Allanza would almost certainly begin to feel soon the muscle aches and the throbbing head preceding delirium, as the deadly fever from the past attacked his body. And somewhere in the city, the family of the sister Augustine Almaviva had come there to visit might have no more than a few days of grace left, if the fever followed an incubation period of roughly seven days, as it appeared to have done with both Guy and Augustine Almaviva.

By tomorrow or the next day, the new sputum cultures should prove whether the microscopic red rods, which had grown so luxuriantly on the culture medium in the small incubator at Casa Yanqui, were indeed the cause of the deadly fever. With that proof—which he did not doubt would be forthcoming—Grant could hopefully start the campaign to control the epidemic before it got completely out of hand.

"Care for a small libation, Dr. Reed?"

There was no mistaking the faint Scotch burr, and glancing toward the bridge, Grant saw Angus Mc-Tavish, the old chief engineer, stretched out in a deck chair where he was protected from the cold sea breeze. On a small table beside him stood a bottle and some paper cups.

"I was enjoying a dram of scotch before going below again," said McTavish as Grant pulled up a chair and poured himself a drink. "The smell from the fish-meal factories stinks up the air around here so much by day that it's hard to get it out of the engine room even after the mills are shut down at night."

"Working late again?"

"Every night lately. Today we managed to weld the cracked cylinder in one engine to where it can furnish maybe a tenth of its normal power, barely enough to get us out of the harbor."

Something in the old chief engineer's voice brought Grant suddenly alert. "Is there any possibility of that happening?"

"You'll have to ask Jack Smithson and Captain Pendarvis about that. They've been talking by radio to Mercy Foundation headquarters in New York about our situation here."

"Asking permission to leave when you're able to furnish the power?"

"What else?"

"But what's the sense in leaving a fine harbor, only to probably wind up drifting helplessly in this open sea?"

"A ship sounding a distress call by radio would bring help from all over this end of the Pacific, Doctor."

"For salvage?"

McTavish chuckled. "Can you imagine a salvage company trying to lay claim to a helpless hospital ship? They'll most likely send a seagoing tug to tow us to Panama; after all, the old girl's going to be turned into scrap anyway when this voyage is over."

"What about the epidemic here at Chimbote?"

"The way I hear it, you haven't proved there's an epidemic, Doctor. So it makes sense—to the captain at least—to get the hell out of here before the port is quarantined and we can't leave."

"But the *Mercy* has the only really decent medical facilities in the area."

"Granted. But the foundation is practically broke, and all the suppliers that sell to us here know it. We're down to bare bones as far as the staff is concerned, too, with most of the volunteers gone, once the malaria epidemic was controlled. That still leaves some seventy-five people aboard this ship, Doctor, counting both complement and crew, and they've got to eat, even if they aren't paid."

"Are you low on supplies, too?"

"We've got enough in a pinch to last maybe a couple of months without taking on anything else. The way Captain Pendarvis looks at it, we'd better use them in getting back to the States."

"Leaving a lot of sick people here to die?"

"Everybody on the ship knows you've probably uncovered a new plague up there in the Callejón de

Huaylas, Dr. Reed, and I can understand how you feel, with your brother responsible. Nevertheless, as chief of the hospital complement, Jack Smithson must ask himself whether it's fair for people, who only came down here to cope with an epidemic of malignant malaria, to be exposed to something that could be ten times worse."

"It may not be quite that bad."

"Your brother's dying of the fever and so's the Indian who was chief of his drill crew. How much chance either can you offer that girl who had the courage to bring your brother down here?"

"I may be able to save her."

"How?"

"Injecting blood from a person who is already immune could do it."

"The only person who's immune, if even he is yet, has to be your brother. Are you willing to weaken his chances of surviving in order to save Lael?"

"That's what's troubling me."

"You know what his answer would be, I'm sure. You also know what the girl would say if she thought saving her from the plague meant taking away his chance to live. So it looks like you're caught in the middle."

"I'm not denying that."

"You love your brother and want to save him. Loving the girl, he would naturally want to save her with his own blood, if he knew it was possible, and meanwhile she would give up her own life to save him, because she loves him. With just one other ingredient, you could have all the elements of a classic Greek tragedy here."

"What's that?"

"If you loved the girl yourself—and that wouldn't be hard to take."

"No," said Grant soberly. "It wouldn't."

"So what are you going to do?"

"Wait until I'm sure the organism we're culturing is what almost killed my brother. When Lael develops the fever, I'll have to decide whether I can be certain I'm bleeding my brother to help his heart failure or to save Lael."

"And if all the answers turn out to be yes?"

"I'll do what I have to do."

"Suppose Jack Smithson and Captain Pendarvis are ordered to take the *Mercy* out of here? Will you go with us?"

"No," said Grant without hesitation. "Guy and Lael were responsible for turning loose a killer microbe that's been lying doggo for five thousand years, since some people with the plague apparently fled to the cave for refuge from the disease, only to be sealed inside it by a landslide. My job now is to contain the plague to this area while it burns itself out—or find a way to protect people from it."

IX

Less than twenty-four hours had elapsed since Grant had injected suspensions of *Bacillus yungay* culture into the ten white laboratory rats—and all were dead. Moreover, sputum cultures from Guy Reed and Augustine Almaviva were already showing a heavy growth of *Bacillus yungay*. Now Grant stood in the well-equipped laboratory of the ship surrounded by a half dozen of the staff.

Dr. Jack Smithson was there, of course, and Dr. Antonio y Marelia. So were the chief nurse, Elaine Carroll, and the head of the surgical staff, Dr. Mark Post, who had performed miracles of plastic surgery on children brought to the ship with birth defects and other deformities. Leona Danvers, the chief laboratory technician, was assisting Grant, and beside Miss Carroll, in an immaculate white uniform, was Captain Harry Pendarvis, with Lael Valdez, looking somewhat flushed and tired, standing behind him.

All of them were staring at the shaved belly of a

dead white rat, attached to a board lying across a metal tray partly filled with a powerful antiseptic. Holding a sterile spatula from a small tray in the flame of a Bunsen burner until it was smoking hot, Grant seared the skin of the rodent's belly to sterilize it, then dropped the spatula into the tray. The sickening smell of burning hair and flesh made several of the onlookers turn away as he picked up a sterile scalpel.

"Yesterday, Miss Valdez and I returned from a visit to my brother's casa at Yungay in the Callejón de Huaylas," he said and continued with a detailed story of what they had found.

Mark Post, he noted, was recording what he said with a small tape recorder but made no objection, since none seemed indicated.

"Cultures from both the camera and the periscope have been made," he said in conclusion. "They show the microbe to be a rod-shaped organism which has not hitherto been identified."

"A new germ and a new disease?" Tonio Marelia asked.

"A very old germ and a very old disease, Dr. Marelia. The report from the Harvard Institute of Radiation Physics of their radiocarbon assay reveals that the specimen of bone and cloth attached to the end of the periscope was five thousand years old, plus or minus about two hundred years—which, of course, are unimportant."

A murmur of amazement came from the spectators.

"As soon as Miss Valdez and I returned yesterday," Grant continued, "I prepared a sterile suspension in salt solution of the organism which had grown out in my brother's cultures. This preparation was arranged by Miss Danvers in ten dilutions, each one-tenth as strong as the one above it and therefore containing one-tenth the number of bacteria.

"One cubic centimeter of each dilution was injected intraperitoneally into white rats yesterday afternoon— ten animals in all—in a standard test to determine the relative virulence of an organism. All the animals died in less than twenty-four hours, indicating an extremely virulent visitor from the distant past. Cultures of the sputum from my brother and the patient Almaviva, using a fresh blood agar medium prepared under my direction, also show a very heavy growth of the same organism."

"Proving that it attacks mainly the lungs but also poisons the rest of the body by releasing a powerful toxin," Jack Smithson observed.

"The rat we are about to autopsy," Grant continued, "received one cubic centimeter of the highest dilution of the bacterial suspension and therefore the smallest number of bacteria—yet it died."

With the scalpel he slit the skin of the rat from neck to groin, opening up the abdominal cavity and laying bare the chest, before dropping the instrument into the antiseptic flooding the bottom of the tray.

Next, using a second knife, he cut through the ribs and lifted off the front chest cage, exposing the major internal organs of the two body cavities, thorax and abdomen, which were seen to be filled with a cloudy fluid. With a small glass pipette, Grant then drew up some of the fluid and let it flow into an empty sterile test tube in a rack beside the table, to be cultured later.

Next he lifted up the spleen, revealing that it was greatly swollen, as were the liver and kidneys. Moving up to the chest, he cut into the lungs to show that they were soggy with what appeared to be the same cloudy fluid the peritoneal and pleural cavities had contained. Working swiftly, he took cultures from the more obviously involved organs. Then, putting the instruments he had been using during the post-mortem examination of the tiny body into the antiseptic solution, he pulled off the rubber gloves he had worn for his own protection and, moving over to the sink, dropped them into a basin of antiseptic before scrubbing his hands and carefully sterilizing the skin.

"Unquestionably, we're dealing with a real killer here," he announced.

"A plague from the past, maybe five thousand years old!" Sweat had popped out on the forehead of the *Mercy's* chief surgeon and his voice was hoarse. "It's incredible!"

"Yet very real, nevertheless," said Grant. "And as virulent today as it must have been when it was sealed in that burial cave by an avalanche."

From behind him came a moan of pain—and fear. Turning quickly, Grant was just in time to catch Lael Valdez as she pitched forward in a dead faint, but his clinical sense told him the collapse was more than just a faint, even before he felt the palpable heat of a high fever from her body.

The plague from the past, as Jack Smithson had named it, had felled yet another victim. And though Grant himself had no way of knowing where it would strike next, he did not doubt for a second that it would.

X

Grant Reed sat beside the bed where Lael Valdez lay sleeping, watching the slow drip of fluid in the chamber of the intravenous setup. Attached to the needle in her arm by sterile plastic tubing was a small flask containing about two hundred cubic centimeters of Guy's blood plasma, mixed with an equal amount of normal salt solution. Beneath his finger, her pulse was racing and the line indicating the body temperature on the nurse's chart had been rising steadily since she had collapsed during the virulence test of *Baccilus yungay* about six hours before.

The question of whether to remove from Guy's circulation the blood, whose liquid portion after the cells were removed was now flowing into Lael's circulation, had been easily settled. Less than an hour after she collapsed from the infection now raging within her body, Guy had gone into acute cardiac failure from the back pressure of venous blood flowing to his overworked heart. Only Jack Smithson's prompt action in removing a pint of dark blood from the desperately sick man's veins had given his heart the temporary respite it needed.

Grant had been notified of the blood removal in the laboratory, where he was busy with Leona Danvers, preparing culture tubes for shipment to Atlanta and the laboratory at the Center for Disease Control there. He had immediately taken the flask of blood mixed with sodium citrate solution to prevent clotting, and divided it between two sterile flasks. Placing these in the high-speed centrifuge Chief McTavish had repaired, he had easily separated the heavier cells from the liquid plasma of the blood.

Carefully removed from the top of each flask, the fluid portion of Guy's blood was now flowing into Lael's body, flooding every cell with fresh antibodies against the toxins of *Bacillus yungay* being liberated by the killer microbe now growing largely unresisted within her body.

Whether the boost in her strength to fight the infection afforded by the injection of Guy's antibody-rich plasma would be enough to tide Lael over the assault of the virulent microbe upon her own body tissues, no one could know. At the first bleeding, Jack Smithson had removed only enough blood from Guy to ease the load upon his heart. Nor had he revealed to Guy the use to which it would be put, knowing the archaeologist would have insisted that a larger amount of blood be drawn, thus perhaps jeopardizing his own rather faint chances of surviving.

While the injection was going on, Jack Smithson came in, studied the chart briefly, and felt Lael's pulse for several minutes. "I wish we could have cultured the blood I took from Guy before you gave the plasma to Lael," he said on a note of doubt. "That plasma may still be teeming with bacteria, you know."

Grant nodded soberly. "It was a case of Hobson's

choice, but she obviously has a severe case of Yungay fever, so the quicker she gets some immune antibodies in her system, the better it is for her."

"Anyway, I'm glad I didn't have to make the decision."

"I'm just as glad I'll not have to make the other decision that's facing you."

"What are you talking about?" the chief physician asked warily.

"Everybody seems to know you and Captain Pendarvis have been talking to the headquarters of your foundation in New York, trying to persuade them to let you sail."

"What's wrong with that?"

"Suppose the *Mercy* manages to clear the harbor and runs into the sort of severe storm that happens frequently in this part of the Pacific? Who's going to be responsible for the seventy-five or so people on your ship then? Pendarvis? You?"

"Our chances would still be better than here, with a killer loose and no way to fight it."

"There may be a way—the one I'm using."

"You know you can't—"

"Lael is sort of a test case. That's why I'm watching her so closely and why I was willing to take a chance and inject Guy's plasma immediately. If his antibodies tide her over until she can produce her own, then plasma or serum from anyone who recovers from the fever can be used to protect the hospital complement and, hopefully, keep them from coming down with it."

"I'd still rather we were out of here," said Smithson stubbornly.

"Don't hold it against me for hoping the foundation turns down your request," said Grant. "If this epidemic follows the course I expect it to follow, I'm going to have my hands full fighting it off the ship. And I don't know of anyone I'd rather have looking after my brother and the girl he loves than you, Jack."

XI

Jack Smithson and Captain Pendarvis were in close conference when Grant came into the dining room for breakfast. Neither invited him to eat with them, so he joined Leona Danvers and Dr. Mark Post, the surgeon, who was hurrying for a cleft palate operation in one of the two main operating rooms on B-deck of the great white ship.

"Are you going to send out the cultures today, Dr. Reed?" the technician asked as she was leaving for the laboratory.

"If you can have them ready by ten o'clock."

"They will be. I'm using extra insulation within the Styrofoam cartons to protect the tubes."

Grant drove to the airport in the Land Rover and gave the package to the pilot of the early morning plane for Lima, with instructions to pass it on personally to the pilot of the daily flight via Braniff to Miami, where it would be transferred to Eastern and on to Atlanta. That done, he drove to the district health office.

A trumpet vine grew beside the doorway to the health office building, its fragrance vying with the strong aroma from the fish-meal factory that hung over the town by day and the smoke from the tall stacks of the steel mills that made Chimbote a miniature Pittsburgh. Dr. José Figueroa, he learned, was still on the tour of inspection with the Minister of Health, but Dr. Tomás Arroya, his deputy, was there.

Arroya listened courteously to Grant's account of the findings in Yungay and the identification of the microscopic invader but didn't seem particularly concerned by the revelation.

"When can you expect a report from the center in Atlanta, Dr. Reed?" he asked.

"Not for four or five days."

"Perhaps they will identify your discovery as an

organism against which a vaccine has already been discovered. Or perhaps it is vulnerable to an antibiotic."

"I'm quite certain this is a new organism, Dr. Arroya. Even if it isn't, you don't have that much time to wait before taking some steps to control it."

"You still only know of three cases, all of the infected at Yungay. Which," Arroya added pointedly, "is in another district for which our office is not responsible."

"The death of Alfaro Mochas makes a total of four cases that we know of positively. Besides, the people who visited him while he was ill, particularly the women who helped prepare his body for burial, will almost certainly develop the fever."

"You can't be sure of that unless they become ill," said Arroya complacently. "To talk of an epidemic now could do irreparable damage to business, both here and in the cities of the Callejón de Huaylas."

"Alfaro Mochas is dead, Dr. Arroya. Augustine Almaviva is dying and my brother and Miss Valdez may both die, too. How much more evidence do you want?"

"That a danger exists in the Callejón de Huaylas, I'm prepared to admit, Dr. Reed," said Arroya patiently. "But that is the province of the district officer in Huarás—"

"Will you notify him then?"

"Of course. What measures do you think he should take?"

"Every new case of any severe fever in the area should be reported—and every death. I will personally go up there and make cultures of any cases he finds. Tell me, what sort of isolation facilities do you have here in Chimbote?"

"Isolation?" Arroya looked blank.

"If the epidemic starts here in the next few days, as I fully expect it to, those patients must be shut away to protect the rest of the city."

"We have a general hospital. But isolation—" Then Dr. Arroya brightened. "There is the *Mercy*."

"It may not be here. Captain Pendarvis is seeking permission from New York to sail for Panama."

"We cannot hold the ship, of course, without closing the port." Dr. Arroya's gesture was as graceful as that of an aristocrat flicking away a bit of dust from his coat. "And that is unthinkable."

"Not nearly so unthinkable as having the world know Chimbote has become a pest city," Grant said pointedly. "That may well happen, too, if my fears are realized."

"Could not your fears be greater than is justified by the evidence, Dr. Reed? After all, you deal with so many epidemics—"

"I have seen many people die—needlessly—because governmental authorities think more of how much the economy of a region will be damaged by an epidemic and not enough of the corpses that will pile up." Grant controlled himself with an effort. "If you'll excuse me, Doctor, I want to visit several people who may already be developing the disease. Then I must get back to the ship and report to the authorities in the Pan-American Health Organization on the danger here."

"Assure them that we will take all steps necessary, once the existence of an epidemic can be proved, Dr. Reed." Arroya was still urbane. "After all we are not like the African nations you have been dealing with. There have been civilizations in Peru for three thousand years."

"Five thousand, Dr. Arroya," Grant corrected him. "And one living thing from the past has just been resurrected to endanger the lives of countless millions all over the world."

XII

Grant Reed hadn't managed to convince Dr. Tomás Arroya of the danger facing Chimbote, but he did gain a new ally in an unexpected place, the barrio. A festering area of narrow streets and slum hovels, it stretched several blocks back from the waterfront on the southern edge of the city. On the way back to the *Mercy* he decided to look in once again on the legless beggar, Manoel Allanza.

It being a fiesta day—one of nearly a hundred such each year—the streets were already beginning to fill with people, many half drunk from drinking chicha and chewing coca leaves. Nobody bothered him, however, when he stopped the Land Rover before the slanting palm that led to Manoel Allanza's second-floor hovel.

Several hailings brought only shouts and curses from inside the small cavern of the hovel, so Grant climbed the slanting palm and, holding on somewhat precariously, looked inside. The den was almost as dark as it was odorous but he did see Manoel crouching against the back wall of the hovel where—though Grant had no way of knowing it—his cache of money was hidden behind a movable brick.

"Are you ill?" Grant called in Spanish.

The question evoked only another torrent of vituperation as the legless one spewed out a veritable vomitus of hatred mixed—Grant's fine-tuned ear could detect—with fear.

"When did the fever strike?" he asked.

This time one word leaped out at him from the torrent of abuse—*maldición,* meaning curse. Esteban had used the word, he remembered now, in connection with the ship, Guy, and Lael. It must be spreading, too, he decided, since he could remember no mention of a curse in his conversation with the beggar several days earlier.

Bending low, he tried to enter the hovel itself to examine Manoel, but a barrage of flying objects, from chicha bottles to empty food cans, drove him back and he was forced to give up the attempt. Besides, judging by the growing number of people gathering around the Land Rover parked at the foot of the slanting palm and the occasional threatening shouts, he realized that

Manoel's screeching was drawing a crowd that was not entirely friendly.

Dodging the barrage still pouring from the mouth of the hovel, Grant began to climb down the slanting palm, but when he reached the ground, he saw a thin-faced man, considerably better dressed than most of the crowd, working his way through the pack toward the front. People were giving way before him with obvious respect, mixed, too, Grant was sure, with fear.

"You are the Yankee *médico?*" Something about the thin man, his air of authority, the hatred in his eyes, told Grant he must be one of the local medicine men, a witch doctor or brujo.

"Dr. Grant Reed, yes. Who are you?"

"Your brother brought a maldición to Yungay," the brujo snarled. "And now you have brought it to Chimbote."

This was the second time Grant had heard the word used today, and he was suddenly alert.

"We brought no curse," he countered reasonably in Spanish. "My brother almost died from a fever he contracted in the Callejón de Huaylas."

"He will die from the curse," snapped the brujo. "And so will many innocent people here in the barrio."

"How do you know that?"

"Because the ship of the Yankee médicos brought sickness to Chimbote but they only take the people of the barrio"—the sweep of the witch doctor's arm indicated the slum behind them—"to use in their experiments and to destroy their souls."

It was the standard accusation with which native witch doctors always greeted medical help, whenever it threatened to break their hold of superstition and fear upon ignorant people. And yet Grant was convinced that this time the word "maldición" had a special meaning, whose source he needed to learn.

"You do not answer!" the brujo shouted triumphantly. "You admit the Yankees of the ship torture the poor—"

"Many of you have been saved from the shaking

fever, the *tercianas,* by the medicines given at the ship," Grant told the crowd. "Others have seen disfigured children cured by the magic of the doctor who remakes faces. Why do you listen to this man, who takes your money like the rest of the brujos when you are sick but lets you die?"

"His brother brought the curse upon us!" screeched the witch doctor. "Do not listen or it will fall upon you."

A growl of anger came from the crowd, and, emboldened by the sound, the brujo suddenly leaped forward and dared to spit in Grant's face. Unprepared, Grant was not able to dodge the spittle but his reflexes were working perfectly, and with a quick punch, he sent the thin man sprawling on the ground.

"Maldito gringo!" the brujo screamed and a flood of other curses followed as the crowd surged forward.

Grant started backing toward the Land Rover, sensing that unless he made his escape quickly, he could be beaten and perhaps trampled to death—exactly the fate the brujo intended for him before any help could possibly arrive. But the crowd anticipated his intention and, spilling around him, shut him away from the car. Surrounding him and the prostrate witch doctor, they were obviously waiting only for an order from the brujo, now scrambling to his feet, to close in for the kill.

While the thin man dusted himself off, Grant tensed himself for the expected attack, but the witch doctor was obviously savoring the way he had been able to stir up the crowd and was in no hurry to have them carry out his purpose for him. Then, just as the brujo opened his mouth to whip his followers into the frenzy of hatred that would lead to the kill, the fingers of a huge black hand closed upon his bony shoulders in a grip that brought a yelp of pain.

"Up to your old tricks again, Santos?" The speaker was a giant Negro, a good six feet four in height, with shoulders—it seemed to Grant—half as wide. His head was bald and a long scar extended from just below the left ear down to the angle of his jaw.

"I thought I told you to stay out of this part of town, Santos." The giant Negro gave the witch doctor a shove that sent him scuttling through the crowd, whose temper changed almost immediately from bloodthirsty anger to amusement. "The folks here know I'm their friend."

Ignoring the crowd, the big man turned back to Grant. "I must apologize for the way my people were about to treat a distinguished scientist and winner of the Nobel Prize." The Negro spoke English with a pronounced southern accent.

Turning to the crowd again, he lectured them rapidly in Spanish, upbraiding them as if they were children.

"I—think you saved my life," Grant told his protector a bit shakily, as the crowd began to disperse. "The man you called Santos was stirring them up to kill me."

"All brujos hate the doctors on the ship. Since they started treating people who aren't sick enough to go into the hospital in the clinic held aboard each afternoon, Santos and the others have lost many patients. By the way, my name is Homer Ferguson, originally from Louisiana."

"How did you happen to come here?" Grant asked as they shook hands.

"I was a rigger in the Louisiana oil fields back home, until I had a slight misunderstanding with another man —over a woman." He touched the scar on his jaw. "A bowie knife in the hands of a Texan did that, but the Texan was white and got in the way of a razor. I left Texas one jump ahead of a sheriff's posse and came down here to work in the oil fields around Trujillo. That was nearly ten years ago, and when the fields began to run dry up the coast. I came to Chimbote to work in the steel mills."

"Do you live in the barrio?"

"The barrio here is like Catfish Row in Charleston, Doctor. You remember Porgy and Bess, I'm sure."

"Very pleasantly."

"The poor down here are ignorant but I picked up Spanish and Quechua—pretty fast so I can do a lot of little things for them. You know—protecting them from loan sharks, unscrupulous landlords, and the like. They even call me El Alcalde Negro," Ferguson chuckled. "Which, when you think of it, doesn't make me seem any better off than I'd be back home—but I am. Once you get to know the Indians of Peru, Dr. Reed, you discover that they're very happy—with a philosophy of life far better than any I was being taught at Tuskegee."

Grant had sensed that the Giant Negro was educated but it was still somewhat of a shock to discover that he was college-educated.

"At the end of my second year at the most famous Negro college in the United States," Ferguson continued, "I stopped one day and asked myself what satisfaction I could get out of teaching young Negroes to look for more in life than they will ever be able to find. The oil business was booming then, so I went into rigging—and wound up here."

"In time to save me from a mob," said Grant gratefully. "Do you mind telling me why you were in this particular spot at this particular moment—unless you're a miracle?"

"Manoel Allanza is a special friend, Dr. Reed. I've been working the night shift at the mill and came by to see how Manoel is this morning."

"I think he's in danger of being very sick, Mr. Ferguson."

"Call me Homer, please. What kind of a sickness, Doctor?"

"A dangerous fever that will soon sweep through the city and perhaps through this part of Peru."

"Is that the curse Santos was shouting about? There's been much talk of a maldición in the barrio lately."

"This fever is no curse, Homer. If you'll go with me to the *Mercy*, I can show you the cause under the microscope."

"But how could Manoel have contracted this fever you speak of?"

Grant gave the big man a quick summary of what he'd learned from the waiter at the cantina on the square about the morning when Augustine Almaviva had collapsed in the fountain, unconscious.

"Could Manoel have become infected merely by drinking from the same glass as the man from Yungay?"

"He also handled money Almaviva had been handling."

Ferguson nodded thoughtfully. "I remember that morning well; it was less than a week ago."

"Four days to be exact."

"Manoel had lost a caster from the little platform he sits on—he calls it his legs. I visited him that evening, but he was already in a drunken stupor from chicha. When he described this Almaviva, I recognized him—"

"You know Augustine Almaviva?" Grant asked quickly.

"He was the guest of honor a few days ago at a fiesta—a party given by his sister and his brother-in-law. They are friends of mine."

"Then you must know their names."

"Of course. It is Torres—Conchita and Juan Torres. They run a cantina at the edge of the barrio. The man is of no consequence, but Conchita—" Homer Ferguson kissed his fingers in a typical gesture, indicating just how much he had acquired of the Latin temperament. *"Une mujer muy appasionada."* By which Grant judged that the big man knew Conchita Torres very well indeed.

"Just last night," the big Negro continued, "Conchita told me she was very much worried about her brother, who left without saying good-by." He slapped a huge leg with his hand and laughed uproariously. "Mainly because he departed for Yungay without paying for the chicha used in the fiesta."

"Almaviva didn't go back to Yungay. He's dying aboard the *Mercy*."

Ferguson's merriment was suddenly cut short. "Perhaps of the same fever you spoke about just now? The one you think may have affected little Manoel upstairs?"

"Almaviva was a drill foreman with a crew employed by my brother in the hills above Yungay to drill a test well. Both he and Manoel contracted the fever from a germ released when my brother opened into a burial chamber."

"No wonder Conchita's brother was talking about a curse. Now all of the barrio is giving it the same name."

"With men like Santos stirring them up against all white men because of it."

"This fever . . . ?" Ferguson's shrewd eyes never left Grant's face as he asked the question. "Is it really dangerous, Dr. Reed?"

"One man who worked on the drill crew—his name was Alfaro Mochas—is already dead of it in Yungay and my brother may still die because of it. Augustine Almaviva is dying on the ship and Señorita Valdez, my brother's *novia,* is also seriously ill with the fever."

"So if Manoel could contract this fever merely by drinking from the same glass as Almaviva and stealing his money, then Conchita Torres and her husband could have it."

"Plus everyone at the fiesta, including yourself," Grant told him. "Can you take me to the Torreses?"

"Of course. Let me speak to Manoel first; it will only take a moment."

The big man went up the slanting palm tree with the agility of a gymnast and disappeared inside the hovel. Grant could hear some explosive conversation in Spanish but it was largely unintelligible. When Ferguson climbed down the palm tree, his expression was grave.

"Manoel is already feverish," he said. "Your curse seems to have claimed another victim, Dr. Reed."

XIII

The Cantina Torres was at the edge of the barrio, a few blocks from the central square of Chimbote. It was closed and Grant half expected to find a wreath of black ribbon on the door like the one they'd found in Yungay at the home of Alfaro Mochas. When Homer Ferguson knocked on the door of the sleeping quarters behind it, a hoarse feminine voice demanded to know who was there.

"It's Homer—with Dr. Reed from the hospital ship."

The door was opened by a very handsome woman of about forty, Grant judged. She managed a faint smile of welcome, but to Grant's highly sensitive physician's instincts, she was obviously already ill—and he had no doubt of the cause.

"The cantina is closed, *querido mío,* do not come closer," she told Homer. "My brother Augustine left a curse on this household behind him when he ran away."

"Your brother didn't run away. Conchita *mía.* He fell into the fountain in the square, unconscious, and the *policia* took him to the hospital ship. This is Dr. Reed from the ship."

"Salud, Señor Médico!" Conchita Torres put her hand against the doorjamb to steady herself. "I'm a little dizzy."

Grant reached for her wrist and felt the pulse. It was racing and her skin was hot and dry beneath his fingers.

"How about Juan?" Homer asked.

"He is worse off than I am. I would ask you in but—"

"May I examine your husband, señora?" said Grant. "Augustine Almaviva is gravely ill and it is possible that you have both caught a serious fever from him."

One glance at Juan Torres, muttering in delirium and already showing the tremors about the mouth that went with Yungay fever, was enough to make the diagnosis.

"This fiesta you had for your brother," Grant said to Conchita Torres. "Were many people here?"

"Fifty or more, I lost count. Señor Guy Reed paid Augustine well." She stopped suddenly. "Did you say you are *Dr.* Reed?"

"Señor Reed is my brother," Grant explained. "Augustine helped bring him to the hospital ship from Yungay suffering from a severe fever."

"Which my brother caught from yours?"

"I think not, señora. Apparently they both caught the fever from the same source."

"The curse for opening a tomb of the ancient people? Augustine was very much afraid of it."

"There is no curse señora; only a new disease. How long was your brother in your home before he disappeared?"

"He came here directly after leaving Señor Guy Reed at the hospital ship, but even then he was complaining that his head ached and his back felt as if men were beating upon it with hammers."

"That explains why the fever is so much further advanced with Señora Torres and her husband than with your friend Manoel," Grant told Homer Ferguson. "They contracted it from Augustine Almaviva as soon as he arrived in Chimbote."

"Then Manoel will become worse?"

"Much worse, and many who were at the fiesta will also develop Yungay fever."

The Negro nodded slowly. "Including me—as you said."

"You and your husband must have treatment at once, señora," Grant told Conchita Torres.

"But Santos—"

"Santos is *fingidor*—a fake," said Homer Ferguson. "You must do as Dr. Reed says, *querida mía.*"

Leaving Homer Ferguson to call the city ambulance and have the Torreses transferred to the *Mercy,* Grant drove back to the dock where it was moored. Lael's temperature had peaked at a hundred and three degrees, he discovered, and her chart had now become almost a plateau. She was semirational, drifting in and out of the delirium that appeared to be a prominent symptom of Yungay fever.

Guy was clear mentally and able to talk much better, but the effect of the bleeding yesterday had obviously been only temporary. The rattle of lung-base moisture was back in his breath sounds, showing that his heart had not been able to gain much, if anything, during the respite afforded by the removal of a pint of blood from his overloaded circulation.

"Dr. Smithson admitted . . . this morning . . . that Lael . . . has the fever . . . ," said Guy. "What . . . are . . . her . . . chances?"

"Good, with the treatment we're giving her—immune plasma I separated from the cells of your own blood we took last night."

"Then why . . . not . . . give her . . . more?"

"I expect to, when we bleed you again. Don't talk now."

"Bleed me . . . now . . . so Lael . . . can have more."

"She'll do better if she has a light attack to stimulate production of her antibodies—the way you've done."

When Grant came out of Guy's room, he saw the ambulance drawn up on the dock in front of the gangplank. Juan Torres was being carried aboard on a stretcher, while Conchita Torres was leaning on the arm of Homer Ferguson. Dr. Marelia had been talking to Conchita and now turned to Grant.

"This woman says you sent her and her husband to the ship for admission, Dr. Reed," said the Bolivian doctor.

"That is correct. The diagnosis is Yungay fever.

"You already know this?"

"Señora Torres is the sister of Augustine Almaviva, Tonio. He was visiting her and her husband when the incident of the fountain occurred."

"Then the epidemic you feared—?"

"Has already begun. The Torreses entertained about fifty guests at their cantina the night before Almaviva was brought to the ship, at a fiesta in his honor."

Jack Smithson came out on deck just then. "What's going on?" he demanded.

"Dr. Reed discovered these two patients with Yungay fever in Chimbote, this morning," said Marelia.

"Are you sure?"

"Absolutely." Grant explained the connection.

"You might as well go ahead and admit them to Isolation, Tonio." Smithson obviously wasn't pleased. "But don't find any more, Grant. We're expecting authority from the foundation to sail by tomorrow or the next day."

"With a full-blown epidemic about to break out in Chimbote?"

"I have my own complement to think of—plus the expense of operating the ship. If the *Mercy* stays in Chimbote another month, we probably won't have enough funds left in the foundation to pay the complement and crew and buy fresh fruits and vegetables for the kitchens."

"Suppose the Health Department of Peru refuses to give you clearance?"

"On what grounds?"

"That the *Mercy* is needed here to help control an epidemic? Then the government would have to pay the cost of operating the hospital."

"Will they bury those of my complement, who'll die of Yungay fever?" Smithson demanded.

"If I can protect you and the rest of those aboard the *Mercy,* would you consider staying in port and functioning as an isolation hospital?"

"You'll hardly be leaving me any choice under those circumstances. The question is, how can you do it?"

"I won't know for another twenty-four hours, until we can be sure just how Lael is responding to the antitoxins we gave her from Guy's blood serum."

Jack Smithson shook his head doubtfully. "Don't get the idea that I'm against using the ship in an epidemic, Grant. Prove to me you can protect my people and I'll even ask the foundation to approve our remaining here.

But at this moment I don't see how you're going to protect seventy-five people when Guy has only so much blood."

XIV

At a public telephone on the dock, Grant rang the health office and asked for the district health officer.

"Dr. Figueroa is attending a conference of district health officers at the Hotel Trujillo, Dr. Reed," he was told by the secretary who answered.

Grant reached Trujillo in two hours of driving. It was a larger city than Chimbote, but since its port of Salaverry lacked the safe harbor provided by the barriers limiting Ferrol Bay, it was not nearly so active commercially. He found the Hotel Trujillo in the center of the town and sent a note in by a bellman to Dr. Figueroa in the conference room where the health officers were meeting.

Figueroa came out quickly and greeted Grant warmly. Short and bald, he was obviously energetic.

"I heard you speak at a Pan-American Health Organization Conference last year, Dr. Reed," he said. "Sorry I wasn't in Chimbote to welcome you."

"I wouldn't disturb you here if I didn't consider the matter urgent, Doctor," Grant told him. "Frankly, I've had some difficulty convincing Dr. Arroya of that."

"My deputy is of the old school, Doctor—and nearing retirement. Perhaps you would explain in detail."

Before Grant was halfway through his account, Figueroa stopped him.

"The conference is breaking for intermission," he said. "I would like for Dr. Huantar, the Minister of Health from Lima, and Dr. Mendoza, the health officer from Huarás in the Callejón de Huaylas, to hear what you have to say."

The four men gathered around a table about ten minutes later while a waiter served them coffee. The others listened courteously while Grant once again recounted the happenings since Guy's drill crew had opened into the burial chamber. When he finished, there was a moment of stunned silence; being trained health professionals, both Mendoza and Figueroa understood fully the significance of what he was saying.

"A bacillus that has lain dormant for five thousand years," said Dr. Huantar. "It's incredible."

"When you see the organism grow in culture, you'll have no difficulty believing it really exists," Grant assured him. "I've worked with strange fevers all over the world and this is easily the most virulent organism I've ever encountered."

"In most epidemics we can count on a certain portion of the population having some acquired immunity, in much the same way the poor often possess more protection against poliomyelitis than the well-to-do," Dr. Figueroa observed. "But with this invader from prehistory, nobody will be immune. It could even attack an entire population."

"The fact that transmission can occur through the air, possibly by droplets, makes it even more serious," Dr. Mendoza added.

"My brother, Alfaro Mochas, and Augustine Almaviva all acquired the infection by actual contact with material in which it had been lying dormant, so you can estimate with fair accuracy that the incubation period of the disease seems to have been almost exactly one week."

"Miss Valdez's case doesn't fit that schedule," said Figueroa.

"Her delay in developing symptoms could be explained by the fact that she didn't handle any of the original material," said Grant. "In fact she appears not to have come in intimate contact with the organism, until my brother became ill and she started caring for him."

"Did she not handle the camera when removing the film?" Figueroa asked.

"My brother took the film from the camera and developed it in their own darkroom. He also prepared the specimens that were sent to Harvard University for radiocarbon assay."

"What is it then that alarms you?" Mendoza asked.

"Manoel Allanza, the beggar, was contaminated only about three days ago," said Grant. "In the case of Señora and Señor Torres, it was perhaps a day longer, yet all three have already developed symptoms. To me, this shortening of the incubation period appears to mean that *Bacillus yungay*—as I call it—is becoming more virulent all the while."

"Then it could already be sweeping like wildfire through the Callejón de Huaylas." Dr. Mendoza's tone was grave.

"As well as through Chimbote and wherever the thief sold the camera and the microscope."

"To sell the microscope for anything like its worth, he would almost certainly have to go to Lima—perhaps to the medical school," Figueroa observed, "spreading the disease even more widely."

"Just how do you propose to rid the world of this monster your brother has loosed upon a helpless people, Dr. Reed?" Dr. Huantar, the Minister of Health, asked rather sharply.

"I think it can be done," said Grant, "but your government may not like the measures I'm going to recommend."

"Why don't you let me be the judge of that?"

Unrolling the road map of the area he had brought from the Land Rover, Grant spread it out over the table, placing empty coffee cups at each corner to hold it down.

"The lay of the land in the region where we already know Yungay fever exists is particularly well adapted to being sealed off to isolate the epidemic in as small an area as possible." With his finger he traced the course of the Santa River through the Callejón de Huaylas lying between the Cordillera Negra and the much higher Cordillera Blanca.

"What happens to the inhabitants during that time?" Mendoza asked.

"Every person who develops fever must be isolated as soon as you can make the diagnosis."

"How can we do that when it begins like any other fever?" Figueroa asked.

"I'll come to that later; meanwhile please examine the map closely," said Grant. "Here is the Callejón de Huaylas with Huarás—your territory, Dr. Mendoza—at the southern end. Only one road comes in from the south toward Lima so a health team could intercept those entering or leaving Huarás by that route and determine whether they have been exposed to the fever or already have signs of it."

"That would mean shutting off all traffic southward toward Lima," Huantar objected.

"But hopefully keeping the organism limited to the valley," Grant reminded him. "The road from Huarás to Casma on the coast would also have to be closed, as would the northern end of the valley at Huallanca. Fortunately, only two routes lead from there to Chimbote, the highway and the railroad through the Cañón del Pato, both of which could be easily controlled."

"You have bottled up the Callejón de Huaylas," said Figueroa. "But what about Chimbote?"

"The Pan-American Highway along the coast is the only route in either direction. Closing it would isolate Chimbote and leave only the port, which the government could also close. That way all of the main routes by which the plague could escape from the two areas where we know it now exists would be contained."

"It is an admirable plan, for a campaign to keep a major epidemic from spreading," Huantar conceded. "But suppose we're able to isolate everyone who shows evidence of the fever? Isn't that better than the economic suicide your plan entails?"

It was an old argument, one Grant had already heard in Africa, as well as almost everywhere else in the world, whenever he proposed an all-out battle to contain a microbe invader.

"That depends on how many thousands of people you're willing to let die so merchants can keep their stores open and hotels fill their rooms with travelers, Dr. Huantar," he said.

The minister flushed angrily. "You take a great deal upon yourself, Dr. Reed. So far you have only identified about a half dozen cases of this fever you describe."

"Believe me, sir, I hope it never goes beyond that. But I've seen battles against diseases lost too often elsewhere in the world to be content with halfway measures."

"What you're saying is that with you it's everything or nothing."

"Not at all. I'm just giving you my expert opinion."

"In this case, you are an *uninvited* expert, Dr. Reed," the minister said coldly. "I don't seem to recall my government asking help yet from either the WHO or the Pan-American Health Organization."

"I have no official status here and have claimed none, Dr. Huantar," Grant said quietly. "My permanent status as a consultant to both health organizations, however, will require me to report the situation here by radio no later than tomorrow—"

"Why?"

"At Harvard University the contaminated specimen my brother sent there for radiocarbon assay was probably examined by several people, perhaps, even more, and whoever touched the material will shortly develop Yungay fever. If a plague is also being turned loose here to invade other countries—and it's probably already loose by now in the United States as well—I shall have failed in my duty unless I notify the WHO and the Pan-American Health Organization of the danger."

XV

It was well after dark before Grant Reed returned to the *Mercy* and he was bone-weary. Going to his stateroom, he washed the grime of the road from his face and hands before checking on Lael and Guy. As he entered Lael's stateroom, he received a shock that drove all thought of weariness from his mind.

Jack Smithson was sitting beside the bed, and a plastic bag, such as was used to hold blood for transfusion, hung from the pole at the head. Plastic tubing connected the bag to the needle in Lael's arm, and a string of dark red drops was visible inside the small glass observation chamber just beneath the plastic flask.

Jack Smithson had been dozing, but roused up at the sound of Grant's footsteps as he moved around the bed. "Where the hell have you been?" he demanded.

"In Trujillo, conferring with the Minister of Health from Lima and with Dr. Figueroa and Dr. Mendoza. What happened here?"

"While you were off playing the prize-winning epidemiologist, Lael went into shock. There wasn't time to separate plasma but fortunately she's a type AB—a universal recipient. I had no choice except to take more blood from your brother to increase her chances of survival."

"You're as qualified to make that decision as I am, Jack."

"Guy asked me to take more when I told him it was for Lael, but it's still a hell of a decision for me to have to make when you're the nearest relative and you're right here in the vicinity."

"You probably saved her life," Grant told him. "I'd have done the same thing you did if I'd been here."

"What did Figueroa and Huantar say about the situation here?" Smithson asked in a considerably less belligerent tone.

"Huantar wants business as usual, until the number of cases gets too high. By that time, things will be competely out of control."

"If you can hold that off for another week, McTavish figures he'll have one engine in good enough condition for us to limp out of here. At least the captain is counting on it."

"Do you think Figueroa will approve that? Hospital facilities in Chimbote leave a lot to be desired."

"Figueroa will probaby do whatever *you* recommend," Smithson said pointedly. "Any idea what that will be?"

"I don't know myself yet. I've got to talk to Atlanta and New York first thing in the morning, and the Pan-American Health Organization in Washington has to be notified. I hope Captain Pendarvis will let me use the ship's radiotelephone."

"That might depend on what you're going to say."

"How can I possibly recommend letting the only laboratory with the kind of facilities I need to study this bacillus and try to control it sail away from here?"

"Even if it means death to a lot of people in the *Mercy* complement?"

"They've already been exposed to Yungay fever with five cases aboard. How about the Torreses?"

"The woman will probably live; she's strong and she told Tonio she's always been healthy. Her husband's a weakling; the wife says he's sick—or claims to be —half the time, so we'll probably lose him the way we're losing Almaviva."

"You haven't heard the worst yet. From all indications, the incubation period of *Bacillus yungay* is getting shorter, which means the bug is gaining in virulence."

"Then you're in as much danger as any of us. How much longer do you think you have before it hits you?"

Grant shrugged. "Two days more than you and some of your complement—the time between my brother's arrival and my own."

"Meanwhile?"

"I'll need Leona Danvers full-time. If we can manage to grow an attenuated strain of the bug, one that will give people a mild case of Yungay fever but not kill, while still stimulating antibody formation, we might be able to immunize your hospital complement before it's too late."

But there Grant lost the battle almost before it began. When he came into the main laboratory, he found the svelte technician with a small bandage on the index finger of her left hand and a worried look on her face.

"I was transferring a culture and a test tube split while I was flaming the mouth," she told him. "A piece of the glass tube nicked my finger."

"Contaminated?"

"I couldn't be sure, so I put some alcohol on it and a bandage."

"How long ago?"

"Just before dinner, maybe a couple of hours."

"We may have time then. Get me some bichloride of mercury and a sharp scalpel."

She only grimaced twice while he crisscrossed the wound with the scalpel until it bled freely. Then he had her soak the finger in the strong bichloride solution, hoping to kill any of the dread bacillus that might still be in the tissues of the small wound. That done, he injected both fast-acting penicillin and the slower bicillin.

"Take a sleeping pill and let me see that finger again first thing in the morning," he told her.

"But you need—"

"No back talk, young lady; show me the cultures you were transferring and I'll take over. I want to try a series with all the mutating agents I can find—on the chance that we'll discover a weakness this organism hasn't shown yet. By the way, do you have any bromouracil aboard? It's one of the best mutagens going."

"I don't think so. The pharmacist would know."

"I'll check with him. Good night, Miss Danvers."

"Good night, Doctor. And good luck."

The next morning, when he glanced at the cultures he had made around midnight, Grant found the tiny volcanoes of *Bacillus yungay* busy pushing up their cones on the Petri dishes and the slanted blood agar culture tubes. Apparently the organism was not at all affected by the chemical agents called mutagens he'd added to the cultures, hoping to bring about a change in the character of the deadly microbe. Fortunately there was still a chance with bromouracil—if he could find any.

As he hurried toward the dining room for a quick breakfast, Grant saw Homer Ferguson ascending the gangplank, carrying Manoel Allanza on his shoulders like the Old Man of the Sea in Sinbad the Sailor's adventures from Arabian Nights. If he had allowed himself to hope the epidemic might still be averted, the appearance of the giant Negro with the crablike Manoel, babbling in delirium, perched on his shoulders, established as nothing else could have done the futility of that hope.

XVI

Grant's call to Dr. Marshall Payne at the Center for Disease Control in Atlanta went through shortly after 9:00 that morning. Payne listened in silence while he gave a rapid account of events since Lael and Guy had opened the tomb above Yungay.

"You're quite certain this is a hitherto unknown strain, Grant?" Payne asked.

"All my cultures here say it is. I sent a half dozen culture tubes to you by air yesterday; they should get to Atlanta sometime today."

"We'll be on the lookout for them."

"You'd better have all the work done in the hot lab," Grant advised. "So far it looks like we'll lose fifty per cent of those with the infection, so this could be even worse than Lassa or Sudan fever."

The "hot lab," a new division of the center sprawled on high ground outside Atlanta, was so designed that everything from culture transfer to microscopic examination could be handled in closed chambers using gloves open only to the outside. Actually the technique had been adapted from that used in handling highly radioactive materials, making it relatively safe for the lab staff to work with some of the world's most deadly disease agents—a group now joined by *Bacillus yungay*.

"I wish you were back here working on a vaccine for Sudan virus," said Payne. "The Nigerian Government reports three villages on the Jos Plateau almost wiped out since you left."

"I could certainly use the centers facilities down here, but I know I can depend on your lab crews to find a weakness in the make-up of this organism."

"Any suggestions on how we should proceed?"

"Maybe you should concentrate on a genetic study. A bacterium that reproduces as fast as this one does and produces such a high titer of specific toxin has to have a few genes carrying those characteristics. If you could somehow modify those genes and pull the teeth of this bug, we might develop an effective vaccine."

"That sounds logical. What else can we do to help you down there?"

"Send me a supply of bromouracil by Air Express, I'm still hoping for a mutation. I'm going to need all the lab facilities I can get and hospitalization, too, when the cases really start coming in. So please contact the Mercy Foundation in New York and have them authorize the captain of this ship to remain in port here in Chimbote."

"I'll do that right away."

"Oh yes. The Radiation Physics Laboratory at Harvard did the radiocarbon assay on a specimen my brother sent there about a week ago. I'm pretty sure the material he sent them was contamina—"

"Good God!" The shocked response of the center director came over the air waves. "Then your prehistoric microbe could already be loose in Boston and Cambridge?"

"I'm sure it is. You'd better warn Professor Mallinson at Harvard—also the health authorities in Boston to be on the lookout for cases of this fever. Tell them to do their cultures on chocolate agar, taking material from deeper portions of the lungs using suction with a small catheter. That way they can identify it in less than twenty-four hours."

"I'll alert them right away. Don't hesitate to call on

us for any help you may need, Grant. This could be serious."

"It already is. Pray for us, Marshall."

As he handed the receiver of the radiotelephone back to the operator, Grant heard a splutter of rage from the doorway behind him. Turning, he saw Captain Harry Pendarvis standing there, his face white with anger and his mustache quivering.

"Dr. Reed!" Pendarvis snapped. "You seem to have forgotten that you're only a guest aboard this ship. I am in command."

"I'm quite aware of that fact, Captain."

"Then by what right do you give orders here?"

"Since you were listening, you know I merely asked the director of the Center for Disease Control to inquire of the Mercy Foundation concerning the possibility of keeping the ship here, where it is certain to be badly needed."

"Dr. Smithson and I will be the judges of that. We're responsible for the safety of the personnel aboard and I have sent a request this morning to the captain of the port, asking permission to sail as soon as repairs on the engines are completed."

"Repairs, Captain? Or a Jerry-built job that will allow the *Mercy* to creep out of Chimbote and become a maritime hazard?"

"Chief McTavish and I will decide that, Doctor. Because of your brother and Miss Valdez, every person aboard this ship is in danger, so you certainly can't blame me for wanting to reduce that danger to a minimum."

"Do you have any conception of what will happen aboard a crippled vessel with an epidemic of Yungay fever running unchecked, Captain? You'll be operating a plague ship."

"What epidemic?" Pendarvis demanded icily. "Your brother is dying as you say and the man who came with him from Yungay is practically dead. That leaves only Miss Valdez with the fever—"

"Two more cases were admitted yesterday and one today—all from Chimbote."

"They can be offloaded to the hospital here. As master of this ship, I have the authority to order you to leave it, Dr. Reed, and I hereby give you six hours to get Miss Valdez and your brother to a hospital on shore. Meanwhile I will request the port captain to remove the Peruvian citizens now aboard pending our sailing. Now if you will vacate the radio room, I will inform the foundation of my decision."

Any further protest Grant might have made was cut off by the sudden announcement from the loudspeaker system: "Dr. Grant Reed—emergency. Please proceed to room B-31. Dr. Reed—emergency."

XVII

Room B-31 was a scene of controlled activity when Grant reached it. Jack Smithson stood at one side of Guy's bed, holding the electrodes of a portable pace-maker-defibrillator against the sick man's chest, and Elaine Carroll stood ready at the controls of the instrument. One glance at the pattern being written on the monitor at the head of the bed told Grant the story. The regular, though hurried, electrocardiographic pattern of Guy's heartbeat had now been replaced by a patternless jumble of peaks and valleys. The picture was characteristic of ventricular fibrillation, the most dangerous—and often terminal—complication of any heart disease.

"On!" said Smithson tersely.

The chief nurse pressed the timed switch, delivering a momentary shock as the high-voltage current raced from one electrode to another, completing the circuit through the heart itself. Guy's chest jerked and his back arched for an instant, before relaxing. At his head, Tonio Marelia had inserted a curved breathing tube to hold the dying man's tongue back and prevent it from obstructing the airway. He had also applied a mask over Guy's nose and mouth and was delivering oxygen under pressure by means of a respirator.

On the master screen, the jumble of peaks and valleys had been erased now and was replaced by a horizontal line indicating no electrical current whatsoever in the heart itself.

"He went into fibrillation about five minutes ago, Grant," said Jack Smithson. "I started defibrillation right away."

"It looks like you stopped the heart this time."

"This is the third time I've achieved cessation, hoping it would resume with a normal beat. Each time the fibrillation pattern was resumed."

"Did cessation last this long before?"

Smithson shook his head. "No. Better switch to the pacemaker, Elaine.

The chief nurse threw the main control switch, and the pattern of a normal heart contraction appeared. This time, however, the rhythm was artificial, the stimulus for each beat being produced by a small jolt of electric current to the heart itself. Under such artificial stimulation the heart could keep on beating, pumping blood through Guy's circulatory system. And since the respirator was mechanically inflating his lungs with pure oxygen, the life-gas was being brought to his cells with each beat of the essentially already dead heart.

But was that really life?

In courts of law throughout the world judges and juries had decided that the electrical activity of the brain itself was the only final arbiter of life, since unlike the pacemaker or the respirator, the electroencephalograph could not be artificially controlled. Once the action currents—tiny bursts of electricity that were the very essence of life—could no longer be detected, the brain itself was dead and with it all life had ceased.

"Want an EEG?" Jack Smithson had read Grant's mind easily, for, like almost any doctor, he'd faced that question himself more than once.

"No."

Nothing was to be gained, Grant had decided, by keeping his brother alive mechanically. A human machine, incapable of maintaining life itself, could not set the minds of students afire with enthusiasm that only a real teacher could excite. Nor could it locate drill sites for tapping vital deposits of oil, or, most important of all, explore the history of civilization through discovery such as had been brought to light in the clean thin air above Yungay.

"Are you sure?" Jack Smithson asked.

Grant understood the reason for that question, too, since his answer would release the chief physician from the responsibility—inherent in the Hippocratic oath sworn by doctors the world over—of keeping Guy Reed alive as long as humanly possible.

"I'm sure," said Grant, but when Elaine Carroll reached for the "off" switch on the pacemaker defibrillator, he touched her arm.

"Not yet, Miss Carroll," he said. "Keep the pacemaker going, please."

"But, Doctor—"

"Guy licked Yungay fever—the only person in the world who's done that for at least five thousand years, so his blood is loaded with antibodies. How many sterile transfusion flasks containing citrate to prevent clotting can you get in a hurry?"

"Maybe two dozen."

Jack Smithson had divined Grant's intention. "Get those transfusion flasks up here right away, Elaine," he said, "with the biggest needles you can find."

The ensuing thirty minutes were hectic. While Grant inserted as many needles as he could into Guy's arm, ankle, and jugular veins, Elaine Carroll was busy connecting vacuum-filled transfusion flasks, with the citrate solution inside to prevent blood clotting, to each needle. Meanwhile, the pacemaker continued to stimulate Guy's long since dead heart muscle to contract driving blood through his circulation and out through the needles, until no more was to be obtained.

In the end, ten pint flasks were filled, five quarts of

blood that would produce roughly two and a half quarts of plasma after the cells were separated. Two pints Grant sent directly to the refrigerator—Lael Valdez, because a gene in her hereditary mechanisms had somehow made her a universal recipient, was capable of receiving whole blood from people of all blood groups and might need some more. The rest he sent to the laboratory, with the instructions to leave it there for him to separate the cellular from the fluid portions, present in roughly equal quantities.

"That took guts," said Jack Smithson when it was over.

"A lot of people would use a more descriptive term —'cold-blooded son of a bitch,'" said Grant wryly. "I'm damned if I know who's right, but it's too late now to mourn for someone you loved very much. The important thing is what his blood can do."

"I know, and so will everybody aboard the *Mercy*. What now?"

"Captain Pendarvis gave me six hours to get Guy and Lael off the ship, but Guy saved me the trouble as far as he's concerned. Now I'll at least have the satisfaction of knowing I've protected the rest of you —for a while, if no longer."

"I'll take care of Pendarvis," said Smithson grimly. "When it comes to hospital patients, I'm the one who gives the orders and he'll take Lael off over my dead body."

"What about Mr. Reed's body?" the chief nurse asked.

"From now on," said Grant, "everyone who dies of Yungay fever will have to be cremated—or buried at sea."

XVIII

It took Grant four hours to separate the cells of what remained of the blood drawn from Guy's body from the liquid plasma, using the high-speed centrifuge.

Unfortunately, Leona Danvers could not help, for her hand was already swollen around the small puncture wound where the sliver of glass had entered the flesh. Moreover, her temperature was rising and Grant was fairly certain now that she had been infected with *Bacillus yungay* in a way characteristic of no other of the victims so far, by direct insertion into the tissues and the blood stream.

Lael Valdez had been able to receive Guy's blood because of her universal recipient type. His cells would, however, cause a severe reaction in any except type A recipients, who occurred infrequently enough to make trying to use whole citrated blood for the purpose Grant had in mind impractical. But plasma—even though, unlike serum which formed when blood was allowed to clot, it contained the fibrinogen that caused clotting —could ordinarily be given to anyone without danger of reaction, and that was exactly what Grant had in mind.

When the plasma separation was completed, he called the chief physician. "Would you have all personnel of the complement and crew gather in the staff lounge after dinner, Jack?" he asked.

"Sure. Need any help?"

"No. Esteban and I can handle it."

Eating a sandwich from the galley while he and Esteban made final preparations, Grant couldn't help thinking how appropriate it was that, after bringing the plague aboard the *Mercy* and placing the lives of everyone aboard in jeopardy, Guy's blood plasma now provided them at least a chance of surviving the malignant fever. His brother, he knew, would have been intrigued by the ethics and the justness of the situation but, tired almost to collapse, Grant couldn't find the energy to consider it more than briefly.

As in nonfloating hospitals, dinner was early aboard the *Mercy*—six o'clock—and the entire personnel of the ship gathered in the lounge shortly afterward. About a third were members of the crew and ship's officers, headed by Captain Pendarvis and the handsome Swedish first officer, Olaf Olsson. Jack Smithson, Mark Post, Tonio Marelia, Isaac Reuben, the dentist, and a half dozen others made up the medical staff. The rest were nurses and nurse's assistants, mainly volunteers from several stateside colleges.

The buzz of conversation ceased when Grant came in, followed by Esteban Gómez carrying a tray containing the flasks of plasma and syringes for injection.

"I think I can at last give you some good news," Grant told the group.

"It's about time, Doctor," said Captain Pendarvis heavily. "So far you've brought nothing but trouble."

"That's part of my job, Captain. It's often the only way I can prevent people from rash acts that endanger their own lives and the lives of others."

Pendarvis only grunted at this implied criticism of his attempt to leave Chimbote with the *Mercy* and did not comment.

"I'm sure all of you know by now that a new and very virulent microbe was accidentally loosed about two weeks ago from a burial tomb in the Cordillera Blanca above Yungay by my brother, while engaged in an archaeological study. As far as we have been able to prove, the organism must have been the cause of an epidemic some five thousand years ago. At least it killed about a dozen people whose bodies appear in photographs taken inside the tomb by my brother's assistant, Miss Lael Valdez. Sealed in the tomb, the micro-organism had apparently lain dormant until material contaminated with it was removed on a special Lerici periscope devised by my brother and the miniature camera attached to it by means of which the photographs were taken.

"My brother is dead, not of *Bacillus yungay*, which he overcame, but from a damaged heart," Grant continued. "Fortunately, he was able to leave behind something that may keep some, perhaps all, of you from developing Yungay fever—the specific antitoxin his own body developed while fighting against the organism. I know some of you thought me callous in draining the blood from his body after he died, and I can understand your feeling. However, that blood has already saved Miss Valdez from the fever, and since Bacillus yungay belongs to a group of bacteria that produce poisons called exotoxins, those who contract Yungay fever will produce their own antitoxins—as my brother did and Miss Valdez is doing."

"If they live long enough," said Mark Post, who was taping Grant's words, as he'd done in the laboratory the morning Grant had autopsied the rat used for the virulence test.

"Of course," Grant agreed, "Fortunately, a relatively small amount of a particular antitoxin will prevent those exposed from catching the disease—in other words, passive immunization against the organism, as opposed to active immunization, when the living body produces antibodies in the presence of the organism itself."

"Obviously you're talking about a serum," said Post. "But is there time?"

"Not for preparing a serum, which would mean injecting graduated doses of Bacillus yungay toxin into a horse until it developed its own immunity, drawing blood from the animal and allowing it to clot, then separating the cellular from the fluid component of the blood—the serum. Fortunately we have a supply of antitoxin available immediately—in my brother's blood —which has already saved Miss Valdez's life and thereby proved its potency."

"She could receive his blood because she was type AB, a universal recipient," Post objected. "But in a group of this size, only a few would be AB's."

"Any of you can safely receive the plasma fraction of my brother's blood containing the Yungay fever antibodies," Grant reminded the surgeon. "And since time is very short indeed, I can see no reason for delay!"

"When?" Captain Pendarvis asked and now there was no belligerency at all in his tone, only eagerness.

"With your permission each of you will be injected intramuscularly with equal amounts of immune plasma," said Grant. "I can't guarantee that all of you will be protected, but most of you certainly will."

"For how long?" Mark Post demanded.

"A few weeks at least."

"And after that?"

"Miss Valdez and at least two of the native patients aboard will have recovered by then and be immune. Besides, I'm expecting more new patients to arrive soon as the epidemic develops. Probably half will survive, which means we should have a supply of immune substances for your own protection, until some other means of controlling Yungay fever can be found—hopefully a vaccine."

XIX

If the paper he was going to present to the biennial meeting of the International Association of Radiation Physicists in London hadn't been the most important one he'd ever written, Professor Philemon Mallinson would never have boarded the big BOAC-747 leaving Kennedy Airport at 7:30 the evening before Grant started immunizing the personnel of the *Mercy*.

Mallinson had felt bad when he'd left Boston that morning and suspected he was developing a case of the upper respiratory infection, known colloquially as flu, that swept through the university and the city several times a year. Fortunately, he had no classes that morning and had stayed at home until time to leave for the airport, taking APC capsules with a half grain of codeine every four hours to lull the headache and the bone ague that gripped him.

As soon as the plane was aloft and the "Fasten Seat Belt" sign had gone off, Mallinson headed for the first-class lounge on the upper deck and started working on his first bourbon highball in preparation for dinner. He'd seen a few familiar faces from the academic world in the departure lounge but hadn't felt like engaging anyone in conversation at the airport, until the combination of bourbon and codeine began to work its magic upon his body, lulling the pain and stirring the appetite.

"Saw you in the airport, Phil." Professor Angus Moriarity, holder of the Stanford University Chair of Radiation Physics, sat down beside Mallinson. "You got away before I could say hello."

"Glad to see you, Angus." Mallinson shook hands with the portly Californian. "I've been feeling pretty lousy all day and my head was aching, so I didn't stop to see anybody."

"You've probably got the three-day flu; it usually sweeps the country in October, but that Kentucky elixir you're drinking should warm your bones. I saw your paper listed on the program; something new?"

"Maybe a small breakthrough. We think we've identified another particle."

"Their name seems to be legion," said Moriarity with a sigh. "I don't even understand quarks yet."

"Who does?"

Moriarity looked up as a tall, bronzed young man of about thirty-five stopped beside them. "Sit down, Puryear," he said. "You know Phil Mallinson, don't you?"

"Heard about you, of course, Doctor," said the younger physicist as he shook hands. "I stopped in Boston to say hello to a cousin who's in one of your physics classes—Sam Judson."

"Oh yes," said Mallinson. "Good boy."

"I almost missed him," said Puryear. "He was leaving tonight for California."

"I know. Judson told me he was going out to Los Angeles for his parents' fortieth wedding anniversary, so I asked him to look up something for me at Cal Tech."

"If you'd called me, Phil," said Moriarity, "I'd have had one of my graduate students look it up for you."

"Young Judson was going anyway and was anxious to do it."

"Sam was telling me about that specimen of bone and fiber from Peru you dated a few days ago," said the younger physicist. "Have you learned any more about it, sir?"

"Not yet, but I should have a letter from Guy Reed when I get back. I've done some dating for him before and he's always furnished me any information I ask for promptly."

Several more of the group of scientists going to London for the famed conference stopped by and the conversation turned to scientific subjects. By the time dinner was announced, the lounge was crowded with scientists, most of them friends of Mallinson's from other conferences and universities.

Lulled by the combination of codeine, phenacetin, aspirin, caffeine, and bourbon, Professor Mallinson slept fitfully after midnight, when the discussions in the lounge finally ended. But by the time the familiar green coast of Cornwall came into view beneath the plane's wings shortly after dawn, he was feeling worse than ever. As soon as he got to his hotel, he took two more codeine tablets and went to bed, ignoring the messages from the Center for Disease Control and the Boston health authorities that has been given him with his room key.

About the same time, Sam Judson was meeting his younger brother in the Los Angeles Airport, having taken the low-fare milk-run flight from Boston to Los Angeles. He was dreading the prospect of a big family dinner at noon celebrating his parents' wedding anniversary, because he was pretty sure he was coming down with an attack of three-day flu that had been working its way through the Harvard University community before he left. But since the anniversary celebration was what he'd come to California for, there was no chance of escaping two or three hours of eating and meeting relatives again.

In the Boston suburb of Waltham, Abraham Haimowitz, another of the students from Professor Mallinson's class, was busy getting drunk at the bar mitzvah celebration of his cousin Samuel Marx. It was a large affair at which spirits, food, and friendship flowed freely— along with a special contribution of *Bacillus yungay* from Haimowitz, who'd had a bad cough all day.

XX

It was nine o'clock when, thoroughly exhausted, Grant, carrying two syringes and the last two doses of Guy's plasma he had saved, entered the ward where Manoel Allanza had been placed. Though the legless beggar was muttering in delirium, his temperature chart had leveled off and there had been no apparent adverse change in his condition during the past twelve hours. Homer Ferguson was sitting by the pipe berth, his big hand upon the outer ring of pipes ready to push the small body back, if Manoel seemed to be in danger of rolling out of the berth.

"What do you think, Doctor?" Homer asked when Grant hung the chart back on the foot of the berth after studying it for several minutes.

"Your little friend is holding his own; if no complications develop, he ought to pull through. I can't say as much for Torres."

"And Conchita?" She had been placed in a ward adjoining the others in a section of the hospital that had been sealed off as nearly as possibly by isolation procedures.

"It's touch and go with her, I'm afraid. The least thing could push her one way or another."

"Can't you give her a push in the right direction, Doctor? She means a lot to me."

"I only wish I could, but I might be able to prevent you from getting the fever."

"By injecting me with your brother's blood?"

"How did you know that?"

"Esteban Gómez told me. He came through here on his way to the barrio right after you gave him the shot tonight."

"Why would he leave the ship at this time of night?"

"I guess Esteban figured the shot you gave him would protect him against the exposure he's already had, and that he'd have a better chance of avoiding any more at home."

"He's wrong," said Grant. "If the epidemic in Chimbote follows its usual pattern, a lot of people should develop the fever within the next few days, starting with those who were at the fiesta with Almaviva."

"I tried to tell him that but he wouldn't listen."

"Dr. Figueroa says the people of the barrio will listen to you if you tell them to bring their sick to the ship immediately," said Grant.

"Is that why you saved a dose of the serum for me?"

"In a way. The barrio is certain to be the place where the epidemic of Yungay fever that has already started will soon explode. You're almost my only pipeline to the people there, so protecting you from it could be as important as protecting the hospital personnel."

"I'd rather you gave it to Conchita, Dr. Reed. She needs it more than I do."

"What I have wouldn't be enough to help her, Homer, now that she already has the fever. But I can protect you for a few weeks and during that time you can help a lot of other people who would otherwise listen to Santos and die."

"All right, Doctor. If that's what you want."

The injection was made quickly, after which Grant gave himself the final dose. "It looks like you and I have been selected by somebody to be good Samaritans, Doctor," said Homer when he finished. "Whether we choose to be or not."

"I think we both know who selected us," Grant told

him, "but just to be sure, I'll ask Father Branigan. He and I still have to take my brother's body to the crematory. The mortician will only operate the furnace at night."

"No mortuary in Chimbote would let you use their hearse."

"So I discovered. It looks like we'll have to do it alone—with the Land Rover."

"After ten o'clock at night in Chimbote the way it is now?" Homer exclaimed. "That would be suicide, Doctor. Santos is just looking for a chance to get at you and I'd be willing to bet he's already learned what you're going to do from the mortician. I'll go with you."

"But—"

"The people of the barrio don't call me El Alcalde Negro simply because I read documents for them. I've also managed to get better working conditions and higher salaries from the plantation owners along the coast and from the hydroelectric plant people in the mountains. No matter what Santos has been telling them, they'll still listen to me."

"You don't have to convince me of that, Homer. I saw it happen when Santos tried to stir them up."

"He'll try again. Maybe tonight."

Homer's prediction of trouble was verified when the Land Rover appeared at the Casa de Fúnebre about half past ten. A sullen-looking crowd was waiting outside and massed around the vehicle, until the big man stood up in the back of the open car with the body of Guy Reed encased in plastic in his arms.

"Dispersar se," Homer shouted to the crowd. "Would you be cursed for molesting the dead?"

The threat cowed even the leaders and the crowd began to fall back, opening a way to the building that housed the mortuary.

"This could be a good time to warn them that anyone who attended the fiesta at the Cantina Torres may soon become ill with a high fever," Grant suggested. "Assure them that they should come at once to the hospital ship."

"I drank pisco and chicha during the fiesta at Cantina Torres with many of you a few days ago," Homer told the crowd. "The *pestilencia* was already in the house then and soon some of you will develop a high fever—a *calenturón* like the one that made Conchita and Juan ill. *El médico americano* will take care of you and treat you if you come to the white ship, but do not delay. Now make way; we must burn the body of Señor Guy Reed so the *pestilencia* within him will be killed."

"What of the devils that placed the curse on him?" a voice demanded from the crowd.

"The only devil around here is named Santos," Homer snapped. "He's afraid you will turn to the white médicos, who stopped the *tercianas africanas* before it could kill us all, and then he can no longer take your money for spells and potions. Go to your houses and stay there. If the fever comes upon you, go at once to the yanqui médicos."

XXI

The temptation was too great for Carlos Ganza to resist: the massive house with all its windows dark, the Rolls-Royce in the garage, the sculptured topiary outlines of the shrubbery. A strong bougainvillaea growing against the wall in the dark corner and the small balcony outside an open window led, almost like a ladder, to what was certainly a bedroom whose partially opened French doors were a further invitation.

Ascending the vine wasn't difficult, though Carlos had to shake his head a few times to clear it of the pain that had been pounding away inside his skull since noon before he reached the rail of the balcony. Climbing over the rail was an ordeal, however, for his muscles seemed to move more sluggishly than was their wont. In fact, he was tempted to give up the venture until he remembered the state of his finances.

The student to whom he had finally sold the microscope yesterday had driven a hard bargain, so he'd gotten only half of what he had expected to get for the instrument. Besides, even a man with an aching head had to live, and the price Ingeniero Jara had given him for the little camera had barely paid Carlos's bus fare to Lima, the rent of a room for a week, and the favors of a tapada, the one thing he'd missed most during those months in the Callejón de Huaylas.

And so, with a final effort, Carlos managed to climb over the rail of the balcony, creating such a racket in the doing that he lay on the floor for a while, holding his head in his hands and expecting to see a light go on in the room indicating that the occupants had been aroused. When this didn't happen, he pushed himself to his feet and slipped cautiously into the bedroom. Taking out the pencil flashlight he always carried, he switched it on, carefully shielding the rays with his left hand while he surveyed the room.

Clothing, both men's and women's, was scattereed all over it, and jewelry lay just where he'd expected it to be, on the bedside table, as if the pair in the bed had undressed in a hurry. In his palmier days, always alert to the possibilities of blackmail, Carlos Ganza might have spent some time searching for identification that would incriminate one of the two at least. But with his head pounding the way it was, he was anxious to gather up the loot and get out.

Perhaps it was his anxiety or perhaps the strange stiffness of his muscles that caused the contretemps. Anyway, as he was reaching for the bracelet and necklace on the table, his sluggish muscles betrayed him and sent the small lamp there crashing to the floor, bringing the pair in bed wide awake.

"My husband!" the woman screamed as she sat up, clutching for the sheet which had been kicked to the foot of the bed.

As for the man, he reacted as any lover would when caught in such a situation. Seizing his pants and shirt from the chair over which he had draped them, he made for the French doors opening on the balcony. In the process, however, he collided with Carlos, who had the same goal, knocking the thief sprawling against the edge of a marble-topped table which, colliding with his skull, brought immediate oblivion.

And so it came about that a groggy Carlos Ganza didn't even remember the coming of the police, or being booked for attempted robbery before ending up in a general cell of the Lima jail together with an assortment of petty thieves, drunks, and other minor miscreants gathered up in the evening police roundup.

Only the next morning, when Carlos was half-dragged before a police magistrate, did anyone realize that the unfortunate thief was genuinely ill and needed hospitalization. Even then, his situation was not much better in the jammed prison ward of the city hospital than it had been in the jail, but that really didn't matter to Carlos, already comatose from the fever raging inside his body.

XXII

If Dr. Rafael Huantar, the Peruvian Minister of Health, was inclined to be dilatory, Dr. José Figueroa was not. Although Figueroa's position in the government required that he pay at least lip service to Huantar's wishes, he had long since become adept at urging a rather somnolent bureaucracy to do at least the better part of what was needed to protect the public health.

Proof of Figueroa's capacity for direct action came the next morning when a military vehicle carrying an officer and two soldiers rolled down the dock to a point opposite the *Mercy* and parked near the Land Rover.

The officer came to the shoreward end of the gangplank, but was careful not to go any nearer to the ship itself. He tossed an official-looking letter addressed to Captain Harry Pendarvis to a deck hand and, this done, marched back to the military vehicle where the soldiers were setting up what was obviously a guard post.

Grant had been ashore, arranging the cremation of Augustine Almaviva and Juan Torres, both of whom had died during the night. When he returned to the ship, he saw the communication posted on the bulletin board near the shipward end of the gangplank. It was in Spanish, which he easily translated.

Port of Chimbote,
October 25, 1975

Office of the Port Captain

As of this date, movement of the hospital ship *Mercy* from Pier 31 is forbidden until further notice.

Dr. José Figueroa, district health officer, will post quarantine regulations as soon as they can be prepared. Only those holding authority granted by the Department of Health will be allowed to enter or leave the ship.

By order of the Port Captain,
Manuel Gonzales, Acting Captain.

"I might as well stop work on the engines, Doctor." The chief engineer was leaning against the rail as Grant came up the gangplank, smoking his pipe while he regarded the soldiers on shore, now engaged in cooking their lunch in a round pot over a small fire. "Looks like we're stuck here for the duration of that epidemic you've been warning us about."

"I suppose everybody is blaming me?"

"A few—Captain Pendarvis and the crew in particular. The medical people know what you're up against."

"I'm glad somebody does."

"Sorry about your brother. I never really got to know him but I had read a lot about him. He seemed to have a nose for oil and that's something we can't have too much of in a tight energy situation."

"Guy had a full life—"

"Which means he was way ahead of the great majority of people who are born, exist for a time without really doing much of value for their fellow men, then shuffle off this mortal coil, as the saying goes, without being missed. Which, when you come to think of it, may be the best sort of immortality—perhaps even the only one."

"Have you seen Father Branigan?" Grant asked. "I've got to cremate Augustine Almaviva and Juan Torres and was hoping he would perform a brief religious ceremony."

"I left him in the lounge just now arguing theology with Dr. Reuben, over pisco sours. They were discussing Maimonides, and from the sound of it, Branigan was losing the argument, so he'll be glad of a reason to break off."

Grant was turning away toward the lounge when he saw Jake Porter, the radio operator, attaching a yellow sheet of paper to the bulletin board with thumbtacks.

"This radiogram just came from foundation headquarters in New York to Captain Pendarvis and he ordered it posted for everyone to see, Dr. Reed," Porter called. "Looks like you've got a lot of moxie back in the States."

The radiogram was longer than had been the order from the port captain but just as much to the point.

14 E. 42ND STREET
NEW YORK, N.Y. 10017
OCT. 24, 1976

FROM: ALLEN J. FLEXNER, DIR.,
        MERCY FOUNDATION
TO: CAPTAIN HARRY PENDARVIS
      S.S. MERCY, CHIMBOTE, PERU
PENDING FURTHER DEVELOPMENTS, THE MERCY
WILL REMAIN DOCKED AT THE PORT OF CHIMBOTE
FOR THE PURPOSE OF PROVIDING MEDICAL ASSIST-

ANCE TO DR. JOSÉ FIGUEROA, DISTRICT HEALTH
OFFICER, AT HIS REQUEST, IN THE EPIDEMIC NOW
AFFECTING THAT AREA. ON REQUEST FROM THE
WORLD AND PAN-AMERICAN HEALTH ORGANIZA-
TIONS AND THE CENTER FOR DISEASE CONTROL,
USPHS, ALL PERSONNEL ABOARD THE MERCY ARE
TO COOPERATE FULLY WITH DR. GRANT REED
REPRESENTING THESE ORGANIZATIONS AND DR.
JOSÉ FIGUEROA AND OTHER PERUVIAN HEALTH
AUTHORITIES.

THIS OFFICE IS NOW NEGOTIATING WITH THE CBS
TELEVISION NETWORK FOR A REPORTER-PHOTOG-
RAPHER TO FLY TO CHIMBOTE. THE REPORTER
WILL FILM FOR TELEVISION AND ALSO PREPARE
COPY FOR NEWSPAPER AND MAGAZINE USE CON-
CERNING THE MEASURES BEING TAKEN TO COMBAT
THE DEVELOPING EPIDEMIC OF WHAT IS BELIEVED
TO BE A NEW AND HIGHLY CONTAGIOUS DISEASE.
THE DIRECTOR AND BOARD OF TRUSTEES OF THE
FOUNDATION REGARD THIS PUBLICITY AS EX-
TREMELY IMPORTANT FOR THE FUTURE ACTIVI-
TIES OF THE FOUNDATION AND THE MERCY. YOU
ARE HEREBY ORDERED TO CO-OPERATE IN EVERY
WAY AND YOU WILL INSTRUCT DR. SMITHSON AND
OTHERS OF THE HOSPITAL PERSONNEL TO DO LIKE-
WISE.

THE REPORTER IS EXPECTED TO ARRIVE TRUJILLO
AIRPORT VIA BRANIFF AND FAUCETT AIRLINES
TOMORROW NOON. PLEASE SEE THAT ARRANGE-
MENTS ARE MADE TO TRANSPORT SAME FROM
TRUJILLO AIRPORT TO THE MERCY AND PROVIDE
ACCOMMODATION ABOARD IN OWNER'S SUITE.

THE DIRECTOR AND THE TRUSTEES FEEL IT IS
INCUMBENT UPON US TO DO EVERYTHING WE CAN
TO ASSIST HEALTH AUTHORITIES IN COMBATING
THIS EPIDEMIC, WHICH IS SAID TO BE HIGHLY
DANGEROUS TO THE POPULATION OF THE AREA.

SINCERELY,

ALLEN J. FLEXNER, DIRECTOR

XXIII

Grant didn't waste time congratulating himself on the victory he'd gained over Captain Pendarvis. He was more concerned about Leona Danvers, whose hand had been badly swollen when he'd looked in on her early that morning. Moreover, her temperature was still rising, in spite of massive doses of penicillin and the broad spectrum antibiotic Keflex, which Jack Smithson had also given to Guy.

He found the technician's eyes bright with the fires of her fever-caused delirium and the muscles of her mouth and throat already beginning to twitch, a sure sign that toxins from the *Bacillus yungay* organisms that had entered her body through the hand wound were already attacking her brain. One thing only could possibly save the girl, he knew; immediate injection of the antibodies contained in Guy's blood, one flask of which was still in the refrigerator.

He tried to find Jack Smithson but was told that the medical director had gone to the port captain's office with Captain Pendarvis, before the radiogram from the foundation had arrived, to protest the quarantine of the *Mercy*. So wasting no time, he put the remaining container of Guy's blood in the centrifuge and separated the cells from the plasma.

He'd already ordered Leona Danvers moved from the small stateroom and adjoining bath that opened off the main laboratory, providing sleeping quarters for the hospital technician so she would be instantly available in an emergency. He was injecting Guy's plasma, mixed with an equal amount of saline solution, into the girl's veins, when Jack Smithson came into the room. One look at the other doctor's face told him there was going to be trouble.

"I just saw the radiogram from the foundation," said Smithson. "Pendarvis says your action in persuading Figueroa to quarantine the ship is the equivalent of mutiny."

"And you, Jack?"

"Right now I'm more concerned about this girl—and the chances of saving her, which appear to be nil." Smithson shook his head in a futile gesture of bewilderment, reminding Grant of an uncertain bulldog. "Look at it from our point of view—mine and Pendarvis's and the rest of the complement—Grant. We've been away from the United States for nearly six months."

"You still have supplies for three or four more."

"Basic supplies, if supplemented from local sources. But if you'll look out there on the dock, you'll see that they've dried up because everybody's afraid of Yungay fever. The ship's under what amounts to a siege."

"Not a siege, Jack—a humanitarian restraint because every indication I know of tells me your beds are going to be filled shortly with sick people, and whatever small percentage of them do recover will owe their lives to the medical skill of your doctors and your nurses."

"Damn it, Grant, that's not our purpose. We've been going to areas that are deficient in facilities for medical care and in medically trained personnel. We treat sick people, it's true, but only as a means of teaching the local medical population to take care of them after we're gone. Besides, I don't have either doctors or nurses enough to operate this hospital ship in the kind of grave emergency you're predicting, and the foundation doesn't have the money."

"The Peruvian Government and the Pan-American Health Organization will find it for you—"

"After a lot of us have died from Yungay fever?"

"I've already taken measures to protect your staff and the crew—"

"I know—and we're grateful. But for how long?"

"I only wish I knew," Grant admitted. "It would make my job a lot easier. By the way, is Captain Pendarvis going to enforce his threat to put me off?"

"The whole thing's out of his hands—and mine—

now that the foundation has ordered everybody on board to co-operate freely with you."

"You can start by examining this girl again, Jack. If you think of anything else to do, for God's sake order it. I'm at my rope's end."

But Smithson could do no more than Grant had already done. In spite of the immune plasma injection, Leona Danvers died in convulsions a few hours later, the final proof that the virulent bacterium that had entered her blood stream when her finger had been nicked by the broken culture tube had gone directly to her brain.

XXIV

Lael's improvement proved to be the only bright note in Grant's day. When he entered her stateroom, she was propped up on pillows, eating a soft-boiled egg and toast. The nurse looking after her had brushed her hair and tied it back with a red ribbon. She'd also given the girl her cosmetic case, and except for dark circles under her eyes, Lael was quite as beautiful as Grant first remembered her when she'd come to meet him at the Chimbote Airport.

"You're getting well fast," he said.

"Thanks to the transfusion Jack Smithson gave me last night. It was the first thing I remembered, after I passed out, and I could almost feel the fever subsiding before he'd finished. By the way, I don't remember seeing you yesterday."

"I was at Trujillo most of the day, locating Dr. Figueroa at a health officers' conference. You were asleep when I left and you were sleeping when I came in last night so I didn't awaken you either time."

"I forgot to ask Jack whose blood he gave me, so I could thank—" She stopped suddenly. "Oh my God! It was Guy's, wasn't it?"

"Yes."

"I remember Guy saw on my passport that my blood type was AB, making me a universal recipient. He said that was fine because if we ever had an accident and I needed blood, they could use his."

"You had three transfusions altogether."

"But how could he spare?" Her eyes were suddenly stricken with pain. "Guy's dead, isn't he, Grant?"

"Yes. Almost twenty-four hours ago."

"You kept the pacemaker and other apparatus in the room the last few days so you could remove all his blood after death, didn't you?"

He nodded. "We gave you one plasma transfusion before he died. Guy wanted you to have more, but we couldn't be sure you wouldn't have a reaction."

He saw the tears fill her eyes and handed her a tissue from the box on the bedside table so she could dry them.

"Poor darling," she said finally. "I brought him nothing but trouble—"

"You can't say that."

"But it's true." When he took her hand to comfort her, she suddenly seized him by the arms, burying her own face against his chest, while she sobbed. Finally, she raised her head.

"Bring me a damp cloth from the bath, please, Grant. Guy taught me to stand on my own feet when I didn't know which way to turn. He wouldn't be very proud of me if he saw me break down like this."

He brought her the cloth and she wiped her eyes and face before handing it back to him.

"Guy would know you were weeping because you loved him, as I did—and because he loved you," Grant assured her. "Before he died, he had the satisfaction of knowing he'd been able to do something for you by giving you his blood."

"Even in death, Guy gave me life," she said softly, then added a stronger note, "which means that one day I'll have to go back into the Callejón de Huaylas and open the tomb, so the world will be able to see his final discovery."

"They may even become as famous as the cave paintings in Spain—and Guy's name with them."

"Promise me you'll be there to help, Grant." She shivered and reached for his hand again. "The thought of facing that shaman painted on the wall of the cave—"

"There *is* no curse, remember? We can see it in the microscope."

The nurse came into the room again. "A message just came for you from the guard station on the dock, Dr. Reed," she said. "Dr. Figueroa wants to see you at the health office right away."

XXV

"You have my sympathy in the death of your brother, Dr. Reed," said the district health officer of Chimbote.

"Thank you."

"I've also been notified that Augustine Almaviva and Juan Torres died."

"We've had still another casualty, our chief laboratory technician. Homer Ferguson brought Manoel Allanza to the ship yesterday, too."

"I hope Ferguson doesn't get Yungay fever," said the health officer. "He's one of the few real defenses we have against the practitioners of witchcraft."

"Like Santos?"

Figueroa gave him a startled look. "You know of him?"

Quickly, Grant gave him a rundown on his own contacts with Santos. When he finished, the health officer was thoughtful.

"The *Mercy* is a threat to Santos's control over the people of the barrio so he would naturally hate you. We've been trying for a long time to convince the people that real medical treatment is superior to Santos's incantations, but so far with little success."

"I gave Homer an injection of my brother's plasma last night when I injected the staff and crew of the ship."

"Pray God it protects him—and all of you," said Figueroa soberly.

"Homer says possibly fifty people attended a fiesta given by Conchita and Juan Torres in honor of Almaviva several days ago. Almaviva was ill with Yungay fever at the time, so all of them have probably been exposed."

"I just finished talking to the Minister of Health in Lima by telephone," said the health officer. "He still refuses to believe this could be a very serious epidemic, but what you just told me may help convince him we're in serious trouble."

"It's the old story of business as usual. I've seen a lot of people die because of it."

"And we'll most certainly see a lot more die before this thing burns itself out, if it ever does. What course would you advise me to take?"

"If the minister refuses to institute a strict quarantine of Chimbote and the Callejón de Huaylas, there's nothing anybody can do except isolate every case of serious fever until sputum cultures can be made on chocolate agar," said Grant. "Fortunately, this organism grows out in about twelve hours and it's easily identified under the microscope without having to carry out a lot of complicated culture procedures."

"And then?"

"Send the patients to the ship, as long as we have beds. Captain Pendarvis and Dr. Smithson have strict orders from Mercy Foundation headquarters to admit all patients who appear to have Yungay fever."

The telephone rang just then; Figueroa picked up the receiver and listened for a moment.

"One moment, Dr. Mendoza," he said. "Dr. Grant Reed is here and I'll put your call on the conference telephone so he can hear. Please speak English."

Figueroa pressed a button on a small speaker upon his desk and the voice of Dr. Mendoza, the health officer from Huarás in the Callejón de Huaylas, sounded immediately.

"I think we have a case of what you call Yungay

fever here in Huarás, a man named Ingeniero Jara," said Mendoza. "I cultured his sputum last night, and an organism resembling your description of what you're calling *Bacillus yungay* is growing heavily on the media this morning."

"Had your patient been in Yungay during the past week?" Grant asked.

"His wife says not, but a cousin named Carlos Ganza came from there a few days ago. Jara bought a camera from him."

"Did you see the camera, Doctor?" Grant's pulse quickened with excitement.

"Only at a distance, Dr. Reed. After your warning about it, I was careful not to touch it, but everyone in Jara's family handled it—"

"Could you tell what make it is?"

"It is a miniature, a Minolta, like the one you said was stolen from your brother's home in Yungay. And Jara's wife says Carlos Ganza is a known thief."

"He may be a dead thief, already, Dr. Mendoza."

"Señora Jara also says Ganza was on the way to Lima, with a larger package."

"The microscope!"

"That was my thought. The situation is bad, no?"

"Very bad," said Grant. "Will you alert the police in Lima to be on the lookout for Carlos Ganza? And also ask the health authorities there to look for any signs of the fever?"

"It has already been done, Dr. Reed."

"One more thing, Dr. Mendoza. Had Ingeniero Jara been in contact with many people since he bought the camera?"

"It was a time of fiesta, Dr. Reed, and Jara was very proud of his purchase," said the distant voice of the health officer. "According to his wife, it must have been handled by dozens of people."

When he returned from taking the bodies of Juan Torres, Augustine Almaviva, and Leona Danvers to the crematory late that afternoon with the help of

Homer Ferguson, Grant received word of Carlos Ganza's death in the General Hospital at Lima from Dr. Mendoza by telephone. With a rising sense of futility, he knew now that *Bacillus yungay* had once again run rings around him in spite of all his efforts.

He would have felt even more disturbed, however, if he'd known that a medical student from Lima named Rafael Solitano had boarded a train that very morning for Cuzco, the ancestral capital of the Inca empire. In an area in the mountains so high that oxygen often had to be administered to the passengers on the train between it and Lima, the city of Cuzco was also close to the fabled Inca fortress of Machu Picchu, a favorite spot with tourists from all over the world.

The train had left very early, and so, although he was quite proud of the bargain he'd been able to drive with a man, who was obviously a thief, for the purchase of a fine binocular microscope, Rafael Solitano failed to see the warning posted on the medical school bulletin board against contact with anyone who might be offering a binocular microscope for sale cheap.

XXVI

Lael Valdez was reading when Grant came into her stateroom, on the way from the dining room on the deck below to the laboratory.

"I was beginning to think you'd jumped the ship," she said with a smile.

"I haven't spent much time aboard today, but you've obviously been getting excellent treatment."

"The transfusions of Guy's blood saved my life; I'll always be grateful to Dr. Smithson." She gave him almost a look of reproach. "How is it that you didn't think of it?"

Grant didn't rise to the opportunity to set the record straight by telling her he'd given her the first injection himself.

"Can't think of everything, I guess," he said. "I've

been busy planning the fight against the coming epidemic with Dr. Figueroa and the rest of the health authorities. By the way," he added, "we've discovered who stole your camera and the microscope."

"Who was it?"

"A thief named Carlos Ganza."

"How did you catch him?"

"*Bacillus yungay* caught him when he left a trail of clues—deadly clues as it turned out. The camera was bought by a man in Huarás named Ingeniero Jara, and Ganza apparently sold the microscope, too, but we don't know who bought it."

"This Ganza. He'd spread the disease wherever he went, wouldn't he?"

"Not any more. Ganza was infected the moment he touched the camera, and by the time he got to Lima, he already had a full-blown case of Yungay fever. He died in the General Hospital there."

"Then I'm the only one of those who opened the tomb that's alive?"

"Yes."

"But how?"

"The whole process is pretty complicated, but I'll try to make it as simple as possible. Most bacteria produce toxins—poisons—some of which are the most lethal substances in the world. For example, only seven ounces of crystalline botulinum type A toxin—an ordinary water glass full—could kill the entire population of the world."

"And what you call *Bacillus yungay* manufactures something as terrible as that?"

"Certainly not as powerful, or everyone who develops Yungay fever would die within a few hours. We know Guy's body did manage to produce enough immunoglobulins to neutralize all the *Bacillus yungay* toxin—"

"My technician training wasn't too thorough. What are immunoglobulins?"

"When stimulated by a toxin—in technical terms they're called antigens—like the ones produced by the tetanus or diphtheria bacillus, and of course *Bacillus yungay,* the body immediately produces large amounts of a special type of white blood cell called plasma cells. These in turn manufacture protein substances called globulins which are part of the liquid portion of the blood."

"I remember that much from a microbiology course I took at Radcliffe."

"Each bacterial toxin causes a specific globulin to be produced that tends to neutralize the poison, rendering it harmless," he continued. "Thus the body develops immunity—hence the term immunoglobulins—to that particular antigen. The immunoglobulins—it's much simpler to call them antitoxins—in turn fight the invading bacteria until they and their poisons are destroyed by the body, or vice versa."

"Then when Guy's immunoglobulins were transferred to my body in the transfusions of his blood, they protected me."

"Correct."

"It's a good thing Dr. Smithson thought of using the blood directly by transfusion, wasn't it?"

"You helped by being a universal recipient, remember? And the fact that Guy had more blood than he needed saved us a lot of time and trouble."

"I don't think I quite understand."

"The red cells of the blood are what cause transfusion reactions," he explained. "The fluid part, either the plasma which contains the clotting agent, or the serum—after the clot is allowed to form and separate out from the serum portion that's left—can be given safely to almost anyone. Fortunately, by putting blood into a centrifuge and whirling it to separate the cells, we can also separate out the plasma of a person who has recovered from a given disease and use it to treat people with the same disease. Then we can mix the red cells with saline solution and inject them back into the circulation of the donor. The procedure is called plasmapheresis."

"My nurse said you gave the rest of Guy's blood plasma to the personnel of the ship, as a preventive against Yungay fever."

"That's true."

"Why not use mine to be even surer they're protected?"

"For two reasons," he explained. "One of them is that I'm not certain you've developed enough immunoglobulins yet to keep you protected. And the second is that if you don't have a sufficient concentration of them, your serum wouldn't be much protection to others."

"But it will become stronger as I recover?"

"Absolutely."

"How can you tell when I'm well enough to help someone else?"

"First, I'll inoculate a rat with *Bacillus yungay* and at the same time give it a small amount of your blood serum. If it lives, we'll know you've produced a lot of immunoglobulins against *B. yungay*. If the rat dies, you haven't, but you couldn't possibly produce enough antitoxin to protect everybody on the *Mercy*, so I'm hunting for other ways to fight this infection."

"Have you found any?"

"No, but I'd better." His tone was suddenly grim. "Or everybody on the ship may still die of Yungay fever—except you."

XXVII

It was tiresome work, and tedious, but there was no way of escaping it and still be certain of the results. In the laboratories of the Center for Disease Control, Grant would have had the technical assistance of sophisticated machinery for studying the production of immunoglobulins. Things like the mechanism of radio-labeled amino acids and their measurement by means of direct radioactive counting. Or the immunofluorescent techniques using an antiserum specific for *Bacillus yungay* coupled to a fluorescent dye, which could then be studied by special chemical tests. And above all, by using the ultra-sophisticated tool of the computer, which could make in fractions of a second calculations that would have taken days to complete by conventional mathematical methods, he could have carried out the studies he was making far more rapidly and far more effectively.

None of these were available to him, however, although fortunately the *Mercy*'s laboratory contained far more sophisticated instruments than any nearby hospital or laboratory. With no one skilled in microbiological technique to carry out routine procedures, too, he had to do it himself. Moreover, for his own protection against an overwhelming infection by *Bacillus yungay*—shortened in laboratory jargon to *B. yungay*—Grant had only his own skill and the knowledge that a shallow cut, perhaps even a pricked finger, could generate an attack of Yungay fever far stronger than the small amount of immunoglobulins he'd given to himself and the rest of the complement could control.

To be closer to the incubators and the cultures growing there, he moved that very evening into the quarters Leona Danvers had occupied adjacent to the laboratory. Though smaller than a regular stateroom, the tiny apartment opening off the laboratory itself did have a bed, toilet, washbasin, and shower, which were all he needed.

Well after midnight he'd finally gone to bed but was up at six for a hurried breakfast with the day shift of nurses going on duty, then back to the laboratory and a new start in the search for something, a vaccine, an antibiotic, even a chemical agent, that could stay the rapid growth of *B. yungay* in culture—*in vitro*—and hopefully inside the body—*in vivo*.

It was backbreaking work and yet exciting because at last he had come to grips with the ubiquitous toxin produced by *Bacillus yungay*. Staring into the eyepieces of a binocular microscope late that afternoon, Grant thought he must be dreaming when the door of the laboratory opened and a familiar voice said:

"Hello, husband dear! Aren't you glad to see me?"

BOOK THREE

ADRIFT

I

Wheeling on the laboratory stool, Grant saw Shirley standing just inside. Apparently she had come in and closed the door behind her while he was half asleep, mesmerized by his own weariness. He rubbed his eyes instinctively before looking again, but she was still there, quite obviously in the flesh. And also fully as desirable as when he'd last seen her in his apartment naked upon the bed, watching him dress with the light of mockery in her eyes.

"It's me, darling," she said. "Not a vision."

"A demon you mean."

She laughed. "Considering what happened when we were last together, aren't you being a little ungallant?"

"How in the hell did you get aboard a ship in quarantine?"

"I didn't ride on a broomstick, if that's what you're implying. Mark Post brought me aboard; I guess the guards didn't think to stop him. I was very sorry to hear of Guy's death; he was quite a man, something they don't make much any more—present company excepted, of course."

She pulled a stool close to where he was sitting and perched on it. An automatic Konica camera with a flash unit hung from a strap around her neck, and a portable tape recorder in a leather case was also slung by its own strap from one shoulder.

"Actually I came the same way you did," she told him. "By Eastern from New York to Miami, Braniff to Lima, and Faucett to Trujillo. But I'm known as

Shirley Ross when I'm working, so I don't blame you for not knowing I was coming."

The truth suddenly dawned on him. "You're the reporter-photographer the Mercy Foundation sent down?"

"CBS paid my way. It's a double assignment, film and narration for the network and features for International News Service. Didn't I tell you in Atlanta I was free-lancing now?"

"I think you did. And I should have known your star would rise very fast."

"What a nice compliment—coming from you. As I remember, you were somewhat preoccupied with another matter at the time."

"How did you—?"

"Get the assignment? Went after it, of course, as soon as I learned from Marshall Payne what you'd run into down here. You called him a few days ago, remember?"

"I suppose you just happened to be in his office?"

"Marshall told me about it over dinner that evening, so I called CBS and INS first thing the next morning. With them behind me, it was a cinch to convince the Mercy Foundation that segments on CBS News and dispatches of INS showing the Mercy and its staff helping the world-famous epidemiologist, Dr. Grant Reed, fight an epidemic here on the coast of Peru would be a perfect opportunity to gain favorable publicity for the foundation—and bring in funds."

"Plus the owner's suite on the ship?"

"I didn't know about that until I came aboard. On the way to Chimbote from Trujillo, I listened to Mark Post's tape recordings of your little speech to the staff before you gave them the protective serum from your brother and I've been busy getting my pictures ever since. The first roll of film and a tape cassette describing what you're doing here went to New York from the Chimbote Airport on the afternoon plane."

"I've got to hand it to you, Shirl"—unconsciously

he used the pet name he'd used while they were still married—"you always were a go-getter."

"I'm saving the best for today—an exclusive interview with the world-famous epidemiologist who feels that this is his own personal fight."

"Why would I do that?"

"Because the archaeologist brother and his beautiful fiancée were the ones who released a plague from the past upon unsuspecting mankind."

She had described his own driving motives since he'd come to Peru more exactly than Grant would have been able to describe them himself, or perhaps than he had ever realized. And knowing it, he couldn't help feeling a reluctant admiration for her—and concern.

"It's also an *imperiled* mankind—including you now that you're here," he told her. "Don't you realize that you've risked your life in coming here?"

"That's in the best reportorial tradition, darling. Besides, I knew you'd look after me."

"With what?" he demanded, angered by his own inability to do what she so confidently expected of him. "I took all the immune blood Guy had and gave it to the staff, what didn't go to Lael Valdez—"

"She's very pretty and very nice; the sort of girl you deserve, Grant."

Her words only angered him more, though he couldn't exactly have told why. "I suppose that idiot Mark Post took you all over the ship."

"Mark is nice. So's Dr. Smithson."

"You mean Jack Smithson didn't warn you about how virulent Yungay fever really is?"

"He didn't have to; I already knew the score from what you'd told Marshall Payne. Besides, we observed strict isolation procedures—you know, gowns, masks, the whole bit. By the way, making the gowns out of paper like that coverall you're wearing is a clever idea."

"A lot of hospitals are using them—it's often cheaper than running a laundry—but I'm afraid in this case the whole bit, as you call it, isn't going to be enough.

Conventional techniques of isolation aren't going to hold *Bacillus yungay* in check. Marshall Payne should have kept you—"

"I knew he'd blackball the whole idea if I told him, so I didn't. It looks like you're stuck with the job of keeping me alive, as you're doing for the others."

"Did it ever occur to you that I'd be considerably better off financially if this fever gets you?" he demanded savagely.

Shirley shrugged. "I learned a lot about you in the five years we were married, Grant. Your conscience would never allow you to deliberately let me die." She reached down and pressed a button on her tape recorder. "How are you going about fighting this new germ?"

"By trial and error. Meanwhile, as people recover from Yungay fever—"

"Has anyone done that?" She was all business now.

"Guy did, but died of heart failure, and Lael's getting well. I hope to get the immune blood plasma I'll need to protect the hospital complement and crew from native patients."

"That's clever. How long will the natives stand for it?"

"I don't have any idea."

"What about this movement against you—by the witch doctor?"

"Who have you been talking to?"

"A gentleman named Homer Ferguson. I'm going to do an entire human interest story on the way he looks after the beggar who doesn't have any legs. It will be the best thing I've ever done."

Grant threw up his hands in a gesture of bafflement. "Manoel's at the height of the fever. If you saw him your chances of escaping infection are practically nil."

"So what are you going to do about me?"

"Ask me that tomorrow. Right now I'm living from day to day."

"And so are a few hundred other people who are

depending on you." There was no mockery in her voice now. "So please don't fail us."

On the way out, she stopped and looked into the open door of the rather spartan quarters provided by the *Mercy* for its laboratory technician. Then, lifting the camera, she took several rapid pictures of it with the strobe flash unit.

"I've already learned that you're *persona non grata* to much of the staff, Grant, but it does seem the ship could provide better quarters for someone as important as you."

"I moved in here after Leona Danvers died of Yungay fever so I could be close to my work," he explained.

"As long as you're satisfied with just a cot, a washbasin, and a shower, it's none of my business," she said. "If you find yourself going stir crazy, there's a supply of bourbon in the owner's suite as long as it lasts."

II

When Grant came into the ship's dining room the next morning, Jack Smithson and Mark Post, both looking haggard, were already eating. He selected his food from the steam table and paused beside them.

"Sit down, Grant," said Smithson. "I guess we've all been in this together since Lael brought Guy up the gangplank a little over a week ago, so there's no use blaming you for the mess we're still in."

"I heard noises during the night." Grant poured coffee from the flask bubbling on the small hot plate in the center of the table. "Did we gain in population?"

"Ten cases. Mark and I were up much of the night."

"How severe?"

"All of them bad. The witch doctors in Chimbote are only letting ones that are obviously in danger of dying come through. They're trying to convince the early ones to stay at home while they use spells."

"That may be the best way." Grant began to eat. "You've discovered by now that there's nothing to be done except supportive treatment and this way we may be able to keep some of the patients we already have alive until they can produce enough immunity to recover and increase our own chances by furnishing immune plasma."

"We're all still going to die when the protection from your brother's blood runs out," Mark Post reminded him.

"You should have thought of that when you brought the beautiful reporter into this pest house, Mark. She could just as well have gone to the Hotel Chimu or, better still, back to the U.S. on the next plane out of Trujillo."

"Mark didn't have any choice," Jack Smithson interposed. "We had orders from the foundation to show Miss Ross everything here and she insisted on seeing it."

"While we're on the subject you might as well know that Ross is only her maiden name. Until about six months ago she was Mrs. Grant Reed."

"I thought her face was familiar!" Jack Smithson exclaimed. "Didn't she come out to see you when we were all together in Indonesia a couple of years ago?"

Grant nodded. "I think that's what started her on the girl reporter kick. She wrote an article on the trip for the Atlanta *Journal-Constitution* Sunday magazine when she got back and the Center for Disease Control hired her to handle public relations."

Mark Post was staring at Grant, his mouth working somewhat like a fish out of water. Finally he managed to splutter, "But—"

"Shirley divorced me six months ago, while I was in Africa, Mark. The decree will be final in a few months. It was what you might call a friendly separation."

"She certainly knows her business," said Jack Smithson. "Three hours after she got here, she had a long dispatch on the way to New York by radiotelephone and a roll of film going out by air mail on Faucett."

"The foundation wants publicity and they're getting it—free." Grant poured himself a second cup of coffee. "Shirley's story should bring money pouring in to keep the *Mercy* going until this epidemic is over."

"From the way it looks now, that's not going to be any time soon," said Smithson. "The ambulance drivers that brought in the last batch of five cases from Chimbote this morning said a convoy is supposed to be coming down from the Callejón de Huaylas with maybe a dozen more."

"The man who stole Lael's camera and Guy's microscope did a good job of spreading the infection but at least we don't have to worry about him any more," Grant told them. "He died yesterday in Lima."

"Have you figured out what to do about protecting your ex-wife?" Jack Smithson asked.

"She's yours and Mark's responsibility."

"You can't just let her take the fever and die," Mark Post protested. "After all, the foundation sent her down."

"They didn't send *me* down," Grant reminded them.

"She's still your wife—"

"Legally, but that's only a technicality. Shirley left my bed and board on her own responsibility."

Jack Smithson had been listening to this interchange and saying nothing; now he spoke.

"Your brother started this epidemic, Grant, so everybody aboard this ship is your responsibility—besides a lot of innocent Peruvians who didn't ask to have a killer microbe turned loose among them."

"That's right," said Mark Post. "You can't just step aside and evade your own responsibility here."

"We've all got jobs to do, gentlemen, so what say we get going?" Grant pushed his coffee cup aside and stood up. "Jack, I'd like to make rounds on those patients who were brought in last night. If any of them pull through, they'll make fine reservoirs of immunoglobulin to furnish more protection for your personnel later on. Then I want to check on Lael Valdez before I talk to Figueroa on the phone and give him an estimate of the situation here."

"Go ahead," said Smithson as they left the room. "You're in charge now—by act of the Peruvian Government."

"When did that come through?"

"By radiogram from the Minister of Health at Lima last night. It should be in your mailbox; didn't you see it?"

"I haven't looked since yesterday—figuring that nobody would be writing me any letters."

III

Manoel Allanza was definitely off the critical list, and so was Conchita Torres, a beaming Homer Ferguson told Grant when he came to the ward. Not so the dozen patients admitted during the night who, with those brought in the day before, now brought the census of fever victims to nearly twenty. Four of those were dying, proof again of the steadily increasing virulence of *Bacillus yungay* as it went from victim to victim.

"Did you get any information about the epidemic in the city from the new patients?" Grant asked Homer, whose help had proved invaluable to the small nursing staff in caring for the seriously ill patients.

"It's bad, Doctor. Very bad. Santos is telling everybody the ship being here is causing the fever."

"How does he figure that?"

"He doesn't need a reason, only an excuse to stir people up with his lies. He's blaming you for most of it."

"I guess he's right at that, everybody on the ship believes the same thing."

"They still know you're our only chance of coming through this alive."

"Right now I don't even know that myself, Homer."

"I heard even worse news this morning," said the

giant Negro. "Remember how Esteban Gómez skipped out, once he got protection for himself with the rest of us?"

"Yes."

"Now he's helping Santos spread word that you're taking blood from patients on the ship and using it for experiments."

"He's partially right."

"He's also saying you want to make a serum and force the government to pay you to keep people from getting the fever."

"He's right about the serum part. Esteban is a smart boy."

"Maybe you and I should make a tour of the barrio and the rest of the town with the loudspeaker truck Dr. Figueroa has," said Homer. "I can tell the people Manoel and Conchita are out of danger, thanks to the doctors and nurses on board the ship. Everybody in the barrio knows them and maybe then they'll start bringing in more of their sick."

"If they don't, conditions in Chimbote will soon be like they were in the plagues of the Middle Ages, with wagons driving through the streets of the city every morning and the drivers shouting, 'Bring out your dead.' "

When Grant called Dr. Figueroa from the telephone on the dock off the ship, the health officer promised to send the truck within the next couple of hours. "Have the patients from Huarás arrived?" he asked.

"Not yet, but the hospital's ready."

"If I could get all the sick to come here I suspect we could fill the ship overnight," said the health officer. "Have you figured out what you're going to do when your wards are full?"

"Commandeer some of the warehouses on the dock, if you can arrange it."

"They'll be yours whenever you need them, but I don't know where we'll get personnel."

"The nurses of the *Mercy* can show native helpers how to care for patients; they've done that before in other parts of the world. The important thing is to keep the sick together and away from the rest of the city."

"Jake Porter was looking for you just now, Dr. Reed," said the seaman standing guard at the head of the gangplank when Grant came back aboard after the telephone conversation. "Said he had a call for you from Atlanta."

It took a few minutes for the *Mercy*'s operator to make the connections with Dr. Marshall Payne.

"How's it going, Grant?" Payne's sharp, incisive voice came to Grant's ears across the crackling static of the air waves.

"The epidemic is spreading rapidly both here and in the uplands. I'm not getting anywhere fighting it, either."

"What about the staff aboard the *Mercy*? Have any of them come down yet?"

"Lael Valdez did but Guy's plasma saved her. The lab technician accidentally became infected, too, when a culture tube broke and a glass sliver cut her hand. She died in convulsions from brain involvement less than fifty hours later."

"Good God! That must be one of the most virulent organisms in history."

"Just about. After all, it's had five thousand years to build on."

Grant went on to give Payne a quick rundown on the measures he had taken to protect the personnel of the hospital ship.

"Good thinking," said Payne, "but that kind of protection will probably last only a few weeks."

"I've warned them of that—and myself as well."

"You're doing all you can, everybody knows that. What I really called about was to tell you Professor Philemon Mallinson died this morning—in London."

"London? What was he doing there?"

"He flew over several days ago for an international conference of scientists—apparently before he got the warning I sent him. A student of Mallinson's named Judson was just admitted to the Los Angeles County Hospital, too, with a raging fever. The people at Harvard told me young Judson handled the specimen of bone and fiber when Mallinson showed it to his class before he had the actual carbon assay dating done."

"There's no telling how many were infected then."

"Everybody in Mallinson's class, for sure."

"Have they been isolated?"

"I got to the Boston health authorities too late for that; it was a holiday weekend up there. Besides the one who went to California, the class is scattered all over the Northeast."

"We'll be hearing from them soon then," said Grant grimly. "Make sure Mallinson's body is cremated."

"I've already arranged for that, and I've warned the Los Angeles County Hospital to keep Judson completely isolated. Unfortunately, he attended a family party—"

"Lord help them."

"The Los Angeles County health authorities will check everyone at the party and isolate them."

"Did you get the cultures I sent you?"

"They came this morning—intact; the hot lab is working on them now. Can you suggest anything else we should be doing?"

"No. I'm making do the best I can with what I have, which is actually pretty primitive. By the way, did you air-mail me the supply of bromouracil I asked for? One of the things I'm shooting for is a possible mutation of *B. yungay*—"

"I've been so busy trying to head off the epidemic up here that I forgot. I'll get some on the way tomorrow."

"Did you know Shirley is here?"

"What?"

"She learned from you about the situation and contacted the foundation, CBS, and INS. Don't be surprised if the story is all over TV and the newspapers by morning."

"How could she have been stupid enough to risk going into a situation like that?"

"The way she sees it, she's got the scoop of the entire century going."

"Not if it costs her her life."

"She's working on the assumption that I will protect her from Yungay fever."

"Any chance of that?"

"Just one, but I think it's a good one."

"You'll save her, if anyone can. Call on us for anything you need."

The telephone clicked off and Grant handed the receiver back. "Thanks, Jake," he said.

"It's I who should be thanking you, Doctor," said the radio operator. "If it wasn't for the shot you gave us, we'd all probably be shivering with that fever before another day's out."

IV

A pall of fear hung over Chimbote like a cloud when Grant and Homer Ferguson drove through the streets in the loudspeaker panel truck. Hardly anyone was about, and in the Plaza Central, even the tapadas, who usually hung around there—looking startlingly like red-winged blackbirds with their dark shawls wrapped around their bodies to emphasize their physical attributes, leaving only one eye uncovered—were gone. Even the tables before the cantinas were largely deserted; only a few of the old men still ventured forth to sit in the sunlight and argue over the events recorded in the newspapers they came there every morning to read, while drinking chicha slowly to make it last a long time.

The wind rustling through the eucalyptus trees and the soft froufrou of the palms were almost the only sound. Even the birds seemed to have been intimidated by the silence hanging over the square and the large yellow posters put up on trees and in store windows by the Health Department, warning people of the epidemic and against congregating.

"Dr. Figueroa's doing his work well," Grant commented as they turned off the street around the square and headed south toward the barrio.

"The fish smell is gone from the air," said Homer. "That means the fish-meal plants have been shut down, too, so a lot of people will be staying home."

"They're liable to go hungry before this is over."

"Better hunger than death, Doctor," said Homer as he picked up the microphone. "I'll get started."

"Bring your sick to the white ship in the harbor," he broadcast to the silent houses, alternating in Spanish and Quechua, as the truck moved along the silent streets. "The yanqui doctors will treat them and some will live, as Manoel Allanza and Conchita Torres are living now. Leave them in the hands of the brujos and all will die."

"Santos and his brethren are going to hate you even more than they hate me, Homer," Grant observed as they entered the barrio.

Normally teeming with life, it, too, was silent, and even the goats and the dogs seemed to be afraid. Here and there, as the truck drove down one street and up another, while Homer shouted his messages through the loudspeakers, they could see frightened faces at the windows—where windows existed. Where they did not, curtains woven of bamboo strips were often pulled aside for the occupants to see out.

They had made a complete circuit through the barrio and started back over the same route when they became conscious of the sound of voices ahead. Only when they neared the crematory however, where the plume of black smoke rising in the air above it bespoke its grim message of death, could they see whence the noise was coming.

A crowd had gathered on the sidewalk and in the street before the building. It wasn't large yet but its members carried clubs and sticks, while some even wielded the long-bladed machetes used in harvesting the corn and sugar cane that grew in the broad irrigated fields around the city.

"Looks like trouble," said Grant. "I'd better turn back toward the dock."

"This is the only street leading directly to it," said Homer. "Let's pretend we don't know what the trouble is and drive straight through. I know most of these people and they may listen to me."

The crowd fell back somewhat when the truck showed no intention of stopping, revealing Santos, the chief brujo of Chimbote, standing on a box beside the curb, shouting and gesticulating. He made a strange picture indeed for he was wearing the costume of the ancient witch doctors, particularly the stag's head mask with enough of the skin cut away to reveal the hate-filled eyes and with the horns still sprouting from the sides, as they had before the animal had died. The rattles in his hands and about his ankles as he danced on the box made a loud drumming sound and kept up a fearful din while he shouted curses at the truck.

"I wish I could knock Santos off that box," said Homer. "He's got his eye on something I want."

Grant didn't ask what that was; with Conchita Torres widowed, there would no doubt be many candidates for both her person and the thriving cantina she now owned entirely.

Under the stimulus of Santos's cursing, some of the crowd moved closer to the truck and added to the torrent of vituperation. They fell back somewhat, however, as the panel truck plowed on and Homer's messages shouted from the loudspeaker tended to drown out the sound of Santos's rattles and his curses.

A rock cracked the window beside Grant's head and he threw up his arm to ward off fragments of flying glass, but continued on as the angry crowd pressed close enough to beat on the back and sides of the truck. When it seemed that they might halt the vehicle, Grant shoved it into a lower gear and gunned the motor but still made only slow progress because he didn't want to injure any of the crowd as the vehicle pushed through them.

In the meantime Santos had stopped his ritual dance and was following the truck, exhorting the crowd to stop it and destroy the yanqui and the renegade. Busy driving, Grant couldn't understand what the witch doctor was saying until the crowd began to move aside. Then there was no misunderstanding the words. *"Sangra!"* And *"palo de sangre!"*

"They're calling us bloodsuckers and vampire bats," Homer translated. "Esteban Gómez started all this."

With the crowd in full cry after them now, people were pouring out of the shacks and houses along the way, making progress even more difficult. Rocks and other missiles rained on the truck, too, as Grant turned onto the street leading to the dock. Only when they drove through the barricade at the guard post protecting the dock was the crowd finally brought to a halt by the leveled rifles of the soldiers there.

Grant parked the truck beside the Land Rover across the dock from the gangplank leading up to the deck of the *Mercy* and drew a long breath of relief.

"That was close, Homer, very close. I thought you said these people are your friends."

"Santos has whipped them up with his stories of blood taken from the sick. When you're afraid, you'll even turn against a friend if he seems to be taking the side of those you believe to be your enemies. Santos is determined now to destroy everybody aboard the ship."

"I can telephone Dr. Figueroa and ask him to have the guard increased."

"Better do it right away, then; they're already mad enough to cut the telephone wires and maybe even the electric cables bringing power to the ship."

"The *Mercy* has its own power plant," Grant assured his helper. "You go on board while I call Dr. Figueroa."

"I'm glad you and Ferguson got out alive, Dr. Reed." The health office sounded harried. "But please don't try anything like that again."

"I can promise you that. Did you know the fever has now appeared in London and Boston, and possibly Los Angeles?"

There was a silence at the other end of the phone, until Grant asked, "Are you still there, Dr. Figueroa?"

"I was just thinking, Doctor. Did you ever see a world epidemic develop so rapidly?"

"I'm afraid not. From now on, nothing this bug does can surprise me."

But there, as it turned out, he was wrong.

V

In the whole picture of the fast-developing epidemic, there was only one ray of brightness for Grant. Lael Valdez was improving rapidly and seemed out of danger. She didn't require a special nurse any longer and was reading when Grant came into her stateroom that afternoon. A glance at the temperature chart hanging at the foot of her bed told him the line was flat, indicating a complete absence of fever.

"You've been neglecting me," she said with a smile.

"You're practically well. My job now is keeping people from getting sick."

"Everybody's wondering what you're going to do about keeping your wife—"

"Ex-wife. Our divorce will be final soon."

"She's very attractive, and an excellent reporter."

"Don't tell me Jack Smithson let her talk to you?"

"Why, yes. After all, she's here to help the Mercy Foundation—"

"She's here to make a name for herself—the intrepid girl reporter, risking her life to report a world-wide epidemic."

He saw by her startled look that she hadn't heard the latest news, and regretted revealing it to her. But now that it was done, he had to tell her the truth. When he finished, there were tears in her eyes.

"Poor Professor Mallinson, losing his life because he did us a favor," she said. "I feel responsible for the others, too."

"I told you once that if you and Guy hadn't opened the tomb when you did, somebody else would have done it later. And nobody could hold you responsible for a thief breaking into your house and stealing contaminated articles."

"That doesn't keep me from feeling bad—and wishing I could do something to make amends."

"You can, if you're willing to take the risk."

"How?"

"Shirley came here without consulting me, assuming that I'd protect her against Yungay fever. But the last dose of Guy's immune plasma was given to Leona Danvers."

"Do you believe my blood would protect her—as Guy's did me?"

"Given early, before an infection attacks the body, relatively small amounts of specific antitoxin will prevent the disease. It's the principle behind the use of immune globulin for people who have been exposed to hepatitis, diphtheria, and some other diseases. I wouldn't even suggest doing it if I thought there was any danger to you."

"Just how would you go about it?"

"I'd draw about two hundred cubic centimeters of your blood mixed with citrate solution to prevent clotting and centrifuge it to separate the plasma from the cells. I'd give her the plasma and then suspend the red cells from your blood in saline and put them back into your circulation. The procedure is called plasmapheresis—"

"I remember seeing it done in a laboratory where I worked in Boston."

"It's widely used to obtain blood plasma for plasma transfusions, so there's nothing unusual or dangerous about it."

"And the body makes new plasma and new anti-toxin?"

"Very quickly."

"I'm ready when you are, Grant. Guy saved my life with his blood, so the very least I can do is to help save someone else."

"We'll probably draw the blood this afternoon and reinject the cells about an hour afterward."

Shirley was in the staff lounge drinking coffee and looking as fresh as if she'd just gotten out of bed.

"I've been talking to Homer Ferguson," she said on a note of reproach. "You could have taken me with you this morning, Grant. A picture of that witch doctor might have won me a Pulitzer Prize."

"Right now I'm more concerned with keeping you out of the obituary column," he said shortly. "Lael's agreed to let us take about two hundred cc. of blood for your protection by plasmapheresis."

"Fine. When do we start?"

"As soon as I can get ready—maybe half an hour."

The injection of Lael's plasma into Shirley's veins and the reinjection of Lael's red cells back into her own circulation was easily accomplished. Grant was working in the laboratory, so engrossed in adding mutants to cultures of *B. yungay* that he didn't even hear the door to the laboratory open, or know anyone had come in, until he looked up to see Shirley standing a few feet away.

"What do you want?" he demanded, irritated that she could look so coolly beautiful when he was hot, dirty, and tired. Besides being, he remembered, badly in need of a shave.

"I just finished thanking Lael for giving me the plasma and came by to thank you, too. The world doesn't know how fortunate it is to have you here in the center of the fight, Grant. It will though—I'll see to that."

"Fame isn't going to save any of the people in those trucks from Huarás that arrived a few minutes ago."

"I want you to know I'm willing to help any way I can—carrying bedpans, giving baths, whatever. I'm not very handy at that sort of thing, but the way things look now, I'll have plenty of opportunity to learn."

"Thanks, Shirl." He saw that she was really sincere and couldn't help realizing how much more attractive it made her than she'd been the last time he'd seen her— in his bed at Atlanta.

"You can help Mark Post with his records," he told her. "He's young and eager and practically drooling over you."

"Doesn't that prospect disturb you?"

"Not any more."

"Then I guess it really is over between us, at last."

"How much longer do you plan to stay here?"

"A couple of more days, why?"

"This plague is spreading faster than any other one in history, and you're the only newspaper reporter who has actually seen what it's like. Now that you're protected for a few weeks at least, you could do a really worthwhile—and newsworthy—job tracing its spread through the world, starting with Professor Mallinson's convention in London."

"Mallinson? Who is he?"

"Not is—was." He told her about the radiocarbon assay and how, because of it, Yungay fever not only had been introduced into the United States but had been carried by the already dying physicist to London, as well as through Mallinson's almost certain contact with other scientists to much of the world.

"That's almost incredible," she said when he finished. "I'll talk to CBS about it tomorrow and see what they say."

She moved quickly to kiss him, and as he watched her walk through the small laboratory and turn to wave lightly from the door, he suddenly wondered if he wasn't a fool to turn down at least one final chance to hold that lovely body in his arms and feel it strain against him at the height of shared passion—perhaps the last chance he'd have in his life to enjoy that experience with any woman.

VI

Jack Smithson's prediction about the rate of admission to the hospital over the next twelve to twenty-four hours proved to be far too low. Cases poured in all afternoon and during the night, many of them from the barrio of Chimbote, where some of the population had apparently been impressed by Homer Ferguson's pleas to bring the sick to the ship.

A steady stream of victims was now pouring down from the Yungay and Huarás areas in the Callejón de Huaylas, too. As Grant had already suspected, the killer microbe seemed to be definitely gaining in virulence, and the incubation period between contact with the fast-growing bacillus and actual development of the disease itself became steadily shorter.

He worked with the staff admitting and evaluating patients, so those who obviously were already dying could be separated from the group who seemed to have at least some chance of surviving the fever. For the latter, supportive measures were indicated, but not for the others, since with medical supplies liable to grow short soon, it was obviously only a waste to use them on those already doomed.

Grant called the hospital staff, including Shirley, to a brief meeting shortly after breakfast. Most of them were bleary-eyed from loss of sleep and weariness; some, he knew, had worked all night.

"I want all of you to know just what we're facing —and that you may actually be better off here on the *Mercy* than anywhere else," he told them. "Centers for spread of Yungay fever already exist in Yungay, of course, but also in Huarás, Lima, and Chimbote here in Peru. Abroad, a real epidemic is already developing in Boston, Los Angeles, London, and elsewhere."

"How could that have happened so quickly?" Mark Post asked.

"An entire class of students attending a lecture on radiation physics at Harvard University handled contaminated material almost a week ago," Grant explained. "The professor who taught the course is already dead in London, where he almost certainly infected dozens of scientists attending an international conference. The students were scattered from the Northeast to California, and during the next week many of the finest scientific minds in the field of radiation physics throughout the world may be destroyed, as well as a number of younger minds."

"It's like a plague from the Bible!" Father Branigan exclaimed.

"When a plague happened in biblical times, it was always considered an evidence of God's anger, but none of these people have done anything to deserve their fate."

"Except your brother," said Mark Post. "And Miss Valdez—but she escaped."

"My brother unwittingly loosed this particular plague upon the world, and by a strange confluence of events, its spread has been very rapid. But someday, another archaeologist would certainly have opened the same tomb, and *Bacillus yungay* would have been reincarnated, so to speak, as a killer. Fortunately, my brother recovered from the fever, only to die from heart failure, so I was able to use his immune serum to give all of you a prophylactic dose of antitoxin against *Bacillus yungay*."

"Just where do we stand now on that score?" Jack Smithson inquired.

"A few of you were probably in the early stages of Yungay fever when I injected my brother's plasma. These may still develop the disease, though I hope only in a mild form from which they will recover and be permanently immune. Others, who had not yet been infected, are probably immune for several weeks, possibly even a month or longer."

"You're the expert," said Elaine Carroll. "Why can't you be more definite?"

"Because we're dealing with one of the most virulent microbes in history," said Grant. "In all of my experiences, I've never run across one like it."

"God help us!" echoed Father Branigan.

"I hope He will, Father," said Grant. "But I hope to help Him a little—with luck."

"How?" Mark Post demanded.

"Two patients aboard the ship at least seem to be recovering from Yungay fever—Manoel Allanza and Conchita Torres. I have no way of evaluating the antibody production in the blood of these patients, but it is certain to be high, since otherwise they would have died. Their blood may be our salvation, but they must be given every opportunity to produce the highest possible titer of antitoxin before we use plasmapheresis to obtain some of their plasma and keep the staff alive longer to help the other patients in the hospital."

"If the admission rate continues at its present level," said Jack Smithson, "every bed and pipe berth in the hospital will be filled by noon tomorrow. What then?"

"Dr. Figueroa will commandeer the warehouses on the dock and turn them into an emergency hospital. We'll have to use the nursing staff in a supervising capacity and enlist close relatives of fever victims for whatever bedside nursing we're able to give them, the way it's done in African mission hospitals. Those relatives have already been exposed, so they'll lose nothing by helping out their loved ones."

"That's spreading the complement awfully thin," the chief nurse objected. "But we'll do everything we can."

"Nobody can do more," Grant assured her.

"One final word," said Jack Smithson before the staff was dismissed. "Don't any of you forget that every patient you save is a potential producer of immune bodies needed to keep us all alive that much longer. So you'd damned well better do all you can to give them every possible chance to live."

VII

Shirley was standing at the head of the gangplank when Grant came aboard the *Mercy* just before dark, after spending the afternoon with Dr. José Figueroa, planning how to turn empty warehouses on the dock into an emergency hospital.

"You were right about CBS wanting me to report on the world-wide spread of the plague, Grant," she told him. "I'm flying to Lima tomorrow afternoon, then across the Andes to Rio and on to London. If you could give me some idea of what you're going to do next, the world outside is waiting to hear."

"It would help me if I knew myself," he said wearily and looked at his watch. "The dining room's open if you care to have an early dinner."

"I promised Mark Post, but I'll have a cup of coffee with you."

"Fair enough."

While Grant ate, she plied him with questions. Shirley at work was all business, not at all the sensuous alluring woman she could be when the mood was indicated.

"Knowing you, I refuse to believe you've given up on finding a way to control this germ besides the immune serum injections," she said.

"Did I say I had?"

"The hospital staff thought you did when you talked to them this morning."

"I don't want them to get false hopes," Grant explained. "Actually, I'm going to start a new batch of cultures tonight using stronger concentrations of formalin mixed in."

"Why formalin?"

"Treating bacterial toxins with formalin often turns them into harmless toxoids, once you get the technique right. The toxoid from a particular organism has the property of acting as an antigen to stimulate antibody formation in the well person."

"Like tetanus toxoid?"

"That's a common one, but there are others. By injecting people with a specific toxoid before they're exposed to the disease—like tetanus from a rusty nail stuck in your foot—and then giving a stimulating dose immediately after the exposure, the antibody levels rise very rapidly and prevent the disease itself."

"Isn't that a long process?"

"It may be a long time before Yungay fever can be eliminated, so anything that might halt the epidemic, even as much as months from now, is worth trying." He looked up from his place to see her looking at him with an odd light in her eyes. "What gives?" he asked. "Don't you believe what I'm telling you?"

"Every word. It's just that if you'd told me things like this about your work long ago—share a little more of your thoughts and convictions—we might have made a go of it."

"I guess I was too busy battling microbes and you were too busy writing publicity releases for the center and promoting academic functions for us to ever get together long enough for anything much besides sex and sleep."

"At least we can remember that both were good," she said with a smile. "Can I ask one more favor?"

"Of course."

"I'd like a few pictures of you working in the lab tonight, to use in a book I'm going to write when all this is over and you win your second Nobel Prize. You won't have to bother with posing or anything like that. I'll just rove around and shoot a few with the strobe unit and slip out when I've finished."

"Okay. I'll be in the lab in fifteen minutes. That way you won't be late for your dinner with Mark Post."

"Mark Post can wait where my work is concerned," she said cryptically. "When you've had a man like Grant Reed—and then lose him—it sort of spoils you for others."

VIII

It was almost midnight when Grant left the laboratory and stepped out on deck. The usual evening breeze, he saw, had changed direction and was blowing now from the northeast. The floodlights that were kept burning from sunset to dawn bathed the long white ship in a soft glow.

On the dock, two other clusters of lights also shone. One was at the guard post across the dock from the gangplank where Grant could see the closed flaps of a tent, but no sign of the sentry who should have been walking his post before it. Farther away, at the landward end of the dock, the glass-walled guard station was also bathed with light.

The northeast breeze brought the faint fragrance of flowers that were approaching the height of their blooming period, a far cry from the usual rank smell of the now silent fish-meal factories and the warehouse across the docks, where guano deposited on the offshore islands was brought in by boat to be bagged and stored.

Climbing the metal stairway to the top deck, Grant looked into the bridge enclosure but saw no one there, not even the crewman who usually stood watch. Captain Pendarvis wasn't running the tight ship tonight he was always boasting about, he thought, and couldn't help wondering whether the depression that seemed to have gripped the hospital staff after his admission of defeat that morning had spread to the crew as well.

As he was turning back to the stairway leading to the lower deck, a sudden booming sound came from somewhere ashore beyond the landward end of the dock. At the same instant lights on the whole dock area, including the ship, went out, leaving the entire area swathed in darkness.

Grant knew enough about the bridge to fumble for the microphone through which announcements were made on the ship's public address system. He found the switch and shouted into it, but, without power, only the echo of his own voice came back to him from the building across the dock. His voice, however, plus the sudden dousing of lights at the guard post, was enough to arouse someone in the tent on the dock. From it came a dim glow of a flashlight, then one of the soldiers threw open the flap of the tent, and Grant saw dark figures running along the dock. He heard a thumping sound several times in succession, too, as if some-one was cutting with an ax on a log, and suspecting what it might be, he started down the stairs.

Halfway down the steps, he ran into the tall figure of Captain Pendarvis on the way up the bridge, his shirt tails flapping while he held up his pants with one hand.

"Rouse Chief McTavish!" Pendarvis shouted, apparently taking Grant for the seaman who should have been standing watch on the bridge. "The natives have cut the power line to the dock."

On the deck below, people were milling about, some carrying flashlights while others bumped into each other in the darkness and confusion. When one flashlight fell on the deck, Grant seized it and turned the spot of light upon the dock to which the ship was moored.

He didn't need to see the steadily widening band of dark water between the side of the ship and the dock, or hear the crash of timbers as the gangplank was wrenched loose from its attachments, to realize the thumping he'd heard had been the sound of ax blades severing the hawsers that had secured the *Mercy* to its mooring.

Chief McTavish's assurance that the old ship could go in a moment's time from external electric power to the current from its own plant wasn't quite realized. Actually, something like five minutes passed before the ship's lights came on again and a powerful searchlight on the bridge began sweeping the dock, now at least twenty feet away, as the ship was steadily separated from land by a combination of the wind and the current setting out to sea. Nor was he surprised to see, outlined by the searchlight as it centered on the shadowy figures moving along the docks, a bizarre sight.

It was Santos in his stag's head mask, his eyes glowing like twin beacons of hate as he capered in frenetic glee. The searchlight held on the brujo while, arms outthrust, he chanted curses, a picture startlingly like the one Lael had taken inside the tomb above Yungay.

Hearing a scream behind him, Grant turned to see Lael swaying in the open doorway of her cabin, staring at the bizzare figure with horror-filled eyes. He moved quickly toward her as he saw her catch the doorjamb for support without, however, taking her eyes from the macabre figure on the dock, reaching her in time to hear her cry: "It's the brujo from the cave, come to haunt me."

Then she toppled into his arms in a dead faint.

IX

Busy examining Lael Valdez in her cabin, Grant could not follow closely what was happening outside, although he could hear it all through the open door. While he was checking her blood pressure, he heard a sudden rumble deep within the old ship, as the engines were started, and felt the drifting movement of the vessel slow immediately when the rusty propeller bit into the dark waters of Chimbote Harbor. Through the open door, too, he saw the light at the end of the long pier sweep by, wondered momentarily why it was moving backward, then realized that the ship was heading toward the open sea.

Noting that Lael's pulse was normal, Grant studied her pupils in its beam and saw them contract normally, telling him there was no actual injury to her brain, like a sudden hemorrhage. In fact, by now he was fairly sure that, in her weakened condition, the shock of seeing Santos, looking strangely like the picture she'd taken of the five-thousand-year-old brujo from the cave, had been enough to bring on the faint.

"I thought I heard Lael scream." Jack Smithson had appeared at the door of the stateroom. "Is she hurt?"

"Not physically. She saw Santos, the witch doctor who has been fighting us, on the dock in his shaman regalia and must have thought he was the one from the tomb, come to haunt her."

"That shock would be enough to make her faint," said Smithson.

"What's going on outside?"

"We're drifting toward Blanco Rock. If Chief McTavish doesn't get more power out of those engines soon, we'll founder right here in Chimbote Harbor."

"We might do worse. What's the depth?"

"How in the hell do I know? It's not my job to run the ship."

Grant threw up his hands in a gesture of hopelessness and left the stateroom. The decks were crowded with people from the hospital staff, many not even wearing life jackets. Obviously nobody was really in charge and everything was in a state of confusion, extending, he suspected, to the bridge. Only the muted throb of the one good engine was reassurance that Chief McTavish, at least, was doing the best he could with his crippled charge.

"Everybody to your stations!" Grant shouted. "I want a life jacket on every one of you and your patients, too."

"Why should we risk our lives for a bunch of dying Indians?" Mark Post demanded. "Besides, you're not in command of this ship."

"I'm in command of everything," Grant snapped. "Are you going to your post or do I put you under arrest?"

There was a moment of indecision, during which Grant didn't even notice the flash of Shirley's camera. Then the hospital personnel began to disperse below to their posts of duty.

"Keep your life jackets on until the emergency is over," Grant shouted after them.

"That was nicely done, Grant," said a familiar voice, and he whirled to see Shirley standing there, without a life jacket but with her camera, as usual, hanging from its strap around her neck.

"Get your life jacket on, too," he snapped. "Damn fast."

"Are we really in much danger?"

"Go ask Captain Pendarvis. It's his job to know that."

She didn't argue, but made her way back along the deck of the now brightly lighted ship toward the owner's suite. Grant went forward to the bow, where the stocky form of Homer Ferguson, his broad shoulders stretching the straps of a life jacket, was standing, looking down at the cutwater below.

"Right now I'd give a lot for a lead line, Doctor," said Homer. "When I was a deck hand on a work boat pushing barges upstream from Memphis, I got to be pretty good at using one."

"Are we in any danger of going aground?"

"The depth is only four and a half fathoms off the end of this pier, and in case you've forgotten how to count in nautical terms, that's eight meters, or a little over twenty-four feet. This tub draws twenty-eight."

"Then we won't make it?"

"The current's in our favor and the wind will be piling up the water between Mount Chimbote there" —he pointed toward a towering hill to the north— "and the dock."

"Maybe Captain Pendarvis should just put her on the shore."

"That's hard to do and keep a level keel, Doctor. Imagine what it would be like operating a hospital with the deck canted to an angle of thirty-five or forty degrees."

"What about the passage out of the harbor?"

"There's fifteen fathoms in the Northern Passage between Blanco Rock and Chimbote Point. Once in the passage, we'd be safe, but it's pretty narrow, with rocky cliffs on each side." He pointed ahead where two flashing beacons could be seen, from that point looking alarmingly close together. At that moment a sudden shudder ran through the ship and shouts came from the bridge, to be echoed belowdecks.

"That's the keel grounding on the shallow place just beyond the end of the dock," Homer explained and looked down. "But she's still moving, so hold your breath, Doctor."

The vibrations imparted to the hull by the laboring engines became noticeably more pronounced and Homer grinned. "If that cylinder head Chief McTavish has been welding on the past few days blows, we'll be sitting here in the middle of Chimbote Harbor for quite a while."

Another shudder shook the *Mercy* and Grant found time to wonder whether plates welded on the hull forty or fifty years ago might begin to open, letting the water of Ferrol Bay pour in. Then the ship moved forward with a jerk that almost threw him off his feet.

"She's off," said the big Negro in a tone of satisfaction. "Which means we're safely over the bar at the end of the dock." He turned to look ahead. "Oh-oh! Santos was smarter than I gave him credit for being."

"Why do you say that?"

"Look ahead where the beacons were flashing a moment ago. He must have sent someone to cut the power to them, too, hoping the *Mercy* would pile up on Blanco Rock at the south end of the channel and sink in thirteen fathoms."

The bridge, finally alert, had apparently spotted the danger, too, for the powerful searchlight that had been sweeping the water in circles now pointed straight ahead. It revealed a narrow channel between the heights of Blanco Rock and Chimbote Point, but both current and wind were pushing the ship on a southerly tack that, it seemed, would throw the old hull against the looming craggy outlines of the rock. Just then, however, they heard the engine room telegraph clang for

more power, and the bow began to swing slowly northward, bringing the vessel more in line with the main
part of the channel.

It was still a race between the force of the current,
the wind swinging the ship southward toward the rock
itself, and the crippled engines trying to turn the old
Mercy more northward to clear the channel. To Grant,
watching from his vantage point at the bow, it seemed
that the engines were losing the battle, as the looming
crags of Blanco Rock outlined in the bright searchlight
came nearer and the roar of the surf against them beat
against his ears.

"If you've ever prayed, Dr. Reed, you'd better give
it the best you've got just now," said Homer Ferguson
at Grant's elbow.

Nearer and nearer the looming heights of Blanco
Rock came as the old *Mercy* crept seaward, with the
full grip of the current flowing through the Northern
Passage of Chimbote Harbor toward the open Pacific
holding it in a firm grip. For a few minutes that seemed
an eternity, it appeared that the ship would certainly
pile up on Blanco Rock. Then, miraculously, it seemed,
the prow of the *Mercy* cleared the rock with not much
more than a few feet at most to spare, and the old ship,
its crippled engines laboring in the extra effort, but still,
mercifully, all in one piece, surged out into the open
Pacific.

"You can go to bed now, Doctor," said Homer. "I'm
going to tell Conchita and Manoel the good news that
we're going to live after all."

X

"Now hear this! Now hear this!" The voice of Captain
Harry Pendarvis over the public address system brought
all hospital activities to a stop about nine o'clock the
next morning.

Grant was in the laboratory, studying the cultures
he'd made the night before, when the call was sounded

but came out on deck, where most of the complement and those of the crew who were off duty had gathered. The sea was quiet and the sun was shining brightly as the white ship plowed slowly northwestward. To the east, the dark line marking the coast of Peru was still visible but details were no longer distinguishable.

"Thanks to heroic work by Chief McTavish and his crew, we were able to negotiate the Northern Passage out of Chimbote Harbor safely last night, after scraping over a bar near the end of the dock," the captain announced. "I've just finished examining the bilges and found no evidence of damage to the hull."

A cheer went up from those on deck.

"Re-entering Chimbote after what happened last night is out of the question," Pendarvis continued, "so our course is northwestward in order to clear the bulge marking the southern tip of Ecuador. Shortly, I will radio the port of Guayaquil in Ecuador, which most of us remember favorably, asking that we be allowed to take refuge there until arrangements can be made to disembark our patients before proceeding to Panama for repairs, and thence home to New York."

Another cheer went up from the listeners.

"That's good news." Father Branigan was standing beside Grant. "These people have been away from home a long time."

"And some of them will probably be away a lot longer—maybe forever."

"You're not making progress then?"

"This bacillus has me buffaloed, Father. I don't have any idea what to try next."

"We had a death early this morning—one of the patients from the barrio of Chimbote," said the priest. "I gave Last Rites, but we'll have to bury this poor fellow later in the morning."

"The quicker the better, Father," said Grant. "Call me when you're ready; oddly enough I've never seen a burial at sea."

"We should be ready about ten o'clock," the priest

promised. "I heard Miss Valdez fainted during our escape from the harbor; hope she hasn't had a backset."

"She got out of bed at the height of the confusion, when the hawsers were cut, and fainted, probably from weakness and excitement."

Jack Smithson came along the deck and stopped beside Grant and the chaplain. "Lael's okay," he reported. "I don't mind admitting I'm damned glad we're out of Chimbote, and the sooner we dock in Guayaquil and off-load these patients, the better I'll like it."

"Do you really think the government of Ecuador is going to let you dock there?" Grant asked.

"Of course. It's the nearest good port and the only humane thing to do. Why wouldn't they?"

"For the same reason I wouldn't let you dock if I were the Ecuadorian Minister of Health."

"That's a hell of a thing to say."

"Put yourself in his place, Jack. Yungay fever hasn't reached them yet; at least I've heard no report of it. If their quarantine measures on land and sea are strict enough, it might miss Ecuador entirely. Would you expose your people to one of the deadliest diseases in the history of mankind if you could prevent it merely by denying the *Mercy* the use of the port?"

"But that means—"

"We're up the creek—and will have to paddle our own way."

"For how long?"

Grant shrugged. "We're barely making way now, so Chief McTavish is probably nursing his engines until the captain can find us a haven somewhere—if he does. How long will your supplies last?"

"Twelve weeks in a pinch. But—"

"It shouldn't take twelve weeks for the patients aboard to either get well or die."

"What about the personnel?"

"I hope to have the answer before then to the whole question of controlling *Bacillus yungay,* but I still don't have any idea what it will be. Meanwhile, like you said the other night, the more patients you can pull through the fever, the more antibodies we'll be able to get to keep the hospital personnel and crew alive."

"If you ask me, this is one hell of a fix to be in." Smithson shook his head like a baffled bull. "We'll probably wind up like the Flying Dutchman, a ship with nobody on it."

"At least we won't starve," said Grant on a philosophical note. "The Humboldt Current brings plenty of fish northward and we can always put out setlines."

"A hell of a lot of good that will do me. I'm allergic to fish."

XI

Jake Porter was busy when Grant came into the radio room but looked up briefly from the chattering keys.

"I'm just getting the reply from the port authorities at Guayaquil to Captain Pendarvis's request to be allowed to enter the port," he said. "Be with you in a minute, Doctor."

"That's all right," said Grant. "I only wanted to read the daily news log."

Several items of particular interest to Grant were in the newssheet printed in the early morning by the radio operator for distribution through the ship. A young man named Sam Judson was reported to have died of Yungay fever in Los Angeles and health authorities there were busy contacting all members of a large family group of which Judson had been a part a few days earlier. London health authorities were also moving swiftly to isolate all those attending the International Conference on Radiation Physics. The Russian Government had claimed that the isolation of their two top men in the field was an attempt by the British to persuade them to defect and had sent a plane to take them to Moscow.

In New York still another supposed victim of Yungay fever named Haimowitz—a student at Harvard home for the weekend—had been admitted to the isolation section of Bellevue Hospital. The Boston Health Department was taking steps to discover and isolate all guests who had been in close contact with Haimowitz at a bar mitzvah ceremony in a suburb several days earlier.

The chatter of the typewriter keys stopped and Jake Porter tore off the sheet with the message that had just been received upon it and handed it to Grant. Only a glance was needed to know that it confirmed what he had just finished telling Jack Smithson:

CLEARANCE TO ENTER PORT OF GUAYAQUIL OR ANY OTHER PORT IN ECUADOR DENIED. UNDER NO CIRCUMSTANCES WILL THE HOSPITAL SHIP MERCY ENTER ECUADORIAN WATERS.

BY ORDER OF THE MINISTER OF HEALTH.
ANTONIO DE QUESADA,
CHIEF HEALTH OFFICER

"The captain will bust a blood vessel when he sees this," said Porter. "Is there anything I can do for you before I take it to him, Doctor?"

"No. I just came to read the newssheet."

"One thing's for sure: Miss Ross is keeping the world informed on what's going on here. She sent a long story to INS early this morning describing what happened last night and she's already changed the name of the *Mercy* to 'Plague Ship.' "

"It's an appropriate description."

"Too bad we don't have facilities for transmitting photographs. I saw her up here on the top deck during all the excitement last night, shooting pictures like mad." Porter stood up. "I'd better get this message from Guayaquil to the captain right away."

"I'll go with you."

At the door of the enclosed bridge, Grant waited until Captain Pendarvis read the message and waved him to enter. The chief officer's eyes were popping with rage as he handed the sheet to Grant without comment.

"It was just coming in when I came to the radio room to read the daily newssheet, sir," he said. "But it was only what I'd expected."

"*You* expected!" Pendarvis purpled. "For God's sake, man! I've got over four hundred people on this ship, three hundred and twenty-five of them desperately ill or dying. And you tell me this denial is what you expected."

"If I were the health officer of any port, I'd deny you entry, too."

"In God's name, why?"

"Jake tells me Miss Ross described us very accucurately in a news report she sent to New York this morning as a 'plague ship,' sir. Would you welcome into a port under your command a vessel that could bring one of the deadliest diseases the world has yet seen into an area where it hasn't struck before?".

"I suppose not," Pendarvis admitted somewhat reluctantly. "But I'm still going to radio all major ports on the Pacific Coast of Central and South America requesting permission to dock."

"I wish you luck, sir."

A seaman appeared at the door of the bridge. "Chaplain Branigan wishes you to be informed that he is about to carry out a burial at sea, sir," he said.

"Tell him to proceed," said Pendarvis. "I'm too occupied at the moment to take part."

"Very well, sir."

The seaman left the bridge and Grant followed down the companionway stairs to the deck below, where a small group had gathered at the stern. The body, sewn in canvas with weights attached to take it to the bottom, was on a stretcher, one end of which hung over the rail while the other end was propped up on a box.

Father Branigan, in surplice and vestments, stood at the head with four seamen, two on either side, ready to tip the stretcher at the proper time and let the body slide into the sea.

Opening the Bible, the priest began to read:

"Behold, I tell you a mystery.
We shall all indeed rise again;
but we shall not all be changed.
In a moment, in the twinkling of
an eye, at the last trumpet: for
the trumpet shall sound and the
dead shall rise again incorruptible:
and we shall be changed.
For this corruptible must put on
incorruption; and this mortal must
put on immortality.
And when this mortal hath put
on immortality, then shall come
to pass the saying that is written:
'Death is swallowed up in victory.' "

Closing the Bible, Father Branigan made the sign of the cross above the canvas-covered body.

"We are gathered to commit to the sea the body of Miguel Olmas, whom our Lord Jesus Christ has seen fit to call to be with Him in His Kingdom. Let no man doubt that Miguel Olmas shall rise again, even from the sea, clothed in immortality and incorruption, at the last day. I now commit to the sea as his last resting place the body of Miguel Olmas."

At a sign from the priest, the four seamen tipped the inner end of the stretcher until the body slid over the rail. It dropped to the sea, where it floated momentarily because of air trapped inside the canvas, bobbing about upon the waves created by the turning of the screw. Most of the watchers were turning away when a sudden cry came from one of the seamen watching the floating canvas-covered body.

"My God! Look!"

Grant turned quickly. The body was barely floating now as water replaced the air inside the canvas covering, leaving a screen of small bubbles in the wake of the propeller. A good hundred feet away but converging upon it from the south was a pair of triangular fins that, to the startled observers, seemed to be taller than an average man's height. One fin was slightly larger than the other, and both were almost white, as they moved with incredible speed toward the body, now barely awash.

Only when they reached their prey did the pair of great white sharks, the most famous killers in the Pacific waters, surface. Huge gashlike mouths gaped wide until the rows of teeth just inside were plainly visible, then the jaws closed upon their grisly target, cutting through canvas and man as if they were sliced by a huge knife.

The body, canvas, and weights disappeared into the giant jaws of the sharks, while blood and fragments of flesh turned the roiled water to a sudden red. Then the giant tails, too, appeared, as the sharks practically stood upon them turning in the water.

The mouths were empty now, the contents of the first bites having disappeared into the huge bodies before the jaws closed upon the rest of what had been a man, but the crunch of teeth against bone and tissue had been plainly audible in the moment before the huge white bodies sounded again to digest their prey in water unroiled by the ship's screw.

"Jesus Christ! In ten years at sea I never saw nothing like that," said one of the seamen who had helped tip the stretcher and slide the body into the water. "They must be twenty feet long."

A low moan came from a nurse who had been standing beside Grant Reed, and turning suddenly, she rushed to the rail to vomit over it into the sea. When he reached out and touched her shoulder to comfort her, she turned instinctively and buried her face against his chest.

"A curse is on this ship, Dr. Reed," she sobbed. "We're all going to die like that man did and be eaten by those sharks."

Father Branigan, almost as pale as his surplice, made the sign of the cross in the air above the after-rail. "God receive the soul of Miguel Olmas," he said, and then in a lower tone, "God save us all."

XII

The grisly climax to the burial had a painful effect on both the personnel and the patients of the *Mercy,* already in the grip of depression and fear. Nor was their depression lessened by the news leaking out of the radio room and into the ship's grapevine, where it traveled almost as rapidly as it had across the airways. News that Lima, Panama, the west coast ports of Mexico, even Los Angeles and San Francisco, had refused entrance to what had now become known the world over as the Plague Ship.

Pushed by the Humboldt Current, the *Mercy* had been moving steadily northward at a very slow speed, with the dark outline of the coast of Peru still visible to the east on the horizon. The first physical impact of their involuntary isolation came that afternoon, when a smaller ship appeared in the distance and bore down upon them rapidly. It hove to just at dusk at least a half mile away and, through high-powered binoculars, could be identified as a gunboat flying the flag of Ecuador, warning Captain Pendarvis that he was now out of Peruvian waters and into Ecuadorian territory.

"Dr. Reed!" came the order over the loudspeakers of the public address system. "Come to the bridge at once."

On the bridge, Grant found Captain Pendarvis, First Officer Olsson, and Jack Smithson, with a seaman who was operating the standard blinker for sending short messages at sea.

"That Ecuadorian gunboat has ordered us to heave to," Captain Pendarvis told Grant. "Since you're technically in charge of the *Mercy* now, it's up to you to decide what we shall do."

"But—"

"Those are our orders from the foundation, Doctor," said Pendarvis, and Grant recognized that the buck was being passed to him.

The blinker on the Ecuadorian boat was sending

another message and First Officer Olsson translated in a strong Swedish accent: "They are demanding to know what we are doing without permission in Ecuadorian waters."

"Ecuadorian waters?" Captain Pendarvis exclaimed. "We must be well over the twelve-mile limit, even though we can still see the coast."

"Ecuador claims their limits extend for two hundred miles offshore, Captain," said Olsson. "They've been arresting tuna fishermen who came in closer."

"We're not fishing," Pendarvis snapped and turned to the sailor at the blinker. "Send that message to them, Jones."

The blinker chattered briefly and was immediately answered.

"They say we have been forbidden to enter Ecuadorian waters, sir," Olsson translated.

"All right, Dr. Reed." Pendarvis's voice took on a caustic note. "The foundation has put you in charge. What do we do now?"

"Test their intentions, Captain. If they refuse to admit us, the whole world needs to know, then maybe some other nation will relent and give us a haven."

"That's a good idea," said the first officer. "Sort of daring them to do something about us."

"Set your course seventy-eight degrees west," Pendarvis ordered the helmsman, who spun the wheel turning the prow of the slowly moving vessel toward the distant shore.

The answer came almost immediately, a puff of smoke from one of the batteries on the gunboat, followed by the report of the gun. The shot itself landed a good mile ahead of the bow.

"They may not be willing to go any farther than a warning shot," said Grant. "I'd hold your course, at least for the moment."

"Where are you headed?" the blinker message came over the mile separating them from the gunboat.

"Guayaquil," said Pendarvis grimly and the message was relayed to be followed almost immediately by the report of another gun from the Ecuadorian vessel. The second projectile landed less than a quarter of a mile beyond the prow of the *Mercy*.

"Looks like they mean business, Captain," said Olsson. "Latins are excitable and not always very accurate with their fire; the next one might be too close."

"I agree," said Grant. "Obviously they're not going to let us into Guayaquil or any other port on their coast."

"Even Hawaii has now refused us refuge," said Pendarvis on a note almost of panic. "What do we do now, Dr. Reed?"

"Obviously nobody is going to allow a 'plague ship' to land, Captain," said Grant. "I'd head for the calmest waters you know of and heave to until we can best this plague."

"Or die from it and feed those sharks," said Olsson.

"Maybe they'll leave us alone now that they've filled their bellies," said the captain.

"There's a sure way of telling—by emptying the garbage." Reaching up to the control panel First Officer Olsson pressed the button that activated the garbage chute, allowing what had been accumulated since the last ejection to slide into the sea.

There was a rumble of machinery in the bowels of the ship, then a splash as the garbage was spewed out of vents at the stern. Stepping from the bridge, Grant looked back and was not at all surprised to see the nearly white fins of the giant killer sharks plowing through the water just behind the slowly turning screw, two wide-open mouths gobbling up the waste that had just been discharged.

"I just hope the son of a bitches get Yungay fever," said Jack Smithson. "We've had another death this afternoon—one of Olma's children—but we're certainly not going to commit the poor little devil to the sea, until it's too dark for the shark to see it."

"What's the course, Captain?" Olsson asked.

"Due west." Pendarvis threw up his hands in a gesture

of helplessness. "There's no land nearby except the Galápagos Islands, but the equator runs right through them, so we're well to the south and in no danger."

There was no merriment at dinner that night for everyone knew the ship was headed out into the vast reaches of the Pacific Ocean with no destination in sight. Meanwhile, one question still had to be answered and that came with the second burial of the day.

The religious service was read after dark, but almost immediately after the small body dropped into the sea, the snapping of giant jaws was heard crunching through the tender flesh and small bones of the child. And when the officer on the bridge swung the search-light to the wake of the ship, everyone could see two giant white tails as the *Mercy*'s grim consorts sounded to digest their evening meal.

XIII

With all hope of finding a haven until the unseen enemy aboard had run its course and, hopefully, de-stroyed itself by stimulating the bodies it infected to produce the chemicals called immunoglobulins, which alone seemed to have the power to destroy it, the *Mercy,* became literally a ship without hope. Life went on while Yungay fever raged mercilessly in its victims until it brought either death or the destruction of its cause. Every day there were more burials at sea and every day the appetites of the huge white sharks seemed unappeasable.

Sometimes the triangular fins, looking at a distance oddly like the sails of small pleasure boats, would disappear for hours. But always, seconds after Father Branigan read the service, which everyone now knew by heart, and the stretcher was tipped, the giant fish would break the surface, jaws open and teeth shining in the sun. For a few seconds, then, the horrible crunching of bones would send a chill through the slowly decreasing population of the old ship, a chill

of fear and a question no one wanted to ask: Who
would be next?

As the *Mercy* sailed westward away from the cold,
north-flowing Humboldt Current, the air began to
grow warm, even hot. To save fuel from the supply in
the tanks, however, the air-conditioning system was not
turned on. Fresh meat was in short supply, too, but
nobody bothered to trail setlines from the stern, for
what was the use of catching fish when the Nemeses
cruising along in their wake only gobbled them up.
Fortunately the staple food lockers had been full when
the ship left Chimbote so suddenly, and since the original patient population of nearly three hundred was now
cut almost in half as Yungay fever took its daily toll,
the consumption of supplies by patients was sharply
diminished.

As to the personnel of the ship itself, everyone aboard
went about their daily—and nightly—tasks like zom-
bies. Only occasionally was laughter heard from the
staff lounge any more, and with no opportunity to
replenish the supply of liquor for the small bar, there
was little to stimulate any gaiety.

Lael Valdez improved rapidly. She was soon sitting
in the sun in a deck chair and taking brief walks along
the deck. Grant saw little of her, or anyone else on
the ship, however. Every waking hour was spent in the
laboratory, desperately seeking some enemy of Yungay
fever that might help provide the members of the hospital staff and crew with protection, when what he had
given them with the original injection of Guy's serum
began to wane. Yet as the days wore on, all his efforts
still proved to be in vain.

Shirley had nothing to do except to give her employers, CBS and INS, a dramatic account by radiotelephone every day of events on board the *Mercy*.
Always active, however, she had volunteered to work
as a clinical secretary to the medical staff, typing
records, keeping track of the steadily declining status
of the ship's stores, and preserving information about
those who died aboard which could be turned over to

health authorities and to their families when, and if, the ship ever reached a port.

A week after the two shots across its bow forced the *Mercy* to turn westward, Lael Valdez appeared in the laboratory, seemingly recovered from her illness.

"Making any progress?" she asked Grant but he shook his head.

"It looks like I've met my match. This bug has had five thousand years to develop a mean strain."

"You're getting hardly any rest at all, either. Jack Smithson says you've been working eighteen hours a day."

"Time is short—except for you and a small number of patients who are recovering."

"I want to help, Grant. I'm strong enough now— and I do remember a little about working in a laboratory."

He gave her an appraising look, then nodded. "I need an assistant all right, but it would have to be for only a few hours in the beginning."

"When do I start?"

"I'm getting ready to transfer some stock cultures of *Bacillus yungay*. Why don't you watch today and tomorrow? Meanwhile you can draw a supply of the paper uniforms we wear at work in your size and start taking care of some of those details yourself."

"The technique hasn't changed much since I worked as a technician," she commented when a rack of tubes had been recultured and placed in the large incubator that served the laboratory.

"Fortunately not. Tomorrow we'll have to make up a new batch of agar slants, so you'd better call it a day."

By the third day in the laboratory, Lael was working smoothly, taking a considerable load of the routine work off Grant's shoulders. She seemed happier, too, which was a definite plus, but not so Jack Smithson, who came to breakfast one morning, looking glum.

"Tonio had a chill last night," he reported. "He thinks he's got the flu or something."

Grant was instantly alert; he'd been expecting something like this to happen. "Who saw Guy first when Lael brought him aboard?" he asked.

"Tonio," said Smithson. "I was ashore wrapping up the Health Department records in the epidemic of malignant malaria we came here to treat and didn't get back until after midnight."

"Then Tonio was exposed to Yungay fever about twelve hours before you were?"

"Something like that."

"He was also the first to see Augustine Almaviva when he was brought aboard the day I arrived, which makes him the prime candidate for the first sign that the protection of the immune serum from Guy is wearing off. What nurse cared for Guy at the start?"

"Elaine Carroll specialed him for the first twelve hours."

"She'd be number two then—and you'd be number three, Jack."

"I'd better order sputum cultures on Tonio?"

"We can't wait for the results. Everybody on board this ship, except Lael, and possibly Shirley, must have another injection of immune plasma as quickly as possible."

"Where are you going to find it? You've already used Lael."

"But not the patients who have been in the hospital the longest and are recovering. The antibody titer in their blood should be high enough to protect the staff and the crew for a while longer."

"How much longer?"

"Until other patients recover. We'll start with Manoel Allanza and Conchita Torres; they're both about well, aren't they?"

"Yes, but Allanza isn't going to like it. He's a troublemaker anyway, always griping about the service and trying to stir up other patients."

"Homer Ferguson will handle Manoel," Grant assured him. "We'll use plasmapheresis, as I did for Shirley, and return the cells to the donor. Shirley can report this so the world will know we're racing against time—"

"You mean against death."

"In this case they're the same thing."

"When they hear the fix we're in, some country might let us land and put these people in an isolation hospital," said Smithson with a note of hope in his voice.

"You could be dooming yourself if you did," said Grant crisply. "Right now our only bet is to keep this tub afloat, while the patients who are recovering manufacture the immune globulins that are going to help the rest of us stay alive." He put down the rack of test tubes he'd been handling. "Let's go check on Tonio and then I'll set Homer to work on Allanza and Conchita Torres—plus any others who look like they're well enough to have manufactured a good supply of antibodies."

Tonio Marelia proved to be sicker than Jack Smithson had thought. The Bolivian had known for several days that his temperature was rising, and the agony in his bones and muscles had steadily increased. Convinced that he was suffering from Yungay fever and dreading even the diagnosis, lest he become yet another feast for the Nemeses that followed the doomed ship, he'd refused to say anything about it.

"He's got Yungay fever all right," said Grant when he and Smithson finished a brief examination.

"No doubt about it," Smithson agreed. "We'd better start drawing blood from Allanza and Señora Torres at once."

"We can't risk that, Jack. Tonio needs blood that contains a maximum number of immunoglobulins to head off what could become an overwhelming infection."

"You mean—"

"Tonio needs my blood, doesn't he?" Neither had heard Lael come in or realized she was listening until she spoke.

"No," said Jack Smithson quickly. "It's too soon after—"

"I can't let Tonio die if I can protect him from that thing waiting out there," said Lael. "This whole epidemic is my fault. I must do everything I can in penance."

Smithson wheeled upon Grant. "If her resistance gets too low from losing blood serum, she's liable to go into a relapse."

"I already know that," said Lael. "But don't rob me of the chance to make the burden on my own conscience a little lighter."

"Actually, you'll not be running any great risk," Grant assured her. "We'll replace the red cells we remove, so on that score you're in no danger. An immunological system that's been stimulated by a powerful antigen like *Bacillus yungay,* as yours has, possesses a remarkable ability to manufacture new immunoglobulins."

"I'll have no part of it, Grant," said Jack Smithson. "If anything happens and we lose both Tonio and Lael, I'll bring charges of manslaughter against you as soon as we reach a port where they can be filed."

"By that time, any charges you or anybody else bring probably wouldn't make any difference," Grant said with a shrug. "Better go to your stateroom and lie down, Lael, while I get things ready. You'll have to stay there for a few days anyway."

As he was working in the lab, preparing the two flasks into which he'd divided the pint of blood he had taken from Lael's veins, Shirley came into the room. Grant had seen little of her since he'd given her Lael's plasma, but although she looked a little tired, as did everyone on the ship for that matter, she seemed to be holding up very well.

"Do you think you can cure Tonio?" she asked when he looked up from the controls of the rapidly spinning centrifuge.

"I don't know. If he'd told me he felt bad two days ago, when his symptoms really began, I'd have a much better chance."

"He was afraid to face the reality of the sharks. We all are."

"Don't tell me you knew he was sick."

"No, but I understand why he wouldn't want to admit it." She shivered, although the room was quite warm and Grant was working in nothing but his paper coverall. "I know I have a better chance of living longer than the rest of you because I got a higher degree of protection in Lael's serum, but the bell will eventually toll for me, too."

"You *could* have the honor of being the last dying American aboard the *Mercy*," he agreed.

"Right now I'd exchange with you if I could."

He gave her a startled look. "Aren't you a little late in reaching that conclusion?"

"Too late. Would it help if I gave Tonio Marelia some of my blood, too? I'm Type O."

"No. Your antibody titer isn't high enough and you didn't manufacture your own protection."

"You told me I'm immune, at least for a while."

"True, but yours is a passive immunity, one you received from someone else. Lael already had Yungay fever when I gave her Guy's blood, so hers is an active immunity."

"And if Tonio survives, his will be active, too?"

"Yes. The dose of Lael's plasma I'm going to give him, as soon as it's separated from the red cells, will merely strengthen his body to fight against the organism and give him time to develop an immunity of his own."

"And then he can give blood to help protect the rest?"

"A few weeks from now, if any of us survive that long." He cut the switch driving the centrifuge and it began to slow down.

"INS reported yesterday that they're nominating my running account of life aboard a plague ship for a Pulitzer Prize," she said.

"I hope you win it—and get there to receive it."

"From the way donations are pouring into the

Mercy Foundation, according to their radio reports, the old ship will be able to sail again, too."

"This is your specialty and I must admit that you're far better at it than I'm proving to be at mine." He was watching the still-spinning centrifuge with a bleak light in his eyes. "By the way, your romance with Mark Post must be proceeding well. He's stopped baiting me every chance he gets."

Shirley smiled. "Mark is a nice boy, too good for a hussy like me. He's only a diversion, though. Anything that takes your mind off these horrors cruising in our wake, even for a little while, is worth the trouble."

"I never take time to think of them," Grant admitted as he lifted one of the flasks from the centrifuge and began to draw off the upper, clear half of its contents, the plasma which had been separated from the packed red cells at the bottom of the tube. "I'm too busy here."

"At that we may be better off than the rest of the globe," said Shirley. "I just received a message from INS about the world situation. The Soviets sent a special plane to London to take their two sick professors back to Moscow, so they've seeded Yungay fever into Russia. Five of the greatest atomic scientists in the world have already died and a half dozen more are gravely ill in London hospitals. The disease is spreading rapidly in Boston, New York, Los Angeles, and a half dozen other cities, too, where the students in Professor Mallinson's class, who handled the specimen of bone from the Yungay tomb, went before you were able to warn Marshall Payne of the danger."

"Have you heard of any progress at the center?"

"I sent a radiogram to Marshall yesterday asking that question. This morning he reported that they seem to be getting nowhere—except that two of the technicians in the new hot lab are sick, presumably with Yungay fever."

"The hot lab contains the finest equipment in the world for the protection of humans against viruses and other micro-organisms," said Grant glumly. "I guess that proves what I've already come to believe here on the ship, that we're dealing with an organism capable of crossing any man-made barrier."

"Which means nobody in the world can be sure they won't one day get Yungay fever?"

"That—and more; our own experience here shows that it becomes more virulent as it passes from body to body." He laughed, but without humor. "At least the no-population-growth advocates should be pleased —if they live through it. Before a year passes, we could see two thirds or more of the people in the world wiped out by a creature so small it can only be seen under a microscope."

XIV

Manoel Allanza was hopping mad. If Homer Ferguson hadn't been holding him down with one large hand, he would long since have jerked from his right arm the needle through which Dr. Mark Post was drawing blood. Blood which, Dr. Reed had assured the recovering patients, would be returned to their veins, once the protection needed again by the nurses, doctors, and crew had been separated from it. Protection which, he had told them, too, their now healing bodies would quickly replace.

"A curse on this ship and everybody on it!" Manoel snapped at Homer. "Including you, false friend that you are."

"Shut up, half a man," said Homer with a grin. "When we get back to Chimbote you will be famous. *La reportera roja* has spoken much of you on the radio and in her writings. Now all the world knows of Manoel, the legless one who is winning the battle with this fever."

"What good will that do when we are all dead?" Manoel demanded. "The yanquis will drain our blood and then feed us to *el tiburón grande*."

"The yanqui doctors made you well," Homer reminded him. "Dont forget that."

"And now they drink our blood to keep them from getting *la fiebre fatal.*"

"At least it wasn't fatal for you, *mi amigo,* so shut up before I throw you to *el tiburón grande* myself, to be rid of your chatter."

The threat silenced Manoel's tongue, at least for a while; if angered enough, he knew Homer could easily toss him over the rail with one hand. But it did nothing to silence his thoughts, which were racing, as the yanqui doctor finished drawing the blood and taped a small dressing over the spot on his arm where the needle had punctured the skin and vein. Or his words, whenever he had a chance to talk to the other patients who were also recovering. For unknown to Homer, Manoel was plotting how to take charge of his own life—and those of the yanquis he hated, even though they had saved him.

The Bolivian doctor who was sick now spoke Spanish, and Manoel had questioned him whenever he had a chance. As a result he knew practically everything that was happening aboard the ship. Besides, the grapevine had already told of the refusal of other ports to let the white ship enter and the decision of the captain to cruise westward in the warm seas around the equator —much more pleasant than the coast and the cold Humboldt Current which had been left behind—until the patients aboard the ship either recovered from the fever or died from it.

No one knew what would happen then, but it was said that among the yanqui doctors and nurses, there was talk that they could go on for a long time on the blood from the *nativos* who recovered. Manoel himself went to the films whenever he could and remembered vividly seeing a white man with long sharp teeth suck on the neck of a beautiful girl, drinking her blood in much the same way the yanquis must be drinking the blood of the dark-skinned ones aboard the ship.

The girl had died, as had others in the film, and

Manoel knew that such a creature would go on drinking the blood of victim after victim unless it was killed by a stake driven through his heart. Aboard the ship, there was little opportunity so far to use such tactics against the gringo doctors and nurses. But when enough of the nativos aboard had recovered from the fever, as Manoel himself had, they would outnumber the *blancos* and could then take over the ship.

Homer Ferguson and a few among the sick, he knew, had some experience in sailing a ship. Once it was under their control, they would steer it to land and then the *blancos* could be taken ashore and killed, one by one, by driving sharp stakes through their hearts as had been done to the vampire in the film.

Yes, it was a good plan, one worthy of a smart man like Manoel Allanza. A man who dwelt above his neighbors in the barrio and who, when the time came, would lead his fellow nativos in taking control and destroying the hated yanquis who had brought this plague to the Callejón de Huaylas and to Chimbote in the first place. He would keep the plan to himself, however, he decided. He would not even tell Homer, who had now gone on with Dr. Post to draw blood from Conchita Torres, until the time came to put it into execution. As for any yanqui who resisted, even Homer Ferguson himself, there were always *los tiburones grandes* following the ship. And between the giant jaws, or doing the bidding of those who controlled the vessel and sailing it to the port he'd already decided upon, where no *cañonera* would put a shot into it, few would choose the sharks.

XV

The second protective injection series brought some relief to the spirits of the personnel operating the *Mercy,* at least ensuring that they had several weeks of safety from the killer microbe. But as the long hot days wore on with the ship now barely making way, the brief lull in the grim depression gripping those on the vessel gave way to the same feeling of hopelessness.

Only the radio, with its daily news bulletins, kept them in touch with the outside world, but nothing happening there was calculated to lift their spirits. Even though brief, the radio broadcasts revealed a steadily rising panic gripping the world outside, as *Bacillus yungay* continued its inexorable spread across the face of the earth. Almost, it seemed, the malignant germ had come to be a true biblical curse, released upon a world where most of the old biblical virtues—as reflected by the Ten Commandments and the Sermon on the Mount—seemed lost on a great portion of the population.

Fundamentalist preachers named it a punishment from God for sin. But for Grant Reed, familiar with similar—though not so violent—plagues in various parts of the world, it was merely another facet in the relentless struggle between man and his environment to stay alive. In Africa, the current villain was Lassa fever; in Argentina, hemorrhagic fever; in Paraguay, still another form he had identified and against which, fortunately, he had been able to devise a vaccine.

That same fortuitous event Grant was hoping to bring about with his work in the laboratory but so far with no glimmering of success. He and Lael, whose donation of blood had kept her in bed only a day, were working long hours together now and she was proving invaluable. As the days of companionship wore on, he was able to see more and more of the qualities in her that had so attracted Guy, qualities far different from the women Guy had achieved liaisons of various degrees with in the past.

She was a quick student, learning very rapidly even the intricate techniques of filtering bacterial cultures through a porcelain filter. Nor was she squeamish about handling the white rats that were used as test animals, holding the squirming animals skillfully, yet gently, while making the injections necessary in the test procedures Grant was following.

At first she was quiet, almost reticent, but as the days passed, she began to open up slowly, revealing things about herself and her relationship to Guy that told him again how much she had loved his brother.

Sometimes, as when she recalled incidents in their trip across the roof of the Western world, she was warm and gay. Grant soon found himself far more comfortable in his relationship with Lael than he'd ever been with Shirley. Yet in her own quiet way, Lael was far more beautiful and, he supposed when he thought of it occasionally as he watched her moving about through the laboratory, fully as desirable.

She startled him one day when they were working side by side, making another attempt to turn the potent toxin obtained by filtering a culture into a toxoid by treating it with heat and formalin.

"You're not at all the way I pictured you before I met you that morning at Chimbote Airport," she said.

"So? How am I different?"

"I guess I thought of you as a medical adventurer, seeking bizarre experiences in different parts of the world and gaining fame you really didn't deserve."

"I never seek them, believe me. They just seem to come my way, as this one did."

"They come your way because you're the one person best trained to handle them; I know that now. Guy boasted so often about your accomplishments that I guess I became a little jealous."

"Is that why you were rather stiff toward me when you met me that first morning?"

"That—and the fact that I had failed to help Guy and had to call on you."

"When you love someone as much as you loved Guy, that's perfectly understandable."

"But not an emotion *you* would feel."

"I'm not so sure of that. While we're confessing, I was quite prepared not to like you that morning, too."

"I know."

"Don't tell me I was rude."

"Not rude—I don't think you're capable of that. But you did think I was an adventuress, didn't you?"

"Only for a little while. Our trip to Yungay and the Casa Yanqui cured me of that."

"I guess each of us learned something about the other up there; the Altiplano seems to bring out the true nature of people."

"Maybe it's the lack of oxygen."

"No. The people up there are more honest—"

"Except Carlos Ganza—and he's dead of Yungay fever."

"I've been thinking a lot these past weeks. When—if—all of this is over, I'm going back to Yungay and the Casa Yanqui."

"You'll be a rich woman in your own right then—and can do pretty much as you please."

"Once you find a way to control Yungay fever, I want to open the tomb. Those paintings should be made available for the world to see and for archaeologists to study. I'm going to make the cave a memorial to Guy."

"He'd love that. I remember his writing me once about visiting the area in southern France where the cave paintings by prehistoric men were discovered."

"We went there shortly after we started living together." The look in her eyes was far away. "Seeing how those artists depicted Cro-Magnon and Neanderthal life many thousands of years ago was so exciting that we decided then and there to follow up on the manuscript I'd already discovered in the archives at Madrid."

"Will you live at the Casa Yanqui when you go up to the Callejón de Huaylas?"

"Yes. We were there almost a year and I love it. Besides, the weather is much too cold at night up near the snow line where the cave is located. Nobody much lives up there."

"I'll try to visit you when the burial cave is officially opened," he promised. "None of that can take place until we've conquered *B. yungay,* though, and as yet there's no sign that we'll do that very soon."

"Do you doubt that you ever will?"

"Very much—at times. Don't you?"

She shook her head. "You're like Guy in many ways; when he started something he always finished it. I think you have the same trait."

"While you're looking into the future," he said with a smile, "it would help if you could give me an inkling of where the answer will lie. I can't even be sure anyone but you and the patients who are getting well will ever get off this ship."

"The *Mercy* will eventually have to make port somewhere; the world couldn't be callous enough to leave all these people to starve," she assured him. "Besides, with Yungay fever already epidemic in so many parts of the world, what's the use of keeping the *Mercy* at sea any longer?"

"I hadn't thought of that." Grant's voice was tense with a sudden excitement as he put the tube of toxin into which he'd been <u>dropping</u> formalin solution back into the wire rack and started washing his hands.

"Where are you going?" Lael asked. "It's too early for lunch."

"To the radio room to send a message to Marshall Payne at the Center for Disease Control. The World Health Organization works very closely with the center, and Marshall can put in a request to the WHO for the *Mercy* to be given a clearance to dock, probably at a U.S. port with facilities for hospitalizing these people."

"Where would that be?"

"Panama is easily the nearest; the Gorgas Hospital there has functioned as an isolation center during yellow fever epidemics. Besides, if we're allowed to dock, I can fly more cultures of *B. Yungay* to Atlanta where the center has the best facilities for discovering how to make either a toxoid or vaccine and stop this epidemic."

In the radio room, Grant wrote out a brief message:

ABOARD SS MERCY
NOVEMBER 1, 1975..

TO: DR. MARSHALL PAYNE,
CENTER FOR DISEASE CONTROL,
ATLANTA, GEORGIA, USA.

SINCE YUNGAY FEVER NOW REPORTED TO BE
EPIDEMIC IN MANY CITIES, NO FURTHER REASON
EXISTS FOR REFUSING PERMISSION TO DOCK.
PLEASE ASK MERCY FOUNDATION AND WHO TO
CONTACT PROPER AUTHORITIES REGARDING PER-
MISSION TO DOCK, PREFERABLY AT PANAMA, FOR
TRANSFER OF PATIENTS TO GORGAS HOSPITAL.
EARLY REPLY REQUESTED.

GRANT REED,
EPIDEMIOLOGIST IN CHARGE

Word of Grant's request spread through the ship in
minutes after the message was sent, buoying tre-
mendously the depressed spirits of the staff and crew.
There was even rejoicing in the staff lounge that night,
and some of the last of the whiskey supply was opened.
The next morning shortly after breakfast, however,
Jake Porter sent for Shirley and Grant and silently
handed each of them a radio message.

Grant's request had been denied, according to Mar-
shal Payne, the reason given being that, with the cultures of *B. yungay* he'd sent from Chimbote already
under study at the center, the U.S. Public Health
Service felt there was no need for the presence of a
large number of patients with Yungay fever at any port.
Besides, authorities in the cities where the *Mercy*
might have been able to dock on the Pacific Coast
were adamant in their decision not to allow any large
number of sick to enter any port.

"It's no go," Grant told Shirley. "Nobody wants us."

"Even though they've already got more cases of
Yungay fever in a lot of cities than the *Mercy* has?"

"I guess the port authorities figure dumping several

hundred patients on them in one lot might make bad matters worse. What about your request to the Mercy Foundation?"

"You won't believe this and they didn't say it in so many words, but you can easily read between the lines," she said. "With contributions pouring in, the foundation never had it so good, so the way they figure it, a plague ship afloat draws dollars, but one tied up in port with no sick aboard wouldn't."

"I guess that makes sense—from their point of view."

"But what about us?" For the first time since she'd come aboard he detected a note of fear—and near hysteria—in her voice. "You've got maybe two hundred natives aboard and barely seventy-five in the staff and crew. Say you lose even another fifty patients before the epidemic burns itself out. How long can you keep drawing blood from those who've recovered, to save Yankees they've been taught to hate since childhood?"

"Who knows?"

"Even if you get rid of Yungay fever, there'll still be a heavy charge of hate aboard the Mercy. Maybe you haven't noticed it, but I have, and that could conceivably be dangerous for the staff and crew."

"I think you're overdramatizing," he told her. "Besides, a revolt would give you plenty of material for INS."

"Right now I'm more concerned about M-E than I am about INS."

"Cheer up," he advised. "If we hold this course westward, we ought to make Christmas Island by Christmas, and Manoel Allanza can be Santa Claus. At least that will be something different."

BOOK FOUR

The
STORM

I

NEWS THAT THE *Mercy* was still a ship without a port doused the brief note of hope for the complement and crew. Not even the recovery of Tonio Marelia, after a stormy week of illness, could elevate their spirits, since it proved that once the killer microbe got a real hold in a body already partly immune, even a large injection of immune plasma might not prevent death. All of which meant that the ship personnel was even more vulnerable than they had realized at first and left the question of how long they could be kept from developing Yungay fever far from settled.

One completely unexpected by-product of Grant's failure to obtain clearance for the *Mercy* to enter a port was the tide of resentment toward him that soon became apparent on the ship. He was puzzled as to how it could occur when he'd done everything he could to defeat *B. yungay,* until he talked to Father Branigan one evening.

Tired and depressed after another failure to achieve a toxoid by treating almost pure *B. yungay* toxin with formalin, he came into the staff lounge for a drink, something he rarely did any more. The chaplain, with the surplice he'd just removed after another night burial at sea hanging over a chair, was having a glass of wine with Mark Post. The plastic surgeon hurriedly finished his drink and made an excuse to leave, while several of the staff who had also been in the lounge when Grant entered gradually filed out, too, leaving him and the chaplain alone.

"Don't mind me if you'd rather go, too, Father," said Grant on a bitter note.

"I'm glad of the opportunity to talk to you, Doctor. The laboratory demands so much of your time that I almost never see you any more."

"Obviously the rest of the ship's complement doesn't share your tolerance." Grant poured himself a drink at the now deserted bar and came over to sit across from the priest. "If you can tell me why, I'd appreciate it."

"The answer is simple. You're the highly touted savior everybody expected to conquer a dangerous disease—"

"I never said I could."

"No, but your reputation went before you. After all, you're not the first savior to be turned upon by the people who needed him. At the trial of Jesus, He was mocked by the scribes and the chief priests who said, 'He saved others; himself He cannot save.' "

"I'm afraid the similarity ends there," said Grant morosely. "I'm an expert in a field where I still have a lot of confidence in my own ability, in spite of the fact that I've come upon a breed of microbe that has baffled me completely."

"Perhaps because of its very age, it doesn't come within the scope of your knowledge. Or again, it could be the will of God that much of the world shall be destroyed by this plague in order that, once purged of its corruption, a new and better race of mankind might emerge."

"I can't subscribe to that theory, Father. Having been trained as a scientist, nothing is more sacred or immutable to me than the basic laws of nature."

"Not even God?"

"I regard the laws of nature as the voice of God. They tell me He exists but they also tell me that, having created something as perfect in its basic laws as nature is, God wouldn't meddle with them except for a very good reason indeed."

"Do you deny the occurrence of miracles?"

"I cannot accept that God will reach down and cure John Smith because a faith healer lays hands upon him or anoints him with oil. To me that sort of a God would be irresponsible and unpredictable, while nothing in the universe could be more responsible and more predictable than the laws of nature itself."

"That I will grant," said the priest. "But surely you've seen patients cured miraculously."

"I've seen religious faith and conviction change the make-up of the body to where it was able to resist and even destroy microbes that attack it. That's what we now call psychosomatic medicine, but what really happens is that emotional changes are reflected in the body chemistry to such a degree that they can change organic conditions. A classical example is elevation of blood pressure from worry, or the formation of an ulcer in the stomach from too much tension and production of hydrochloric acid."

"I remember a surgeon in World War II telling me they couldn't cure a stomach ulcer that occurred in a soldier while under tension. Yet as soon as he was discharged from the service, it would heal of itself almost overnight."

"That's the sort of thing I'm talking about," said Grant. "The longer this ship is free to cruise without a destination and those animals are waiting there behind us, the more emotionally related ills we're going to see in both complement and passengers—possibly even some real psychoses may develop in time."

"At least you've kept us alive."

"Just now I'm not sure I can take much credit even for that. Jack Smithson is a very capable doctor; if I hadn't been here, I'm sure he would have thought of giving immune plasma to protect the staff and crew."

"But early enough to save Miss Valdez and Tonio? Everybody knows Dr. Smithson was angry at you for what he thought was an unnecessary risk you took in giving Miss Valdez your brother's blood without doing a culture first."

"He was right about the risk; the necessity was something I had to decide on the spot."

First Officer Olsson had come into the lounge and, going to the bar, poured a drink before turning toward the table where Grant and Branigan were sitting.

"Mind if I join you, gentlemen?" he asked.

"Bring the bottle, please, Oley," said Grant. "I feel like hanging a small one on."

"Wish I could do the same thing myself." The tall blond officer was very popular on the ship and rumor said he'd slept with half the women aboard. "The radio reports a considerable storm several hundred miles to the northwest. It's coming our way and I'm on duty. Besides, I've just inspected all decks and the natives are restless tonight. Once or twice I had the eerie feeling that someone might clobber me in a dark spot."

"I've had that feeling myself, both as to the restlessness and the possibility of being mugged," said Grant. "But of course this isn't Central Park and people recovering from a severe disease would have no reason to turn on their benefactors."

"I'm not too sure of that," said Olsson. "I understand enough Spanish to know they're blaming you because you weren't able to arrange for us to dock somewhere."

"Looks like the club's getting bigger every day," said Grant bitterly. "Next, I suppose everybody'll be blaming me for the storm that's coming."

"With that much warning in advance, can't you go around it?" the chaplain asked.

"At five knots?" Olsson shrugged. "Besides, if we turn north we'd run right smack into the Galápagos Archipelago. The farther south we go, the more of the storm we might escape, but we'll have that much farther to limp back, if the authorities ever do relent and let us land somewhere."

"So you're heading south?"

"I've already changed the course. Captain Pendarvis is otherwise occupied, but lately he's left the running of the ship largely up to me anyway."

"That shot from the Ecuadorian gunboat sort of took the starch out of the captain," Father Branigan agreed with a chuckle.

"As well as a lot of others," said Grant.

"How is all of this going to turn out, Dr. Reed?" Olsson asked. "Can you ward off the fever indefinitely with these injections you're giving us?"

"With a germ as potent as this one is, the patients who get well are probably permanently immune, which means we can use their blood indefinitely," said Grant. "I'd say the real limiting factor is the amount of food and fuel supply aboard."

"That gives us a little under two months if we cut down on the rations toward the end." Olsson drained his glass and stood up. "I'd better go up and see if Jake has anything new on the storm. We'll track it by radar when it gets nearer. Our range isn't much over a hundred fifty miles, though, and by the time we see it the situation will probably have worsened considerably. Good night, gentlemen."

"Better get a good night's sleep, Father," Grant advised. "If a real Pacific storm hits us, we're all liable to be in the drink by tomorrow afternoon, and our friends the sharks back there are going to have a smorgasbord."

II

Lael had returned to work in the laboratory two days after she'd given the blood plasma to Tonio and the red cells from her blood had been reinjected into her veins. She appeared to be none the worse for the experience, and the fact that she had undoubtedly saved the life of the Bolivian doctor, who was very popular with everyone aboard, including the patients, had buoyed her spirits considerably.

"Some of the staff were saying at breakfast that we may be caught in a storm," she told Grant when she came into the laboratory, where he'd been working for several hours, getting started on still another attempt to make a toxoid from the toxin of *B. yungay*.

"Oley Olsson told me about it last night. We're heading south in an attempt to avoid it, but the storm is moving from the northwest, so we may be near a collision course."

"Couldn't Chief McTavish get more speed out of the engines?"

"Not without risking a breakdown, I gather, and he can't take a chance on that. Even at five knots, the ship could be headed into the storm when it strikes, giving somewhat the same effect as putting out a sea anchor. Drifting helplessly, though, it could take a pretty bad dusting."

"Jack said at breakfast that the *Mercy*'s been through a couple of Pacific typhoons, so she ought to be all right."

"Just the same we'd better get everything movable in the laboratory fastened down," he told her. "Check your stateroom, too, before dinner, and make sure no bottles or jars are left on your dressing table to go flying around the room when the ship starts pitching and rolling."

The work of securing the equipment took most of the day, but when he surveyed the laboratory late that afternoon, Grant could see that it was shipshape. Chemical reagents were stored on shelves in their bottles, with a four-inch board in front of each shelf to keep the bottles from sliding off in a rough sea or being tipped over. Glassware such as culture tubes and Petri dishes were something of a problem, until he corralled all the blankets he could find. Since they were still only a few degrees south of the equator, although moving steadily southward, bed covers weren't needed any more. Carefully wrapped in blankets, the glassware would, hopefully, withstand the tossing about sure to happen as the ship labored through a storm.

Between times, Grant was busy timing the application of formalin to the *B. yungay* toxin and injecting rats with the mixture at various intervals to test its virulence after treatment with the potent germ killer. He looked up once to see Lael moving around inside his small adjoining cabin. When she came out, she was shaking her head.

"You're as untidy with your personal things as Guy was," she said. "I wrapped your shaving lotion bottle in a towel and put it in the dresser drawer. Your vitamins, too; you seem to have quite a supply."

"I always carry concentrates with me. The average native African diet of roast rat and beans isn't exactly vitamin rich."

"Ugh! Gerald, the medical student I was engaged to in Boston, came from the South and loved things like fried rabbit, squirrel stew, and opossum with sweet potatoes and collard greens."

"You can get that at some of the Atlanta restaurants. It's called soul food."

"It only made my soul want to vomit. Do you have any idea when we're liable to be hit by the storm?"

"I'm going up to the radio room in a few minutes to look at the radar screen. If you like, we can go to dinner when I come back."

She gave him an odd look. "Do you know that's the first time you've asked me to have dinner with you?"

"I haven't paid much attention to eating since I started looking for a crack in the armor of our microscope enemy."

"Why now?"

"Perhaps because we may be in greater danger for the next twenty-four hours than we've been before, and nobody enjoys facing danger alone."

"That's also the first time I've ever heard you admit you were afraid of anything. It makes you much more human."

"Have I seemed less than a human to you before?"

She smiled. "A little. Sometimes you're like a scientific machine—one of those gadgets that perform so many tests per hour."

"Is that why the others have been avoiding me?"

"No. I think they expected more from you in the crisis than you were able to deliver."

"Sort of a savior who turned out to be a failure?"

"Is that what *you* think you are?"

"Father Branigan says people often turn in a crisis on somebody who appears to have the answers to everything but fails to deliver."

"That really isn't fair," she protested. "If you hadn't taken steps to carry out passive immunization, everybody on this ship would now have Yungay fever and some of them would be dead."

"I'd better go up to the bridge and see if they know where the storm is," he said. "Shall we go to dinner when I get back?"

"I'm sorry, Grant, but I promised Jack Smithson this morning that I'd have dinner with him. If you'd asked me last night—"

"It took me till nine o'clock to finish treating that batch of toxoid I was working on with formalin. After that I had to settle for a couple of drinks and a handful of peanuts with Father Branigan and Oley Olsson in the lounge."

She laughed. "No wonder you need vitamins. Will you have dinner with *me* tomorrow night?"

"Unless our escorts have us both for theirs."

She shivered. "If the storm somehow drives those monsters away, it might even be worth going through it."

"Take a couple of Nembutals and you'll sleep through it," he advised.

"Is that what you're going to do?"

"No. You've done a fine job in here of battening down the hatches, but if the sea gets really rough, something still might break loose. I'll stay up and try to catch it before it can do too much damage. If our cultures of *B. yungay* should be destroyed, we'd have to start from scratch culturing the patients."

"They wouldn't like that, particularly Manoel Allanza."

"Homer can handle Manoel and besides, most of them are about well now."

"Would the organism grow out with all the antitoxin they've developed in their bodies by now?"

"Everyone who's had Yungay fever—you included —will be a carrier for at least a month or six weeks. That's the real reason why none of the public health people I radioed would advise their governments to let us land."

III

When Grant climbed to the bridge, he saw that the wind had already risen sharply. Tall rollers were rushing down upon the ship from the northwest, causing considerable pitching and rolling, since the course of the old vessel, as it fled from the storm, made them following seas—the worst kind. Spray was blowing even across the top deck and he had to hold on to the railing as he made his way from the top of the stair to the radio room where the radar screen was located.

Jake Porter—otherwise known, like radio operators the world over, as Sparks—was sitting in front of the screen with Captain Pendarvis looking over his shoulder. The captain looked up when the door opened letting Grant in along with a blast of wind and spray. He nodded, though with no detectable welcome in his manner.

"How's it going?" Grant asked.

"A lot faster than we are." Jake Porter pointed to the screen where, in the northwest quadrant, a white shadow could be plainly seen with each swing of the antenna rotating outside.

"On this course, the full force should strike the ship around midnight," Captain Pendarvis added. "Sometime before then, we'll have to head northward to face into it, so she'll ride better."

"Any chance of skirting the heart of the storm?" Grant asked.

"That's what we're trying to figure out."

Jake Porter pointed to a chart lying on the table beside him on which were traced two lines. One obviously was the course of the *Mercy* and the other equally obviously the path of the storm, but the way the two were converging made collision seem impossible to avoid.

"I'm going to change our course to due west and try to skirt the storm," said Pendarvis. "Even at full speed, we probably won't be able to sail clear of it, but at least on a westward course, we'll be heading into the storm more and the pitching from following seas ought to be easier."

Pendarvis left to order the course change, but Grant stayed on awhile to watch the progress of the storm on the radar screen. The abatement in the pitching of the laboring old ship was immediately evident when the course was changed, but so was the distance between it and the storm—a steadily narrowing space as the shadow on the screen grew larger.

The dining room was almost filled with people when Grant came in. Being veteran sailors, most of the complement were able to take the pitching and rolling of the old ship without becoming casualties to seasickness. Jack Smithson and Lael, he saw, were at a small table in the corner with a bottle of wine between them.

Shirley and Mark Post were at a table for three with an empty chair. When she waved an invitation to him, he brought his tray over, but the plastic surgeon looked a little surly, though he didn't object.

"The ship's riding a lot easier," said Shirley. "Are we going to miss the storm?"

"Captain Pendarvis has set the course due west to try to miss the center so there's less of a following sea," Grant explained, "but we'll probably still be hit by the full force."

"When?"

"Around midnight, he thinks."

"I've never been in a storm at sea before," said Shirley. "It's very exciting."

"And also dangerous," said the plastic surgeon. "If the old tub should break apart, the lifeboats would never stay afloat in such a rough sea."

"Don't be such a killjoy, Mark," said Shirley. "Grant's not afraid, are you?"

"I'm scared stiff, and if you'd seen what I saw just now on the radar screen, you would be, too."

A sudden lull in the conversation at the tables around them told him he'd spoken more loudly than he'd intended. In the lull, Captain Pendarvis's voice was easily audible from a nearby table where he was sitting with Elaine Carroll.

"Spoken like a true landlubber," he said contemptuously.

The conversation in the room was resumed on a more subdued note, and to cover a sudden burst of anger, Grant picked up his coffee cup, spilling half of it in his saucer. As he was pouring it back into the cup and dabbing at the overflow with a paper napkin, he looked up to see Shirley's eyebrows raised in a gesture of surprise.

"I didn't think anything could make you blow your cool, darling," she said lightly. "Which means something besides a storm at sea has got you hot and bothered. Is it something I should know?"

"Nothing you're *going* to know."

Just then, Grant heard Lael's gay laugh above the hum of conversation and looked quickly at the table where she was sitting with Jack Smithson. Her cheeks were flushed, her eyes bright with laughter at something the bearded chief physician had said, and watching her, Grant was certain he'd never seen her look more beautiful.

"Well, well!" Shirley's mocking voice interrupted Grant's thoughts, and he turned back to her quickly, hoping she hadn't noticed—but she had.

"What *has* been going on in the laboratory in the past week or two, darling? A little hanky-panky among the bacilli?"

Grant couldn't help laughing. "She's a bitch, Mark.

You might as well know it now, in case you're thinking of marrying her when our divorce becomes final. But an exciting bitch."

"Thanks for the compliment." Shirley's voice had a remembered edge to it now. "And don't listen to him, Mark; I'm really a very retiring person. Which reminds me, why don't we retire to the owner's suite and my last bottle of bourbon. I've never been high in a storm and it might be quite an experience."

"Don't mind me, Mark," said Grant when the other doctor hesitated. "There's nothing between us any more except a few months we have to kill. And *one* of us might as well enjoy it."

Dinner over, Grant took the stairway down to the ward where Conchita Torres, Manoel Allanza, and Homer Ferguson were berthed. Both Conchita and Manoel were practically well now but the legless man was very seasick. Taking pity on him, Grant went to the ward medicine cabinet and poured a couple of Dramamine tablets out of a bottle. Taking them back to Manoel's berth with a cup of water, he handed them to the beggar.

"Take these," he said in Spanish. "They're good for seasickness."

"Maldito gringo!" Manoel drew back his hand to throw the water in Grant's face, but just then Homer, coming up on the opposite side, reached over and seized his arm.

"Do as he says, you legless fool! The doctor is only trying to help you." Homer's tone brooked no resistance and Manoel obediently swallowed the tablets.

"How is Conchita?" Grant asked.

"Right as rain, Doctor. When you need more blood for the doctors and nurses, she'll be glad to give it. So will Manoel here."

The assurance brought a flow of curses which Homer stopped by putting his hand over the small one's mouth.

"Don't pay any attention to him, Dr. Reed," he said. "He's possessed by a demon."

"How about the rest of the patients? Are many of them seasick?"

"Quite a few, but this small devil here has been hopping about, telling them the doctors wish only their blood, so they're afraid to take the Dramamine."

"You'd better persuade them to take it. The going will be even rougher later on tonight."

"When the course was changed just now to due west, I thought we might escape the storm."

"Captain Pendarvis is trying to skirt it, but the radar screen looks like most of it will still hit us."

"Pray God this old tub holds together."

"Exactly my thought. Do the best you can to ease the fears of the patients, Homer, and tell them to take the Dramamine. Being scared doesn't help seasickness."

"The first storm I was in at sea, I damned near puked my guts out, but when it was over I told myself nothing else could be worse than that. I haven't been seasick since."

IV

By ten o'clock when Grant, a raincoat thrown over his paper coverall, went up to the radio room, the wind felt as if it had achieved the force of a real hurricane. Huge seas were breaking over the bow as the old ship labored into the storm, drenching even the bridge with spray. Each time the hull slid into the trough between the waves, it seemed to hesitate, as if uncertain whether to try, in its agony, to surmount the following crest or to plunge on into the depths and thus achieve peace. A life raft had broken loose and was banging against the side of the ship, held only by a few ropes, while the davits by which the lifeboats were raised and lowered creaked like the wails of banshees as the wind howled in demoniac glee.

Climbing the stairway to the upper deck was like riding a bucking horse, and Grant was fairly winded by the time he pulled open the door of the radio room and jumped in. Jake Porter looked up from the radar screen and grinned.

"You should have stayed in that snug harbor you've got off the lab, Doctor. As my grandmother used to say back in North Carolina, ' 'Tain't a fit night out for man nor beast.' "

"I hope two beasts take the hint and head for quieter waters," said Grant. "Is this the worst, or is more coming?"

"These Pacific autumn storms don't have a well-defined eye like the typhoon would. It's practically all over the screen now, but Oley thinks it'll be another hour at least before we reach the center."

"How about coming out? Is it as bad as going in?"

"Maybe—for a while. The storm will be going away from us at the same time we're leaving it, so there's hope—if we're still afloat. Much damage out there yet?"

"One life raft's about to blow away."

"We'll be lucky if we lose only one. How about inside? You've got a lot of fragile glassware in the lab."

"Miss Valdez and I wrapped most of it in blankets this afternoon. I plan to stay up until the worst is over, so I can catch anything that breaks loose before it does much damage."

"Good luck."

Going back to the laboratory wasn't nearly as difficult as climbing the stairway. Since the *Mercy* was heading into the wind it almost blew Grant down the metal stairway. The raindrops had much of the impact of bird shot against his face and hands, however, and even with a raincoat, his coverall was damp when he got back to the laboratory about ten-thirty.

He was locking the door from inside so it couldn't blow or be washed open, if a wave somehow managed to smash against it, when he heard a footstep behind him and turned to see Lael. She was standing in the door of his small cubicle, still wearing her daytime working garment, her body braced against the doorjamb as the ship pitched and rolled, making standing without a support almost impossible.

"What are you doing here?" he demanded. "I told you to take some Nembutal and go to bed."

"I knew you'd be working here—and I was afraid." The tremor in her voice told him she was speaking the truth.

"The storm hasn't reached its height yet."

"Then I'm glad I came."

"You were lucky not to get washed overboard on the way, but since you're here, you'll have to stay. It's getting worse out there all the time."

"Are we going to founder?"

"Jake Porter's been with the *Mercy* through several storms worse than this. He says not."

Just then a small reagent bottle fell from the rack that had been holding it, crashing upon the steel floor.

"Don't move," he warned when Lael instinctively started toward it. "It's only formalin. I must not have put the bottle back securely when I took some out this afternoon."

It took him several minutes to mop up the pungent liquid. By the time he finished, the acrid reek of the chemical filled the room but they couldn't open a porthole. As he was moving back, the ship lurched suddenly and he slipped on the wet floor, bringing him up beside the door where Lael was standing with a crush that left his shoulder numb.

"Are you—hurt?" she asked.

"Just bruised, but neither of us had better try that again. If anything falls, we'll just let it lie."

The words were barely out when he heard the crash of breaking glass, as something outside struck one of the fixed portholes in the laboratory wall back of the shelf holding a row of large bottles containing reagents. Instinctively, he moved to protect her against this new danger when a stream of water pouring through the broken glass of the porthole, struck the upper part of what he saw was a bottle of sulfuric acid.

Realizing the danger, Lael had left her place in the

door before he could shout a warning, and when the
acid bottle toppled out of the wooden rack to crash on
the metal table top and spray the corrosive fluid, both
were in the path of the deadly droplets.

Throwing an arm around Lael, Grant pulled her
head down against his chest to protect her from the
chemical and fragments of glass, even as he felt the
acid strike his coverall in a dozen or more places. In
the instant before the flickering light suddenly went out,
too, leaving them in darkness, he saw wet spots upon
the paper garment Lael was wearing.

"The acid, Grant!" she cried. "It burns."

Feeling the sting of the corrosive chemical on his
own hands and on his skin through his paper coverall,
Grand realized what had to be done. Moreover, it
must be done quickly if they were not to suffer severe
burns. His prompt action, he hoped, had saved Lael's
face. Her body, particularly her back, however, had
been in the path of the acid, just as his own had been.
Unless it were washed off immediately, it would eat
through the paper and skin to the flesh beneath, causing
fearful burns that were both hard to heal and very
deforming.

"The shower—quick," he told her.

When she didn't seem to understand, he propelled
her bodily toward the door of the adjoining stateroom
and the shower that could be their salvation. She did
not resist, although they bumped painfully against the
door.

"Peel your coverall off and get into the shower," he
directed, pushing her toward the stall.

When she still seemed dazed by the suddenness of
the catastrophe, he seized her paper coverall at the
collar and, jerking downward, ripped it from her body,
pushing her under the shower at the same time and
reaching for the handle that controlled it. An instant
later he felt down along her back with his left hand and
ripped away the bra and briefs that had been her only
remaining garment.

The light came on for an instant just then, giving

him a glimpse of her lovely nude body, flinching instinctively as the cool water struck it. Then he was tearing at his own coverall and stepping out of the shorts he wore under it.

The water was spraying down, washing the acid off Lael's body as he stepped into the shower. Crowding her against the side of the stall, he fumbled for a bar of soap in the holder recessed into the wall of the shower. Rubbing the cake frantically to produce suds, he handed it to Lael and began to soap her back and shoulders. By now, however, she had realized what he was doing, and even though they were crowded in the shower, she began to soap her own body.

"Thank God the pumps are still working," he managed to say. "Is your skin burning now?"

"A little—in spots."

"Your face?"

"I don't think any of it hit there."

Busy soaping her back under the shower, Grant was vividly conscious of the lovely body pressed against his by the narrowness of the stall, the warmth of her flesh in spite of the cold shower.

"Better soap the front of your body again." His hand touched her breast in the darkness as he handed her the soap, and he felt the nipple suddenly become erect and hard beneath his touch telling him that her body, at least, was as conscious of their proximity as was his own.

"A spot back there between my shoulder blades still burns," she said.

He rubbed the spot vigorously and was fumbling to put the soap back into the rack when the ship lurched into a trough between two huge waves.

"Hold me, Grant!" Lael turned and threw herself into his arms, clinging to him in the agony of fear, as the old ship plunged deeper until they were half prone upon the now almost horizontal side of the metal shower stall.

For a long moment it seemed that the dive would never end. Then as the old vessel sluggishly righted herself, Grant guided Lael out of the narrow confines of the metal stall, against whose walls their bodies were being battered by the agonized thrashing of the ship. Falling upon the narrow bed, they clung together while the *Mercy* continued to resist the attack of the storm and finally drifted off into exhausted sleep.

The pitching and rolling of the laboring ship had lessened considerably, Grant realized when he awoke. Lael was still asleep in his arms, her breath soft and featherlike against his temple, her body warm and dry from its own heat. His left arm was partially numbed from the pressure of her body, and when he shifted it a little, she stirred against him, moving closer until her lips found his in the darkness.

"Guy! Guy!" she murmured in her sleep.

Still not fully awake, she strained against him while her mouth became a warm, fragrant cavern in which he lost all sense of time and responsibility. Obeying a basic instinct, her body moved against his in a rhythm of passion neither could—nor wanted to—deny, and he responded, no longer caring that, half asleep, she had apparently thought he was his brother.

V

Grant awakened when the lights in his stateroom and the laboratory outside its open door suddenly came on again. He was instantly aware that the motion of the ship had abated considerably and when he looked at the clock, was startled to see that it was six. Light was already beginning to break through the portholes of the laboratory and the stateroom, but Lael was gone and along with her, the garments he'd torn so hurriedly from her body last night.

In the mirror on the door of the stateroom, he examined his naked body but could see only a few red spots, mainly on the backs of his hands and between his shoulder blades, where the acid had splattered. None appeared to be deep enough to cause a permanent burn, and since the acid had been washed off Lael's body before his, he judged that she would be even less likely to suffer any permanent scar from it.

Putting on a pair of shorts and a fresh coverall, he stepped through the door into the laboratory.

The place was a shambles, bottles broken, the floor and the table tops slippery with sulfuric acid and other reagents. The larger of the two incubators had been smashed, and broken culture tubes and Petri dishes were everywhere.

All the tubes from the series he had been working on the day before had been broken, too, and the rats he'd injected with the formalin-toxin mixture were dead. The cage in which they'd been placed had fallen during the storm, however, so whether the animals had died from the toxin of *B. yungay* or from the dousing with sea water pouring through the broken porthole, he couldn't tell.

Fortunately, the rest of the animal cages had remained in place, and since they were elevated, the occupants had not suffered very much. Weeks of work had been destroyed by the ravages the storm had inflicted upon the laboratory, however, leaving him no alternative except to start over—or give up.

Unwilling to tackle the mess in the laboratory, particularly with the ship still rolling considerably more than normal, Grant went to the dining room. A few nurses were there, getting breakfast before going on duty in the wards. Seeing Angus McTavish sitting at one of the tables with a cup of coffee before him, while he smoked his pipe, Grant drew a cup of coffee for himself and picked up some toast before joining the old chief engineer.

"Get any sleep last night, Chief?" he asked.

The old Scotchman shook his head. "I was too busy nursing our one working engine to think of sleep, Doctor."

"You brought it through, that's the important thing."

"The Lord brought us through, which can only mean He must have something left for us to do."

"Is the ship damaged much?"

"One of the life rafts blew off and the water in the bilges has risen a little. Several portholes were broken, though, and some could have come in that way."

"Much of it may have been through the laboratory, after something broke the glass covering one porthole," said Grant. "The place is a shambles."

"We'll get a patch over that porthole when the sea quietens down a little more," McTavish promised. "Is any water coming in now?"

"No."

"Good. Sparks tells me the radar shows clear weather ahead."

"I'll need it to get my work started over again."

"Any progress?"

"Nothing definite, but what I've really been doing so far is feeling out the enemy. You always do that when you tackle a new microbe or virus."

McTavish nodded. "I was a pretty good boxer in my youth. It takes the first few rounds to find your opponent's weaknesses, but if you don't find it then, you're liable to end up on the canvas with the referee counting over you."

"I'm down, but I'm not counted out."

"Just like that old engine we welded together at Chimbote," said McTavish, with a chuckle.

"How did it feel around midnight to know three hundred-odd lives depended on what you and your engine could do?" Grant asked.

"About the same way you must feel, when you're keeping us from dying of that fever you discovered. Any idea how much longer you can keep it up?"

"No more than you have about your engine," said Grant. "But until I find a vaccine or toxoid for *Bacillus yungay,* we'll be better off out here on the ocean with a shipload of immune passengers to draw blood from for our protection than if we made port and they were taken off, leaving us without any reservoir of immunity."

"When will we be due another shot?"

"Probably two weeks from the last one. Several more of the Indians are well enough now to supply immune plasma and I don't want anybody else to have the close shave Tonio Marelia had."

"I guess we all know now how Damocles felt with the sword hanging over his head." McTavish knocked out his pipe and put it in his pocket. "Take care of yourself, Doctor. You're the only thing that's holding up this particular sword."

Shirley came in as the engineer was leaving. She looked a bit hollow-eyed but managed to smile when she sat down across from Grant with her own coffee and toast.

"I just came from the radio room," she said. "Jake says we're going into clear weather ahead."

"What are you doing up so early? I thought you were going to celebrate the storm with a binge."

"No such luck. My drinking companion got the shakes, so I put him to bed and dictated a running account of the storm." She smiled crookedly. "I don't mind admitting my voice was quaking a little about the time the old girl took that nose dive around eleven. Were you still awake?"

"Yes. Something cracked the porthole and let a lot of water into the lab about then."

"Any damage?"

"The place is a mess."

"Wish I'd known about it. I could have put it in the account I just radioed to INS."

"Was that what you were doing in the radio room this early?"

"Sure. By nightfall the American people will know what the *Mercy* and its personnel have been going through." She gave him a quick appraising glance. "You don't seem so broken up about your laboratory, though. Why?"

He shrugged. "When you've been knocked down as many times as I have in the past month or six weeks, you become accustomed to it."

"Maybe having a beautiful young assistant helps, too?"

Grant laughed. "Fishing again?"

"Not this time. I really owe you a lot, Grant, and, like I once said, Lael's the sort of girl you ought to marry. Don't let her get away. I'd hate to see you strike out twice in a row."

VI

On the way back to the laboratory, Grant stopped at the drug room. Taking a bottle down from the shelf, he poured some tablets into his hand and wrapped them in a piece of tissue. He was working in the laboratory about an hour later when the door opened and Lael came in.

"Good morning," she said, looking around. "The storm really did a job in here."

"Are you all right? No acid burns?"

"I found a few red spots when I was dressing and put some cream on them. Nothing deep, but I would have been scarred for life if you hadn't stripped me and put me under the shower."

"I had to fortify myself with some breakfast before I tackled the job of cleaning up here." Grant changed the subject firmly. "And even now I shudder at the idea."

"Don't touch any of the culture tubes or Petri dishes," she said quickly. "A small cut on your finger and you could die like Leona Danvers did."

"It's still got to be done."

"Let me do it then. I'm already immune."

"I'll find you some tough rubber gloves somewhere so you won't be running much risk of contamination," he said. "I don't like your doing it, but I don't know any other way to get all the broken stuff cleaned out so we can start new cultures."

"Jack Smithson was in the dining room just now," she said. "He said he came to my stateroom at the height of the storm last night to see if I was okay, but didn't find me there."

"Did he suspect——?"

"I told him I was with you in the lab, trying to protect the equipment and the cultures."

"Do you think he believed you?"

"I really don't care. After all, I *am* a grown woman with no obligations to anything but Guy's memory —and to you for saving my life when I developed Yungay fever. I suppose it sounds strange but I can't seem to separate the two of you in my mind—or want to."

"I still blame myself for what happened last night."

"Don't, Grant." She smiled. "As I remember, you didn't meet any resistance."

"For God's sake!"

"Face it. We're normal people and that *was* an unusual situation."

"You can say that again."

"So let's put it down to proximity, being scared— a lot of things all happening at once—and think no more about it."

"That may be a little difficult, but I'll give it the old try. Incidentally," he added, removing from his pocket the tablets he'd taken from the drug room and handing them to her, "you'd better take these."

She looked at the small tablets in the tissue and then back to him. "Is this some kind of a birth control pill?"

"Diethylstilbestrol—popularly known as the morning after pill; it's about as near a hundred per cent protection as you can get." He turned toward his stateroom. "I'll get you a cup of water."

"I'd rather not take it, Grant."

He turned quickly, staring at her in disbelief. "Why?"

"Guy wanted us to have a child but he must have been sterile. He examined his semen under the microscope once and found no spermatozoa, but I'm sure he'd approve of an ovum of mine being fertilized by one of yours."

"We could be on the *Mercy* for months yet," he

protested. "Everybody would know, in fact, Shirley suspects already——"

"Nothing had happened until last night, but it has now—and I'm glad." She tossed the tablets into the sink. "You tried to protect my reputation, Grant, so your knightly duty is done."

"That doesn't help my conscience," he admitted wryly. "And besides, how could you be sure I'm not sterile—like Guy?"

"Shirley told one of the nurses she had an abortion right after you left for Africa six months or so ago."

"That could have been another man's child."

"She said it was yours—and she ought to know."

He shook his head slowly. "My father used to say the hands that tie the apron strings rule the world, but I never knew exactly how right he was—until now."

"If I do have a baby I can still say it's Guy's," she assured him. "I'm going back to the Callejón de Huaylas when I leave the ship, so nobody need know any different."

"Except you and me." He studied her for a long moment, but she underwent the scrutiny with a smile which, when he thought of it later, reminded him of nothing so much as the inscrutable smile of the Mona Lisa.

"Tell me one thing," he said at last. "When you came into the laboratory last night during the storm, you expected what *did* happen to happen, didn't you?"

"Yes. But not quite the way it did."

"What does that mean?"

"With that conscience of yours, I thought I might have to convince you. But when that porthole glass broke, the whole thing was settled."

"I'll never understand women," he admitted. "Not even if I live as long as Methuselah."

"It's really very simple, Grant. Guy's child or yours would have many of the same inherited genes. I wasn't being untrue to Guy in coming here last night—intending to seduce you. I was only trying to give Guy something he wanted badly, the final proof, you might say, of how much I loved him."

"I loved him, too. Did I betray him?"

"Of course not. Some people might not see it that way—"

"Nobody else would *ever* see it that way."

"Nevertheless we both loved Guy enough to want to do something for him he wasn't able to do for himself." Her smile was like the sun breaking through a cloud. "And he would be the last one to condemn us for enjoying it. Now let's get busy and clean up this mess so we can go back to work."

"You forgot one thing," he said with a wry smile. "It's the man who's supposed to seduce the woman. So what does that make me?"

"A very satisfactory lover," she told him. "That should satisfy your pride."

VII

By midafternoon, the *Mercy* was headed north toward the equator west of the Galápagos Islands in seas that grew calmer by the hour. Shortly after noon, the garbage chutes were emptied, while most of the complement and many of the recovering patients watched from the afterdeck to see whether the hated white forms of the killer sharks would rise to engulf it. The garbage only bobbed on the broad V of the ship's wake until it was out of sight, however, and as the *Mercy* moved on, a ragged cheer rose from the watchers.

At midafternoon, Grant made an inspection tour with Jack Smithson, Captain Pendarvis, and Angus McTavish in order to assay the condition of both complement and patients. The glass had been smashed in a few portholes, a life raft lost, and a section of rail torn away, but none of that was serious; it could be repaired in a few days when they reached a calmer area. The pumps were already lowering the water in the bilges to its normal level for the old hull that was far from watertight, so they had no need to worry on that score. And judged by the way the patched-up engine had performed last night, it could keep on going until they ran out of fuel.

One of the native patients had suffered a broken arm when he was tossed out of his pipe berth by the fury of the storm, and several others were enough washed out from seasickness to require intravenous fluids. But all were improving rapidly, and the knowledge that they had lost the Nemesis that had been following them made the *Mercy* an almost happy ship.

The inspection tour finished, Grant returned to the laboratory, where Lael was still cleaning up the damage from the storm. He was depressed by the thought of having to start over in his attempts to produce a toxoid from the toxin of *B. yungay* but could think of no other route by which to approach the problem of producing an active immunity to the plague from prehistory in the endangered personnel of the *Mercy*.

Lael had a smudge on her nose and her hair was tied up in a kerchief, giving her a gamin look that made it even more difficult to remember she was his brother's widow, even though last night she'd been a naked wanton in his arms. To keep the memory out of his mind, he got busy mopping up the metal floor with a strong alkaline cleaner to neutralize whatever remained of the acid from the broken bottles. Each time he saw her pass, however, slender and lovely in the heavy paper coverall, he was all too conscious of the body beneath.

It was almost five o'clock and she was putting the last of the broken glassware in a bucket to be emptied over the rail when she called to him from the other side of the lab.

"Come here, please, Grant! I've found something interesting."

At the table where she was working, she pointed to the bottom half of a Petri dish she had just placed upon it. The culture of *B. yungay* growing upon the chocolate agar had apparently been doused with sea water last night, for crystals of salt had formed across the surface of the agar and inside the rim of the shallow glass plate. Several colonies on the surface of the agar were entirely covered with the salt crystals, but near the center of the dish, one colony appeared to have broken through, as the culture had kept on growing in the warm atmosphere outside the incubator. Seeing it, Grant felt a sudden sense of excitement begin to rise within him.

"Get me a fresh Petri dish from the small incubator, please," he said.

Reaching into the instrument rack, he took up the magnifying glass they used in transferring very small colonies to fresh culture media. Switching on a bright light over the table, he placed the intact dish she brought and the half dish with the salt crystals side by side.

"The colonies are a different color!" Lael exclaimed. "The one the sea water almost destroyed is a bright orange."

"Have you ever seen an orange-colored colony of *B. yungay?*"

"No. It's always brown." She looked up suddenly, her eyes bright with interest. "Could this be a mutation?"

"It's possible. Are those fresh tubes and plates of chocolate agar ready yet?"

"I took them from the autoclave over an hour ago, the agar should be cooled and solid by now. Are you going to reculture the organism?"

"Right away. Then I want to examine it under the microscope."

"But if it's a mutation, how could it have happened when the culture itself was almost destroyed by sea water?"

"We'll worry about that later."

A half hour later, Lael carefully placed in the small incubator that was still working a rack of culture tubes and Petri dishes, each inoculated from the orange-colored colony. Meanwhile Grant was using the oil-immersion lens of the microscope to study a stained slide of the strange orange-colored culture.

At first glance, it seemed to be just another preparation of *Bacillus yungay,* but as he examined the organisms more closely, subtle differences could be seen. The rods of the new growth were a little thicker and somewhat shorter than the true *B. yungay.* The staining was deeper, too, as if the mutation—for that was what it now appeared to be—possessed even more growth energy than its parent, if that were possible. Moreover, the bacteria in the smear seemed to have lost the tendency to expand into bulbous ends and form spores.

"Take a look," he told Lael, sliding off the stool in front of the microscope.

While she was examining the slide, Grant took a sterile pipette and dropped about half a cubic centimeter of sterile water on what remained of the orange culture, stirring it with the tip of the pipette until the resulting suspension was orange-tinted.

"What did you see?" he asked when Lael finally looked up from the microscope.

"It's a gram-negative rod, like the other, but it's different, too."

"How?"

"I didn't see any spores for one thing. Did you?"

"No. But it's a young culture."

"And the rods look fatter, maybe not quite as long either."

"You're a good observer," he told her.

"What is it? What happened?"

"Get me a rat. I'll explain while I find a sterile syringe.

"If this is what I think it is," he said as he was drawing part of the orange suspension into a small syringe, "something has knocked a gene or so out of the BNA chain characteristic of *B. yungay,* leaving an offspring with different characteristics."

"Then it is a real mutation?"

"I think so, but I won't be sure until morning."

Holding the wriggling white rat in his left hand, he

inserted the needle at the end of the syringe through its abdominal wall and into the peritoneal cavity. After injecting some of the new organism into the small furry body, he replaced it in the metal cage from which she had taken it and put the syringe into a glass dish containing bichloride of mercury, a powerful disinfectant.

"If the rat lives," he added, "it means something last night pulled the teeth of our old microscopic enemy."

"And then?"

"If the mutation doesn't produce Yungay toxin, it might possibly act as an antigen and stimulate the body to produce antitoxin."

"The vaccine you've been looking for!" Her eyes were shining. "Oh, Grant, wouldn't it be wonderful?"

"Right now it would be a gift from the gods. And with both of us praying for it, that just might happen."

VIII

Grant was awake at dawn and, stepping through the door into the laboratory, went first to the animal cages. The rat he'd injected with the orange-colored mutation was frisking about in the cage, apparently none the worse for the injection. When he opened the small incubator, he could see bright orange colonies of the new strain already growing on the dark brown surface of the agar, as well as on the slanting surface of the medium inside the culture tubes.

He fed the animals and was singing in the shower when he heard Lael's cry of joy in the laboratory outside. Turning off the water, he wrapped a towel around his middle and looked through the door to see her standing beside the animal cages, looking at the busy rat as if she couldn't believe the evidence of her own eyes.

"It's alive, Grant! The mutation didn't kill it!" she cried. "I looked in the incubator, too, and the new organism is growing all over the place."

"Have you had breakfast?"

"No. I couldn't eat before I came to see what happened."

"Wait till I pull on a coverall and we'll go together."

"Okay. I'll just stand here and look at the rat. It's the most beautiful thing I've ever seen."

Right now, you're the most beautiful thing I've ever seen, was Grant's thought, but he put it from him.

Jack Smithson came into the dining room as they were putting down their trays. "What are you two looking so happy about?" he asked.

"Come join us and we'll tell you," said Grant.

"Grant's found the mutation he's been looking for," said Lael when the bearded chief physician joined them with his own tray.

"At least it's breeding true on reculture," Grant added. "And a rat I injected last night with the organism is alive this morning."

"When did all this happen?"

"Sometime after the porthole broke in the lab night before last," said Grant. "One of the Petri dishes in the incubator that was smashed got doused with sea water, and yesterday afternoon Lael found a bright orange colony growing right through the salt. Its microscopic characteristics are slightly different from *B. yungay* and it doesn't seem to form spores."

"Which proves nothing yet."

"Oh, Jack! Don't be such a killjoy!" Lael cried. "At least we know the new bug doesn't produce Yungay toxin."

"Or any toxin that's lethal," Grant added.

"Which means it may not act as an antigen—and is worthless," Smithson reminded them.

"At least we're further toward an answer to Yungay fever than we've ever been before," said Lael.

"What do you think happened?" Smithson asked.

"I've got a hunch the mutagen that caused the change may have been bromouracil," said Grant. "I was trying to get some from Atlanta before we left Chimbote but it didn't arrive in time. Sea water contains a lot of bromide compounds, though, so it's logical that one of them should be bromouracil—which is one of the best mutating agents I know of."

"I'd still hate to see the complement and crew develop false hopes and then be knocked down again," said Smithson. "We've had too much of that already."

"So far you, Lael, and myself are the only ones who know there's even the possibility of a vaccine. I think we should keep it a secret between us and meanwhile everyone should have an injection of immune plasma right away."

"I'm for that," said Smithson. "Several of the patients are in good shape now, so we ought to be able to get enough plasma without any difficulty—especially if we reinject the cells. The centrifuge wasn't damaged, was it?"

"No," said Grant. "I ran a check on it yesterday while I was cleaning up."

"There'll be some squawking from the patients," said the older doctor. "Manoel Allanza is a devil; he's been telling everybody we're vampires and need blood to stay alive."

"He's almost right. Immunizing everybody again will give me about two weeks to test the mutation. If it stimulates the production of immunity, we won't need any more blood from the patients."

"When you tell the world you have a vaccine that lasts, surely they'll let us land somewhere to protect themselves?" Lael added.

"No doubt about it. The radio newssheet was full of new attacks of Yungay fever every day until we got into the storm, so there'll be plenty of need for the vaccine—if we have one."

"Jake just posted another bulletin," said Jack Smithson. "Something like panic is spreading over the world even faster than Yungay fever is. When Shirley Ross sends the message announcing your vaccine, a lot of stations will pick it up and the news service she represents will make it public all over the world. It will be the news beat of the century."

IX

The third series of immune plasma injections, and with them the assurance that the complement and crew were reasonably safe from Yungay fever for another two weeks, if not longer, buoyed their spirits considerably. It also stirred even more resentment among the natives, confirming—in their eyes at least—Manoel Allanza's charges of vampirism. As the ship plowed on in ever quieter seas, music and some laughter was heard again in the lounge, though not belowdecks, but the meager liquor supply still dampened somewhat the capacity of the complement to enjoy themselves.

With few patients still sick enough to need nursing care, the work load on the professional staff had lightened markedly. Afternoons always brought a gathering on the afterdeck, some to play cards, others to enjoy deck tennis or simply sunning. Tonio Marelia, completely recovered now and safe from any further attack, shot skeet with Mark Post off the afterdeck. Of the group, Shirley was the most restless, for nothing was happening to enliven her reports by radio to her employers.

Grant was working day and night now, injecting laboratory animals with increasing amounts of the culture suspension of the new *B. yungay* mutation, trying as rapidly as possible, with the rather primitive facilities at his disposal, to determine whether antitoxin was being produced. He came on deck for a breath of fresh air several days after the discovery of the mutation to find Shirley talking to Homer Ferguson.

Manoel Allanza was riding on the big Negro's shoulders, and the two of them made a startling sight. While Homer talked to Shirley, Grant could see Manoel's dark eyes studying the trap that threw the skeet targets high up in the air above the ship's wake and the double-barreled shotgun Tonio and Mark Post were using to shoot the clay targets down.

"Who's winning?" he asked Tonio.

"Mark, at the moment; I'm still off my game from that bout of fever. Give me another day or two and I'll beat him."

When Grant appeared, Shirley broke off talking to Homer, who started back to the bow with Manoel still perched upon his shoulders. She came over to where Grant was standing and leaned against the rail beside him.

"A rumor's going around that you've discovered something," she said. "Not holding out on me, are you?"

"If I find anything worth letting the rest of the world know, you'll be the first I'll tell."

"Promise?"

"Of course."

"How about giving me a hint?"

He shoot his head. "I've thought I had something and failed too many times to go off half-cocked. Where did you hear the rumor?"

"From Jack Smithson. By the way, where's your beautiful assistant?"

"In the lab—working."

"You two spend a lot of time together in there."

"She's very capable."

"And also attractive?"

Grant laughed. "Mirror, mirror on the wall—"

"Oh, shut up! All I want is to get off this ship. At first it was exciting, but nothing happens any more."

"That could be our salvation."

"Stop being so infernally right! It isn't human."

"Not many people aboard this ship agree with you about my being right, either. Most of them resent me."

"Then they're damn fools."

"What were you talking to Homer about?" he asked.

She shrugged. "Just human interest questions. I'm still trying to build a story around Manoel Allanza but can't seem to get a good lead. Homer claims he's very intelligent but all I can see in him is hate." She shivered. "I guess he's given me the heebie-jeebies."

"Maybe I'd be sour on the world, too, if I could

only get around by riding on someone's shoulders or on a little cart with casters for wheels, while I begged for a living." Grant looked at his watch. "I've been out here too long. Lael and I have to make some injections before dinner."

"Go back to your old rats then," said Shirley crossly. "And don't kill too many of them; before this thing is over, we may be eating 'em to stay alive."

X

Some five days after the discovery of the mutation, Grant was working in the laboratory late one afternoon, preparing to make the first injection of the *B. yungay* mutation into his own body. Three successive injections into two series of animals had caused no symptoms, beyond some swelling and local irritation for about twenty-four hours at the injection site, with slight perceptible warmth over the area of swelling. Since the reaction in the animal tissues was about the same he'd experienced after the standard cholera and yellow fever vaccine injections he'd taken before going to Africa the last time, he had every reason to believe a human could tolerate the mutation as well as the animals had done.

As yet he had no evidence that the immunizing injections were actually producing protection against the deadly microbe that produced Yungay fever. Proof of that could only come with the final test, injection of the virulent organism itself into the animals, but several more days were necessary before the immunity he sought could be expected to develop.

Pulling up the sleeve of his paper coverall to bare the surface over the deltoid muscle just below his shoulder, he set the needle against his skin and pushed it about an inch and a half into the muscle itself beneath it. Then with his thumb over the plunger, he injected a half cubic centimeter of the orange-colored culture.

The injection finished, he dropped the disposable plastic syringe into a waste container and strapped a small dressing over the puncture site. As he was pulling down the sleeve of his coverall, footsteps sounded behind him and he whirled to see Homer Ferguson standing in the middle of the laboratory.

"What the hell are you doing here?" he demanded angrily.

"I knocked but nobody answered, so I came in to see if you were here."

"I certainly didn't hear you."

"Occupied as you were, I can understand that. Mind telling me why a simple hypodermic injection, even into your own arm, would require such intense concentration?"

"Nobody likes to feel the pain of a needle prick."

"This would seem to be more than just a needle prick—unless you've taken up drugs."

"Go to hell!" said Grant, and Homer grinned.

"So I'll put two and two together. A rumor's been going around that you're on the verge of a discovery and I'll lay you odds this is part of it. Am I right?"

Grant studied the big man for a moment, then came to a decision. "How well can you keep a secret?"

"Better than it's being kept right now."

"The day after the laboratory was wrecked by the storm, Miss Valdez discovered a new organism growing in one of the culture plates that had been flooded with sea water. It closely resembles the bacillus that causes Yungay fever, except that its teeth appear to have been pulled by the action of something in the water."

"How do you know that?"

Grant took down a small wire cage and lifted the white rat that had been given the first injection of the mutation out by its tail. "About a week ago, this little fellow received a half cc. of the same culture you saw me inject into my arm. If the new organism—it's called a mutation—had possessed even a fraction of *B. yungay's* virulence, the rat would have been dead the next day, but it's had two larger injections at two-day intervals since—as have a dozen others—without any ill effects."

"Does that mean you're waiting now to see whether the mutation—as you call it—will produce immunity in the human body?"

"Exactly."

"Why try it on yourself before you make the final test with rats?"

"I can't test the animals for virulence for another two days at least. Their antibody level would hardly be high enough before then to make it a valid test of immunity. Meanwhile, having had two injections by then I'll be at least two days ahead toward finding out whether or not we've got a vaccine against Yungay fever that works."

"You're a brave man, Dr. Reed." Homer started rolling up his own sleeve. "But two human subjects will be more convincing than one, whatever happens."

"I can't argue with that, but I didn't ask for volunteers."

Homer shrugged. "A friend of mine, who was a student at Tulane Med School, once told me no doctor should draw conclusions from a series of one case. Get the stuff ready, friend, and stop wasting time on semantics."

"One thing I don't quite understand," said Homer after Grant had made the injection. "You and I have each had three shots of immune plasma already. How do you know we aren't protected anyway against an injection of the real thing?"

"The dose of immune plasma we've had would keep us from getting Yungay fever through the ordinary routes of transmission, but I'm sure they wouldn't protect us from a living culture of *B. yungay*," said Grant. "Miss Danvers, the hospital technician, proved that when she developed an explosive case of Yungay fever after a few living organisms were injected accidentally through a wound in her finger."

"That makes sense. When do I get another one?"

"The day after tomorrow, about this same time. I'll

send Miss Valdez to her quarters about five, so no one will know you're part of the experiment. Thank you, Homer. If both of us survive the ultimate test, it will be conclusive evidence that we've licked Yungay fever."

"You don't have to thank me, Doctor. If you hadn't recognized the condition of Conchita and Manoel in time, they'd both have died, right?"

"No doubt about Conchita. Manoel might have made it on his own. He's ornery enough."

"Just one more thing. All told, there are about a hundred and fifty patients aboard, in various stages of recovery, not including myself. What's going to happen to us?"

"If the mutation should turn out to be effective as a vaccine, I'll notify the Center for Disease Control and the World Health Organization. They'll probably land a helicopter on the upper deck from an air force base at Panama and take cultures of the new organism back to the States for testing. They're already working on *B. yungay* in Atlanta and several other places, trying to discover a way of controlling it."

"How long could that take?"

"A month at least—for the kind of tests the health authorities would insist on making. You realize of course that I've been working with very primitive conditions aboard the *Mercy*."

"The irony of the whole thing is that you've done what none of the fancy labs have yet been able to do."

"It's even more ironical that we were floating in the middle of the one thing I needed to bring out the mutant—sea water."

"Why wouldn't the authorities let us dock somewhere, once you give them the mutation?" Homer asked.

"They probably will when they're sure there's an effective vaccine. But like I said, that would take several weeks at least."

Homer shook his head slowly. "Keeping all these people cooped up on a small ship all that time wouldn't be right, Doctor. They didn't mind it when they were sick or even during the storm, but now that most of 'em are well, something's got to give."

XI

Four days after Grant had made the first injection of the mutation into his own tissues and those of Homer Ferguson, he was ready to make the final tests on a half dozen laboratory animals, each of which had been given three injections of the mutant. He knew he was pushing his luck in making the injections so close together. Two weeks apart was the usual period for the doses of an ordinary vaccine like typhoid, but signs of discontent were growing daily among the now largely recovered native population of the floating hospital.

Even without Homer's warning, Grant recognized that the sooner he was able to announce to the world the achievement of a preventive measure against Yungay fever and the ship was allowed to proceed to a port to disembark its passengers, the better off everyone—and the world—would be. Meanwhile, the *Mercy* was plodding along through quiet seas and the heat of the equator west of the Galápagos Islands.

"I'm scared, Grant," Lael said as she lifted the first of the white rats from its cage by its tail for the final test injection of a pure culture of *B. yungay*. "Suppose this fellow's dead in the morning?"

"Then we'll just have to start over."

"From the beginning?"

"Maybe not quite that far back; the dose of living organism we're going to inject into these animals would be fatal to a human being without any protection, so we're asking a lot of the rat's antibody level this early in the game. If these animals die, I'll autopsy them in the morning and we'll do bacterial counts on the body fluids. If the count is notably low, it could mean the animals developed a significant degree of immunity, but the test dose of *B. yungay* was too high. Or the period between immunization and testing could have been too short."

"Then there would still be hope of developing a vaccine?"

"Some, though an apparent failure at this time would be very disappointing. That's why I've insisted on keeping our work secret."

"All sorts of rumors have been flying around. Several people have tried to pry some information out of me—but without success."

"I'm sure of that. Only you, me, Jack Smithson, and Homer—"

"Homer Ferguson! Why him?"

"He came to the lab the afternoon I was giving myself the first injection of the mutation culture and figured out part of what was happening. I had to tell him then and he volunteered as a subject for the experiment."

"When will you make the final test?" An odd intentness in her voice made him glance up from the rat he was injecting, but she was looking away and he couldn't see her eyes to measure the degree of her concern.

"We get our third injection of the mutation this afternoon," Grant said. "And four days from now—"

"I'm afraid, Grant! Isn't there some other way to test the immunity except by taking a chance on losing your own life?"

"If these animals live, there should be no danger," he assured her.

"But if they don't—"

"Then neither Homer nor I should take the risk."

"When's the big test, Doctor?" Homer asked as he rolled down his sleeve after the third immunizing dose of the mutation.

"Four days from now—unless these animals die." Grant nodded toward where the rats he'd injected were moving about, eating the food Lael had put into the cages and apparently none the worse for the relatively massive dose of *B. yungay* they had received that day.

"If they do, we'll keep our mouths shut, while Miss Valdez and I go on working."

"Everybody aboard is pretty jittery, and right now any bad news would just shake them up even more. At that though," Homer added on a thoughtful note, "I guess everybody in the complement and crew— including me—are better off here, where we can get protective injections, than we'd be out in the world with the plague raging. The radio news these days is full of it."

"I can't remember any disease spreading so rapidly since the 1918 influenza epidemic," Grant agreed.

"Doesn't it sometimes bug you to have the fate of maybe the whole world resting on your shoulders?"

"I'd be a frail Atlas indeed to carry the weight of the world, Homer, so I just limit my world to this laboratory. By the way, have you noticed any side effects from the injections?"

"Nothing except a sore arm—and I've had worse from a tetanus shot."

"Pray God that's all we will have," said Grant soberly. "There's no time left to wait for any long-range ill effects of the mutation on humans to become evident, so we'll just have to take a chance at that."

"I've gambled all my life, Dr. Reed, but compared to the gambles you've been taking in here every day, I'm just a piker. See you in four days—I hope."

XII

When twenty-four hours passed and the injected rats were still apparently healthy, in spite of having received a dose of a *B. yungay* that would have been fatal to a human being, Grant dared to believe he had really found the answer to controlling the scourge Guy and Lael had loosed upon an unprotected world. Only the final test remained upon human subjects—with but two available, himself and Homer Ferguson.

"When are you going to give Homer the test injection?" Lael asked as she was preparing to leave the laboratory late on the afternoon of the fourth day following the last injection of the mutation culture he'd given Homer and himself.

"He's due here at five-thirty. I'm going to prepare the two injections—"

"Two?" She turned abruptly to face him, her eyes wide with concern. "Surely you can't risk—"

"I couldn't ask Homer to be a human guinea pig for this experiment, Lael—and take such a risk alone."

"But if it fails, what's going to happen to all these people on the ship?"

"The center in Atlanta has microbiologists who are just as capable as I am when it comes to developing new vaccines. They'd find one eventually."

"You haven't even thought about what's going to happen to me, have you?" The concern in her voice had been replaced by a note of anger.

"You've already made plans—"

"Oh, why do you always have to be so infernally right?" Turning on her heel, she left the laboratory, slamming the door behind her and leaving Grant to remember that only a few days earlier, Shirley had said the very same thing.

"I guess some sort of speech would be appropriate for an occasion like this, Doc," said Homer when he arrived a few minutes later. "The only one I can think of is the salute of the gladiators. I seem to recall that it went something like '*Morituri te salutamus.*'"

"Stop being a philosopher and let's get this damned agony over with."

The injections were quickly made and Grant dropped the plastic syringes into bichloride solution.

"How soon will we know the verdict?" Homer asked.

"If you're not delirious—or dead—by daylight, you'll know the vaccine works."

Lael wasn't in the dining room when Grant went there for an early dinner, and since he didn't feel much like socializing, he ate hurriedly and went to his room. His arm was a little painful where the puncture wound of the injection showed on the skin below the shoulder and he felt a slight headache, so he took a couple of aspirins, peeled off his clothing, and went to bed early. The course the *Mercy* was following had brought it to a point only a little south of the equator, so he'd been sleeping nude for the past week because of the heat in the small stateroom off the laboratory.

The moon had risen and was shining faintly through the porthole over Grant's bed when he was awakened by a hand upon his forehead. Moving quickly, his fingers closed around a slender wrist, and a voice that he recognized as Lael's cried out softly from the pain of the sudden pressure.

"Lael!" He released her wrist and sat up. "What in the—?"

"I had a nightmare. In my dream I came into the lab and found the rats all dead—and when I looked into your room, you were dead, too." She sat down suddenly on the narrow bed, burying her face against his bare shoulder. When he put an arm about her reassuringly, he was disturbingly conscious that she was wearing only a sheer silk nightgown.

"I'm very much alive," he told her. "What time is it?"

"About four o'clock. Oh, Grant! It was terrible, seeing you there—after I'd been so nasty to you in the lab yesterday afternoon."

"I'm all right, Lael." He took her hand and put it to his forehead. "See? No fever at all. If our prehistoric enemy was going to bother me, I would have been delirious now. Everything's going to be all right."

"Oh, darling!" She caught her breath quickly. "What will you think of me?"

"I already think you're sweet and quite the loveliest thing I've ever known." Still holding her hand, he placed it against his lips and kissed it. "Now, you'd better go back to your cabin before anything else happens."

"But I don't want to go." She stood up suddenly,

in the faint glow of the moonlight, the white gown giving her almost the appearance of a wraith. Then she bent with a quick movement, followed by the whisper of silk falling to the floor at her feet, and he saw that she was far from ephemeral. Instead she was a lovely nude statue for an instant, until she moved to lie beside him on the narrow bed. His arms went around her then and his mouth found the warm, fragrant cavern of her own.

Since neither he nor Homer Ferguson had suffered any ill effects from the injection of a virulent culture of *B. yungay* by late afternoon, Grant called a meeting of the staff and crew for that evening, planning to announce the success of his venture and allow Shirley to make the broadcast of the news the following morning. Still at work about five o'clock, transferring cultures of the mutation so there would be plenty of it to start immunizing the complement and crew, he was startled when the ship's loudspeaker system suddenly exploded into speech.

"Dr. Reed and Dr. Smithson to the bridge!" The voice was that of Captain Pendarvis and the tone was hard and angry.

As Grant came out of the laboratory and started up to the bridge, he was startled to find the top deck crowded with patients, most of them wearing hospital pajamas. Nobody seemed to be in charge, however, and the sound of the Quechua dialect was deafening as all of them appeared to be talking at once.

No one barred his progress to the bridge until he came to the door, before which one of the natives he remembered seeing several times with Homer and Manoel Allanza stood holding the shotgun Tonio and Mark Post had been using to shoot skeet off the afterdeck. The guard stepped aside when he recognized Grant and opened the door, to reveal a tense scene inside.

Homer Ferguson was standing with his back to the

opposite wall, while Manoel rode upon his shoulders. The big Negro was holding a pistol in his hand.

"Come in, Dr. Reed," he said. "As you see, the patients have taken over the ship."

Jack Smithson arrived just then and was also ushered into the enclosed area of the bridge, but when Shirley tried to follow him, she was stopped by the guard.

"What the hell does this mean?" Smithson demanded.

"I was just telling Dr. Reed that the patients have taken over the ship, Dr. Smithson," said Homer pleasantly.

"You're not a patient."

"I represent Manoel here, and he speaks for the patients aboard the ship."

"Damn it!" Captain Pendarvis spluttered. "This is mutiny."

"Perhaps you're right, Captain; I'm not a sea lawyer," Homer agreed. "But you have my word that there's no reason to be disturbed."

Pendarvis wheeled upon Grant. "You called a meeting for tonight, Doctor," he snapped. "Was this what you planned to announce?"

"I can assure you that Dr. Reed had no part in planning what you call a mutiny, Captain," Homer interposed. "If you'll all just calm down and listen, I'm sure we can arrive at a reasonable solution to the problem that will be good for us all."

"What problem?" Jack Smithson demanded. "All your people are well, many because of treatment given by me and my staff. Is this the way you thank us, Ferguson?"

"I regret very much that such drastic steps had to be taken, Dr. Smithson. The patients *are* grateful, but we have no wish to stay shut up on this ship any longer than we have to."

"You know I've asked permission to enter every port in the area and off-load the sick," the captain protested indignantly. "No country will receive us."

"That's exactly why we've taken control," said Homer. "And incidentally, why you and the rest of the complement and crew should co-operate with us."

"In a mutiny? You're mad."

"On the contrary." Homer Ferguson was still patient. "We've been planning this move for some time, but until today I couldn't be sure I would be immune from Yungay fever, so it would be safe for me to leave the ship."

"How can you be more immune than the rest of us, Ferguson?" Jack Smithson demanded. "You had the same injection of blood plasma we did."

"Dr. Reed can answer your question."

"Late yesterday afternoon I injected a half cubic centimeter dose of pure *Bacillus yungay* culture into Homer's arm and my own," Grant explained. "It was enough to kill anyone else on this ship, but as you see, we have suffered no ill effects because I had taken the precaution of actively immunizing us both beforehand."

"Then the mutation you discovered is really an effective vaccine?'

"No doubt about it—unless some delayed side effects appear. And there have been none in the laboratory animals."

"Thank God!"

"Obviously the situation has changed radically, Dr. Smithson, not only for the world but for the ship," Homer pointed out. "However, Dr. Reed must first convince world health authorities that he really has succeeded before the ship can dock and unfortunately that will take some time."

"A commission will have to be appointed, tests run, and the usual routines followed," Smithson agreed. "It could take weeks."

"Meanwhile you must all remain aboard the ship," said Captain Pendarvis. "We have no choice."

"Maybe *you* have no choice, Captain," said Homer, "but we who now control the ship do."

"Over my protests," said Pendarvis.

"Granted," said Homer. "We accept the fact that

the officers of the *Mercy* cannot take her into any port forbidden to them without being subject to having charges brought against them. Or even risking an attack upon the vessel. But mutineers can force you to send the *Mercy* wherever they wish."

"This is outrageous! I—" Captain Pendarvis protested but Grant spoke before he could finish his tirade.

"Just where did you have in mind taking the ship, Homer?"

"Where else but the nearest land? The Galápagos Islands."

"They're controlled by the Ecuadorian Government, and Ecuador has refused to let the *Mercy* dock."

"The islands are sparsely populated and have several well-protected deep water harbors, Doctor. If the authorities in Guayaquil and Quito don't know we're headed that way, they won't be able to stop us before we touch land. Then it will be too late to keep anyone who wishes from going ashore."

"You've evidently devoted a great deal of thought to this plan," Grant conceded.

"It was Manoel's idea. I merely put it into English for him."

"What exactly *is* your plan?" First Officer Olsson asked.

"Merely to sail this ship to a place where we can disembark," said Homer. "What you and the hospital complement do after that is your own affair."

"That sounds reasonable. After all, you do have the weapons."

"I hope we don't have to use them, Mr. Olsson," Homer said pointedly. "But don't think we won't if we have to."

"How will you prevent Captain Pendarvis from notifying port authorities in Ecuador by radio?" Grant asked.

"If you'll look into the radio room, you'll see that Mr. Porter is already under guard, Doctor. One of the recovered patients has some knowledge of electronics and is even now removing a transformer from the sending apparatus. It will be returned to Mr. Porter when we leave the ship in the Galápagos, but until then his equipment can only receive, not send. Miss Ross will no doubt be disappointed that she can't immediately broadcast the news of your discovery, but that, too, will have to wait."

"One more thing," said Jack Smithson. "It's been over a week since the complement and crew had an injection of immune plasma. Will the patients agree to furnish enough to protect us until you leave the ship?"

Homer spoke briefly to Manoel Allanza in Quechua. Even though none of the others on the bridge could understand the answer, however, there was no doubting its nature from the flood of invective the questions brought forth.

"He says no more blood," Homer reported. "But then, Dr. Reed's new vaccine works swiftly, as I can testify, so the rest of you will have no need to worry."

"Pray God you're right, or our deaths may be on your conscience." Smithson turned to Captain Pendarvis. "As medical director of the *Mercy*, I vote to accept their terms—as gracefully as we can."

"And I," said Grant.

Pendarvis chewed his mustache for a moment. "In fifty years at sea, I've never had a mutiny aboard, and I don't propose to connive in one now," he said at last. "Mr. Olsson, you'll take charge of the ship."

"Aye, aye, sir," said the first officer briskly.

BOOK FIVE

The GALAPÁGOS

I

FROM THE DECK of the *Mercy*, the members of the complement and crew watched the motor-driven lifeboat return from its final trip ashore, carrying the last of the patients. Those already on land were racing up and down the sandy beach, or frolicking in the clear waters of Santa Cruz Island at Academy Bay, near the village of Puerto Ayora.

By approaching from the northwest, they had met no interference, as they threaded a course through the Galápagos Archipelago toward Santa Cruz, the most thickly populated of the islands and site of the research station for studying the giant tortoises of the Galápagos. Since some housing and supplies would almost certainly be available there, Homer had selected that island as their point of debarkation.

Acting Captain Olsson, as directed by Homer and Manoel Allanza, who were now technical masters of the ship—though without opposition—had carefully avoided San Cristóbal, some fifty miles to the east, in order to avoid any contact with Ecuadorian governmental authorities there.

Before departing, the mutineers had collected all the money aboard, so they could purchase supplies during their stay on the island. Before climbing down to the waiting lifeboat, Homer handed Jake Porter the missing transformer that had rendered the radio equipment incapable of transmitting, although still able to receive frantic messages from both political and health authorities as they tried vainly to locate the *Mercy*.

Daily news bulletins had also been received, telling

of the rapid spread of Yungay fever through a now fear-gripped world and concern for the missing *Mercy*. At a meeting the night the mutineers took over, Grant had recounted in detail to the complement and crew the discovery of *B. yungay* mutation by Lael and his subsequent experience with animal injections, as well as the final tests upon himself and Homer Ferguson.

"I'd like to say that took guts," said Mark Post. "Some of us, including me, have resented your being aboard, Dr. Reed, but I guess we've shown it. For myself I want to apologize and tell you I'm damned glad you were."

"Thanks, Mark," said Grant. "Can I assume that you'll be the first among the group to take the new vaccine?"

"Put me down for the first dose."

"I'll take the second," said Jack Smithson, and after that no one had made any objection.

The first injection for immunizing the entire hospital complement and crew, including Lael, who had insisted upon taking it, too, as well as Tonio Marelia, had been carried out the next morning. As he had done with the animals and also with himself and Homer, Grant elected to give three doses, two days apart. And since no one had developed symptoms of Yungay fever, though most of the recovered patients were still carriers of the deadly microbe, as proved by Grant's cultures, the preliminary tests of the *B. yungay* mutation as a vaccine could be termed an unqualified success.

Now, as Grant stood on the deck near the radio room where Jake Porter was starting to reassemble the broadcast equipment with the missing transformer, Shirley came up the stairway and paused at the rail beside him. She was carrying both her still and movie cameras.

"I've been photographing the departure of our captors," she said. "You should have seen Manoel preening himself when Homer told him his picture's going to be shown on American television, in that special I'll be doing for CBS when I get back to the States."

"Always in there pitching, aren't you?"

"So are you. Thanks to that, all of us are still alive."

"Are you going to say that on your broadcast?"

"Of course. By the way, what's going to happen to them?" She nodded toward the former patients, who were still gathered on the shore.

"I doubt if living on any island of the Galápagos is going to be the bed of roses they think it is," said Grant. "From what I've read, they're not the most fertile places in the world, and with nearly two hundred people turned loose on this particular one, it's going to be a little crowded. Somebody will soon go hungry and that's liable to cause trouble."

"What about the population of that island? None of them will have any immunity to Yungay fever."

"Tomorrow morning Captain Olsson and I will go to San Cristóbal and report our landing to the Ecuadorian port authorities. If they give me permission, I'm going to offer immunization with the vaccine to the population of Santa Cruz."

"What about the other islands?"

"There's no communication between them except by boat and radio. If the authorities follow my recommendation and clamp down a tight quarantine on Santa Cruz, the disease shouldn't spread to the others."

"Where's the airport?"

"On a small island called Baltra just north of Santa Cruz, but the same quarantine procedures will apply to it. The Galápagos will suddenly lose all its tourist business, but, from what I've been reading, the government wouldn't mind that. They're trying to preserve what's left of the conditions Darwin found here in 1835."

"Will you have enough vaccine to immunize the population on the island?"

"I hope so. Lael and I have cultures growing on all available tubes and Petri dishes. The mutation multiplies very rapidly so, as fast as we use up a culture, we can start another fresh one on chocolate agar."

"You think of everything, don't you? I guess the real

reason we couldn't get along is that you always seem to end up by being right."

Grant laughed. "You're pretty successful, too, you know. I wouldn't be at all surprised to see you get a TV special on the Galápagos out of this."

"Not this time. From what we've been reading in the daily radio bulletins, millions of people in the world are scared to death rght now. They're waiting for something they can't see to strike them down, and if they know a way of protecting them has been found, it's going to bring a lot of comfort to them."

"No doubt about that."

"Unless someone is selected to direct the world attack on Yungay fever, who isn't afraid to face down timorous government officials like so many I know of in the USPHS and the WHO, a lot of people are going to die because of the delay. I guess you know who should get the job."

"Lael says very much the same thing."

"By the way, what are her plans when this is all over?"

"She's going back to the Callejón de Huaylas to open the tomb she and Guy discovered to the public as a memorial to him. Have you seen the photos she took with the periscope?"

"Yes."

"She's convinced it's what Guy would want her to do."

'It probably is; they're spectacular enough." Shirley gave him an appraising look. "Jake Porter expects to start transmitting by morning. Do you want to go first?"

"No. Get your work over with and then I'll talk with Marshall Payne. I want him to get a group of experts together and fly down to look over my records and take cultures of the mutation back to Atlanta for study in the center laboratories."

"Can I make the announcement of your discovery?"

"Go ahead. It may speed things up a little if we put pressure on the health authorities from both sides."

II

Shirley came into the dining room as Grant was finishing breakfast the next morning.

"The air waves are all yours," she told him. "CBS News taped my report for use on all their broadcasts today and wants me back in New York as soon as possible to start putting the special together. I also filed a long dispatch to INS for the afternoon newspapers; you'll be front-page headlines before night."

"You didn't talk to Marshall Payne did you?"

"No, that's your job. I don't work for the center any more."

Jake Porter was sending the last of Shirley's INS dispatch when Grant came into the radio room. He looked up and grinned.

"You're a cinch to win your second Nobel Price, Dr. Reed," he said. "Miss Ross really laid it on—and well deserved, too."

"Thanks, Jake. Can you get me Dr. Marshall Payne at the Center for Disease Control in Atlanta?"

"Right on, Doctor. When I opened up this morning, the mainland operator in Panama nearly dropped her teeth. They had us down as being lost at sea and it took me a minute or so to convince her I wasn't some ham trying to pull a hoax."

"Is it really you, Grant?" Marshall Payne asked. "We'd given all of you up for dead."

"We're very much alive, Marshall. When you hear Shirley's report of what's been going on the last month, you'll know the details."

"I turned on the car radio this morning as I was driving to work and got the last few sentences of her broadcast from the *Mercy*. It all sounds like a suspense novel."

"I'd like for you to fly down here and bring the president of the Mercy Foundation—plus one or two well-known epidemiologists and, probably, the director of the WHO. You can take cultures of the mutation back with you."

"If you're immune—as I gather Shirley indicated—why not fly up here? I can get the air force to send a helicopter over there to pick you up."

"When the mutineer patients landed on Santa Cruz, they put everyone on the island in danger of death from Yungay fever, so I've got to get them immunized immediately. As soon as I finish talking to you, I'm going to the Ecuadorian authorities on another island to arrange it."

"That's a wonderful opportunity to give your vaccine a thorough testing on the island population. You can set up a double blind test procedure, immunizing half of them and injecting the other half with sterile water—"

"If you'd seen as much Yungay fever as I have and as many people die from it, Marshall, you wouldn't sentence half the population of Santa Cruz to possible death just to have an experiment on record." Grant's tone was firm.

"But the vaccine has to be tested."

"It's already been tested, right here on the ship. With the facilities at your command in the States, you can produce a more accurately calibrated vaccine, as far as the number of organisms is concerned, but you won't make a better one. Take my word for it."

"Are you prepared to take charge of the entire program?"

"If that's the way the WHO wants it."

"They will, and the Public Health Service will be behind you, I'll see to that. I'll also get a commission together and ask the air force to lift us from Panama to the deck of your ship with a helicopter. That way, we can avoid a lot of complications with the Ecuadorian authorities."

"Let me know by radio when to expect you."

It took most of the morning to make the run from the anchorage of the *Mercy* in Academy Bay off Santa Cruz Island—called Indefatigable by the early explorers and buccaneers who had used the Galápagos as hiding places—to San Cristóbal, or Chatham, where the governor of the archipelago had his seat at the village of Baquerizo Moreno. Volcanic in origin like the other islands, San Cristóbal boasted a mountain almost twenty-five hundred feet in height, and its green-clad slopes were a beautiful sight in the bright morning sunlight.

Having reassumed command with the departure of the mutineers, Captain Pendarvis was an imposing figure in freshly pressed white ducks. Tonio Marelia went along to interpret, in case the Ecuadorian authorities spoke a Spanish dialect. They found the governor, a perspiring plump Ecuadorian in dingy white ducks, having a drink at the local cantina.

At first the governor wasn't interested in the presence of strangers in the islands. Cruise boats now made regular runs through the archipelago from Baltra, where the airport was located, several times a week. Besides, yachts were always stopping to see the giant tortoises that had given the Galápagos its name, as well as the famous iguanas, relics of an era many times older than the micro-organism Guy and Lael had discovered in the cave above Yungay. At the mention of the word *Mercy,* however, the governor jumped to his feet and quickly put the width of the room between himself and the visitors.

"Please, señors," he said. "The Plague Yungay has not come to these islands. If you have anything to do with it, you must go away."

Tonio Marelia explained in Spanish how the ship had come to be anchored in Academy Bay off the coast of Santa Cruz.

"By what right did you bring your plague ship to these waters?" the governor protested angrily. "You must leave at once!"

"My ship is in no condition to sail," Captain Pendarvis assured the official. "The engines will barely turn over and we are low on supplies."

"Buy what you want on Santa Cruz, then. Hunt

wild pigs on the mountainside, even kill some horses and goats if you wish, but leave before you bring the plague down upon us."

"The plague is already there," Grant told him in Spanish. "Although the mutineers have recovered from it, they still carried it in their bodies when they went ashore."

"These men you call mutineers, you say they are capable of spreading the fever?"

"Yes. They are carriers, for perhaps a month after they have recovered."

"Then everyone on Santa Cruz Island is in danger?"

"Grave danger. That's why I need your order authorizing me to vaccinate everyone on the island."

"But what shall I do about the mutineers? I have no police to bring them in and no prison that would hold them. If they are running all over the island, property will be damaged; the farms of settlers around Bella Vista on the slopes of the mountainsides may even be ruined."

"All the more reason why the Peruvians should be taken off Santa Cruz as quickly as possible," Grant urged.

"And prosecuted as mutineers?" the governor asked hopefully. "That would put them under the jurisdiction of your captain."

"I intend to bring no charges against them," said Captain Pendarvis quickly. "They escaped because they were afraid of having their blood taken to protect the crew and the personnel of the hospital."

The governor looked baffled, obviously with no solution to the problem.

"Since Captain Pendarvis has no intention of bringing a charge of mutiny on the high seas against the Peruvians, why don't you contact your government in Quito?" Grant suggested. "Ask them to enter negotiations with the Peruvian Government in Lima."

"For what reason?"

"These people no longer have Yungay fever but many in Peru still do, particularly in the area of Chimbote and the Callejón de Huaylas. The mutineers are not a menace to that part of Peru where the disease is spreading, even though they are carriers. If a request goes from the government of Ecuador to the government of Peru, asking for a plane to remove the Peruvians and take them back to the mainland at Chimbote, it should be honored."

The governor brightened for the first time since the conversation had begun. "I will send such a message at once," he said. "Meanwhile, what about the people on Santa Cruz?"

"Dr. Reed has developed a method of preventing Yungay fever," Captain Pendarvis explained.

"There is no *prevención*."

"There is now," Grant assured the governor. "I tested it on myself first and then on the hospital personnel and the crew of the *Mercy*."

"This *prevención*"—the governor was obviously still doubtful—"what is it?"

"A vaccine—for injection. It will keep the fever from developing."

"You have taken this injection yourself?"

"Yes. And so has everybody now on the *Mercy*."

"It is a strange thing, señors. On the radio, we hear the plague kills the people in many parts of the world, yet you say you have a *prevención* there on the ship."

"The vaccine was discovered in the laboratory of the *Mercy*. In a few days, a commission of health experts from the United States and elsewhere will fly to the ship, to witness this vaccine I have developed. I will go back with them to the United States to make it available all over the world."

"It will be a fine thing," the governor agreed. "And save many lives."

"Right now I'm concerned with the people living on Santa Cruz Island," Grant told him. "If you will give me an order for everyone on the island, except the mutineers, to be given injections of the vaccine, I will undertake to prevent anyone on Santa Cruz from getting Yungay fever."

The governor frowned. "How can you get this vaccine if you are still on the ship?"

"We're making it there, in the laboratory, but as soon as the commission visits the ship, it will be manufactured in the United States and elsewhere to control the fever all over the world."

"Is this then a test that you wish to do? On the people now living on Santa Cruz?"

"The vaccine has already been tested on the ship's company," Grant assured the official. "If it keeps the people on Santa Cruz from developing Yungay fever, that will be even greater proof of its worth."

"How long will this vaccination take?" the governor asked.

"About a week. Everyone on the island must have three injections."

"I will issue the order, señor," said the governor. "But I will not go to Santa Cruz."

III

The motor-driven lifeboat bearing Grant, Captain Pendarvis, and Tonio Marelia, and several sailors arrived back at the *Mercy* by late afternoon. After dropping the captain and Tonio off at the ship, Grant was taken ashore in a lifeboat. He went directly to the Darwin Research Station, which had been established in a joint venture between the Ecuadorian and other interested governments, with UNESCO. The director of the station, a young American from the Middle West, greeted him politely but was obviously concerned.

"The governor's lieutenant for the island received a copy of the order for immunizing the people immediately after you left San Cristóbal, Dr. Reed," he said. "We had already learned of your discovery of a method for preventing Yungay fever from Miss Ross's broadcast."

"Then you monitored it?"

The young scientist nodded. "We recognized the ship

as the *Mercy* before it dropped anchor. Many people in the settlement fled to the interior, where some Norwegian immigrant farmers have a small village in the foothills."

"I'd heard the soil of the Galápagos wasn't very fruitful and that there is almost no rain."

"That's true generally, but on the lower slopes of the mountains there are pockets of fairly fertile earth. Mists settle there practically every night, too, providing enough water for crops, but elsewhere the islands are quite dry."

"The governor said there'd been no Yungay fever on the Galápagos," said Grant. "And I hope to keep it from developing."

"Pray God you can," said the young American earnestly. "I have a wife and children here. Quite a number of children are in the settlement, too, and a few white people besides us live here on the island. From what I have heard about Yungay fever, it can be devastating."

"We lost almost fifty per cent of the patients that were aboard the *Mercy* when the mob cut it loose at Chimbote and we were forced to flee into the open Pacific."

"What about the mutineers?" the director asked. "When they came through here right after you'd landed, I noticed that a few of them were being carried —one in particular."

Grant smiled. "Believe it or not, the legless one was the instigator of the mutiny and the friend who carried him is an American Negro. All of the natives who were aboard have recovered from Yungay fever."

The young scientist shuddered. "It's a terrible plague. How soon can you start immunizing the population of the island?"

"Tomorrow morning if you will send word out telling people to come here. I believe that would be better than trying to visit them in their homes."

"Much better. The road to the farms is rough, and when it rains, which it occasionally does, part of the area becomes a sea of mud. I'll undertake to have everyone in the settlement who'll take the vaccine available tomorrow morning. We should be able to get word to the ones living nearby tomorrow and also bring the others down from the hills at least by the following day."

"The governor on San Cristóbal is going to try to get the Peruvian Government to fly the mutineers back to Chimbote or to Lima."

"It can't come too soon," said the young biologist. "I suspect some of the mutineers know that Galápagos tortoises are an excellent source of meat. We've been breeding some of these animals for many years, and if they're killed, our research could be set back many, many years."

"A commission of scientists from the United States and elsewhere will arrive at Baltra or on the ship by helicopter in three or four days," Grant assured him. "I will see that the need for evacuation of the Peruvians is made one of the first orders of business."

IV

Assisted by Lael Valdez, Jack Smithson, and several of the other doctors and nurses, Grant began the immunization project the following morning. Tonio Marelia was of considerable value because he was able to act as interpreter with the Santa Cruz inhabitants, as was Lael. Most of them were Indians but a number were blond Norwegians from the mountain settlements in the foothills of the two mountains that made up the highest portion of Santa Cruz.

Lael prepared the suspensions from cultures of the mutation. As soon as one culture was used up, the container was put aside to be taken back to the ship, where the tube or plate was resterilized and filled with fresh chocolate agar medium ready to be inoculated with the orange-colored organism. By nightfall of the first day, most of the population of the settlement at

Academy Bay and quite a number of those from inland had received the first injection.

The colonists who had fled from the inland farms and small villages called Bella Vista and Miramar reported that the escaped Peruvians had caused no particular problems, except to pigs, wild goats, horses, and a few tortoises and iguanas. At the moment, at least, the ex-patients appeared content to gorge themselves on meat and some of the vegetables grown by the diligent Norwegians of the Miramar settlement. What might happen later, when the mutineers became bored with the island life, no one could tell. But the reports filtering down along with those colonists who came to be immunized seemed to indicate that, for the moment at least, Homer and Manoel were firmly in control.

On the second day of immunization, Lael remained aboard the ship, making up new batches of medium and transferring the mutation culture so as to have an adequate supply for further injections. Fortunately, it grew rapidly, doubling in size of the cultures every forty-eight hours until the limit of available nutrients in the tubes and Petri dishes brought growth finally to a halt, so Grant could see no probability that they would run out of the vital vaccine material.

On the afternoon of the second day, the sound of a rifle shot stopped all work and a tall figure was seen approaching the settlement. When Grant focused his binoculars upon it, he easily recognized Homer, with Manoel Allanza in his usual position upon the black man's shoulders.

"I'll go and talk to them," he said.

"Are you sure it's safe?" Jack Smithson asked.

"Homer is my friend. He knows I saved his life by insisting that we all be immunized. Take charge here, please, Jack."

Homer and Manoel looked well fed when Grant toiled up the rocky volcanic slope to where the two stood waiting. The Negro was carrying the shotgun used aboard ship for shooting clay targets, but he didn't hold the weapon in a position of menace toward Grant.

"Will you be able to immunize the people of the island, Doctor?" Homer asked. "We wish no harm to come to them."

"We're finishing the first set of injections this afternoon. The others will follow according to schedule."

"Good. What of your proposal for a commission to verify that you have produced a true prevention for Yungay fever?"

"I expect to hear from the Center for Disease Control and the World Health Organization by tomorrow at the latest. I've asked them to fly a group of scientists here by helicopter, possibly from one of the air bases on Panama."

Manoel broke into explosive speech, which Grant recognized as Quechua, but Homer translated. "He wants to know what the Yankees are going to do with the Peruvians you lured aboard the ship to take their blood," he said.

"I'm afraid Manoel saw too many vampire films in Chimbote. I'm trying to arrange for the Peruvian Government to fly all of you home from the Galápagos."

"To be charged with mutiny?"

"Captain Pendarvis will not press charges against you."

Homer grinned. "More of your backstage finagling?"

"The captain is as anxious as the rest of us to wind this business up. The big job is yet to come—that of removing Yungay fever from the world by means of the new vaccine."

"And that's going to be given to you—unless somebody in Washington has rocks in his head."

"I'll probably get the job," Grant agreed. "What did you want to speak to me about, Homer?"

"We want you to get us off this island and back home, Doctor. The way my friends and I see things, it was your idea to concentrate the sick people on board the *Mercy*, so you're responsible for us all."

"I'm doing my best to get you off," Grant protested, "but it's a little hard to communicate with you—"

"That can be handled easily. The signal gun aboard

the ship fires flares; if you want to talk to us, just fire the gun. When we hear it or see the flares, Manoel and I will meet you here."

"Agreed," said Grant. "Do you have enough food for everyone?"

"There's goat and horse meat aplenty, but I'm afraid the Norwegians won't have many chickens left after we've gone. In a pinch, though, we could shoot a few wild horses and some of these big tortoises, so we'll make out for at least a few weeks, while you try to figure out some way to get us off. *Vaya con dios,* my friend."

V

On the third day after the *Mercy* dropped anchor at Academy Bay, Grant was notified by radio that the Yungay Fever Commission, as it was to be called, would be landed by helicopter on the ship about noon the following day. When the big helicopter appeared, having refueled at Guayaquil and also on Baltra Island, a cheer went up from among those on board the ship.

The first passenger off the big helicopter was Dr. Marshall Payne, from the Atlanta Center. Next came Dr. Eric Brechter, a Swiss epidemiologist who was secretary of the WHO. Representing the Pan-American Health Organization, to Grant's surprise, was Dr. José Figueroa. The last member of the commission was the chairman of the Mercy Foundation Board, Mr. Godfrey McCausland, a pudgy little man who was obviously out of his depth in such a situation.

Grant shook hands with those he did not already know, and with the others, all of whom had been compatriots of his in other attacks upon disease. Figueroa was the last to be greeted.

"I was as surprised as you to find myself selected for this honor, Dr. Reed," said the Peruvian. "The Minister of Health would have come himself but he figured I had more experience with Yungay fever."

"Next to me, I suppose you've seen more cases than anybody else in the world," Grant agreed. "I'm glad Dr. Huantar realizes your worth."

Figueroa grinned and Grant knew they both understood the reason why the Peruvian Minister of Health had chosen not to visit the ship.

"Well, gentlemen," he said, "the first order of business will be to give you an initial injection of the mutation in order to start protecting you from Yungay fever."

"We'll take your word for its efficiency, Grant," said Dr. Brechter. "But I wish we could have had a double blind test of the vaccine's value here."

"We're running what amounts to that on Santa Cruz, Dr. Brechter. With the entire population immunized and the risk quite heavy from contact with the mutineer carriers, the results should be quite conclusive."

"I suppose we'll have to accept that proof," said Payne. "What do we see first?"

"Miss Valdez is waiting in the lab to demonstrate the cultures we've made and the growth of the mutation."

After the session in the laboratory, where Lael worked quietly and effectively, the commission moved on to inspect the vessel itself. When they finished, Grant took them ashore to the research station to see the immunization process going on there. They came back on board in time for dinner and afterward adjourned to the small lounge that was part of Captain Pendarvis's suite.

Present at the conference, in addition to the commission and Grant, were Jack Smithson, representing the medical staff of the *Mercy,* Captain Pendarvis, First Officer Olsson, and Elaine Carroll, the head nurse. As master of the ship, Pendarvis opened the discussion.

"You've seen the ship and the work Dr. Reed has been doing, gentlemen," he said. "What are your impressions?"

"In the first place," said Dr. Marshall Payne, who

was acting as chairman of the commission, "there's no question about the fact that Grant and his assistant have done a remarkable job in isolating the cause of Yungay fever. Moreover, it would appear that they have found the answer to controlling this fever in a remarkably short time through the discovery of a mutation."

"We can thank sea water for that, and probably the bromouracil contained in it," said Grant.

"Whatever the cause, the event itself was certainly fortuitous and of great importance throughout the world," said Payne. "There remains now the tremendous job of initiating a world-wide immunization project using the Yungay mutation. That sphere of activity, of course, will have to be moved from the *Mercy*."

"Right now, those of us aboard are more interested in getting the ship to a port," said Captain Pendarvis.

"I'm afraid that isn't going to be very easy," said the Disease Control Center director. "In order to have at least a tentative answer to this question, I asked Dr. Figueroa, representing the Pan-American Health Organization, to consult the various governments on the Pacific side of the hemisphere and inquire which of them would be willing to let the *Mercy* dock at one of their ports. Perhaps we should have his report at this point."

"The simple fact is that nobody wants your ship, Captain," said Figueroa.

"In God's name, why?" Pendarvis demanded. "Judging from the reports we've been getting by radio, Yungay fever is raging now in just about every major city in the hemisphere, so no one aboard this vessel is a menace any longer."

"When I certify, as I certainly shall, that the personnel aboard the *Mercy* are immune to Yungay fever and thus pose no threat to any other people, I'm sure your people will be allowed to go wherever they wish. This ship is another matter."

"Are you saying the *Mercy* will be refused admission

to any country, while her complement and crew will not?"

"That's what it amounts to."

"I'll be damned if I see their reasoning," Pendarvis exploded.

"I think I do, Captain," said Grant. "When my brother accidentally loosed *B. yungay* upon an unprotected world, the germ had been in a state of what may be called suspended animation for five thousand years. During the past several months we have treated over three hundred patients with the disease aboard this ship, so the physical facilities of the vessel itself are heavily contaminated with the most dangerous organism now known to man."

"What about fumigation?" the president of the Mercy Foundation asked.

"Dr. Brechter has had considerable experience with that sort of procedure," said Grant. "I'd rather he would answer your question."

"It would be a waste of time—and money," said the WHO secretary without hesitation. "With such a virulent micro-organism, no one could ever be sure every germ was killed, no matter how heavy a fumigation was carried out."

"I guess that leaves only one alternative," said Pendarvis. "The sea."

"We had agreed upon that even before we landed on the ship," Marshall Payne told him. "No other solution seems possible."

"The *Mercy* was to be scrapped anyway when she reached port after this final voyage," said Godfrey McCausland. "The foundation will lose the amount of its value as scrap, of course, but that cannot be helped."

"Are you going to replace her?" Jack Smithson asked.

"We're negotiating with the navy to take over one of its hospital ships that was about to be put in dry storage," McCausland told him. "The cost to the foundation will be nominal."

"And with Shirley Ross photographing and describing the death of the old *Mercy,* after its sea cocks are opened," said Marshall Payne, "the publicity value of its sacrifice to the foundation should more than compensate you for its loss."

"We considered that factor, too," McCausland admitted.

"Which leaves us two things to be decided upon," said Grant. "When the personnel and crew can be taken off by way of the Baltra Island Airport. And what to do about the mutineers."

"I have told the governor of the Galápagos that I will not bring charges of mutiny against the former patients," said Captain Pendarvis.

"A wise decision, I'm sure," Marshall Payne agreed.

"I have contacted the air force at Panama," McCausland added. "A transport plane will be sent to Baltra Island, when we request it. It will take the former patients to Chimbote, where Dr. Figueroa will see that they are returned to their homes. On the way back, it will stop at Baltra to pick up the personnel and crew of the *Mercy* and fly them to Panama."

"I guess that winds up the affair except for one thing," said Marshall Payne. "We're all in agreement that Dr. Reed should head up the world-wide campaign to eradicate Yungay fever by immunization with the mutation. How about it, Grant?"

"I started the fight to control it the day I landed at Chimbote, and I have a habit of finishing what I start."

"Good! We'll leave tomorrow morning by helicopter. Can you go with us?"

"I have an obligation to see Miss Valdez safely back to Yungay. Once Dr. Figueroa has Yungay fever under control in the Callejón de Huaylas, she plans to open the tomb she and my brother discovered as a memorial to him. I would like to fly to Chimbote with her and the patients and continue on to Atlanta by commercial plane."

"That sounds reasonable," Marshall Payne agreed, "provided, of course, you prepare the second and third doses of the mutation for the members of the commission to take to complete the series."

"Miss Valdez is working in the lab now, preparing fresh cultures for the third and final dose to be given to the people of Santa Cruz," Grant assured him. "There'll be plenty left for all of you."

VI

The conference finished, Grant went in search of Lael but didn't find her in the laboratory, her stateroom, or in the staff lounge. There a merry celebration was in process, stimulated by the news that they were going home and by a supply of rum brought from the cantina on Santa Cruz by the group who had been immunizing the inhabitants. Climbing to the top deck, he saw her at the stern, where she was standing in the shadow of one of the lifeboats.

"Conference over?" she asked.

"Yes."

"I hope everything worked out the way you wanted it to."

"Not quite. A transport plane from Panama will take the Peruvians back to Chimbote and then return to Baltra to pick up the ship's complement and crew. I can arrange for you to go on either flight."

"I want to go back to the Casa Yanqui.'

"I'd go with you if I could."

"I wish you could, too. You didn't have a chance to see how lovely the Callejón de Huaylas really is, but you must go on fighting Yungay fever."

He smiled. "My infernal rightness again?"

"Thank God for it."

"They've asked me to take charge of the immunization program throughout the world for the WHO."

"Guy would want you to do that."

"I'd still rather be with you. People who love each other should be together."

"What we want—and I want to be with you as much as you want to be with me—doesn't have to be considered now, Grant. Not as long as what Guy and I started the day we drilled into the cave above Yungay is left unfinished. Dr. Figueroa says there's still a lot of Yungay fever in Chimbote and the Callejón de Huaylas."

"I don't doubt it; they were the hotbeds of the organism's growth in the beginning, so it would take time for it to burn out."

"Dr. Figueroa stayed behind and talked to me in the lab," she told him. "He wants to get started immediately on the production of the mutation vaccine in Peru without waiting for any more tests, like you'll be doing in the States. And he wants me to take charge of producing a vaccine for immediate use—"

"It could be done, but I'll hate to see you—"

"We'll start culturing the mutation in the laboratory of the Health Department at Chimbote from the cultures Dr. Figueroa takes back with him. Since I'm familiar with the way the mutation grows and you'll be busy with the larger job of working out methods of wiping out Yungay fever on a world scale, I'm the logical person to help attack it where it started. There's a question of responsibility, too. You know, the original contamination with *B. yungay* came from my camera and the periscope I persuaded Guy to make so I could photograph the inside of the tomb."

"I'd rather not see you take the risk."

"There isn't any risk, darling. I'm immune to *B. yungay* and I'll keep my immunity up with occasional injections of the mutation."

"You still intend to make the cave a memorial to Guy, don't you?"

"Of course. But first I have to be sure the people who do the work of opening it are immune, too. The natives around Yungay know me and they know I recovered from the fever, so Dr. Figueroa thinks I'll have no trouble persuading them to be immunized."

"Promise me one thing: When you're ready to open

the cave, send me a cable. I want to be there to see that nothing happens to you, but, more than that, your immediate job will be finished then and I can take you back with me to wherever I'll be working."

"I'll be living for that day," she told him, "and I'm sure Guy would want it that way. Sometimes I wonder how much of our loving each other stems from the fact that both of us loved him so much."

"A great deal—as far as you're concerned." He was remembering the night of the storm. "But I'm not at all certain I didn't fall in love with you when I first saw you, hurrying through the airport at Chimbote to meet me that first morning."

She laughed softly. "You put me in my place right off—by telling me I resented you at the start."

"When did you come to know better?"

"That night at the Casa Yanqui, of course. It was the first time I realized how much like Guy you really are, deep inside."

"And I guess that was the first time I was really convinced you weren't simply a younger woman, attaching herself to an older man for what she could get out of him."

"I knew you felt that way at first. It was still another reason why I was prepared to dislike you and found myself able to for a while—even after the Casa Yanqui."

She looked across the anchorage to where a few lights were still burning in the Academy Bay settlement. "Is it true that the *Mercy* will be sunk? I looked in on the staff lounge before I came up here and they told me Mr. McCausland said it probably would."

"There's really no other answer, even though I still hate to see it go, if for no other reason than because it brought us together."

"I guess at that, the ship would rather rest in the sea than be cut up for scrap. I'll still hate to see her go, after what I've found here—not only you, but I've discovered so much about myself that I wasn't aware of before."

"You need never feel insecure again," he assured her. "Once the story of the Peruvian mutation is finished, you're going to have a full-time job looking after me."

"I was thinking about that before you came up here. I'd really like to be a part of your work, as well as your wife."

"You're already a better than average bacteriologist; there's no reason why we can't go on fighting the *B. yungays* of the world together."

"Thank you, darling." She stood on tiptoes to kiss him, and when he took her in his arms, her lips were soft and warm beneath his, but with no hint of the passion he knew they were capable of developing.

After a moment, she pushed him away. "There," she said. "That should remind you of what you'll be coming home to someday."

VII

The big air force transport plane trundled down the runway on Baltra Island, built by the army and navy during World War II, and took to the air. While the team from the *Mercy* had been completing the immunization program for the inhabitants of Santa Cruz Island, Grant himself had gone into the interior to tell Homer Ferguson and the Peruvians they would be transported back to Chimbote, if they wished.

The few days the mutineers had spent on the relatively inhospitable Galápagos island had been enough to convince them they wanted no part of it. All had trooped meekly down to the harbor the next morning, where they were transferred to the *Mercy* once again. Weighing anchor, the vessel had steamed northward around Santa Cruz to the smaller island of Baltra, where the airfield was located, and anchored there awaiting the arrival of the plane.

Early that morning, everyone had left the ship, except Oley Olsson, Angus McTavish, and two seamen who were to sail it out into deep water northwest of the Galápagos and open the sea cocks before being picked up by a helicopter which had been sent from Panama. Now, late in the afternoon, the big transport was on the first leg of its job taking the ex-patients back home before picking up the crew and complement and carrying them on to Panama.

Grant and Lael were sitting in the front of the plane with Homer and Manoel Allanza across from them. Gaining altitude, it circled in a wide arc that took it over the northernmost island of the Galápagos Archipelago—Genovesa, called Tower Island by the buccaneers.

Looking down at Tower, Lael shivered. "It looks like the TV pictures from the moon."

"Only more desolate," Grant agreed. "Charles Darwin landed from the *Beagle* in 1835 at the small bay you see between two headlands. He didn't think much of it either."

A sudden babble of voices in the Quechua dialect broke out among the Peruvians in the after part of the plane. Grant looked out the window beside Lael and saw the *Mercy* far below them, with the helicopter carrying the small crew that had sailed the old ship to her final resting place circling above the vessel itself. The lower decks were already awash as water poured in through the open sea cocks and the old vessel was settling comfortably into the sea, as if glad to be going to her rest at last.

"I guess Shirley's in the helicopter, taping a description of what's happening," said Lael. "But I'm glad we're not waiting to see the ship go under."

"So am I."

"How long will it take for us to reach Chimbote?"

"A couple of hours at least."

"I think I'll take a nap then." She reached over to pull his arm across her shoulders and settled herself comfortably against him. Then in a whisper she added, "It may be a long time before I can sleep in your arms again."

VIII

It had been summer when Grant told Lael good-by at the Chimbote Airport, before taking a local flight to Quito, Ecuador, and thence on to Atlanta to begin the campaign against Yungay fever. Now it was midwinter, but because of the proximity to the equator —only eight or nine degrees south—the change of season had brought little change in climate.

In the preceding six months since Grant had landed at Atlanta, the immunization campaign had moved at a swift pace. Only once in medical history—when the mass production of penicillin, newly discovered by Dr. Alexander Fleming, had been made possible by the work of researchers E. Chain and H. W. Florey—had a crash campaign of such dimensions to manufacture an antibacterial agent been undertaken.

Grant Reed's tireless energy had sparked the campaign to the point where fatal Yungay fever was now under control in all of the major centers of the world where it had broken out—Boston, Los Angeles, London, Paris, Lima, and Moscow. Moreover, his campaign to eradicate the disease was now being hailed as one of the major exploits in the history of epidemiology and its director had already been honored by half a dozen nations.

Lael's letters kept Grant informed of the rapid progress she and Dr. Figueroa had made in eliminating Yungay fever from Chimbote and the Callejón de Huaylas by not waiting for commercial production of the new vaccine. She had moved back to the Casa Yanqui several months after he had left her at the Chimbote Airport to begin arrangements with the Peruvian Government to open the tomb.

News that the gift had finally been accepted, along with the setting aside from Guy's considerable estate of a trust fund for maintaining it as a memorial, reached Grant in Geneva—where he was conferring with Dr. Brechter of the World Health Organization

—in an article from the London *Times*. And when he reached his hotel that evening, a cablegram from Lael was waiting.

The night had found him on a Lufthansa flight to South America, thence by Varig to Lima and the morning local flight to Chimbote. He had cabled Lael that he would rent a car at Chimbote for the trip to Yungay and the Casa Yanqui, but as he came through the airport, he saw hurrying toward him the girl who, less than a year ago, had met him in the same spot.

Where on that earlier meeting her greeting had been cool and distant, however, this time her eyes were shining with happiness. And as he hurried to take her in his arms, he was even more certain than he'd been on that earlier morning that she was the loveliest thing he'd ever seen.

What's more, the warmth of her kiss told him she was now his and his alone.